The Liar's Wife

The Liar's Wife

MARY GORDON

PANTHEON BOOKS

New York

I would like to thank Leslie Vosshall of The Rockefeller University,
who talked to me about mosquitoes, and Meredith Martin,
who talked to me about art.

Grateful acknowledgment is made to Regal Literary for
permission to reprint an excerpt from "The Problem of Freedom:
The Crisis of Democracy" ("Das Problem der Freiheit"),
by Thomas Mann, copyright © 1939 by Bermann-Fischer Verlag.
All rights reserved by S. Fischer Verlag GmbH, Frankfurt am Main.
Reprinted by permission of Regal Literary.

Library of Congress Cataloging-in-Publication Data
Gordon, Mary, [date]
[Novellas. Selections]
The liar's wife : four novellas / Mary Gordon.
p. cm.
ISBN 978-0-307-37743-2 (hardcover).
ISBN 978-0-307-90888-9 (eBook).
I. Title.
PS3557.O669L63 2014   813'.54—dc23   2013043926

www.pantheonbooks.com

Jacket design by Linda Huang

Printed in the United States of America
First Edition

2   4   6   8   9   7   5   3   1

for David Plante

Contents

The Liar's Wife

A YELLOW TRUCK WAS PARKED across the street, in front of the Chelford-Johnsons'.

It looked all wrong.

It was a delivery truck, but if the Chelford-Johnsons were having something delivered, why wasn't the truck parked in the driveway?

The truck, parked where it was, made Jocelyn uneasy. She was alone in the house. She had just come in from the back garden, closing the curtains for the night. Until she saw the truck she had been happy.

It was early evening, August 7. She had been standing out on the lawn, holding her glass of wine, lifting it up so that the sun's last rays were trapped in it.

Summer evening, her favorite kind of weather.

Heat was a presence, a companion, but not, as in the daytime, an oppressor. And the heaviness was potent; it reminded you that you were a creature with a body, and sometimes it made the body's longing sharp for sex, food, simple touch, and sometimes it made the body feel at peace with itself. Sometimes a warm breeze skittered along the surface of the skin like a flame along pavement, a match dropped onto a thin, invisible stream of gasoline.

When she was younger, these summer evenings had everything to do with sex. She had felt herself desirable on evenings such as this. Her sense of her own desire and her own desirability made her feel the simultaneous heaviness and lightness that made her love this weather. When no one was looking, she would fall to the ground, crouch on the grass or roll in it, or sometimes she literally flapped her arms, expecting to take flight.

But that was over. She had the compulsion neither to drop down nor to fly up. Still she was happy. Very happy here, tonight.

"Jossie," her mother would call out from the back porch when Jocelyn was standing here among the trees, wanting to fall or fly. "Come have some lemonade."

She had loved her mother.

I couldn't sell this house because I loved my mother.

Her mother. Always when she thought of her mother she thought of her lovely hands, always cool and the beautifully shaped nails, polished with clear varnish, and the exposed half-moons that she, as a child, had traced with her small, shapeless fingers. Her hands had become her mother's, and she was grateful that, like her mother's, her hands had not grown gnarled or twisted or spotted as she aged. She thought of the cool feeling of her mother's hands on her forehead when she had a fever. And her mother sitting in her study, bent over her work. She made anatomical drawings to illustrate medical textbooks. As a child, Jocelyn had loved watching her create veins and arteries, then the larger projects: kidney, liver, lungs. Jocelyn couldn't draw "for beans," as she often said, sometimes wondering what beans had to do with it, and who had originally been paid in beans.

Her mother had been dead two years. She had died in the house, her house, but not in her own bed; it was a hospital bed, metallic, mechanical, which had been brought in to replace the beautiful mahogany four-poster with the pineapple corner posts. But at least she had died among her own things. Her silver-backed hairbrushes, her scent bottles on a lace cloth on top of the Sheraton chest, below the oval mirror. The mirror in which her mother had seen herself a young bride, a young mother, then aging, and finally, old, near death. It would have been sensible to sell the house when her mother died, but Jocelyn had not. Because she hadn't wanted to. Simply, she hadn't wanted to give it up. She didn't want to give up what she thought of as *her* trees: chestnut, oak, hickory, sugar maple. She didn't want them to belong to someone else.

So she had made up a kind of story. First to herself, and then she began saying it aloud. "We're keeping the house in New Canaan as a weekend house. A getaway from the city. Nantucket is just too far." Her husband's family had bought a house on Nantucket in the thirties. Richard had inherited it.

"It's that damn ferry," she would say, as if she needed to justify herself, though no one had accused her. "You wouldn't think of going there for a weekend, even a long weekend, even a very, very long weekend," she would say, cocking her head as if to make a joke of her own position, which she knew to be extreme. "This way, we can just nip up here anytime for a little R & R. Just a nip," she said, using, she knew, the alcoholic's diction of evasion. Just a nip.

Her next-door neighbor, seeing her at the house, had brought a small bunch of sweet peas. She'd been moved by her neighbor's kindness. Janet Wilkinson, who had lived next door for more than twenty years, and kept an eye out, always, for Jocelyn's mother. What was her work? Jocelyn tried to remember. Telecommunications. That was the kind of word that stopped the mind making pictures. Or at least her mind.

The sweet peas were a dark purple that seemed almost navy blue, almost not a proper color for a flower. Such a saturated darkness, and weren't flowers supposed to invoke brightness, not the dark? But they were lovely in their saturated darkness, and the graceful folding of their petals, leaning inwards, almost touching, tender on their light green, fragile stems.

Janet Wilkinson had brought her purple sweet peas in a plain glass bottle which might very well have once held medicine. But the shape was pleasing.

What did Janet Wilkinson make of Jocelyn's uneven habitation of the house? It almost shamed her, with its hint of wastefulness, of laxity. The house was large. A large house in New Canaan, Connecticut. "Worth a fortune" is the phrase she knew would come first to people's minds.

"I love the scent of sweet peas," Janet Wilkinson had said, putting her face (which was almost a perfect oval, tan now: she'd had two weeks in Martha's Vineyard) close to the elegant flowers. Jocelyn had been surprised. She hadn't thought of sweet peas as having a scent. And the scent was, in itself, surprising. Neither sweet nor sharp, subtle but direct, a kind of simple presence with a plain insistence on itself.

People didn't credit the sense of smell nearly enough. Jocelyn believed that firmly. For thirty-five years, she'd worked in a lab that was involved in the study of mosquitoes, and the life, the fate, the impact on the world of mosquitoes was inextricably connected with their extraordinarily well-developed sense of smell.

Standing on the back porch, Jocelyn could see Janet Wilkinson walking around in the half-light of her kitchen. Had Janet Wilkinson ever married? She had come to Phillips Road as a woman in late middle age. She could have married and divorced; somehow it was something that neither Jocelyn nor her mother had felt free to ask, and Janet had never spoken of it. Was Janet Wilkinson a lesbian? Or not very sexual? Or just unlucky in love? Not being very sexual was, Jocelyn had come to believe, a much more common, much more deeply kept secret in these post-Freudian, post–sexual liberation days. She had come to believe it only recently, when she'd experienced it herself.

She preferred to think that Janet loved women. She preferred thinking of it that way, she didn't like the word "lesbian," with its swampy sound, although she liked lesbians, had loved some, though she hadn't gone so far as to make love to another woman. Not yet, she'd always said. Certainly the excitant of a loved, an admired woman, made the skin ripple in a way that was something like what one felt for a desired man. But only something like. Well, she would never know now. Although she'd seen surprising things among her cohort, she believed there would be no new surprises in her life. Not good surprises, anyway. It was, perhaps, another instance of her lack of courage.

Was it lack of courage that kept her from selling the house?

She had long ago come to terms with the idea that she was not a courageous person. A courageous person would not be made uneasy by a yellow truck parked on the street. But the truck had wrecked her peace; she could no longer keep herself from peeking from behind the curtains to see if the truck was still there.

It had not moved. In the dim light she could make out the writing on the truck's side. FRITO-LAY, it said. The words alarmed her. There was no reason for a Frito-Lay truck to be parked on Phillips Road in New Canaan, Connecticut. Dire thoughts raced through her brain. She began with the simplest. They were burglars. Or it could be much worse. They could be kidnappers; the Chelford-Johnsons were a young couple; they had two children, both, Jocelyn was sure, under ten. Or it could be even worse than that: perhaps they were terrorists, perhaps in the yellow body of the enormous truck there was an arsenal that would destroy the neighborhood, the town. She saw the street littered with arms and legs strewn on the pavement like leafy branches after a violent storm. She thought of calling Janet Wilkinson. But that would be absurd, it would be shaming. She was seventy-two years old, and at her age, one had to be careful of many things, not the least of which was appearing to be a scared old lady. A crazy old lady. A crackpot. A pain in the neck.

She forced herself to go back outside. She forced herself to think of her mother, her mother's calmness. And her father, who, with every breath, every step, conveyed the sense to Jocelyn that she would always be quite safe.

She turned on the back porch light. The air was saturated with the seductive scent of nicotiana, tobacco plant. It was a scent her mother had loved. She walked into the dimness, comforted by the presence of her beloved ghosts.

We were a happy family, she thought, holding her glass to catch the last light, feeling the presence of her parents, loving ghosts, hovering beside her. There was a literal sense, she thought, in which she was trying to catch the last light, to make it sink into the gold of her wine so she could take it in, swallow it along with her Pinot Grigio. Quiet, quietly affectionate . . . perhaps a bit undemonstrative. No, she'd be honest.

We were stingy in our expression of affection. She'd learned that from Richard's family, Jews from Poland, Russia, who praised and kissed each other loudly and loudly argued and accused.

We were a loving family. And yet, she thought, somehow it seems that I was often sad.

Days spent sitting under the stairs sorting remnants of fabric her mother had saved for her. The sense that a day of clouds was her appropriate weather. The choked silence in the school yard: what if no one likes me? A desire to hide from the signs of misery: from the Down syndrome cousin, fully adult and yet a child. A story in *Life* magazine about a girl in an iron lung. The sound of the word "refugee" and images of piled bodies in concentration camps, and her night terrors that she would be taken, she the daughter of prosperous parents, and she knew she was not one of the marked ones, the ones who had been taken, so she was ashamed of her own terror, her own fear, ashamed to cry out, crying silently, both in fear and taken over by the question: What if the world is not a good place? So her parents had grown vigilant. She'd heard them: "Don't let her see that—keep it away from her." The time she wept for the children in a puppet movie of Hansel and Gretel was a family joke. She'd cried because in winter the swings in the playground had been taken down. Where had they been taken? She hadn't believed her mother when she said, "You'll see, they'll be back in the springtime like the flowers and the birds." She had believed her mother was trying to protect her, because she believed that her mother was very kind. But her deepest belief was that there was no real protection, no possibility of being fully safe.

Where had it come from, this overriding lack of courage? This sense the worst could always happen. Not from her parents: her forthright, accomplished father, who had been in the War, and liked nothing more than a good laugh. Her gentle mother, who she believed was always humming under her breath, a tender song, maybe something from an operetta or a ballad popular in the late nineteenth century. Nothing later than 1925.

She had not been courageous.

Her life had turned out to be far happier than what she had feared would be her fate.

A happy marriage. Healthy children, happier themselves than not. Work she enjoyed. More than enough money. And yet, sometimes, inexplicably, this sadness, this fear: What if the world is not a good place? What if the worst came to the worst?

It never resolved itself into a wish for death. Rather, now that the children were grown, the thought descended on her lightly, like a warm cloak on an early autumn day: It would be all right to die now. I wouldn't mind. I have had, in many ways, enough.

Enough is enough.

She had often heard her mother use that expression and only recently had she the impulse to ask the ghost, who was her mother: What does that mean, "Enough is enough"?

She had enjoyed her life, more than not. But she could not say she was avid that it should go on forever. She didn't think anything happened to you after death. She supposed it was something like sleep. That was all right; often, she quite enjoyed sleeping. She hoped it would come before she ended up like her mother, her sweet mother, who had died demented, raving, furious. From this she had learned that there were many things worse than death.

Was it all about sex? Was the sense that you'd had enough of life connected to the knowledge that sex was finished? People would be surprised how ardent she had been for sex. How she had loved the bodies of men. At a friend's sixtieth birthday party, to which only women were invited, some of the guests had carried on about their dislike of penises. When some of them—perhaps having had more wine than they were used to and feeling free because they were only with other women—had spoken of their distaste, she, perhaps a bit drunk herself, had said, "I have to say that when it comes to penises, I'm a fan." And everyone had laughed, because she was pretty sure they hadn't thought of her as a passionate person. Even someone much interested in sex. "A cool customer," she'd heard someone say about her once.

But when she was young, she felt herself often in the grips of something she thought was an ugly word: "lust." The final letters, "ust," so unlike the crackling or flaming of what she felt. For a long time, having sex itself was wonderful; it took a while to realize that there was good sex and bad sex, that there was a range of performance options.

Oral sex, for example, was something she'd had to work up to slowly, whereas now it seemed to be the first thing teenagers did, and they didn't even think of it as sex. It wasn't until she'd married Richard that she'd become in any way expert.

And then, as strong as sex, as violent, as entirely absorbing, there'd been the searing love of children. Nothing of the nursery pastel about it: rich, dark as blood. In her work with mosquitoes, she had identified with the maligned female, who, in order to reproduce, required what was called a blood meal. When she first heard the words she found them exciting, arousing even: they seemed so plainly brutal. Blood meal. Each word one syllable. Each suggesting what was necessary to maintain life. Blood. Meal. Violent, destructive, voracious. Mother love.

Her children were grown now, and if she died now their lives would not be ruined. She worried about them less, but they were always at the front of her brain. Erika, headstrong, prone to wildness, an economist now, specializing in microloans for African women. Herself the mother of two sons, Benjamin and Nathan, twelve and ten. Vincent, her son, at thirty-nine, had not yet married. Drawn to beautiful, self-dramatizing girls (with whom Jocelyn always sympathized): none of them good candidates for happy marriage. She hoped he would someday be a father; she knew he would be wonderful at that. He worked too hard. He said he liked being his own boss. A landscape gardener. How much she'd learned from him; he'd allowed her to become a gardener herself, rather than simply reiterating her mother's old plantings. He was always bringing things to delight and surprise her. Deep red dahlias. Blue-black salvia. Left with a note on the table, "Mom: enjoy."

It was possible he would not have children, and then she would never have a granddaughter. The female line ended. Perhaps it didn't matter. She adored her grandsons. The love of grandchildren—embarrassing almost to speak of it, as if you were putting yourself in the category of retirees on tour buses, eating dinner at 5:00 p.m. It was not the tearing love of a mother: it lacked the element of terror, it was not up to you to keep them alive. Rather it was a swim in a temperate sea, with the occasional intoxicating, gentle swell. When they were babies, she could reenter the blissful moments of her own young motherhood; put her lips to their heads and necks, breathe in the yeasty smell and feel the old swoon. But they were twelve and ten now, and she couldn't think of taking them in her lap. Their embraces now were rushed and guarded. As they should be. But it was another loss.

She would not allow herself to go into the house to check to see if the truck was still there.

Taking a drink from her glass, the glass that had been her mother's, hearing the light breeze soughing through the trees, the trees she had loved as a child, she knew that she was happy. Now happiness felt like a piercing, a sharp point pressed against the heart, relieving some pressure, creating another kind of lightness: a relief from something, a suggestion of something. And accompanied by words now, "Thank you" (but to whom?).

The doorbell's ringing startled her. No one came to this house spontaneously; no one who knew anything about anything would ring this bell without a call first. The doorbell ringing at seven o'clock in the evening could only signal something wrong. An emergency. Her mind went first to her grandchildren. Then to Richard. A heart attack. A car accident. It was too late for Jehovah's Witnesses. She walked quickly from the backyard to the front door, and with each step the two words pressed into her brain: *Something wrong. Something wrong.*

She ran to the table in the front hall to get her cell phone. The doorbell rang again, louder this time, three rings now, more insistent. Then a woman's voice. Southern. "Jocelyn. Yoo-hoo."

It was quite possibly a trap. She wouldn't open the door. She went to the window, opened it a crack, and shouted, "Can I help you?"

The minute she'd said these words, she felt a fool. Can I help you? Can I help you steal my things and leave me tied to the dining room chair? The woman knew her name. Was this a good sign or a bad sign?

She switched on the porch light. The woman wasn't young, although Jocelyn couldn't quite fix her age. Her hair was blond, but badly dyed. "Tortured" was the word that came to mind. It looked fried: or like a kind of scorched grain. She was wearing low-rider jeans and a T-shirt that said BORN TO BE WILD. Her breasts were very large, disproportionately large for what seemed an almost distressingly thin body. Now that she was in her seventies and the looks of people her age varied so dramatically, Jocelyn often felt stumped to guess people's ages. She's my age, Jocelyn thought. Maybe a bit younger. Or older. But what did it matter? she asked herself. She could still be a gangster's front woman, the granny who softened the potential victim.

Whoever she is, Jocelyn thought, she doesn't belong here. Whatever she's doing here, she's out of place on Phillips Road.

She was struck with displeasure at her own snobbishness. This feeling took its place beside two other conflicting feelings: the terror of being hacked to death with a meat cleaver and the terror of seeming rude.

"Now I know I'm a stranger," the woman said, or shouted, "and believe you me I know it's a little odd and I understand your suspicions, believe you me I do. A woman alone can't be too careful. Who knows who's out there these days?"

If the woman was trying to reassure her, she hadn't succeeded. How did she know Jocelyn was alone?

Jocelyn allowed her tone to become sharper.

"What is it that you want?"

"I have a message from a friend," the woman said, stepping back into the porch light. The yellow light was disastrously falling on what Jocelyn could see was a set of very bad false teeth. The overwhite smile made Jocelyn want to turn away.

"A friend?"

"A very old, very dear friend," the woman said. And then, stepping back as if she were about to break into song, she dropped her arms to her sides, raised her palms to the porch ceiling, and said loudly,

"Johnny Shaughnessy."

Jocelyn sat down heavily on the sofa.

It was impossible.

Johnny Shaughnessy.

Her first husband.

Her first love.

She hadn't seen him in fifty years.

She had known him less than two.

She had run from him, run away leaving only a note on the white deal table, "I had to go home."

She was suddenly struck at the oddness: in the years that had gone by, she had rarely thought of Johnny.

How could it be that you had married someone, loved someone, and then never thought about them?

And now, after all this time, he was here. Of course she'd have to let him in the house.

But how would she say this in a way that was neither unwelcoming nor encouraging of too much—what? Intimacy? Friendship? Time? What could she say? "Bring him in. I'll see him now. I'm ready." What she decided to say was not quite true, but it had the virtue of seeming inoffensive.

"I'd like to see him. Of course I would."

The woman reached into the back pocket of her jeans. She took out a lime green cell phone and pressed one key.

"It seems you're as welcome as the flowers in May, as one of your old songs goes," she said.

She stood on the porch, beckoning Johnny in, as if it were her house, as if she were the hostess. Jocelyn stood behind her, still in the living room.

The door of the truck opened. The driver's door. He walked towards the house.

It was too dark for her to make out features, but even in this light his walk was familiar to her, that mix, that had once so aroused her, of confidence and hesitation, born of the sense that was nearly but not quite absolute: everyone would be glad to see him. And there was no need to thrust or push or even rush to make his presence felt. He was still thin; and although you heard that in age people got shorter, she hadn't noticed it yet in her friends, and she didn't see it in him. He had all his hair, and it hadn't seemed to turn gray; it was still blond, golden even. He was wearing jeans and a T-shirt whose inscription she couldn't read . . . did it match the woman's? Like her, he wore cow-boy boots. The buckle of his belt was elaborate, but Jocelyn couldn't read the lettering. Why was he trying to pass himself off as a cowboy? She remembered that he'd loved American Westerns, loved the part of America that she felt no connection to, that slightly embarrassed her. Elvis, for example. He was crazy about Elvis, whom she considered at best mildly mortifying, at worst a bore.

From this distance, he appeared to be much younger than she knew he was. She saw that he had his right hand in his pocket, and she knew what he was doing; playing with a coin, turning it up and down. It was what he did when he was nervous, and of course, he would be nervous seeing her.

He jumped up the three porch stairs—still, she thought, the master of the boyish gesture.

"Well, Jossie, if you're not a sight for sore eyes. You haven't changed a bit."

And you're still a liar, she wanted to say, surprised at her own bitterness.

"Won't you sit down," she said, indicating the couch to them, dis-pleased at her own diction.

The woman sat down and patted the chintz fabric of the couch. "Johnny was as nervous as a cat that you wouldn't want to see him. I said, 'Johnny if she don't want to see you we just start up the truck and just take off, like we never been here.' But he says to me, 'Linnet my love,' he calls me that, I think it's the Irish way, 'Linnet my love,' he says to me, 'you go in first, to pave the way.' I said to him, 'For Lord's sake, Johnny, after all this time there's bound to be no hard feelings.'"

Hard feelings. Jocelyn thought. No hard feelings. What would be the opposite of hard feelings? Soft feelings. The truth is, Linnet my love, she wanted to say, I have no feelings at all.

She felt ashamed at her own nullity of heart. In place of sadness or regret there was simple curiosity. Johnny Shaughnessy was seventy-five. He'd been twenty-five when she'd last seen him. In her mind, he was still twenty-five, and Johnny had always been much more boy than man. And so, like some joke speeded-up film, the boy in her mind was the old man in her living room.

"It means the world to him," Linnet said. "I can tell you that for sure."

Johnny seemed to want to let Linnet talk. He was looking down at the carpet, as if the pattern were a code he might, with luck, break.

"Linnet," she said. "That's a lovely name. Unusual."

"My father was Canadian."

She wondered what that had to do with anything. She tried to remember what a linnet looked like, but she was pretty sure it was a small bird, rather delicate. But there was nothing delicate about this woman, with her tortured hair, her oversized breasts, her Born to Be Wild T-shirt, her long red nails. The stench of cigarette smoke clung to her. Jocelyn wondered if her breasts were real. It seemed unlikely, given the smallness of the woman's frame. But what did it matter if she'd had—a phrase Jocelyn loathed—a boob job? She wouldn't be spending enough time with her for it to matter one way or another. A few minutes, half an hour perhaps. Then she'd be gone from Jocelyn's life, as quickly and easily as she'd entered it. Taking Johnny with her. Quickly and for good.

"You're probably surprised to see an old Frito-Lay's truck parked in front of your house, on your nice street. But it's our job. It's a pretty common job for senior citizens. Pretty common for retirees trying to supplement a pension. Cross-country hauling, I mean to say. Of course we're not exactly retirees. A musician never retires. For a musician, retirement and death are the same word. And the Lord knows neither of us have a pension."

"You're still playing and singing, Johnny?" Jocelyn asked, glad to think of something to say.

"We both do, Jossie," Johnny said. "We call ourselves Dixie and Dub."

"On account of he's from Dublin and I'm from Tennessee."

"Oh, yes I see," she said, wanting to add, You were better than that when I knew you.

It was the fourteenth of July, 1962, the day she met him. She remembered it was Bastille Day.

He had come into their lives because her father had met him on the train. His usual train, the 5:38. Johnny had sat down next to him, out of breath, having only just made the all-aboard. She always imagined a conductor shouting "All aboard" and Johnny running down the track, jumping onto the train at the last minute. But she wasn't really sure if anyone shouted "All aboard" on suburban commuter trains.

Johnny had engaged her father in conversation. Had her father been reluctant, putting his face in his *New York Times* to seem discouraging? But no shield could withstand the thrusts of Johnny Shaughnessy when he was determined to make contact. Of course her father had been charmed. Perhaps it was his voice, the beautiful Irish cadences, making you feel you'd never heard English spoken properly before. Her father had been seduced. Johnny was a seducer. His seduction of her was in a way the least spectacular of the many she'd observed. He had seduced her, but it had been he who'd been abandoned. There was a category "seducer," but none for the abandoner. That is who she had been.

Johnny had missed his station: New Rochelle. What had got into her father, that he'd invited Johnny home for supper? It was quite unlike him; he was a careful, a reserved, a predictable man. But he arrived at the door with Johnny, Johnny with his rucksack and guitar. Like the wanderer in an adventure story.

She had wondered later about her father's unusual impulse, inviting a stranger to dinner. Was it a vestigial longing for the wildness and camaraderie of the War? Lieutenant Pemberton. Stationed in France 1941–45, an orderly in a wartime hospital. He never spoke of it.

Or was it that in Johnny he saw the son he'd always wanted, lighthearted, free, so different from the careful women—wife and daughter—he'd come home to after the War?

Summer of 1962. It might have been one of the best summers in the history of the world to have been young and in love. If you were healthy, prosperous, American.

She had just graduated from Cornell, B.S. in animal physiology. She had wanted to be an entomologist, wanting to work in a laboratory, but not like her father: he was involved in cancer research, and she didn't want to work at something where so much was at stake. She preferred the nineteenth-century model of scientist, naturalists they were called, whose métier was slow observation and precise recording. She took the job in the lab of Dr. Probst, her father's friend, just to give herself time to figure out her next move. "Rest, you need your rest, after the ordeal of senior year and all those exams," her mother said, having no real idea of what Jocelyn's college life had been. She had worked hard, but certainly not to the point of exhaustion, like many of her friends. She never left things to the last minute, and she wasn't given much to late nights. She dated, but the men she met didn't interest her enough to become seriously involved. She was famous for refusing a fourth date, although if they were handsome she enjoyed the light kissing and fumblings in the backs of cars, the incomplete expressions of desire in the dormitory "parietal hours." But no one interested her enough to give up her virginity, which was still, in 1962, something of a big deal for someone like her.

She enjoyed working in the lab; everyone was young and enthusiastic. Often they went out for drinks after work. She couldn't remember what they talked about. Nothing very serious. Five years later, it would have been impossible not to talk about politics. But in June 1962 it was certainly possible. It was, in fact, the norm. John Kennedy was in the White House. Everything would be all right.

Her work was interesting but not taxing; her colleagues were pleasant, but she knew that none of them would be lifelong friends. What pleased her most was walking the streets of New York, and having a paycheck. And it was pleasant to meet her father for a drink at Grand Central as they got on the commuter train together, workers on their way home for a good meal. She hadn't been on the train with her father the day he had met Johnny. If she had, things would have been very different. She would have been sitting next to her father. There would have been no free seat beside him for Johnny to fall into, at the last moment, in the nick of time. Her life would have been different. Although she wasn't sure how very different it would be. If her marriage to Johnny had changed her very much. She was not sure it had changed her at all.

———

She thought it was important to set the right tone. She didn't want to sound unfriendly. But how did she want to sound? She didn't want to spend much time with him, but to turn him away would be to suggest something that was not true: that what had happened had been powerful enough to cause her to recoil. He had once been part of her life. No, she told herself, tell the truth: he had once been her whole life. Was it possible that he was nothing to her; was it possible that memory, which was meant to be so powerful a force, growing stronger in its pull with every year . . . was nothing to her? She had to understand that, in fact, she didn't remember him very well.

It had been nearly fifty years ago. Their time together had been only seventeen months.

Three months in New York City and New Canaan, Connecticut. July, August, September 1962. And fourteen months in Dublin, October 1962 to December 1963. What fraction of her life was that? Less than one seventieth. Still, she had loved him. They had been married. She ought to be feeling more than this.

When he smiled, she saw that, like Linnet, he had a very bad set of dentures. For the first time, she felt sadness. She remembered she had loved his mouth; the slight upper lip, the very full lower, which expressed his moods much more clearly than his eyes: sad or delighted, she could tell in a moment by his mouth. When he was troubled, he jutted his lip out, and tucked his upper lip behind it. And when he was happy, the lip seemed to grow even fuller, as if his joy in whatever was pleasing him had spilled over and filled that lovely lower lip.

But now his mouth was just the mouth of an old man with a bad set of dentures. She remembered he had always complained about his teeth, envied hers. American dentistry, she'd said, apologizing for her lack of dental troubles. Our greatest achievement. Sure, we gave the world the atom bomb, but we're second to none in orthodontia. But then she'd come to understand, he brushed his teeth only rarely. She'd worried about this, urged regular toothbrushing on him. With horror, she remembered herself testing his toothbrush for wetness in the morning. Well, he'd paid for it now.

She didn't want to be thinking this way, thinking about toothbrushes and dentures when she ought to be feeling something great.

But she couldn't get thoughts of teeth out of her mind. She remembered a conversation she'd once tried to have with her dental hygienist, whom she very much liked. She'd said, "So much comes down to dentistry. I mean, if you have good teeth, you are sexually viable, young, employable, socially acceptable, and if not, well, not. What we're doing, you and I, Suzanne, is in some way unnatural. At my age you're supposed to be dead or wearing dentures."

The hygienist, who was very young, looked at her strangely and began blinking hard. "But you don't want to die and you don't want to have dentures. So it's all good, right?"

Jocelyn had regretted the conversation, because she liked the girl, and she thought she had made her uncomfortable, feared that perhaps Suzanne would now find Jocelyn strange and they would lose the easy bond she had enjoyed. And so she said, "Right, Suzanne. All good."

She felt she'd been standing silently, looking at Johnny for much too long. Finally she thought of something it would be all right to say. If she had been a religious woman, she would have offered up a prayer of thanks. But she was not a religious woman, so she put it down to luck.

"What brings you to this part of the world?" she said, in a tone that she believed was light but not dismissive.

"Well that's a story in itself, Jossie, and like all my stories, as I'm sure you've not forgotten, not a short one."

She turned on the living room light. She would have to offer them something to drink.

"A beer would just hit the spot," he said, settling back into the couch.

She put her hand to her throat, feeling his request as an accusation.

"I'm afraid I don't have beer," she said. "We're not beer drinkers, my husband and I. Wine, though, we've got lots of wine. Or scotch, vodka, or bourbon, any of those. Only we just don't have beer. My husband has to worry about his weight. Or not really, he's not heavy, but, you know how men of a certain age put weight on in the gut, and that's a danger, increases the risk of heart disease."

She felt her words had a slightly hysterical edge, and she sat in what had been her mother's chair to calm herself.

"What are you having, then? Let's just be easy. But I'd say you don't have to worry about weight, you're as slim as a girl."

She knew that wasn't true. She'd put weight on in the thighs, in the midriff, in the upper arms, but she could dress to conceal it. She wondered what he thought of her, in one of her fifty identical Eileen Fisher outfits, neutral colors, linen or cotton, loose pants, flowing tops. There was nothing loose or flowing about Linnet and Johnny in their jeans and T-shirts. She admired them for it; she was sick of those ads for Viagra showing older couples in matching white outfits, heading, hand in hand, for twin bathtubs with a beautiful view of the sea.

"Neither of us seems to gain an ounce," Linnet said. "It's all that good living, I guess."

"We're very happy to drink whatever you're drinking, Jossie," Johnny said. "Whatever's easy."

What in the world would make you feel this could be easy? she wanted to say, but mentioned, instead, Pinot Grigio.

"Is that a dry wine?" asked Linnet. "I like a dry white wine."

"Yes, yes, quite dry," Jocelyn said, in the same slightly hysterical tone. "It's one of the driest, really."

"Because I just can't stand sweet white wine. It just makes me feel terrible."

"No, no, it's not the least bit sweet. It's very dry. I'll just get you some."

She had to keep herself from running into the kitchen.

She wanted to phone Richard and demand that he come down from Nantucket, instantly, to rescue her. But of course that wasn't possible. This will be over soon, she told herself. She thought of her mother's words, when she was trying to instill courage in her timid daughter. "Think of it as an adventure," her mother had said. Well, she had thought of her marriage to Johnny as an adventure, and it hadn't turned out well.

"I didn't know you were back in America," she said, placing the glasses of wine on the coffee table.

"Oh, Joss, the truth is, I wasn't long following you back here. I've been back and forth home and here over the years, but mostly here. Harder to make a living there, even now.

"*Sláinte,*" he said, raising his glass. The Irish toast she hadn't heard since she'd left Dublin, fifty years before. She hadn't thought about

Dublin; she had not thought about it at all. She would have to think about it now, because he was here, reminding her of a part of her life that she had simply amputated. Or no, that was too dramatic. Once again she thought of teeth. It was as if she'd extracted a troubling, a painful tooth, a rear molar, something whose absence would not be visible, even when she smiled, and the emptiness something she got used to so that, even running over it with her tongue, the emptiness seemed the norm, and so, forgotten.

Dublin. When she thought of it now she thought of watery skies, larger than the skies of any city, and the lettering on shops: gold against black, that had so pleased her, and the shop windows, flat-faced but friendly on the quay, and the beautiful ornate ceilings in the great houses, and the great high staircases, and the places he had taken her, pubs on the waterfront, Howth, she remembered it was called, where old men and women sang songs that had made everybody weep.

Before she met Johnny, and had believed she'd be living there for a long time, she hadn't thought of Dublin as European. Europe was Paris, where she had traveled with her parents, or Rome or Venice, where she'd been one summer with her roommates, staying in hostels, eating delicious food. London was still Europe, but only just. They spoke English, but they had had the War. Good behavior during the Blitz. Dublin had not had the War; it was only one of the reasons that Dublin wasn't Europe; it was Ireland, a place you didn't need to learn about, or learn from.

What had she expected? She landed in Shannon, surprised, even though every cliché she'd ever heard should have prepared her for the striking, the overwhelming green. Taking a train across the country and then landing on the other side, in what was a city, whose elegance impressed her . . . because she'd expected only a small town, a market town perhaps. She was delighted by the long wide streets, though surprised at their treelessness, and the fronts of the houses and the fanlight windows. Perhaps it was Europe after all.

Fifty years later, images come to her mind. Two young men riding on one bicycle, one pedaling for dear life driving the bicycle, the other perched on the saddle nonchalantly, languid as though in a chaise longue, his legs trailing along the cobbles.

A shop called Junk and Disorderly.

Gypsies, or were they called tinkers, now they were called itinerants, with shockingly beautiful faces, wrapped in blankets with their babies inside, thrusting their babies in your face, a penny for the babby misis (this was not America). They frightened her and made her feel ashamed, and she fled from them as if they were a plague that would infect her with their anger and their thrusting and their poverty and their insistence that they would not wish to be like you, but you must pay them, somehow, for the very things that frightened you and made you feel ashamed. And the women selling fruit and vegetables shouting in voices coarse and aggressive, then, when you bought, suddenly maternal, tender, calling you dear, and then possibly breaking, for no reason she could tell, into song, and breaking the song off for no reason.

But now when she thought of that time, what came to her was not what she saw, but what she heard. Her days were days of talk, a paradise of talk, a wilderness of talk. Or like a large dark room full of old furniture, in which she stumbled, sometimes crashing into a broken useless piece, sometimes coming on something of astonishing grace, heartbreaking proportion. She felt herself getting drunk on their talk, on the large words they felt free to use, "death" and "betrayal" and "mourning," the large categories: "life," "truth." The rage at the church, the playing with all kinds of anarchisms. She had to learn that republicans were not the people of Dwight Eisenhower but revolutionaries, and some of the people she met in the pubs had been imprisoned by the British for their political activities, some of which, she later learned, had ended in violence. Strange, she thought, she had no sense in 1962 that the question of a united Ireland, of getting the British out of the north, was anything that occupied people's minds very deeply. Was that another kind of untruth, another kind of burying of the reality . . . that people didn't talk about it? Or at least to her. Ten years later would be Bloody Sunday, and it would be all anyone would talk about. Oh, they sang revolutionary songs at some of the pubs Johnny performed at, but it seemed an anachronism, a nod to a long-distant past.

Johnny was performing almost every night, usually in pubs. And she was always with him, so they always went to bed late and got up late . . . it had taken her a while to get used to that. And then she had "her job," 12:00 to 4:00 p.m., helping Maeve Riordan organize her memoirs. Or not organize them, actually, talk about organizing them. Maeve Riordan, still beautiful at—what would she have been then?—seventy-eight. Not much older than I, Jocelyn thought now and yet presenting herself as an old lady. That was your only option then. Whereas she and her friends were doing Zumba and yoga and having things done to their eyes and lips and wondering whether it was unseemly for them to be wearing bikinis at their age. She thought of Maeve Riordan's hands, with their prominent veins and their twisted fingers and her sapphire ring, and her emerald, and she looked at her own hands, which were not yet old. When are we allowed to get old now? she wondered. Some days she thought that might be a luxury; to give it over, this pressure to appear, if not young, then not yet old.

Maeve Riordan, who was a much younger friend, an "associate," of Constance Markevwicz, despite her name an Anglo Irish aristocrat turned revolutionary suffragette: first woman elected to the Irish Parliament and the Irish cabinet. Yeats had written about her and her sister, "Two beauties / One a gazelle." And so Maeve Riordan had known Yeats ("He liked being called Senator,") and AE, "a great windbag," and to listen to her might have known Cathleen ni Houlihan and Wolfe Tone. Jocelyn never knew what of her stories had really happened, and nothing ever got written, not a word. Maeve would shuffle papers, pat them into piles, put rubber bands around them and then take rubber bands off others. But nothing got written. As far as Jocelyn knew, it never had. And yet, Jocelyn thought, I spent days with someone who thought of herself as a friend of Yeats and of the woman Yeats has described, she and her sister, "both beautiful, one a gazelle."

Johnny had told Maeve Riordan that Jocelyn was a direct descendent of Rogier van der Weyden, and she had believed him, and Jocelyn didn't know how she could possibly say, "But that's not true." He'd got the idea because in one of his friend's apartments the van der Weyden portrait of a lady was hanging on the wall, and he'd pulled it off, dancing around with it, and said, "Isn't it just the spit of Jossie here? Couldn't this one be the great-great-great-great-grandmother of my beautiful wife?" And everyone had been taken up by his enthusiasm and had said, yes, look at the high forehead, the shape of the mouth.

But Jocelyn hadn't seen herself in the beautiful woman with the transparent headdress, except that she had always thought her forehead too wide. She assumed that in the fifteenth century it had been fashionable. But in 1962, it was, for her, only an annoyance.

Every evening was spent in talk with Johnny's friends, and the whole of Sunday, from waking to sleeping, was full of talk.

And amidst all the talk she would want her own silence; there were places she could go to escape. The beautiful park, called Stephen's Green if you were Protestant (which she was), St. Stephen's Green if you were Catholic. She wrote a letter to her mother, sitting on a bench there, describing a well-dressed matron on her knees, looking around her like a thief, taking a cutting from some plant with a nail scissors, sticking it in her fancy handbag and running out of the park as if the police had given her chase. And she would treat herself to a coffee at Bewley's, as much for the coffee (she missed American coffee) as for the beautiful stained glass window, rich deep colors, which you had to describe in terms of jewels, ruby red, emerald green, sapphire blue, tropical birds with long curling tails, bright rampant flowers, butterflies, solid as shining rocks, flashes of orange against a muted yellow and green background. And sometimes, when she was very lonely, stealing comfort from the Madonnas tucked into the corners of buildings, a comfort to which she knew she had no right.

Because she wasn't Catholic, and although she had been told different, she believed everyone else was. And she could never be, and so would never be of the tribe. Her parents had been nominally Episcopalian; she'd been confirmed in the Episcopal Church, but they were scientists, rationalists. They went to church because they thought it was something good to do. A kind of placeholder. No word of religion made its room in the house.

The tribe. She did feel she had been brought, provisionally, into a tribal society. And that was how she knew she'd have to live. She was unprepared for the shock when she realized the depths of what had been kept from her.

In all the talk, a central silence, and in the end it was why she had to leave. She was never sure she really knew what people meant. A mania for secrecy, for keeping things mysterious. Women in stores whispering their orders, so you thought they were asking for some illegal drug when they were only ordering toothpaste or stamps.

She had the sense of walking always in a fog, a fog in which the features of the landscape were unrecognizable, and there was in the offing no sun which would have presented the slightest hint of a burning off, a hole even through which there might be visibility. These people lived by words, and yet their words were, she came to see, of less and less use to her.

She began having headaches. The dampness made her headaches worse, the daily rain no longer an emolument but another problem to be got around. Another lie, "It's a soft day," meant the rain might possibly let up by two, and with the sun setting at four, she found no softness, only a heaviness pressing on her head, on the bones of her face. She was always cold; she remembered the heater with its single insufficient orange bar.

Until one day, she left.

She couldn't wait any longer; she felt she had to know, and that enough time had passed so that she wouldn't seem impolite.

"How is that you happen to be in New Canaan?"

"Well the truth is, it's our last stop before we leave the country. Back to Ireland, Jossie, maybe this time for good. We drove this load from Ohio we have to leave off in Long Island, and I don't know why, we were driving through Connecticut and I got this idea in my head, I knew it was a chance in a million but I said to Linnet, Let's go for it, let's drive by Jocelyn's old house. Just for old times' sake. And who knows when I'd ever be back on this part of the road. Of course Linnet knew all about you and she's always up for anything, aren't you, girleen?"

"Yup. I just said, Hey, Johnny, go for it. Though I didn't think there was a snowball's chance in hell that you'd be here. But that's Johnny. Born lucky."

"Right you are," he said. "Wasn't I lucky to find you, Linnet?" He turned to Jocelyn. "The two of you as a matter of clear fact."

Jocelyn raised her glass. She hoped her displeasure wasn't visible. She didn't want to be linked to Linnet. Not in any way. And certainly not by the suggestion that they had anything like an equal place in Johnny's life. It wasn't that she wanted a larger share than Linnet; she wanted a smaller one. Clearly, this woman was his partner, in a way that she had never been. What had she been to him? A ghost? A dream?

"It's sort of a miracle I'm here, actually," Jocelyn said. "I mean, we don't really live here, Richard and I. It's not really our home."

"Richard, that's hubby then, Richard."

"Hubby." She hated that word, as she hated the words "boob job." Maybe, she wondered, they both had too many b's, and too many b's were an ugly sound.

"Yes, Richard Bernstein. He's a lawyer."

Why did I say that, she asked herself . . . why did I say he was a lawyer? Nobody likes lawyers; nobody likes a lawyer's wife.

"He specializes in intellectual property. Actually, he's very concerned with the protection of the rights of musicians, with the new technology, the whole issue of copyright is completely up for grabs, and people aren't paid for what they've created."

"'Intellectual property,' that's a term that could only have been made in America," Johnny said, but not unkindly. "As if what came from your mind was something like a house that you could put a fence around. I'm sort of in favor of everybody having access to all the music in the world. Though it's not in the interest of me and my friends' pocketbooks to say that. But I've never been a great man for the pocketbook."

"That's for sure," Linnet said, snorting, and patting his knee.

"And what about you, Jossie? Are you still working? Still the mad scientist following in the footsteps of Madame Curie? Or is it just that you're about your father's business? The science business, I guess it was a natural for you; if he'd been a cobbler you'd have spent your life mending shoes."

"Johnny said you were a real career gal," Linnet said. "He said you were real devoted to your work. It must have been real challenging, being a scientist and all."

She knew that people only used the word "scientist" in that way when they really knew nothing about it. "I've been retired for six years now. And I wasn't really a scientist. I was more a high-level technician."

Those were the words her daughter, Erika, had used once, in a daughter's anger: "You're nothing but a high-level technician."

She had felt her daughter's words flung like sharp pebbles against a window that would not break, but might be pocked. "You're like one of those people in the ads you see on the subway," Erika had said, "for places like Voorhees Tech. *Love animals? You could be a veterinarian's assistant.* Meaning you can clean up shit while other people do the real work and get the real money. You are allowed to breed mosquitoes and feed mice so that the real scientists can get on with their work, and love you, and tell you how grateful they are. Call you the mother of the lab. Whereas if you'd had any guts or gumption you'd be doing what they do."

Useless to tell her daughter, "But I didn't want to." Sometimes it was painful to examine why it was that she was telling the truth when she said, "I didn't want to."

She didn't want to because she didn't want the struggle, the push, the hardening over that would be required if, as a woman of her generation, you wanted to protect yourself from the insults, the slights, well meaning or not, patronizing or malicious. And she didn't want a life like her father's—late nights, the sense that your work is never enough and never done. She did not want to be the only girl. It had been hard enough at Cornell, a major in animal physiology. "You're such a pretty girl, why do you want to be fooling around with rats and mealworms? Or don't you ever feel bad taking up a place that should go to a man, who really needs it to support a family? You'll just do this as a game, then marry a doctor and stay home with his kiddies."

Her years at Cornell: 1958–1962. Ten years later it would have been different. Twenty years later, unrecognizable. But she had been born when she had been born. She could only be of her time. It was all anyone could be. Except the unusually gifted, the unusually courageous. And she had known that she was neither of those things.

And after she came back, after "that year," it was easier for her to take a job in Stanley Probst's lab. Stanley Probst, a colleague of her father. Working with mosquitoes, working in an infectious disease lab. Dealing with terrifying illness. Malaria. Dengue fever. Even now, she couldn't hear the words without an accompanying sense of doom.

And yes, Erika was right. She was a high-level technician in a way, B.S. Cornell, the servant of her betters. But she'd liked her work.

Lately Erika had been kinder about it, understanding now that she herself had children and was rubbed raw with exhaustion. "I think you made the wise choice, Mom, particularly for the time. Why get involved in that macho rigmarole? For the glory. Well it's true, you never got the glory, but you made important work possible and that's the real thing, isn't it? Maybe we need to start questioning 'what price glory.'"

Jocelyn wished she could have been entirely pleased with what Erika had said. But she knew that underneath her daughter's loving words there was a brackish stream of condescension that in its turn activated Jocelyn's shallow stream of cynicism. Erika had begun meditating and taking yoga. She talked a lot about compassion. In many ways, Jocelyn preferred the older, harsher version of her daughter. She wanted to say to Erika, "Why are you saying things like 'what price glory'? It sounds like a movie starring Victor Mature."

She'd never liked to talk to anyone about her work, and Johnny and Linnet were the last people she would have wanted to talk to about it. It had always been difficult, even when people were genuinely interested, which she was sure these two were not.

"I work with mosquitoes." The minute she said that, whatever the season—it could happen in a dinner party in January, at a formal dance in March—the sentence would cause the people across from her to reach under their protective clothes and scratch.

No, she couldn't possibly say what she really felt. That she loved mosquitoes. Found them beautiful. The delicate wings. The complicated mouths. The fragile, articulate legs. The multiple sensitivities. And yet, along with rats, they were the most despised species in the world. A pest. Responsible for hundreds of thousands of deaths a year. How could she explain what she felt when she went on the Internet looking for popular sites about mosquitoes when an expert opined, "No one would mourn the complete disappearance of the mosquito from the face of the earth."

But I would, she had wanted to write in to the chat room. How relieved she'd been when an entomologist asserted that the disappearance of mosquitoes would be disastrous to the ecosystem.

Her mosquitoes made her feel protective, maternal, as if someone had suggested that her juvenile delinquent son be sent to the electric chair.

And yet she could never forget that they were responsible for the deaths of millions, and had always been. She had read somewhere that our primate ancestors were recognizably malarious before they were recognizably human.

Malaria. The labs she worked for had concentrated on studying malaria; she was faced daily with its devastations. Once a conference speaker, an epidemiologist, had appeared onstage standing before a blank screen. "I am now going to show you," he had said, "the image of the person responsible for more African deaths than any dictator." He pressed a button, and on the screen appeared the face of Rachel Carson. Because of her campaign to ban DDT, he said, the number of deaths from malaria in Africa had increased tenfold.

This was the kind of thing that made Jocelyn glad she had decided to retire. She often wondered if most people were tormented by these thoughts as she was, or if she was unusual. Because these weren't the kinds of things people talked about. And while she was doing her work, breeding the mosquitoes, providing their food, or their blood meal from the rats she also tended, recording their movements—she wasn't thinking about these ideas. But when she wasn't directly performing the tasks connected to her work, and when the labor of tending young children was over, she had become, for many years, almost obsessed with what her poor, beautiful, murderous mosquitoes suggested about life.

They supported life; they destroyed life. They could cause the death of some splendid person and then minutes later die themselves, replaced by indistinguishable millions of their species. They were the necessary food of songbirds. She had often thought, after that conference, of the face of Rachel Carson, who, when Jocelyn was a young girl, she had thought of as a hero. But was that wrong; was the right thing to consider her a villain? And who was right, the environmentalists who said it was wrong to grant the human species a privileged position in the civilization and so opposed DDT and other large-scale measures to extinguish the mosquitoes, or the epidemiologists, with their images of the stricken dead, of suffering children? Nothing, they insisted, nothing should get in the way of preventing this.

"So because I'm retired and Richard is sort of semiretired, we kind of divide our time between this house and his family's house on Nantucket and our place in New York."

She felt ashamed of her own prosperity. Deeply ingrained had been the Yankee sense of thrift. There was no luster now to being a WASP. She was all too aware of the horrors perpetrated by her forebears. But if there was something admirable in the stock, it was a horror of waste, a commitment to keeping your word. Well she had flown in the face of both of these. Holding on to the house was an extravagance.

She, or she and Richard, was the owner of three abodes. The apartment on East Sixty-Seventh and Lexington. The house on Nantucket—Richard's, left to him by his stepmother; it had been in her family for years. Richard was clear that no Jew would have owned a house on Nantucket before quite recently. But it had been wonderful for the children, and Richard loved to sit on the deck and read, watching the light on the ocean. He'd majored in philosophy, and now, not quite retired, but almost, he reveled in the difficult large questions he had given over when he'd taken up the law. His secret, shared only with her: he was writing a book on the Renaissance philosopher Giambattista Vico. His ideas of time.

One of the great pleasures of their marriage was sitting next to each other, each absorbed in reading. Perhaps occasionally saying, "May I read you this?" He was interested in Renaissance philosophy, she, increasingly, in the nature of language, its acquisition, its implications. But five years ago, she had had to have skin cancers removed; from her forehead, her shins. They had returned; she'd had them removed again. So she didn't feel quite safe on Nantucket anymore; she felt protected by the trees in the backyard here that had been her place of safety in childhood. But Richard loved the ocean, and she felt ridiculous saying, "Can't you come to New Canaan so we can read under my trees?"

She could say to herself that actually two of the houses had been inherited: they hadn't actually gone out and bought anything, except the apartment, which they needed, because New York was where they worked. So it was not a luxury, nothing to have to explain. People had to live near where they worked.

"Where's your place in New York, then?" Johnny asked. She was grateful that neither of them had remarked on what they must think of as excessive real estate holdings.

"East Sixty-Seventh Street."

"Oh, East Sixty-Seventh Street," Johnny said. "That's very posh."

"Oh, you'd be surprised, Johnny. When we were young the Upper East Side was the big thing. Now it's considered rather dowdy, a grey lady. All the young people want to be downtown. They have all these new names for places you'd never have heard of, Johnny. Soho. Noho. Dumbo. And young people all want to live in Brooklyn."

She knew she was babbling. It was because she was ashamed. These were people driving loads of potato chips across the country, who couldn't afford proper dental care.

"And have you children, Jocelyn? That is to say, are you a mother?"

"Yes, I have two," she said, not wanting to give details of her children's lives for fear of exposing more prosperity.

"Boy, girl?" asked Linnet.

"One of each."

"The king's set," said Johnny.

"That's not an expression we use in America, Johnny," Linnet said. "We don't have a king. What would you say, that's the president's set?"

Jocelyn wondered if children were a sore subject between them.

"I have only the one, a daughter," Johnny said. "I'm afraid I had not much to do with her rearing. Her mother didn't want me to have anything to do with her after we split. We weren't a good match, Ashley's mother and myself. She was a woman with no sense of humor. Now Linnet here is a woman with a fantastic sense of humor. Fantastic."

"Oh, Johnny," Linnet said, with a girlish tone Jocelyn found mortifying.

"No, I'm afraid I hadn't much to do with Ashley's bringing up. But then a miracle happened. Just two years ago, she found me. She friended me on Facebook. Are you on Facebook, Jossie? I'd like to friend you."

What could it mean, she wondered, to friend someone, to use "friend" as a verb? Did it mean the same thing as "befriend"? No: friending meant nothing, or it meant that what happened seemed to happen with no one taking the lead, just some sort of vague mutuality, housed in cyberspace.

"No, I'm afraid I'm not."

"You must, Jocelyn, you really must. You never know who'll turn up, like me and Ashley. So Linnet and I visit her whenever we're on the West Coast. She lives in San Francisco. She and her husband are both in computers. I have three grandchildren, Jocelyn. Can you imagine? Three little girls."

"Mine are two boys," Jocelyn said.

"Ah well, we must arrange a betrothal before too much more time is lost," Johnny said.

Grandparents. They were grandparents. They had been young lovers.

Her eyes fell on Johnny's hands. They were battered, damaged. The nail on his left middle finger was split down the middle; the others were ridged and cracked. His knuckles were overlarge—was it arthritis? They were not the hands of a young man. She remembered his hands, hairless, girlish even, how they had given her pleasure that had astonished her; she'd learned on her skin, from his hands, the meaning of the word "swoon."

Were these the same hands now? Was her body the same body? The skin had been long ago sloughed off. Many times. Was it every seven years you got a new skin? Or was that an old wives' tale? She should know better than this, with her training; she should know better than even to entertain such a thought.

They were grandparents. They'd been young lovers.

And at once, like the seven skins she'd shed in fifty years, the past fell from her and she was back again in that first summer, twenty-two years old, in love with Johnny. In love with Johnny and his miraculous hands.

It wasn't possible that in that summer they had never been indoors, but that is how she remembered it. He met her every day for lunch;

they walked west to Central Park; he brought sandwiches, every day the same, ham on white bread with butter. Never had any food seemed so delicious to her, sweet and salty, the thick yellow butter, the soft gluey bread, and they would lie in the grass after they'd eaten their sandwiches, quickly, very quickly, and then kiss for forty minutes straight until it was time to go back to work. Now work was a trial to her; only an enforced waiting, four hours to be lived through till she could see him again, when there would be more kissing and then parting in Grand Central, her body sluiced with pleasure, dreaming of him the whole way home. Unless he was performing somewhere that night and then she would stay to see him sing. But never once had she spent the night with him. She actually had no idea where he lived. When she asked him where he lived, he said only "here and there," and gave no particulars. Soon he was spending the weekends with her family in New Canaan. Her parents were delighted with him. Or her father was.

She hadn't looked too closely at what her mother thought of Johnny. She hadn't asked. She hadn't, perhaps, wanted to know. She and her mother would be in the kitchen, making supper, doing dishes, whispering like girls, and they would hear Jocelyn's father laughing as they had never known him to laugh with them, and get almost sick with laughing at dinner over Johnny's stories. Story after story; they poured out of Johnny like grain from a sower's hand, or from a chute. But she couldn't now remember a single story. Not one. Oh, yes, she could bring one up now. Something about some IRA soldiers who were lying in ambush to kill a wealthy Anglo Irishman, only to find out he wasn't coming out; he'd been laid up with a cold. "The poor fellow," the soldiers had said to one another. "Terrible thing, a summer cold. Please God he'll be all right tomorrow." Tomorrow would be the day that they would shoot him. Yet for tonight, he would be in their prayers.

Later, when she'd tearfully asked her mother, "Why didn't you warn me?" her mother had said, "I hoped for the best."

Certainly, her parents had been welcoming. Too welcoming? Had her father offered her up on the altar of his own desire for a lively son?

He took him to the country club; he taught him golf. Johnny seemed to learn the game instantly. "A natural," her father said. "As if he'd been born to it."

"Well I'd hardly say that," Johnny had said.

And there was the music. When he came to New Canaan he always brought his guitar. And after dinner he would sing for them. It was summer; the evenings were long, the light stretching out, it seemed, forever. "I'll sing the darkness in," he'd say, sitting on the back porch, and they were all at peace, and happy, but she was enormously aroused and couldn't wait for her parents to go to bed so she could be in his arms. Right there on the couch; was it this couch? She had remained a virgin. She can't imagine now how that could have been. She can't imagine that she thought it normal that she would wear a girdle when her stomach was perfectly flat.

The music. She was for that summer, for the whole next year, the singer's girl. Gigs they were called; it was a word she heard for the first time then. An endless series of Irish pubs that seemed to her indistinguishable from one another. The Shamrock, the Blarney Stone, Paddy's Galway Bay. Smelling of beer, the bartenders not knowing quite what to make of her nursing a single gin and tonic—she'd do better now, she thought. As she aged, she'd learned to like drinking more and more. But then, she was the girl at the table, sitting, holding her drink, smiling, but full of anxiety—would they like him, they had to like him, she would kill them if they didn't like him, how could they not like him, he was entirely lovable, entirely desirable, entirely gifted. Or if they didn't like him enough, enough for him to say, "It was all right, then," he would be cast down, his lower lip thrust out, his upper lip tucked behind it, in need of endless reassurance. "You were great, Johnny, they loved you."

It was hard, sitting at those tables, to keep her face in what she imagined was the right way. She'd tried to remember the faces of the girlfriends of singers in movies. But they had it easy: they were only required to keep their faces right for a minute or two. She felt the responsibility of it, sometimes for hours. Fifty years later, she can remember the strained muscles in her face. Trying to keep it right.

She remembers the music, not the people he gathered around him, droves of them, not the people, not the stories. Because even then she didn't quite believe the stories. Sometimes she was embarrassed to see some of the people again, because he'd told them things about her that weren't true. At first she thought he'd misunderstood when he told people her ancestors had come over on the *Mayflower*. That her father had been one of the soldiers to land on D Day.

He'd ended each of his sets with the same song, which he dedicated to her each time.

"To my very special lass here, who puts up with me." He'd strum a few chords and then warn the audience that this was the last song of the evening. Then he'd put down the guitar and step forward and begin Prospero's speech from *The Tempest*, "Our Revels now are ended," pausing a moment after "We are such stuff / as dreams are made on, and our little life / is rounded with a sleep," to say, "This is Shake-speare's way of saying, 'Have ye no homes of your own to go to?'" Then after the laughter, a few more chords and the song that brought tears to everyone's eyes, even hers, genuine tears, every single time.

> *Will ye go, lassie, go*
> *And we'll all go together*
> *To pull wild mountain thyme*
> *All around the blooming heather.*

And the second verse, even more beautiful:

> *I will build my love a bower*
> *By yon pure crystal fountain*
> *And on it I will pile*
> *All the flowers of the mountain.*

It was only later that she discovered the third verse, the one that made a mockery of eternal love. "If my true love will not come / I will surely find another."

He never sang that verse. She didn't know about it till years later, after she'd left him. She heard a record of the Clancy Brothers on the radio. That was when she discovered that he'd stolen the "Revels now are ended" bit . . . and have ye no homes of your own to go to . . . from the Clancy Brothers, a straight-out theft. How could he have done it, riding as he did on the coattails of the Clancy Brothers, riding the wave of the craze for folk music? But in 1962, she'd never heard the songs before. She thought they were original with him because she thought everything about him was miraculous. And so it seemed a miracle to her when he told her he loved her and when, that September, he asked her to marry him. Who would refuse a miracle? Would she, he asked (he was literally on bended knee), go back with him to Ireland?

Was she disappointed that her parents seemed so delighted? Or was it just her father? Her mother busied herself with plans for the wedding, only a few people, a judge who was her parents' friend, right in the living room. Right here, she thought, I married him right here. She wondered if he remembered.

"We have a favor to ask you, Linnet and myself, but we'd like to think we'd be able to do something in return."

Here it comes, she thought. How much money would he ask for? How much would she give him?

"Could we park the truck here and spend the night in your home? We'll be out of your hair in the morning. It's nice for us to rest our old bones in a bed from time to time instead of dossing down in the back of the truck. And we'd be pleased to take you to dinner. We've just made great friends with Tony, who owns a fabulous restaurant right here in town. Of course you know it. The Tower of Pizza. Fabulous Italian food."

"No," she said, feeling as if she'd missed something right under her nose, something wonderful he'd seen the first minute he laid eyes on it. "Richard and I rarely go out to eat when we're here."

"Well then you've a treat in store," he said, rubbing his hands. She understood that he understood that she'd already agreed to their spending the night. She couldn't say no now without making a much larger point than she wanted to. And really, her impulse was to agree.

"I wonder if I could bother you to use the powder room," Linnet said.

"The powder room." The words made Jocelyn sad, making clear

the woman's unease, her desire not to appear unrefined, and the use of the words was the very thing that revealed their class differences, as if a spotlight had been shone on them.

"Of course," Jocelyn said, "I'll just get you a hand towel."

"She's a great girl, Linnet, a great soul, really," Johnny said when the bathroom door closed. "The soul of loyalty. The most loyal woman I ever knew."

Did he mean that as an accusation against her? She knew very well that with Johnny anything that was hurtful was not meant. Unconscious malice, it might be called by a certain type. Passive-aggressive by another. But Jocelyn believed that neither of these terms applied to Johnny. No, it was simply a certain absence of mind. A certain lightness, a tendency to shift attention.

But meant or not, the word "loyal" could not have been applied to her. She had left him. After only a little more than a year of marriage.

"We'd better get a wiggle on," Linnet said. "It's after seven and they don't serve all night. And we need to get an early start in the morning."

"I'm thinking you'd prefer to take your car than ride in the cab of the truck," Johnny said.

"Yes, certainly," said Jocelyn.

"So if you'll move your car out of the driveway, I'll just pull the truck in. We don't want to leave it parked on the street. The last thing we need is a whopping great parking ticket."

"Of course," Jocelyn said. She realized that, since they'd arrived, she'd done nothing but do what they asked. And why not? Everything they suggested made the best possible sense. But what sense did it make that she was driving her ex-husband and a woman who either was or was not his wife, fifty years since she'd last seen him? It made no sense at all.

She realized she hadn't called Richard to tell him where she was. She hoped he wouldn't worry. Of course he wouldn't worry. There was no reason to, no reason whatever.

The restaurant was near the railroad station, the part of town, in all the years she'd lived in New Canaan, that Jocelyn had approached most rarely. The town had a dirty little secret, perhaps not well kept. Every-one thought of New Canaan as the home of upper-class WASPs, but there was a part of it that was not WASP at all, that had been, for many years, primarily Italian. None of her parents' friends lived in this part of town. "They" had their own church, their own schools; as a child she'd seen other girls her own age in plaid jumpers and brown oxfords, the boys in blue jackets and grey trousers. In high school, some of her good friends had been Italian: Barbara Valone, who'd been her partner in the science project—she remembered it was something about bats—that had won them third place in the state finals, and Arthur Calonna, who sat next to her in Chemistry and taught her how to use a pipette. But when it came time for college, Jocelyn and her friends went to Ivy League schools and Barbara went to Manhattanville, Arthur to Ford-ham. It was understood that they would go to Catholic colleges. Jocelyn had never seen them after high school graduation. Not once. If they came home to visit their parents, it would have been to quite another part of town.

"Right here," Linnet said, indicating a neon sign that flashed TOWER OF PIZZA. How had she never noticed it? She noticed once again that Johnny had, if not actually lied, then exaggerated. He'd certainly got the name wrong. It wasn't an Italian restaurant. It was a pizzeria. But when they approached she saw that the menu on the door indicated that lasagna, manicotti, and baked ziti were also served. So perhaps she was being unfair.

Johnny and Linnet walked into the restaurant ahead of her. She saw how he did it, making an entrance, certain that everyone would be glad to see him. And the owner came out and put his arms around first Johnny and then Linnet. "I was so afraid you wouldn't show up," he said. "We've got everything all set up for you."

He pointed to two chairs and a microphone, a small table, a pitcher of water, a vase with two daisies in it, and an overlarge chrysanthemum.

"This is the friend I told you about," Johnny said. "Do you believe she's lived in New Canaan all these years and never been here?"

"It's just that we're only here on weekends and, well, we like to stay at home."

"No problem, honey," the owner said. "Anything you do is fine by me, after what Johnny told me about you. By the way, say hi to Mick next time you see him."

Jocelyn nodded, not knowing what she'd agreed to.

"What did he mean by that, 'Say hi to Mick'?" Jocelyn asked.

"Well, I just told him a little story, just to pass the time. I told him you and I had been friends when you were traveling in Europe in the sixties, boyfriend and girlfriend I said, but I told him you left me to go off with Mick Jagger. Before he joined the Stones."

"Why would you do that, Johnny?" Jocelyn said. "What can I possibly say to him if he asks me?"

"Just say everything was great, that Mick was great, a very sensitive fellow," Johnny said.

"Isn't he just a hoot?" Linnet said, putting her arm around Johnny's waist.

"You see, now, Tony has a story to tell his family and you'll always be welcome."

"Except, Johnny, that it just isn't true," Jocelyn said.

Johnny shrugged, and a waitress came up with two menus.

"Katerina, love," he said, kissing her on the top of her head, "great to see you. I was hoping you'd be on. Katerina's from Romania."

"I understand the song 'Ruby Tuesday' was written for you," she said.

"I guess so," said Jocelyn. It was a set of muscles she hadn't used for fifty years, the muscles that allowed her to pick up the thread of Johnny's stories so that no one would be embarrassed, disappointed, shamed. Linnet started singing "Goodbye, Ruby Tuesday" and Johnny joined in, and then Katerina, and then Tony, the owner. Jocelyn looked down at the floor, hoping to suggest that the memory was bittersweet.

When she sat down, she realized she was trembling. She was slightly shocked at how glad she was to see Tony approaching with a bottle of wine and three glasses.

She drank rather faster than she was used to. Johnny and Linnet were holding hands. She found this vaguely embarrassing, and she disliked herself for the feeling. She felt that the silence made their handholding more portentous than it might have been. She noted that neither of them had asked her anything about herself. And then she remembered;

the Irish didn't ask you about yourself, they considered it rude. But of course Linnet wasn't Irish, but maybe she wanted to let Johnny take the lead. Well, Jocelyn told herself, I'm not Irish, and there's no one but me to take the lead. And there were things she wanted to know. She felt she had a right to know certain things; they had imposed upon her privacy, her hospitality. She should get something in return. She should be given information about the last half century of her ex-husband's life.

"How long have you two been driving trucks?"

"Well, not that long, it's just our latest way of surviving," Linnet said. "We met when we were working a county fair in Wisconsin; we were an introductory act for Arlo Guthrie."

"Oh, yes," Jocelyn said, "Alice's Restaurant."

"Fabulous guy, fabulous. He wasn't just a one-trick pony. He's really grown as an artist. Great stories, great stories. Great gas it was being on the road with Arlo."

"Don't say 'great gas,' I told you that, baby," Linnet said. "It makes people think you've got a flatulence problem."

Johnny laughed and kissed Linnet on the mouth. Jocelyn remembered she had thought the same thing fifty years ago in Dublin when people said "great gas," when they meant they were having a good time.

Jocelyn felt herself laughing more than she knew the comment was worth. Why not enjoy the evening? she asked herself. There's nothing wrong with it. It's good to widen your horizons. Get out of your rut. God knows, Johnny was never in a rut.

"For a while, we had a really good gig, a good paying gig, not a musical gig but, you know, like a job. We had it for two years. We were a live-in couple for a terrific old lady. We really loved her. Out in New Mexico, near Taos. Beautiful country. I just love the desert," Linnet said.

"I do too," said Jocelyn, with an enthusiasm that suggested that the bond between them was profound.

"Adelaide Harrison, what a great lady. A really great lady. We lived in, you know. I was the handyman and Linnet did the cooking and cleaning and the errands—she had a gorgeous place near Taos, incredible views of the desert, unbelievable sunsets. We lived there for two years, and we were like family. We couldn't do enough for her, she couldn't do enough for us," Johnny said.

"It's because of her we have this nest egg," Linnet said, reaching into the neck of her T-shirt. She pulled something out, a silver chain, and lifted it over her head, cupping it in her hand as if it were a literal, fragile bird's egg, robin, perhaps, or plover, Jocelyn thought. She brought her hand close to Jocelyn's face and then opened it slowly. "This is our nest egg," she said. Attached to the chain was a diamond ring; the stone, Jocelyn could see, even in the darkness, was enormous.

"Adelaide gave this to me and Johnny. It was her engagement ring. She said she'd give it to us if we'd promise to make it legal someday. We said we would, although, as a matter of fact, that's not going to be happening anytime soon, because neither of us is exactly what you'd call divorced."

"Ashley's mother?" Jocelyn asked. She was listening to what they said as if they were people with whom she had no connection, from another very distant country, with another set of customs, fascinating, but far from her concern.

"No, no, Ashley's mother was much too organized not to get properly divorced. You were organized in that department, Jocelyn, or I guess the family lawyer was. I was quite grateful at how easy it was."

She'd had to sue him for desertion, and she'd disliked that very much, because he hadn't deserted her, she'd deserted him, although she found the word grotesque, as if they were infants left on some doorstep. She knew that he wouldn't mind, though, and it was much easier. Quite easy, in fact, she remembered now.

"No, it was a lady named Melody, but we did not make beautiful music together," Johnny said.

Linnet raised her glass, and they clinked.

"And me," she said, "well I got out by the skin of my teeth, let me just tell you that. I don't know what it was but for a while there, bipolar types just levitated towards me."

"I think you mean 'gravitated,' sweetheart," Johnny said. "Although knowing you, you're such an angel, maybe they did levitate."

"Whatever," Linnet said. Jocelyn noticed she took no offense at

Johnny's correction of her diction. He had cared about words; she wondered if Linnet's carelessness with language was troubling to him.

"But you let your friend Adelaide think you would get married
someday."

"Well, we didn't want to worry her. It would have just worried her if
she knew about all our legal complications. And she was worried about
what to do with the ring. She knew her daughter didn't want it. She
kept saying, 'Rowena's just too sporty for this kind of ring.'"

"What she meant," Linnet said, "was that she was a lesbian."

"Rowena was a great girl, her and her friend Beth. We had some
marvelous evenings with them, watching the sun go down with a glass
of wine. It was great crack, great crack."

"That's another thing you can't say, Johnny, like I've told you maybe
like, what, a million times. You can't say 'great crack.' People will think
you're a drug addict."

Jocelyn laughed out loud, a laugh she thought would have embarrassed almost everyone she knew. It would definitely have embarrassed
Richard.

She was feeling dizzier now, and her sense of well-being had suddenly
disappeared, replaced by a disturbing notion that if she got up and tried
to walk she would fall down. She remembered feeling that way all the
time in the last days of her marriage to Johnny. It was navigating the
choppy seas of what they would call stories and what she could only
call lies. Not knowing what was firm, dependable ground, the ground
of fact, the ground on which words and facts met—it had made her
woozy; some days she felt she could do nothing but take to her bed. It
was why she'd needed to leave him; she needed to be on firm ground
again. And she had been, living her life, one foot before the other on
the sweet firm earth. Until tonight. Once again she had to navigate
the sea of untruths. Johnny telling the restaurant owner she had been
Mick Jagger's girlfriend. Pretending that she wasn't more than slightly
queasy about the way in which they'd got their "nest egg," this extraordinarily valuable ring. He had pulled her back, back into those treach-
erous waters.

They never called anything a lie, but they lied all the time, even to each other, even to their best friends. Lying to each other didn't seem to tarnish their sense of friendship. But she had believed that if you were really friends with someone, you didn't lie to them, and so if you lied to someone, that person could not be a real friend. She thought she had made real friendships until the end, when she couldn't believe anything, when she thought nothing was real, and she had been terrified and fled for home.

She had thought Claire and Moira were her friends. She was fascinated by them, by a way she'd never known of being a woman. They talked as she had never heard women talking before. In the fog of talk, the tempest of talk, the tornado of talk, the furniture shop of talk, the flood of talk, the firestorm of talk—men talking, talking, these two women would send up a flare, and there would be a clearing because always they were surprised that it was a woman talking. And the talk of these women was deliberately not kind.

She and Johnny had lived first with Claire and her husband, Diarmid, when they arrived in Dublin. The ease, the kindness of Claire and Diarmid ... "You're very welcome," they had said, and she did feel welcome, nothing begrudged, everything offered—laughter, talk, cigarettes, whiskey, wonderful brown bread and butter-boiled eggs for breakfast; tea, which she had to learn to like, and did. They had actual jobs; they left the flat early ... Claire to work at *The Irish Times,* Diarmid at his architectural firm. He was taking a courageous position, a position against the time of the tide: trying to preserve the beautiful old Georgian buildings against the rush of new development, buildings of a shocking ugliness, an ugliness, he said, that gave him a physical pain, made him want to take to his bed. He was quieter than Claire, and Claire talked even more than Johnny. But she, Jocelyn, was the quietest of them all. She thinks now that with her, Claire took on the male part: the talking part, and she became the woman, the wife, the little sister, listening. Listening to the real story. What was really there behind the ornate, colorful, so decorative screen.

Claire and Moira: best friends since childhood. Jocelyn came to see they didn't really take men seriously. For them men were always boys to be put up with or put off or teased or indulged. A luxury item. They never asked men for advice; they never asked men their opinion. And they had important work, Claire at the paper, and Moira a doctor. How surprised Jocelyn had been that someone her age, twenty-three, would already be a doctor. The training was different, she learned soon; you trained as a doctor the minute you entered college. Tropical medicine was her specialty. And Rory, so in love with her, getting his Ph.D. in French, but film was his passion. What was most important to him was writing film criticism for small journals. They were all mad about film . . . Sometimes they forgot themselves and pronounced the word "film" with two syllables—"fillum," they would say. There were enormous queues around the cinemas that showed the latest films from Europe. The whole town seemed movie mad. But no one was more mad about films than Rory. Serious, always the butt of their jokes, perfectly accepting, even relishing in his role as the one to be teased.

So much is coming back to her now. She remembers Moira making fun of an article he had written. "Marian Imagery in the Work of Ingmar Bergman." He had asked if they would listen to it, give him "constructive criticism." Jocelyn had no idea what the words "Marian imagery" might mean. It became clear to her (she had learned by then not to ask, to wait until she got the code) that it meant something about the Virgin Mary.

And Moira had said, "Oh, for God's sake, Rory, will you give over that pious shite. Bergman has no more interest in the Virgin Mary than my arse."

"I've heard your arse is quite interested in the Virgin," Claire said.

"So it's well ahead of Bergman."

Claire, with her girlish, breastless body, her cap of tight curls, wearing only the lightest shade of pink lipstick, cutting her nails like a boy's. And Moira with her thick black hair, in a single plait, and the black eyes and the un-Irish olive skin. "My tinker blood," she'd said, proudly.

Jocelyn had thought they were her friends. But in the time when she felt she was going mad, because she didn't know what anything really was, what was really happening, when she couldn't believe anything anybody said . . . she felt that even Claire and Moira, if they hadn't exactly lied, had presented her with some version of untruth.

One day, she'd run into them coming out of a store that had always puzzled her. The mannequins were nuns, deliberately unsexy, block-shaped rather than curvaceous. She had found the window display sad: garments meant for concealment rather than allure; serviceable, unadorned, unlovely.

She couldn't understand what Clare and Moira were doing coming out of that store, their arms full of packages. Her puzzlement must have showed on her face because Moira had said, "Shopping for my trousseau, don't you know."

And Claire had said, "We'll have a drink to celebrate the dear about to be departed. Only keep it under your hat."

Moira was going to be a nun. She was leaving for something called the novitiate in six weeks.

Jocelyn was appalled. It seemed appalling to her; beautiful, brilliant Moira throwing her life away, hiding herself behind stone walls. She had suggested gently, she hoped, that perhaps it hadn't been quite fair to Rory, to let him go on thinking there'd be a chance they'd spend their lives together. Moira's lips had thinned almost to invisibility and she'd said, "There are some things too deep for words, too complicated for words. It wouldn't have been telling the truth to talk about it, because I didn't know yet what I felt and I could only decide in the privacy of my own heart. Privacy is not concealment. It is not untruth."

But they had never been quite comfortable with each other again. Because what Moira was doing seemed just too strange to her, too difficult for her to understand in someone whom she had believed to be a friend. Now she wondered: was there a kind of jealousy of it? A jealousy that her friend had a secret life, deeper, richer, more glamorous than any life she had access to? It made her friend unknowable to her; as if she were someone who had been born in another century, and the person Jocelyn thought she had been speaking to was only a phantom, a chimera, the product of a dream.

"We'd better drink up, because this one won't be getting the water of life too much from now on. We won't be able even to see her in the first year, while she's in postulancy. But I'd say in the novitiate they'll ease up on you."

They were using these strange words, "postulancy," "novitiate," as if they were ordinary, as if they were saying "knife," "fork," "glass," "spoon."

"God knows what you'll be up to without me to keep an eye on you. I suppose the sky will be the limit with you and the French fella."

"Well, Jesus, what would you have me do? Join you in the sister-hood of perpetual Irish virginity?"

Jocelyn was completely confused. They had had a lot to drink. They saw that she was lost, and she could see them sharing a look that meant, "Shall we let her in on it?" And then they decided that they would.

"You see, my wild American rose, my husband isn't so much for the below the waist business. It seems I haven't the right equipment. Not like your Johnny."

How long did it take her to understand that she was saying that Diarmid was homosexual?

"I love him with all my heart, you see. My best friend. We're the greatest of pals."

"More than you can say for the President of the Holy Name Society and his lovely wife, Prefect of Sodality."

They threw their heads back and laughed at a joke whose meaning Jocelyn had no access to.

So the friends she thought she had made had all been lying to her. And lying to each other.

But she should have known, because almost from the beginning her friendship with Moira had been marked by lies. The first had turned into a joke. Jocelyn had invited Moira for dinner one night when Johnny was meant to be working late. She had bought what she would have called lamb chops, what were in Dublin called mutton chops. They had just moved into their own apartment and she was excited about cook-ing for another woman, a woman whom she liked, whom she admired.

But before she could serve Moira, Moira grabbed her stomach and said, "Oh, dearie, I'm afraid my girlfriend has just arrived."

And Jocelyn didn't know what she meant, so Moira had to explain, her "time of the month," and she ran out of the house saying she'd come by tomorrow, and they'd have a great time then.

When Johnny came home, and she heated over the lamb chop for him, and told him what had happened with Moira, he bent over laughing. "Oh, God, Jossie, you were going to serve her meat on a Friday and she just couldn't do it, under pain of mortal sin; she lives by that kind of thing, even though she thinks it's tosh, she says she still has to live by it. She didn't want to embarrass you so she pretended to be ill."

"She lied to me?"

"Oh, why would you put it that way? Think of it as a sign of her regard."

"But she wasn't telling me something I needed to know. I could have gone on making the same mistake over and over again."

"The thing is, Joss, we believe people will twig sooner or later. But in their own time. We're not great believers in rushing things here."

"You can say that again," Jocelyn said, because the inability of all her Irish friends to get anywhere on time, to do things when they said they would be done had been a source of great vexation to her, and her vexation was a great source of amusement to her friends. And so, when she said, "You can say that again," Johnny picked her up in his arms, threw her on the bed, and said, "We're not great believers in rushing things here," and made love to her slowly, quoting from Beckett, " 'With a slowness that would arouse an elephant.' Not that you're an elephant, you're my lovely kitty cat, my sweet, fastidious pet."

He was so generous in his praising of her body. What he loved, he said, was the contained whiteness of her body. "Like a lovely, peeled almond," he said, kissing every inch of her, and that, she could remember fifty years later, was a pleasure so complete that she thought she might be carried away somewhere. Love unto death, she remembered thinking. But it hadn't been unto death. It had, rather soon, been over.

She believed that he loved her body. But after a while, she didn't know what she could believe.

She looks over at Johnny, an old man now, perhaps still handsome, but all his freshness leached. She had not been able to bear being married to a liar. She could no longer avoid the truth of it, after the big lie had been unmasked. Is a fifty-year-old lie still a lie? Or has it become just a story?

"I'll need to be packing a bag, Jossie. I'll be needing to go to a funeral."

She was rather excited; she'd been told that funerals, rather than weddings, were the great social events for the Irish.

"Oh, no, my love, it's a long tedious journey. To Longford City. Changing buses, all of them uncomfortable, and then there'd be nothing for you to do ... it would just be family telling stories and drinking too much and I don't know where we'd stay. No, you're much better off staying here in our cozy nest that you've made so wonderful. But I'd appreciate it if you'd do me the favor of packing my bag."

He was always impressed by her packing skills. "Aren't you great," he'd say, every time she folded a shirt or found a place for socks in a corner of the bag. But she was disappointed that she wouldn't be going to the funeral. And for the first time, he became impatient with her when she told him of her disappointment. "Will you give over, I'll be back before I'm gone."

A little shocked, a little bruised, she complained to Moira and Claire when they met in the pub, just the three of them. "I just can't understand why he acted so unlike himself," she said, coughing a little from the cigarettes which she was trying to learn to smoke, particularly around Moira and Claire, who smoked, as they said of themselves, like chimneys.

"Well, I'd say his father's death came as a shock. Though I am surprised he wouldn't have you with him at the funeral."

"What do you mean?" she asked, absolutely puzzled. "Johnny's father's been dead over ten years."

Moira and Claire looked at each other uneasily. "Well then somebody died again with his name just yesterday," Claire said, and Moira laughed, but the laugh wasn't their usual laugh and there was unease in the smoky air.

"It's his father's funeral he's going to, pet."

Jocelyn felt herself falling through, as if the wood of the pub floor, which she believed to have been firm enough to support her, had suddenly rotted, and she was dropping straight down, plumb, to some dark place, but no, the drop down wasn't straight, she was twirling, head over heels, heels over head, with no sense of a final landing, only that the landing, when it came, would be painful, hard.

All she could do was say some words which she knew would make her pathetic to these two women, her friends.

"He told me his father died when he was a teenager. An accident on the farm, something about a tractor."

Claire and Moira tried not to laugh. "Oh, Lord, Jossie. Johnny's father wasn't a farmer, he owned a draper's shop in Longford City. Johnny wouldn't know one end of a cow from the other."

Jocelyn tried not to cry. She remembered being a child in school, not knowing an answer and knowing that tears would only double her humiliation, but the child she was couldn't keep tears back, made fists of her hands to dig her nails into her palms, but it was no use, the tears spilled out, hot, choking: she was helpless, weak; the tears would not be stopped.

"Why would he have done that? Why would he have told me those things when they weren't true?"

"Probably because he wanted them to be true, and he thought you'd like to hear them."

"But what do I do now?" she said, looking at her friends with a desperation. "What do I do next, how do I tell him that I know he lied to me?"

"I wouldn't be so quick to be telling him," Moira said, and Claire nodded her agreement.

"But I have to tell him. I couldn't have this secret between us. It would poison everything."

"Only if you let it," Claire said. "What would poison everything is if you shamed him. You have to understand the Irish, Jocelyn. We're easily shamed: it's usually our first response to nearly everything. We're a nation of shamed children, shamed by our parents, the church, the British, maybe even the land itself. And when we're shamed we want to flee from what's shamed us, flee as if we were running for our lives. And then we want to hurt the thing we've fled. No, Jocelyn, you mustn't let him know you know. You mustn't shame him."

"I can't," she said, suddenly dry-eyed, suddenly certain. "It's not a way that I can live."

"Well, my love, I'd say then it's your funeral. And it will be no Finnegan's wake, let me tell you. There won't be lots of fun at this."

And of course they were right, because it was the death of their love. She couldn't sleep, and when he came home, late, the cold of the early fall on his rough cheeks (his beard was always rough by nightfall), which he rubbed against her to wake her, he thought for love.

She had to say it, she had to speak the words, and she was compelled, as she had felt her body compelling her to weep. She had to say what had to be said.

"Why did you do it, Johnny? Why did you lie to me? About your father?"

And he stood and paced up and down the small room, pounding his fist into his hand, walking in smaller circles.

"It just happened, somehow. Because I didn't want to burden you with the real sordid story. That I hated my father. That he was a brute to us, my sisters and my mother, hoarding his money, refusing to get someone in to help her when she had a weak heart, never the slightest word of praise, only the cutting edge of his tongue, cutting you down to size."

"Why did you tell me you grew up on a farm?"

"Because I hated where I grew up. The oh-so-respectable draper's shop selling the oh-so-respectable clothes to the oh-so-respectable women who only wanted to pass for English, and the town with nothing in it, I couldn't wait to get out. And so I made, what we call in the catechism, a mental reservation. What they would tell you, even the priests and the nuns, especially the priests and the nuns, was that, for example, if someone came to the door, a salesman or a Jehovah's Witness, that your mother didn't want to speak to, you could say, without sinning, 'My mother isn't home,' and you made the mental reservation, 'My mother isn't home *to you.*' So I made a kind of mental reservation: my father is dead, and in my mind I said, 'My father is dead to me.' And I said, 'I grew up on a farm,' and what I said in my mind was 'I grew up on a farm in my dreams.'"

"But you made me believe things that weren't true, Johnny. You made me think you were a person that you're not."

He knelt down on the floor beside her and took her hands, began kissing them. "No, Jossie, I am the person I told you I was. What I'm not is the son of a mean, pious, begrudging bastard who grew up in an ugly, dead town. I'm much more the person of the stories I told than the person of the circumstances of my birth."

She felt her mouth go dry, the skin at the base of her throat go cold, her hands freezing; she took them from his hands and put them under the covers. Was he mad? What he said made a kind of sense, but it was the sense of a madman. Once again, she felt the floor on which her bed rested falling through, but the insubstantial flooring didn't make her fall down; she was carried aloft, and she saw herself, in her white night-gown, in her white bed, whirled through the heavens, with no prospect, ever, of landing on any firm place she might know.

"Will you forgive me, Jossie? I never meant to hurt you. I wanted to make things easier for you, lovelier for you, happier for you. Can you forgive me for that?"

She felt the boy in him, the suffering boy, and she could not keep back forgiveness from this wretched child. But he could never be the man she loved once; that man had been a phantom, and had been carried away, as she had felt herself carried away, into the heavens, only she had come back now, but he was gone forever.

She wonders now if things would have been different if, a week later, John Kennedy had not been assassinated.

A cliché of her generation: you always remember where you were when you heard the news of John Kennedy's death. And yet when Americans were recently asked in some survey about the television images that had most gripped their imaginations, the Twin Towers came first, the death of John Kennedy falling far below the first man walking on the moon. It was another thing that made her feel old, and outside the center of the world. No images were more deeply incised in her mind than the Dallas motorcade, veiled Jackie elegantly grieving, John-John's salute.

She had been in a pub when she heard of it. The shock of it, the greatest of a series of shocks that had made her feel alone. Moira leaving for the convent; Johnny's lie, the many lies, about his father, his whole past; even Claire's revelation about Diarmid and then their insistence to her that it was all right to cover up, to hide, to change the truth if it wasn't what you liked.

Her sense of her own strangeness, of her own exclusion, of not belonging, bubbled up, in the days following John Kennedy's death, overflowing into a froth of primitive possessive rage. He is not yours. He is ours. America's.

She felt enraged at his being claimed by the Irish as one of theirs. *Our dead.* That was a primitive idea; the words were primitive, she knew. And yet they lodged in her mind and would not be uprooted. *Our dead,* she wanted to cry out to the weeping crowds.

His youth, his beauty, his voice and gestures—she could hear him saying the word "vigah," his hopefulness, his belief in change, in progress, these belonged to America, not Ireland. And all of them seemed to be rushing into churches, all of them, the most vehement atheists, and the most scurrilous insulters, reveling in every blasphemy, hurtling now into dark, cold buildings where they could hunker and mumble in Latin. There she would not go. She'd believed what they said about the church, it had been her only source of knowledge about it. She'd believed what they said those buildings represented. She could not now so easily unbelieve. But what did they believe, most deeply, what did they value in the bottoms of their hearts, underneath all the bluster, the bravado-filled, rebellious striking out? Then, shuffling out of churches to pubs to sing "The Minstrel Boy" and weep and drink and cross themselves again.

A lie, a lie. He is not yours. He's ours. Our dead. America's. She wanted to stand up on the bar and sing "America the Beautiful." Shout it like a madwoman over the Irish words. She wanted to say, Did you know, any of you, that I wore a straw hat with his name engraved on it, ringing doorbells in Republican New Canaan, arguing at night with my parents, begging them to vote, to vote for me, winning them over: he was Catholic—oh yes, my friends, it bothered them . . . they feared he would be taking orders from Rome; my mother, who had volunteered for years at Planned Parenthood, feared what that meant especially. I convinced my father first; he was a war hero, Dad, and then my mother: Mama, look at Nixon's eyes. He's not an honest man. What she did not say to him: he is making it possible for us, all of us Americans, to live in a new, larger way.

Youth and beauty and hope and then the other faces as deeply incised: Lee Harvey Oswald, his face a blur of disappointed failure, and then impossible to believe, he is shot by Jack Ruby whom she can only think of in movie terms. Cheap hood. All of us American. Not Irish. All of it ours. Not yours. Ours.

Hope and the dashing of hopes, rubbed out by blurred failures, cheap hoods. The hope. Ours, not yours. And the loss ours.

Those days, those weeks of hurtling and falling, spinning, dropping, her head always aching and the bones of her face always fragile-feeling. The command in her mind when she woke next to Johnny, the voice saying: *Flee, flee.* He was a stranger to her now as she realized herself a stranger, and so one day she told Johnny she'd be coming home for Christmas and would not come back.

She left a note on the deal table, "I had to go home," and from America sent a letter in which she said, "It isn't possible for me to be your wife. I must stay here. I don't belong with you, or in Ireland. This is my home."

Did she imagine he'd come after her? No. They had become ghosts to each other in the weeks starting with his father's death, leading to John Kennedy's death, even as she was living in the rooms she shared with him, sleeping with him, sharing meals and making love, she was not there and he was not there. They were two ghosts, eating, sleeping, making love. Only one of them knew who she was. A ghost.

Somehow the legalities were sorted out. They were divorced. The grounds: desertion. The word stirred her; it was simultaneously true and untrue. She did not desert him, as you would desert a child, leaving it on a doorstep. But it was true, deeply true. She had deserted a belief. A dream.

And here they were now, fifty years later.

Half a century.

A lifetime.

"What made you decide to go back to Dublin now?" she asked. She was feeling pleasantly light-headed, pleasantly irresponsible, knowing she was risking seeming prying, even rude. But she wanted to know. Alcohol is a disinhibiter, she told herself, and I am giving up my inhibition against possibly rude curiosity.

But seeing Johnny go silent, she regretted that she had asked.

"A lot of things, Jossie. A lot of things coming together all at once."

"Oh, come on, sweetheart, there's no sense not being straight. It's a little late for that. And Jocelyn can take it; I can tell she's no wilting flower."

"No, certainly not," Jocelyn said. "Certainly not." Why did the two of them always make her feel unnatural in her speech? Why did they always seem to make her repeat clichéd phrases, so that they were twice as unnatural, twice as bad?

"We don't need to trouble her with our woes, Linnet," Johnny said. "Not on our one night together."

"Well you have to tell her now. But I know you; you never want to be a downer. I'm not that polite though; I'm just going to barge right ahead like I always do. I'll tell you why we're going back to Ireland, Jocelyn. It's the Big C."

For a minute, Jocelyn thought they were talking about the circus. The Big Tent. The Big C. She saw a big neon "C" in front of a tent, and then she saw a "C" in the sky, smoky, and a plane making the letters. Skywriting. Then it occurred to her, and she was ashamed at her own delay. She had to say the word.

"Cancer," she said. "Oh, Johnny, I'm sorry."

"Lungs," he said. "Well, I came by it honestly. A lifetime of Marlboro Reds."

"We don't have insurance," Linnet said, pronouncing the word with the accent on the first syllable. "And in Ireland, it's all on the state. The state'll take care of him. It won't cost him a thing."

Johnny. Cancer. She looked at him more closely now. She had to think of him differently, as someone who was dying. Was this why he was so thin? But why did he still look so young, so vital? Was this just another of his lies?

She put her hand on his, and he squeezed her hand. The touch was so familiar, and so strongly evocative of youth and past love, that tears came to her eyes, and she didn't try to stop them. He took several napkins out of the dispenser on the table and wiped her eyes.

"I hate to break this up," Tony said. "But it's time to sing for your supper."

He handed Johnny a guitar, which he'd clearly left the last time he'd been here. Was it lunch, only a few hours ago? Had he earned such a welcome in one lunchtime, two or three hours? Tony walked up to the microphone and tapped it twice, making an unpleasant click.

"I've got a special treat for you tonight. Just to show that we're not stuck in the Italian ghetto, we've got two real special people for you, singers on their way to Ireland from sunny California. Ladies and gentlemen, let me introduce Dixie and Dub."

Linnet ran to the stool and hopped on it like a girl. Johnny said, "Good evening, folks. We'd like to start out telling you a little bit about ourselves." He struck a few chords, and then they began, "We got married in a fever / hotter than a pepper sprout . . ."

They begin with a lie, Jocelyn thought, but she realized she didn't care. They weren't married. They would never marry. What did it matter? What had it ever mattered? The song made everybody happy; Johnny made everybody happy. And he was dying now.

The next song was Linnet's. The tough girl singing "We got married in a fever" had disappeared; the purity of her voice was shocking, piercing, disturbing coming from someone with that ruined hair, those disproportionate breasts, the Born to Be Wild T-shirt. "I am a maid of constant sorrow. I've seen trouble all my days."

Jocelyn believed that she had seen trouble, that they had both seen trouble. She felt suddenly smaller than the two of them with her safe life, her safe home, her safe marriage. The light fell on them, and she noticed that their hair was exactly the same color, and she wondered if that was why Johnny's hair hadn't greyed; because he dyed it. She saw them buying Clairol in a drugstore and grooming each other in the tiny bathroom of a cheap motel. She touched her own hair, disliking it now, disliking everything about herself.

The next song was Linnet's too, and she was a different person yet again. "Stand by your man," she sang or belted, defiant, proud. And then Johnny took the mike. "This is for a very special lady, and some very special memories."

She knew what it was from the first chords. "Oh, the summertime is coming / and the trees are sweetly blooming."

She was glad that the restaurant was in the dark, because she could feel free to weep without constraint, invisible.

He invited people to sing along, and they did, a surprising number of them knowing the words. And then he put down his guitar and stood by the mike. "Our revels now are ended," he said, and went into the speech from *The Tempest,* ending the way he always had, "Which is Shakespeare's way of saying, 'Have ye no homes of your own to go to?'"

She let the tears flow, and looking around, she could see others were weeping, though none of them would know what she was weeping for, and she didn't know why they wept. She looked at Johnny and Linnet. What did it matter that their hair was dyed, that their teeth were false, that her breasts were silicone, that they'd abandoned wives and husbands or been abandoned by them, that the "nest egg" that settled itself between Linnet's false breasts might have made its way there by less than entirely honest means? They had made something happen in this ugly room, with its turquoise faux leather benches and its plastic gondolas. They had given people something; whatever else was false, the tears were real, real tears. What was it they had given? Hope? Belief? A sense that we are not alone, that we will not be left, finally, unaccompanied.

> *Our revels now are ended. These our actors,*
> *As I foretold you, were all spirits and*
> *Are melted into air, into thin air:*
> *And, like the baseless fabric of this vision,*
> *The cloud-capp'd towers, the gorgeous palaces,*
> *The solemn temples, the great globe itself,*
> *Yea, all which it inherit, shall dissolve*
> *And, like this insubstantial pageant faded,*
> *Leave not a rack behind. We are such stuff*
> *As dreams are made on, and our little life*
> *Is rounded with a sleep.*

Johnny was dying.

And he had come back to her. To say goodbye.

The place went wild. Tony came up to the mike. "You've got to let them go. You don't want their manicotti to get cold."

And he escorted Johnny and Linnet back to the table, where Jocelyn sat, as she so often had, not knowing what to do with her face.

Katerina, the Romanian waitress, kept bringing them plates of food, variously shaped pasta covered by tomato sauce. Jocelyn enjoyed everything she ate, much more than the pan-seared scallops or chicken under a brick she might have had in the restaurants she and Richard occasionally went to on the other side of town. People from adjoining tables kept coming by, slapping Johnny on the back, the men kissing Linnet, the women kissing Johnny. "Fabulous." "Fantastic." "When are you coming back?" people were saying.

"Ah, well, you never know," Johnny would say.

And she wanted to say: You're never coming back. You're dying.

But that of course could not be said. And maybe it wasn't even true. Maybe he wouldn't die anytime soon. Maybe a miracle would happen. Maybe he would be back. And why would anyone say anything to leave everyone unhappy? Everyone in the room was so happy now. Johnny had made them happy. Johnny and Linnet.

It took them a very long time to get out of the restaurant. She remembered it always took forever for Johnny to leave a place because no one ever wanted to let him go. Everyone always wanted to hold on to him.

Except for her. She had run from him as if she were running for her life.

And she had always believed it was a good thing, the only thing for her to do.

She fished for her keys at the bottom of her purse. She hoped she was all right to drive. She thought it was at least possible that she wasn't. Well, it wasn't very far. She prayed the police wouldn't stop her.

"I must get you fresh towels," she said, the moment they got in the door. In the bathroom, she turned on the light and stood at the sink, splashing cold water on her face. The sight of her face disturbed her.

She looked florid. Wild. She turned out the light and reached for the towels in the dark.

"I'm going to turn in," Linnet said. "We've got to get a really, really early start."

"Yes, well, good night then," Jocelyn said, admiring Linnet's tact, thinking how kind it was for her to give her and Johnny some time alone.

"Would you like some ice water?" she asked.

"You were always mad for ice water in Dublin and no one could understand your craving for it. They thought it was very odd of you Americans, this mania for ice."

"And I couldn't get used to drinking tepid water. Although I remember there wasn't much water drinking in your crowd."

"Have you ever gone back to Ireland?"

"No, Johnny, I never wanted to."

"Do you think about it much?"

"No," she said. "I don't."

She wondered if that sounded brutal, but it was just the truth.

But she was back there now, that young girl, Johnny's wife. The American girl. The deserter. The one who fled.

"I don't go back much myself," he said. "And when I do, I don't stay for long."

"You'll be all right going back there now?"

"Oh yes, right as rain. You remember Moira O'Connell. She'll look after me."

"I thought she was a nun."

"Well she is, but you know she's a doctor, too. And quite the media star. She was in Africa for many years, and very involved with AIDS work. Came back to Ireland, stood up to the bishops about condoms and their treatment of AIDS patients. And your woman Claire, you know she was an anchorwoman on the TV, she did a film about Moira, put her on the map. The two of them, thick as thieves, like always. No, Moira's taken me in hand, she's got all kinds of treatments and places set up for me. Practically the whole of Dublin eats out of her hand, and the ones that don't eat out of her hand do what she wants because they're afraid of her. Funny, she and Claire and Diarmid are big wheels in AIDS things in Dublin. It turns out Diarmid is gay. Would you have credited it, Joss? Diarmid's a homosexual."

"Oh," Jocelyn said. "But he and Claire are still married?"

"Happiest couple I know, though God knows it's not in the ordinary way. I'd say Claire's known her share of happiness outside the marriage. They're great pals though, great pals."

She remembered that that was what Claire had said of herself and Diarmid. That they were great pals. She wondered if that was to be hoped for in a marriage, that after fifty years you could still say you were the greatest of pals.

"And Rory?"

"Moved to Australia. Teaching something there. I'm afraid he fell out of touch, the only one of us not to keep in touch. I suppose he was bitter about Moira. But you know that was a foolish thing to do, a waste of time and energy. No sense being bitter about the past, Joss. The past is the past. You let it go, or it just eats at you."

"Yes, I suppose you're right," she said, not knowing if she believed what she was saying. She would have said you had to hold on to the past, or you'd keep repeating the same mistakes. But she'd let go of the part of her past that was Johnny . . . and it had, after the first little while, not been difficult at all. She didn't know what that meant. About her. Or the past.

"I suppose I've been given a death sentence, Joss, but you see I just don't believe it. I just don't think it will end like this. I can't believe that I'll just give it up. Life, I mean. I love it so much. I can't believe it will be over. Not when I love it so much. Always have, Joss, always have. I can say that about myself, I've always loved life."

She closed her eyes.

"I've always loved life," he'd said, and for once she knew she could believe him.

What she didn't know was whether she could say the same words herself and know that she spoke the truth.

She knew she had been fortunate, been spared the larger, more dramatic tragedies. War, illness, natural disaster, fire, flood, the deaths of children. She would say she had been happy. But always she felt that her luck was just a trick. It wasn't that life was good. It was that she'd been lucky. And at any time the luck could run out.

And often now, she was tired of making it up. What was called a life. A life of meaning. Children, grandchildren, a husband, houses, gardens, friends, her pitiful efforts at volunteering (trying to tutor inner-city kids in science). When she thought of life as a pile of coins or a necklace of pearls, she never had the image of abundance. Everything in her life had been carefully chosen, carefully tended. Contained.

Johnny had not contained his life or been contained. He had loved women, left them and been left. He had a child whom he hardly knew. He hadn't even enough money for proper medical care. His musical dreams had ended up in what he had to know was an embarrassment: an opening act for a minor star at county fairs in parts of the country no one but the natives knew about. And ending up with Linnet, with her fried hair and her fake breasts and her tacky clothes and her murdering of the language. But that was not all Linnet was. Linnet was that and then there was the Linnet of the miraculous voice, clear and pure, light on water. All that that voice suggested and called up. So he had had that too. They had had it. The both of them.

He had loved life. He had lived it abundantly. "Brimful" was a word that came to her. No, not just brimful, she thought; over-flowing.

And of herself, the words that came were "meager." "Mere."

She thought of the fable of the grasshopper and the ant. Maybe it was all wrong. Maybe the ant withered away alongside his store of dried-up grain. Sated but desiccated. Maybe the grasshopper got some other creature to take him in at the last minute, glad of the company, happy to provide.

She could not have made a life with Johnny. And yet he had made a life. A life he loved.

"I've always loved life." She would never forget his saying that. And behind those words other words came to her, from where? The Bible? Some long-dead poet. Love casts out fear. If love casts out fear, does it follow that fear casts out love? More than loving life, she'd feared it, not what it was, but what it could bring. She had not been able, ever, for long, to put out of her mind the things people had to endure. The things they lost.

Perhaps it was genetic; perhaps she was born the child who wept when the swings were taken down for the winter.

She had always somehow known that life was capable of striking blows that crippled, mauled, maimed, even killed. Always she had been prepared for the great blow.

But the great blow had not come. Rather there had been a series of diminishments. She couldn't say, if she were honest, that age brought anything but loss. The muscle's firmness, the keen tooth of desire blunted or ground down, the ardent flame of the first years of marriage banked, coals in a stove, the heat steady, dependable, the embers lively, but the flame, the flame, the thrilling dangerous climb and crackle nowhere to be seen. And the soaring love of children, the exhausting days when you wept for sleep that you couldn't have, days when you knew every act was meaningful—diluted now to a weekly call, a monthly visit. The belief that the work that you were good at was somehow important, mattered terribly to the fate of the world—you knew others would take up what you'd done, perhaps be better at it, or perhaps the work would become obsolete, and no one would remember what you'd done or how you did it. And the fate of the earth itself, degraded by the greed, the carelessness of people who would not see. Would her grandchildren kill or be killed for drinking water? Would New York be drowned? She often had these thoughts, and when she did, what she hoped was to die before these things happened, before she had to see the horrors that she knew might come.

She believed that the best possible course in the face of these things was to see clearly, to see what was there. Not to pretend that what was there was not. So that you wouldn't find yourself ambushed, struck down on a dark road. She had tried to see clearly. And because of this she couldn't say, "I love life."

As Johnny could.

My life, she wanted to say, not even knowing what she meant, my life. "Sometimes I think I don't understand anything about life, Johnny," she said. "Nothing at all."

"Isn't that the great thing, then," he said. "Isn't that the great thing about it. Anything can happen, you never know what it's going to mean."

She felt quite light-headed, and she very much wanted to be outside. "Come outside with me, Johnny," she said. "Let's have a look at the moon."

The moon was three quarters full. It fell on the blue-black grass, it lit the peach-colored geraniums so that they seemed newly daring; the yellow hibiscus blazed, remembering its jungle home. The white hydrangeas seemed larger than they had in daylight; someone's cat slunk into a bush; there seemed to be no stars.

They were standing in the moonlight; they would not see each other again. It ought to have been a solemn moment, but she felt not solemn at all, but giggly. She very much wanted to dance.

Through her mind went the words of the nonsense poem, turned into a song she'd sung for her children. "They danced by the light of the moon, / the moon, / the moon, they danced by the light of the moon."

She heard herself beginning to sing.

"Would you dance with me, Johnny?" she said.

"Delighted, madam," Johnny said. "I'd say Tony's Chianti did you no harm."

"I never sing, Johnny. I have a terrible voice."

"There's no such thing as a terrible voice if you have the love of singing."

"Well, Johnny, that's just not true," she said and began giggling, letting him twirl her across the dark lawn.

Suddenly she felt quite dizzy. "I must sit down," she said.

"And I must say good night." He kissed the top of her head.

"Joss, you're a great girl, a great girl. You always were. We had some great times, didn't we, lass? No regrets."

"No, Johnny," she said, "no regrets."

And she knew she'd spoken truthfully. She would have been less had she never known him, without the glimpse of something offered, something she knew she couldn't hold on to. Didn't want. Without Johnny she wouldn't have known, really, who she was. Because he had taught her who she was not.

And by coming back, he'd done something else for her. Some lightness had come about, as if heavy branches had been cut down, changing the whole look of the house.

He had changed something. Moved some rock that had sealed something over. The sealed-up understanding that she'd had, as if she knew what life was and would always be.

She thought of the word "unsealed," and the thrill of it made her feel even more dizzy. But the dizziness pleased her now.

She was awakened at 4:30 the next morning by a sound she couldn't place: it was loud, unaccustomed, misplaced in the grey air which ought to have been still. She was unwilling to unloose the grip of sleep; she couldn't yet commit to wakefulness. Alongside the loud noise, which she gradually understood to be the sound of an engine, or rather, underneath it, two words thrummed or drummed in her sluggish brain. Blood meal, someone was saying. A woman's voice, no one she knew. Blood meal, the voice repeated. And then, hovering above it, the sound of Johnny's voice singing, "We'll all go together" and then Linnet's, "I wonder if I could bother you to use the powder room." And then Johnny's voice, speaking this time, "Our Revels now are ended."

She forced herself awake, and then walked quickly to the window. The yellow truck was driving down the street.

She felt a chill in the air. The sun hadn't come up yet and the air was damp.

He'd gone now. She remembered that he never liked goodbyes.

She wouldn't see him in her life again.

She would have to explain to the neighbors why a Frito-Lay truck had been parked in her driveway.

Of course she could never go back to the Tower of Pizza again. Or maybe she would, with Richard, and if anyone said anything about Mick, she'd just put her finger to her lips and then wink.

But how could she tell anyone about what had happened last night? The visit of these two. Quite out of nowhere.

People might say she'd dreamed it.

But no one would suggest she'd made it up.

No one would think she had it in her.

Simone Weil in New York

She looks ridiculous.

Only a ridiculous person would be dressed like that.

The black cape, overwhelming her in the high wind.

The flapping trousers.

The white hand, holding down the black beret.

The wind has overwhelmed her.

She is standing in the middle of the sidewalk, overwhelmed.

Waiting for someone to tell her what to do.

Her cape, that looks like it is good for nothing, certainly no good for protection from the cold. Or good only to carry her off.

Away somewhere.

Aloft.

And then smashed down.

And her trousers, as if they, too, were in the business, the enterprise of forcing her to take flight.

Forced into flight when what she wanted was just: gravity.

The wind is strong but her clothing makes the wind a much greater problem.

Overwhelmed.

Unfit.

Unsuited.

Genevieve doesn't know: Does Mlle Weil see me? Or does she not see?

Genevieve cannot order her impressions. Which was first?

"This figure, man or woman, I can't tell, is ridiculous."

"I will not grant this ridiculous figure the expenditure of my attention. Even for a second glance."

Or was it: "That is Mlle Weil, whom I refuse to see."

Or was the first impression not in fact a sight, but a cry, audible despite, or perhaps because, of the high wind.

"Geneviève. Geneviève."

Her name pronounced as she had known it until two years ago. "Jahn, uh, vee, evv."

Her American friends call her "Jenn uh veev."

Her American in-laws, strangers to the French, but not the Yiddish tongue, prefer to call her Jenny.

There is nothing to be done. She can't run; she is pushing a perambulator.

If she hadn't had the baby with her, would she have run?

Probably not. She is not that sort of person. To run. To run away from someone she had known, who calls her name. And she would not have run, because of that woman's force.

A force from whose field she had believed she had long ago freed herself. Mlle Weil, her teacher. Her revered teacher in the *lycée* of Le Puy, in the south of France, thousands of miles away. The year was 1933. Nine years ago. Now she is twenty-four, no longer Genevieve Le Clos, now Genevieve Levy. The wife of Dr. Howard Levy, fighting in the army of the South Pacific. The mother of a thirteen-month-old baby. Aaron. Her son. No longer the girl she was.

And Mlle Weil? Is she the person she was in 1933?

It is impossible to believe that Mlle Weil would not be the same.

Genevieve waits for the light to change. Mlle does not wait; she is running. Even across the width of Riverside Drive, Genevieve can see the plain happiness on her face. *Can she be smiling like that when I am feeling nothing but the urge to flee?*

She had known that Mlle Weil was in New York. Friends of friends had told her, colleagues of her brother, Laurent, professor at the university. Columbia, Department of Psychology. Mlle Weil is here because of her brother. The great mathematician André Weil. Older brother of the younger, in some ways more famous, sister.

Mlle Weil is here with her parents. Saved from the fate of French Jews, sequestered on account of her brother's gift for mathematics. In the safe bosom of the American academy. Teaching in a college in Pennsylvania, Genevieve had heard. But the Weils, Mlle Weil and her family, are living, she knows, quite near where she lives. On the same street, though perhaps a quarter mile away. Riverside Drive. To herself, though she never says it aloud, Genevieve thinks of it as Riverside Boulevard.

Genevieve had been afraid of just this moment. This moment of encounter, not only with this woman whom she does not wish to see, but with the whole of what has been lost.

Of course her losses are not singular. The War. The War has stolen whole lives. Whole cities. Ways of living.

But the sight of Mlle Weil reminds Genevieve that the loss had come before the War. And *was* in some ways singular. A loss unlike others brought about by the War. Perhaps not a loss, rather a relinquishment. A gift freely given. A relinquishment, yes, but drawn up from a well of love.

Genevieve thinks of the sign over the door of Mlle Weil's classroom in the *lycée*. ONLY MATHEMATICS MAY ENTER HERE. And yet she taught not mathematics but philosophy.

It has been a very long time since Genevieve has entertained a dream of mathematical or philosophical proficiency. She can only even recall it vaguely: a dream figure walking on a shoreline, almost entirely consumed by fog.

The light changes. Green to red. The cars stop; it is now legal for Mlle Weil to be crossing the street.

Before Mlle Weil reaches the sidewalk, the baby cries. *My baby. My baby cries.* The cry an entirely meaningful utterance. Or: an utterance with a few possible, radically limited meanings, but each entirely meaningful. *I am hungry. I am cold. I am dirty. I need to be held.*

Meaningful utterance.

The meaning of meaning.

Those kinds of words indicate a habit of mind Genevieve has long since given up. Brought back by the sight of the ridiculous woman.

Mlle Weil.

"Genevieve."

The harsh voice, a crow's, as her flapping cape makes her a crow. Worn out, worn down. Abraded. These are the words for the skin on her face. Too many cigarettes, too much shouting at workers' meetings, shouting over the heads of those who probably don't understand her.

And there had, of course, been illnesses. Mlle Weil suffered from headaches. Her mother had told Genevieve's mother that she suffered greatly.

But how had Mlle Weil even recognized her from so far away? It has been nine years. Nine years of the difficulties of war, of terrible displacements. Genevieve knows that she has aged. Sometimes, looking in the mirror, she doesn't even recognize herself. And yet Mlle Weil had known her.

"Genevieve."

Now they are on the same side of the street.

Mlle Weil's fierce eyes, unblinking behind thick glasses.

Seeing everything.

Except what she doesn't wish to see.

"I knew, Genevieve, that you were living here. Close to where I am living. I knew, even, your address. But I didn't want to contact you. I was afraid you wouldn't want to see me."

So she has said it: the most uncomfortable thing. The thing that ought not to be said, that no one would say. The truth. Plain. Causing the greatest possible discomfort. Did she consider discomfort a form of suffering? She had understood the contemplation of suffering to be her life's work. Of course, she wouldn't consider discomfort. She would consider the consideration of discomfort a form of self-indulgence. Bourgeois falsity.

Mlle Weil had almost been fired from the *lycée* for referring to marriage as "legalized prostitution."

What would she know of it? Of any of it? Marriage. Prostitution. Even, perhaps, the law.

Most likely she believed in some universal law that had never been seen or practiced on this earth.

Genevieve would honor her old teacher by not telling a polite lie. She would honor her by silence. And by making a simple statement of fact.

"And so, we meet here."

The present tense. Suggesting a continuum.

Eternity.

Genevieve remembers that among those who mocked Mlle Weil, and there were many, were those who called her the Red Virgin. Because of her left-leaning politics, because of her refusal of traditional feminine allure, feminine attachment. They thought it doubly amusing to call her the Red Virgin, because in Le Puy, the town where Mlle Weil was teaching in the *lycée,* the town that was the home of Genevieve and her mother and her brother, there was a statue of the Red Virgin, the Madonna. A mother but still a virgin. This was called a mystery, but you had to believe it or be guilty of sin. It was for things like this that Genevieve's family counted themselves among the non-, or unbelievers.

The statue had been cast from iron that came from guns taken at Sebastopol. An abomination, Genevieve's mother had called it: abominable to form a statue of a mother, the source of life, from the machines of death. Genevieve's mother did not believe, but, a mother herself, though not a particularly tender one, she liked the tenderness suggested by the idea of the Madonna.

As a young child, Genevieve had done what many children, she later learned, had done. Made a list of words representing her place in the universe: the universe being the highest possible term in her imagination.

Genevieve Marie Le Clos

14 Rue de la Gazelle

Le Puy

Haute-Loire

France

Europe

The Earth

The Universe

It was beautiful, Le Puy, the town where she had been born, the town that it was very possible she would never see again. A region of stone: the stone faces of the houses, the climbs up and down the stony streets. She had loved the high outcroppings, the cascades.

Her mother had admired Mlle Weil. She had been amused by Mme Weil, Simone's mother.

Mme Weil had confided in Genevieve's mother, who was a teacher in the *lycée* where Mlle Weil taught, where Genevieve was a student. She had come to Le Puy for a visit. That is what Mme Weil had said, but really she had come to check up on her daughter. She was very worried. Her daughter took shockingly little care of herself. She was eating only boiled potatoes. She liked to think of herself as living like the poorest workers, but the truth, said Mme Weil, was that her palate was quite refined. Especially sensitive. If there was the smallest spot on a piece of fruit, she couldn't even touch it. And she could tolerate only the finest cuts of meat. Would Mme Le Clos consider helping Mme Weil—of course, it was really her daughter who would be helped, though it would involve some subterfuge. Would Mme Le Clos give some extra money (provided to her by Mme Weil) to the butcher so that when Simone ordered horsemeat she would be given filet mignon?

Mme Le Clos laughed, and Mme Weil laughed with her. The two mothers were laughing.

"Of course, Mme Weil. And I will do more than that. When she comes to give lessons to my son, I will provide her with dinner. And I will make sure it's something that she will like to eat. I will tell her it's horsemeat, of course."

"She particularly likes my way of cooking mashed potatoes," Mme Weil said and made some notes on the back of a used envelope. Which Genevieve's mother put in one of the kitchen drawers. The one where string was kept, along with the screwdriver and pliers.

And Genevieve had been appalled. Tormented that she was somehow involved in deceiving Mlle Weil.

Whom she revered.

Whom she admired.

Whom she loved.

Was it possible that Mlle Weil was the only person at that time not related to her by blood whom she could say, in complete confidence, that she loved?

She loved her mother.

She loved her brother.

But her mother was her mother.

Her brother was her brother.

And Mlle Weil was . . . what?

Her teacher.

A hero.

A saint.

She could invoke that category, although she was an unbeliever. Mlle Weil was a saint of the mind.

And yet she had always seemed in need of some protection.

It had to be said that what Genevieve felt for Mlle Weil was a kind of love.

They had all loved her. All her students, all Genevieve's friends. The combination of her extreme purity of mind, her extraordinary learning, her extreme devotion to them, her students, and her clumsiness brought out the gallantry that rests in the hearts, Genevieve had come to know, of all young girls. Behind the eyes of each French girl: *La Pucelle. Jeanne d'Arc.* The dream of knighthood. A participation in a valorous undertaking. The vulnerable foot shod in iron, ending in a metal point, knife sharp, pressing hard into the soft earth. Relinquishing her girlhood, the girl sheds, Genevieve had come to understand, her dream of armor. She takes on breasts, hips: no longer the valorous knight. So perhaps Mlle Weil brought out our early gallantry, or we gave her the last of it, before it was required to transform itself into the smaller compass of maternal ardor.

She had demanded a great deal of them. Everything. And she would give them everything. She was, for all her brilliance, surprisingly patient. Generous with her time, never humbling the slower girls, always kindly. Yet rigorous in her pursuit of truth.

Only mathematics may enter here.

Her idea was that the mind could be best trained by geometry, geometry as it was practiced by the Greeks, that the attention required to solve a problem in geometry was the best possible training for any kind of difficult intellectual work. She had talked often about the virtue of attention. She had described it as a moral good.

But sometimes she was ridiculous. One day she came to class with her sweater on backwards.

Genevieve had been the one to see it first, had been the one to rise to her feet. She gestured to her three best friends: Hélène, Colette, Chantal. Where were they now? Starving? Dead? Collaborators with the cabal of Pétain?

They made a guard in front of the blackboard so that Mlle Weil could disappear behind it and turn her sweater around.

Had Mlle Weil laughed?

Made fun of herself?

Genevieve cannot remember seeing Mlle Weil laugh.

But no, that isn't true. She *had* seen her laugh. She had laughed that day . . .

She had come from behind the blackboard with the sweater on the right way and said, "Young ladies, you have spoiled my great effect. Do you not know that the most fashionable women in Paris are wearing their sweaters backwards this season?"

Yes, she had laughed.

And the students had laughed.

But Genevieve had not laughed, because she hadn't thought that what Mlle Weil said was funny, or not funny enough to laugh at, and she was afraid that the others felt the same and were just pretending. And this would have been, this pretending, this deceiving of Mlle Weil, this would have been below Mlle Weil's standards for truth.

And if Mlle Weil didn't know that she was being deceived, being humored, what could that mean? About her intelligence, her wisdom, her knowledge of the world?

She didn't know that her mother and Genevieve's mother were in league to deceive her.

Genevieve understands that this is why she had not liked to remember that Mlle Weil had laughed.

Mlle Weil isn't laughing now. All the expression on her face is taken up with the effort of furious blinking. The sun is very bright; it is high noon; the vivid colors of the leaves exaggerate the brightness.

How weak her eyes look, as if seeing must be, for her, a perpetual strain.

Her eyes are tired.

Her glasses are the thickest Genevieve has ever seen.

And now something must be said. Something ridiculous.

"How are you?"

Without a pause, as if waiting to speak had nearly suffocated her, as if she were taking her first breath in much too long, "I am trying to get out of here. I must get back to Europe. To join de Gaulle and the Free French in London."

"And will that be difficult?"

Mlle Weil makes a face—screwing up her tired eyes, tightening her thin lips—that suggests that the idea of difficulty is in itself ridiculous.

"And is this child yours?"

"Yes. My son, Aaron. He is thirteen months old."

Mlle Weil bends over the baby, puts her face close to him. She makes cooing noises, as anyone might with a baby. This surprises Genevieve.

"A fine little man," she says. "And so you must be well. But Laurent, I have thought of him often. How is your brother?"

Laurent. One of the afflicted, his body broken from birth. *My brother, for love of whom, in outrage on whose behalf I refuse to bend the knee to any God.* Any God who would have allowed the fate of Laurent's body could only be a monster.

Misshapen in his mother's womb.

Our mother, in whose womb I was, strictly by chance, not misshapen. Cerebral palsy.

Sporadic control, only, of his limbs. A bent spine, so that most days he presents to the world the shape of an upside-down L, his spine a flat table, parallel almost to the ground. Usually, he tried to talk to people only when he was sitting down, but if he had to talk to people when he was standing or walking, he would have to awkwardly twist his head, look up at them from a sidewise angle. Which made people more uncomfortable still.

Genevieve can only love people who are able to look at Laurent without looking away.

"I was quite fond of your brother. I would like to see him."

Genevieve takes the words as a command. Now there is no choice. Because of the way she had been with Laurent, Genevieve would owe Mlle Weil fealty.

I love my brother.

I love my brother without question.

I may have loved my brother from before my birth. From my time, well formed as he was not, in our mother's womb.

Of everyone whom she had observed in Laurent's presence, Mlle Weil seemed to have the least trouble looking at him. She had appeared to have no trouble at all. Of everyone who had looked at him, only with Mlle Weil had there been no catch, no taking hold of the reins to check the horse of recoil, of revulsion, the impulse Genevieve had seen so often. The effort to control disgust. Genevieve had many times tried to understand the position of people seeing Laurent for the first time. Tried not to judge them, to forgive their look of shock. But she could not forgive. She knew that Laurent saw it, was hurt by it. So how could she forgive?

Was it possible that Mlle Weil didn't notice Laurent's distorted body? That she saw only his mind?

Yes, this was possible. For this, Genevieve would always owe her fealty. Beyond question. A knight's fealty. Unto death.

It was how Mlle Weil had first come to their house. She had, of course, been Genevieve's teacher. But there was a distance there, a formality. People were careful not to bring the scent of home into the clear air of the *lycée*. It would be like whispering about your boyfriend as you knelt in church. Not that she had ever knelt in church, coming as she did from a family of unbelievers. Nevertheless, there were things that, as a native of the land of France, she had always known.

Mlle Weil was also the colleague of Genevieve's mother, but even that would not have meant that she would have entered the house.

It was because Laurent had been quite ill with pneumonia that winter of 1933, and had missed so much school. (He was always susceptible to illness, particularly of the lungs.) He was falling behind in Greek.

Their mother would not allow that anything connected to Laurent's illness would result in his falling behind. And so she had hired Mlle Weil to tutor him in Greek.

Only Mlle Weil would not take money.

And so, their mother had said, then you must take your evening meal with us.

And Mlle Weil had said, "Sometimes I do not like to eat."

How Genevieve's heart had beaten, so painfully, when she waited for Mlle Weil's knock the days she came to tutor Laurent. Waiting to answer the door, waiting to be *the one,* and yet feeling as if, in doing so, she overstepped some mark. Stole grace.

"Answer the door, for heaven's sake," her mother had said, settling Laurent against pillows on the sofa.

"I am very much looking forward to seeing Laurent," Mlle Weil is saying, nine years later, older now, looking older than she really is—thirty-two is it, thirty-three? Her shoulders stooped, her back bent like an old woman's.

Genevieve wonders what it is that Mlle Weil sees. Is it more or less than what others see? The real, true, deep, high reality . . . or is it a kind of careless seeing . . . not noticing that people are selling you filet mignon and calling it horsemeat. Not noticing that you are wearing your clothes backwards, that you are ruining your health. Not seeing what is being done for you, what people are doing for you so that you can see only what you want to see. Rather than trying to get the truth of what is there.

Once, this question would have mattered to Genevieve. She had believed, once, that it was possible to grasp reality through thought. That it was a human being's most important responsibility: to understand reality through the labor of the mind.

She no longer thinks this way.

What has taken its place?

Something she calls getting on with life. Something she calls, now, living.

And yet the other was a kind of living.

Does it mean that she has lost a life?

Yes and no.

It was fortunate that there had been no need to choose.

She has not lost her mind. She is not mad, or entirely incapable of thought. In the first moments of waking, when she nurses the baby, in the moments stolen for reading while he sleeps. And there is her study of the Hebrew language.

She had set Laurent the task of finding someone who could teach her Hebrew. Rabbi Cohen, on the faculty of the Jewish Theological Seminary, two blocks from her apartment, where he comes once every two weeks, surprised that a woman, a non-Jew, is interested in the Hebrew language. He is kind about the slowness of her progress, and impressed, she thinks, in spite of himself, at her determination. He assumes that she is studying the language out of intellectual curiosity. What she does not tell him: her motive is not primarily intellectual. She is doing it to make a connection with the Jewishness of her husband and her son, without ever invoking the name or idea of God. She loves the look of the letters, the sound of the words in her throat: coming from someplace deeper than French words, or English ones.

And so she knows her mind is still alive. In some ways more than ever. But she knows, too, that she *makes* nothing of what is done with her mind. The work of her mind leaves no trace. The fact of there being no product of her mind's work does not mean that the work has not been done.

Like Mlle Weil, Genevieve knows herself the inferior younger sister of the brilliant older brother. Laurent's career at the *lycée* was brilliant, despite time lost from illness. His career at university was brilliant.

Because he would be studying at the University of Bordeaux, she and her mother move there, too. Pull up stakes. Her mother, the lioness mother of the wounded cub, makes it all happen, as she always made everything happen for Laurent. She gets a job in the *lycée,* once again teaching chemistry, and finds a place there for Genevieve. They leave the town where all of them have lived all their life for a new life. For Laurent's new life. Not questioning, even for a second, whether it was the right thing to do. Not worrying if it would cause problems for Genevieve. Only now does it occur to her that perhaps, in this way (were there others?), she had been neglected.

He studies psychology. He turns his attention to people who have afflictions, but have not been given the gift of language, as he has. He begins with veterans of the War, and moves on to those struck from birth.

He perceives that severely disabled people, who were thought to have no intelligence, no mind even, in fact had intelligence, had mind, only they had no access to language, and were imprisoned by this lack. He invents both an object and a technique that gives these people, who were as good as dead, a new life. Language. He invents what they come to call the board. They call it that, as if it were a domestic animal that had become part of their daily life. They say "the board" as other families would say "the dog."

It is because of "the board" that they are where they are. Safe in New York instead of in ravished France. That she is Mrs. Howard Levy, mother of Aaron, of the beautiful perfect limbs, traceable to her brother's broken body.

Her husband, Howard, a neurologist, had written Laurent from America. He had read an article Laurent had written about his work. His board, his great invention. Howard had traveled to Bordeaux just to meet Laurent. 1937. This is how it had happened.

In some ways, a love story, like any other.

But strangely brought about.

A love story linked to the tragedy of a brother's broken body.

She is thinking of Howard's body. How aroused she had been when she first knew him by the sight of him walking down the street. She would sneak out the door so she could watch him from the back without his knowing. His walk was the first thing she desired. His long loping strides, eating up the road, so American, so confident of his getting to the place he meant to get to. A walk far more horizontal than a Frenchman's. Compared to Howard, she had thought then, most French men walked as if they were riding a unicycle: excessively vertical, their torsos stiff, their arms immobile. When she watched Howard walk she thought: this is a man who never thinks of distance as a problem. As the sister of Laurent, she had always had to calculate the possible negative implications of any distance. When she took her first walks with Howard she felt, for the first time, that she could, for a little while at least, stop doing that.

She thinks of his comically long, thin legs, the line of dark hair traveling down his chest—so black against the surprisingly white skin, the line of black making its way in an even line exactly halfway between his nipples, which were a dark maroon. Now that she is nursing, she thinks how odd it is that men have nipples. What do they need them for? But she had been fascinated by the look of Howard's torso, as if it were a map of something, a blueprint, a chart. And she loved his thin fingers, almost feminine, except for a thumb that was surprisingly wedge-shaped, blunt. And how shockingly aroused she had been when he rolled up the sleeves of his shirt to help her with the dishes. His chin: perhaps too pointed for real beauty, maybe his worst feature. And the enormous eyes, dog's eyes, he called them, but she said, it was a very intelligent dog, a good dog, a faithful dog.

Now he is fighting in the South Pacific, or because he is a doctor perhaps not fighting but tending the shattered bodies of the fighters. She believes that he *is* faithful. She will not allow herself to think of it. She understands that in some ways they don't know each other very well. She knows him first as her brother's friend, a kind man (he, too, does not look on her brother with revulsion; he is one of the rare ones who does not find Laurent impossible, even difficult to look at). An American. Is it that they both liked the way their bodies took up space in relation to each other's, she containing space, and he expanding it, the easy way their footsteps chimed as they walked up the stony streets? He found her pretty. She thought that was a less satisfactory word than *jolie* or *mignon*. "I think you may be the prettiest girl I've ever seen," he said to her in English, though sometimes they spoke in French. And he would laugh at her inability to make anything of his name except Ow Ard, and she liked the way he would play with her glove when she laid it on the table in the café, after he'd placed their order.

But did they know each other? What did it mean to know someone? Certainly she did not know him as she knew Laurent. And would he be the same person when the War was over? And who did he think he'd married? A pretty French girl. The kind, caretaking sister of his afflicted friend. Sometimes they talked about books. She was impressed that he, an American, had read Proust; he was impressed that she, a woman, knew Descartes more thoroughly than he, and that she adored geometry. He did not know that both these things could be traced directly to Mlle Weil. She had never mentioned Mlle Weil to him.

She is used, now, to living in the house with Laurent and Aaron, walking the New York streets, a wife without a husband, the mother of a child who doesn't even know his father's face. Would she like it better when she had to consult, to compromise? Would the assuaging of her loneliness be worth her loss of authority? Of course. Of course it would. She couldn't wait to see Howard. She longed for him. But who was the man for whom she longed?

She thinks of "the board," made of highly polished, highly finished wood—oak, she guesses, though it's not the kind of thing she ever asked herself before. Two feet square, three quarters of an inch thick. Two painted lines divide the surface into four squares. Within each square there is a sort of square dish, a depression six inches square and a quarter of an inch deep, its bottom edges smooth and polished.

The blocks are arranged in sets of four, each set constituting a puzzle. She remembers how Laurent explained it to her for the first time. "Listen, GeGe," he said (as if she had ever not listened). "Three of the four blocks show an image closely related in type or subject to the others, but the fourth block, though resembling the others, has some feature that does not fit. Four blocks would represent foods, but three are fruits, the fourth a vegetable. Three blocks will show a problem of addition: $2 + 6 = 8$, $22 + 20 = 42$, $9 + 3 = 12$. The fourth block will be a problem in subtraction: $14 - 2 = 12$. I set up the blocks, then I ask the person, 'Which doesn't fit?' He or she need not speak. All he or she has to do is make a crude gesture towards the block that doesn't fit. If he or she can't even gesture, I or one of the assistants can do the pointing, only asking for responses by the blinking of eyes."

Genevieve thinks of how her brother is described. A hero. A revolutionary. A savior of the disabled, disabled himself. He is, in Mlle Weil's terms, one of the afflicted. Terrible in his afflictions. His mind: brilliant; his nature: kindly, except for outbursts of unaccountable pique, often connected to food. Only Genevieve knows about this. Laurent may not be aware of it himself. And so it isn't even a shared secret, only hers to keep. She had shared the secret with her mother.

It had been their secret, almost their joke, although they felt disloyal in it, would not have called it a joke or even acknowledged the complicit smiles that passed between them when Laurent would complain about the saltiness of the soup or the piecrust's failure at an ideal of flakiness. An unspoken understanding: food is the only physical pleasure unequivocally open to him. And so we must see that it is a source of great, unalloyed pleasure.

Now, years later, in a place thousands of miles distant from Le Puy, or even Bordeaux, now that she is a citizen of wartime New York, the problem of Laurent's pleasure in his food has become a great headache for Genevieve. Rationing! The calculations, the little stamps and stickers: red for meat, blue for milk and butter. Sugar like gold. She imagines that her mother would have been better at it. Her mother. Their mother. Impossible, sometimes, to believe that she is dead, by which was meant no longer in this world. Her mother: sharp, competent, almost not maternal—parsimonious with caresses, creating a determination in Genevieve to be extravagant in caresses with her son. Her mother: the chemistry mistress, *la maîtresse de chimie.* Stricken with stomach cancer, said to be the most painful of all cancers. Her greatest concern when dying: that Laurent would not be properly cared for, that Genevieve on her own would not measure up. Along with her stifled groans and cries, the constant anxious articulations: *You'll make sure he'll be all right.* No question, then, they both knew, of Genevieve going on with her studies at the university. She had a place in the Department of Philosophy, although she would have preferred literature, but understood that, for her mother, literature was not serious: a leisure pursuit. She consoled herself that, not studying at the university, she would have more time to read the literature she loved. She would be keeping house.

Keep house. Keep the house from what? Keep the house as shelter for the afflicted body, the broken body. They would be orphans now. As a family they had been unlucky. She had never even known her father. A victim of the terrible influenza epidemic. One of the dead, not the war dead, but the plague dead. 1919. Genevieve had been less than a year old. Laurent, three: he had some memories. A tall man, kindly. The physics teacher. *Le maître de la physique.*

When their mother died, everyone—the aunts and uncles, her mother's colleagues, Laurent's friends—was so worried about Laurent that there was no worry left for her. The concern that trickled in her direction was just runoff from the mighty river whose source and mouth, whose whole course, was Laurent. If some concern splashed onto her—well, that was incidental. So Laurent's professor had arranged for her to have a job as a secretary in the Department of Psychology, so she could be near to Laurent. In case anything happened. By which they meant: in case they could not cope.

Those years were difficult, although there were not many of them: only two between her mother's death and her marriage to Howard. They had seemed much longer. When her mother was alive, the care of Laurent had seemed quite possible. Sacrifices were required, thought had to be put into things, but it had not been crushing. She and her mother were a team. Perhaps, she thought, a couple. She was, in a way, her mother's wife, her mother, the breadwinner, the forceful one in the outside world, Genevieve not taking the lead, but following, proud of her quick ability at picking up her cues. Had she ever really been a daughter? Ever really been the child of the house? It didn't matter; she had felt safe, they had been happy. She heard from her friends stories of quarrelsome families: brothers and sisters squabbling or involved in terrible exhausting disputes with no beginning and no end. She and Laurent never quarreled. His nature was, above all, patient. Patient but with outbreaks of acerbity. Great patience was required for him to get on with his life, to not be overwhelmed by his affliction. Patience and bravery, which, in their turn, nurtured in Genevieve and her mother, patience and admiration. Love.

They had been, as a family, afflicted. But none more so than Laurent, unable to control his hands, the muscles of his face, the thrashing of his limbs. But his words are luminous, a tongue of silver in a broken mouth. When Mlle Weil first arrived to tutor him, she had seemed not to notice his flailing arms and legs, the drinks spilled, the objects broken. She seemed not to take it in. Simply, she enjoyed him. She found him interesting, a gifted pupil whom she tutored in the Greek language, which they both loved.

Mlle Weil was only twenty-three that year, Genevieve thinks. Eight years older than I. Could I have been just fifteen then? I saw us as inhabitants not only of different countries but of different planets, different universes even, separated by a distance traversable, sometimes, in the imagination, but only with the understanding that the distance was real and not in any way insignificant. A distance made up of knowledge, wisdom, moral greatness. The heroic, radically separated from the ordinary.

Nine years later, thousands of miles away. Mlle Weil cannot control her blinking. She cannot control her garments. Her cape, the loose legs of her trousers, her beret, which she must hold against her head with one hand.

"My brother is well. He would be glad to see you. He is working at the university. Columbia. The Department of Psychology."

She explains the outlines of Laurent's work, which calls forth a smile. Pure. Radiant.

"When can I see him?"

"Could you come to tea tomorrow?"

"Yes, I would like that." It had not occurred to Mlle Weil to thank Genevieve for the invitation. Well, Genevieve thinks, perhaps no thanks are required. Perhaps it is no more than her due. And perhaps it is I who should be grateful.

She wonders what Laurent will think of the prospect of having Mlle Weil to tea.

Entering the dim apartment from the blazing autumn day, she has put the baby down for a nap and, having a little time, looks in the trunk that stores what she has brought from France that is of no immediate use. She knows that among things she has brought with her are notes she took in Mlle Weil's class. Her essay topics. And the extraordinary letter. She recalls the process of selection, what would be brought forward to the new life, what left behind. What would be brought forward included a connection to Mlle Weil, a connection she had thought she no longer believed in.

She opens the large envelope with a mixed sensation of curiosity and resentment. What is in these papers that she had saved, transported? She resents having to remember the girl she was: serious, scholarly even, with an appetite for abstract philosophy. A Platonist, she had thought of herself then. How ridiculous to apply that term to herself now. Having seen what she has seen, lived through what she has lived through, horrors she could not have imagined when she was Mlle Weil's pupil. And now: a life composed of caring for an afflicted brother, and a baby whose very life depends on her attention to his physical needs—all this makes discussions of the beautiful, the view outside the cave seem infuriatingly beside the point. She is a cave dweller. She cannot now imagine a time when she will not be.

She opens the envelope. The heading on the first sheet she comes to: "ESSAY TOPICS."

What are the main forms courage takes? Do they have anything in common?

How does Plato define justice in the *Republic*?

Attention is what above all distinguishes man from animals. Is it something which belongs to the mind or the body?

Is it possible to know oneself and how?

What is there in common between the self of a year, a month, a day, an hour ago? Is there a fragment of the self which continues to exist from one moment to the next? What is lost in doing away with the self?

She wonders: Were these questions that any teenager should be expected to answer? Were they too far above us, way over our heads? Was Mlle Weil mad to demand a response to these kinds of questions from young girls? And yet, she thinks, I believe we rose to the occasion.

She had not saved any of her own essays, but she remembers getting them back from Mlle Weil, covered with her small handwriting, the corrections clearly an immense labor of attention. She had been honored by the attention: it inspired her to give her utmost.

She sees, on another page, some notes she took from Mlle Weil's lectures.

All belittling of oneself is bad. Sacrifice is related to suicide. It is always something bad to injure one's power of thought, since thought is the condition of all that is good. Any ability which is not directed towards conscious thought (even philanthropy) must be condemned.

The general character of human misery and greatness. One has the impression of being sometimes at the center of the world, and sometimes of being nothing in contrast with it.

An artist creates a state of silence for himself and so the soul's forces are marshaled together, but he is not responsible for the inspiration itself: it is this instance of suspense that it creates.

Genevieve experiences the sensation of seeing someone from a great distance, through a thick fog; she knows that this is her handwriting, that she, Genevieve, wrote these words, or rather took them down. But just as her handwriting has changed (it is smaller now, there are fewer loops and curlicues), she has changed fundamentally. She is no longer the person whose mind would seriously engage with these kinds of ideas. And yet, the question: what is there in common between the self of the present moment and the self of a year, a month, a day, an hour ago—this question seizes her as she sits in the soft chair beside her bed. What she has lost: the faith that such a question is answerable. Or perhaps, more accurately, answerable by her.

Inside there is another envelope, a smaller envelope, with her name and address written in Mlle Weil's tiny handwriting. It is the letter. The extraordinary letter.

My dear Genevieve:

As regards love, I have no advice to give you but at least I have some warnings. Love is a serious thing and it often means pledging one's life and also that of another human being forever. Indeed it always means that, unless one of the two treats the other as a plaything, and, in that case, which is a very common one, love is something odious. I can tell you that when at your age, and later on, too, I was tempted to try to get to know love, I decided not to, deciding myself that it was better not to commit my life in a direction impossible to foresee until I was sufficiently mature to know what, in a general way, I wished from life, and what I expected from it. I would add that love seems to me to involve an even more terrifying risk than that of blindly pledging one's own existence. I mean the risk, if one is the object of a profound love, of becoming the arbiter of another's human existence. My conclusion (which I offer to you solely for information) is not that one should avoid love, but that one should not seek it, and above all when one is very young. At that age it is so much better not to meet it, I believe. What matters is not to bungle one's life.

To bungle one's life.

Has she bungled her life? She, Genevieve, who had been given a life. To do . . . what . . . with?

"Bungle," a luxury word. A peacetime word. Useless now in a time of war, a time of horror. Although she remembers Laurent and How-ard laughing at a word newly invented by soldiers, snafu. An acronym: Situation Normal All Fucked Up. It was Laurent who said aloud the word "fucked." Howard is too embarrassed to use that word in front of her. But "snafu" suggests a jokey situation, a shared understanding of an almost comically omnipresent chaos. To bungle, however: that is a solitary act. Bungle, as if, at the mouth of hell you worried if your hat and gloves were quite appropriate. Bungle. It suggested a faux pas, a minor error, a clumsiness, a malfeasance. As opposed to a devastation. Her world had been devastated. By history. By the forces of evil. Her life had been overturned, uprooted. By history. By the accidents of dis-ease. It had not been her doing.

Or was it better, perhaps, to say: to have survived means you had not bungled.

But there was more, much more to her life than to say she had not bungled.

She had loved greatly and been greatly loved.

She had her child.

Ashamed that Aaron has been so long out of her thoughts, she goes to him, straightens his blankets, risks waking him. By doing this she has traveled very far from the place she was when she was reading Mlle Weil's letter. Aaron's mother is no longer simply Genevieve. She is Aaron's mother.

And Howard's wife.

Mrs. Howard Levy.

Not Mlle anybody anymore.

It was an extraordinary letter to write to a sixteen-year-old girl.

She can no longer remember who it was that she wrote Mlle Weil about.

Why had she asked Mlle Weil's advice about love?

Because she had adored her. Because she had believed her the font of all wisdom, the source of all true knowledge, knowledge that could be trusted to be absolutely true.

Whom had she been in love with then?

She can no longer remember even a single feature, to say nothing of a complete face. Or a name. And yet at that time it must have seemed of the utmost importance. Or she would not have written to Mlle Weil.

Genevieve knows this of herself. From her first awareness that she was no longer a child, she had been in love with someone or other.

Someone or other. As appropriate to call them someone or other as to give them proper names, individual names. Because the truth is, they were interchangeable. They must have been, or she would be able to remember at least one face.

It must have been love she loved.

The idea of love.

I HAVE LOVED GREATLY AND BEEN GREATLY LOVED.

Had she, defying Mademoiselle's advice, sought love?

Or had it sought her?

Had she met love?

Or had it met her?

And if, as Mademoiselle said, it would have been better not to have met love, had she done wrong in meeting it, in allowing it to be met?

Love sought me.

Love met me.

She smiles to herself, at her use of the words of a cheap song. The words are cheap. Mlle Weil's questions are absurd.

I HAVE LOVED GREATLY AND BEEN GREATLY LOVED.

These words are not cheap. Nothing about them is absurd.

She thinks of Howard's body. Possibly in terrible danger. Possibly shattered. Possibly not even in this world.

Sitting in her bedroom, beside their bed, in the middle of New York, in the safety of America, she thinks of her husband's body, which is not safe. Of his body, beside her in the bed.

I HAVE LOVED GREATLY AND BEEN GREATLY LOVED.

She hears Laurent's key in the door. He is fumbling it. It is taking him a good deal of time to get the door open. This means it is one of his bad days. But she knows better than to try to help him. An important part of her life is pretending she is not seeing what she sees. Pretending that Laurent's hands and limbs aren't being taken over by tremors, pretending that he isn't failing at a simple task. Because tomorrow he might not fail, tomorrow it might be different, and they can only have the kind of life they want if they live this way. She wonders what Mlle Weil would think of this, she who is so devoted to the truth. This willed blindness. This evasion of the real.

And what would Mlle Weil think of the love she has for her son, that she would strike to the death anyone who raised a hand against him? She would do so without even a thought. Without a single thought.

Maternal love, she wants to tell Mlle Weil, makes a mockery of the idea of universal love. Of the idea of impersonal love. She would like to ask Mlle Weil if she thinks that maternity disqualifies a mother from participating in what might be called the moral life.

Or does the category of the moral life need to be expanded to include maternity?

These are things she will never ask Mlle Weil. Among other reasons: the echo of the conventional, the official woman. The proper woman. The kind who Mlle Weil imagined would tell ardent girls, tell all of us: Don't read, don't study. You were born for only one thing: mother love.

And so she will not speak of it. Perhaps she will whisper it into Aaron's ear. Perhaps in the form of a song. But that will only be possible until he understands. After he understands, she will go silent.

She stays in the bedroom until she hears that Laurent has settled himself in his chair, until she hears the rustle of the newspaper. And then she cannot wait. She is impatient as a girl to tell him. "I have seen her, right here on Riverside Drive. I have seen her. I have seen Mlle Weil."

"Here? On Riverside Drive?"

"She's coming to tea tomorrow."

"It must be as if you'd just run into Marlene Dietrich. Or Mrs. Roosevelt. At one point she was the center of your life. You loved her very much."

"No, Laurent, it wasn't like that, it wasn't like that at all. I wanted to run away from her. I was hoping she didn't see me. I dread having to spend time with her. It brings back too much. Too much I'm not strong enough to think about. A person I no longer recognize whom I have, somehow, to understand is still myself. I think I will be a very great disappointment to her when she learns about my life. I didn't pursue my studies. I can hardly remember a word of philosophy, to say nothing of mathematics. My days are spent trying to make sense of my ration books, studying various ways of curing colic."

"Caring for your brother, a helpless cripple."

"Laurent, I hate it when you talk like that."

"My bitterness, Mama called it. She would say, 'Bitterness curdles the digestion, Laurent.'"

"You aren't often bitter. You are very good."

"I am not very good. I am, however, often a good actor. Unlike you, I have no mixed feelings about seeing her. She was an extraordinary teacher. When she was with you, you felt you had the attention, the complete attention of an incandescent mind. She was tremendously patient. And when she would quote the *Iliad,* her face—which I never,

I must confess, thought beautiful—was also incandescent. I knew what it meant when people said a person was lit up. But you, my God, GeGe, you worshipped her."

"It was very long ago."

"It was a different world."

"She'll be very interested in your work. She has no small talk, and I don't think she'll care to hold the baby. So I will make tea, try to find something for her to eat—although as I recall she almost never ate—and I can disappear and leave her to you. Bring the board home tomorrow. It will give you something to talk to Mlle Weil about. So I won't have to think about it."

OCTOBER 8, 1942

Genevieve knows she is spending more time than it is worth considering what to serve Mlle Weil. It will be tea rather than coffee; coffee is severely rationed, and Laurent absolutely needs his morning coffee. She decides that she will serve peanut butter on crackers; this will be an entirely new food for Mlle Weil, and, when she is told they are eating peanut butter as part of the war effort, she will be enthusiastic. Genevieve will take special care making the tea, in the way that an English friend once taught her. She will use her best china. She is very aware that it is likely Mlle Weil will notice none of this.

Laurent has arranged for one of his students to help him home, to carry "the board." The young man sets up the easel on which the board rests; he places it in the direct center of the room. Like a god to be knelt to, worshipped.

The student, whose name Genevieve doesn't know, goes out to the hall and brings in a wooden box of wooden blocks. She's met him before and, knowing that she should know his name, can't ask it again, and so she doesn't address him, just nods and smiles like a simpleton. Perhaps he thinks her English is very bad. Well, let him think that; that would be better than his believing she is rude, or knowing that she has forgotten his name. He has not taken off his hat, and he tips it to Genevieve and then backs out of the room, uneasily, as if he were ashamed to have entered the private quarters of the Master. The student has been gone less than five minutes when the bell rings.

"Mlle Weil at the gates. *En garde,*" says Laurent.

She is wearing exactly what she wore the day before. Her clothing gives off an unfresh smell. She takes off her beret and cape and hands them to Genevieve without a word, without even a greeting. She heads directly for Laurent, her hand outstretched. Genevieve wonders if she notices the spasms that are racking his body, whether she will acknowledge it in shaking his hand, or in withdrawing her extended hand because of it. But no, she seems to be unaware of the tremors. Or she is a very great actress indeed. But Genevieve knows that is impossible; dissembling, dissimulation are simply not things that would occur to Mlle Weil. It must be that she is unaware. Unaware of her unawareness. Always. Yes.

"Genevieve has told me about your wonderful work," she says, cutting right past any pleasantries, any inquiries in regard to health, any comments on the weather, even the state of the larger world.

"I brought my board along to show you. I was hoping you would be interested," Laurent replies, taking up her tone.

"Indeed, I am extremely interested. I have been looking forward to learning about this very much. Please explain everything to me, slowly. I am not very good at understanding things in space. With time, I am much better."

Is Mlle Weil making a joke? In case she is, they should laugh. In case not, they ought not to. Genevieve says, "I am going to make tea." She leaves the decision to laugh or not to laugh to her brother, whose face, often distorted, is sometimes incapable of clear signals, in this case, a mercy.

Mlle Weil sits on the couch next to Laurent's chair. He pulls the easel closer to both of them. He reaches into the box and takes out one of the blocks.

"The blocks are six inches square. Any one of them can be placed into one of the depressions on the board, where it will rest secure because the board is leaning back. The block can be easily grasped and removed because it protrudes slightly above the face. This is important for the people I work with; the articulation of their fingers can be very limited."

"Yes, yes, go on," says Mlle Weil, lighting a cigarette.

"Would you like to try using the board?" he asks.

Genevieve is happy to be in the kitchen, watching the baby play on the floor. She has seen the demonstration a thousand times. She continues to be deeply moved, enormously proud of the work her brother has done. Giving hope to hopeless people. Giving language to the entirely mute. Freeing them from a terrible prison. But she doesn't need to see the demonstration yet again. Whereas every action of her beautiful baby—rolling a ball, hitting a pot with a spoon—seems to her entirely riveting.

Mlle Weil, though, is entirely absorbed.

"Mlle Weil is a good pupil. She has gone through three sets. She seems to be baffled. You would do better, Mlle Weil, if you had begun at the beginning and progressed to this point."

"Well, then, let's start again."

"Next time," Laurent says. "Next time we'll begin from the beginning. For now, tell us about your time in New York."

Genevieve pours the tea. She passes the plate of peanut butter and crackers.

"This is a new food. It is called peanut butter. It was just recently invented, meant to encourage people to eat less real butter."

Mlle Weil picks up a cracker, looks at it as if it were an exotic, possibly dangerous animal, and puts it back on the plate. She lights yet another cigarette. Genevieve sees that her two middle fingers are stained brownish yellow from nicotine.

"I fear I have made a very great mistake in coming to New York. I did it because I feared my parents would not leave France without me, and I didn't want them to be in danger. I, of course, know it is my duty to be in danger, but I also know it is not their duty. So while I am here, all I do is try to make contacts that will allow me to leave and go back to Europe. I have worked on a plan for parachuting nurses into very dangerous battle zones. At the moment, I am taking a training course in first aid myself, because I wouldn't dream of proposing a scheme in which I was unable to take part. I have written to many people, seen many people. I am at the French consulate almost daily. I have been in correspondence with a very fine naval officer, an Admiral Leahy. I have written to President Roosevelt. His office wrote back, expressing interest, but offering no help. I am even in touch with a French naval officer on a ship in Cuba. If I had to pretend to be a Nazi to get back to Europe, I would do it."

Genevieve and Laurent do not even want to meet each other's eyes. "We will talk later," they say silently, without gesture, in the way of brothers and sisters. The baby fusses in Genevieve's lap.

"I myself have just had a little niece. My brother's child. I call her Patapon. She is in Pennsylvania."

"Are you fond of babies, Mlle Weil?" asks Laurent.

"Simone, you must call me Simone. Of course I am fond of babies. Do you think of me as that unnatural?"

The real answer to that, Genevieve thinks, would be yes. It is the answer that Mlle Weil would give. But Laurent only laughs, and Genevieve says, "I'll put him down for a nap." She will never be able to call her Simone. She will address her as nothing. But in Genevieve's mind she can only and forever be Mlle Weil.

"Ah, then we mustn't wake him. But I hope I will come back. Tomorrow, perhaps."

"Unless President Roosevelt agrees to meet with you," says Laurent.

"No, that will not happen, I'm afraid."

"He's rather busy," Laurent says.

Genevieve makes a threatening face at him: Don't tease, the face says, and he can read it, and is silent.

"Tomorrow, then," says Mlle Weil.

Most people, Genevieve thinks, would wait to be invited. But Mlle Weil is not like most people. She is entirely herself. Unlike anyone else. Barely human. Barely inhabiting the world.

OCTOBER 9, 1942

She comes the next day, at teatime. Four o'clock. Genevieve wonders if she understands that tea is rationed and her coming for tea means there will be less for her and for Laurent. An old instinct of hospitality makes her hope that she does not realize it, and the same instinct brings to birth a clutch of shame that there is nothing good to serve with the tea. It should make things better that Genevieve knows Mlle Weil would probably not eat anything with her tea. She remembers that Mlle Weil ate almost nothing that was served to her by Genevieve's mother, who was, she very well knows, a much better cook than she. She is used to believing that, but now she wonders: How would my mother cope with wartime New York? Would she do better with rationing than I? With almost no butter. With bread so soft you could squeeze it to nothing in your hand.

"I see your brother is not here. I was hoping he and I could work again with his board."

Genevieve tells Mlle Weil that Laurent should be home shortly, but that he will probably not have his board with him, since he has to enlist a student to carry the board when he wants to bring it home.

"That is too bad. I am disappointed," she says.

Genevieve is annoyed with Mlle Weil's self-absorption, but she has to remind herself that no one who has not lived with a disabled person understands the endless calculations that must be made, how to ask for help without overstepping some kind of mark. A mark that is invisible, but once crossed, impossible to cross back over.

"I am eager to talk to you about my plan to parachute nurses into battle zones. But we will wait for your brother."

This is my home, Mlle Weil, she wants to say, and you are taking it over, dictating terms. She hears Laurent's key in the door, and her relief is enormous. She hates the thought of being alone with Mlle Weil.

"I will just get the tea," she says, and Mlle Weil waves her away like a distracting fly.

When she comes in, she sees that Laurent is beginning to be bored, has nothing to say when Mlle Weil asks him if he knows a place she could train as a parachutist. She thinks of Mlle Weil's clumsiness and she can't imagine her being able to open a parachute. Laurent's boredom can be a danger in a social situation. When he's bored he becomes sarcastic. Ironic, he calls it: my knife of irony cutting through the fog of excess and confusion. He teases. And Mlle Weil is not a good person to be teasing.

The doorbell rings. Genevieve doesn't know who it is, but whoever it is, the air in the room will be changed, and there is very little air that is right for Mlle Weil to breathe. She answers the door, and her heart contracts.

Joe and Lily. Of all people, the wrong ones to be in a room with Mlle Weil.

Usually, Joe is the person she most wants to be in her home. He laughs, he makes Laurent laugh, he praises her hair, he throws the baby in the air and catches him as Laurent cannot and as she is afraid to do.

Joe owns a beauty parlor on the East Side. She would love to go there sometime, but he has told her it's very "pricey" and so she would never suggest paying a visit.

What will Mlle Weil make of Joe and Lily? Genevieve hopes she can count on him not to start talking about his great love, the miracle of his great love for the beautiful Lily, who enters on his arm, and then almost leaps across the living room to kiss Laurent. Lily, beautiful Lily, never seems to actually walk anywhere. She leaps, she floats, she dances. Lily, young as Genevieve knows herself no longer young, with her wonderful, full, red lips and her hair like a glossy chestnut and the whites of her eyes so clear, never reddened by fatigue, and her black emphatic eyebrows. Lily, Joe's mistress, twenty-five years younger.

Genevieve prays to a God in whom she cannot believe that he won't talk about the wife he loathes, with whom he lives most of the time in an overlarge apartment in the Bronx, a section he calls Belmont ("'Beautiful mountain,' right, isn't that French?"), his children grown and gone. That he won't talk about the apartment upstairs he rents for Lily. "Imagine me, a grandfather and madly in love with this princess here." And she hopes, desperately, that Mlle Weil won't question whatever it is that Joe has in the paper sack, treats he always brings from "his cousin who owns a farm in New Jersey." She and Laurent speculate that Joe has contacts in the black market, but they agree not to look into it too closely. She tells herself that Mlle Weil isn't familiar enough with the ins and outs of American rationing to notice anything amiss.

"And how's the most beautiful mama in New York?" he says, kissing Genevieve on both cheeks.

"Joe, this is our old teacher from France, Mlle Weil," Laurent says.

"Uh-oh, I'm in for it. My French is lousy. I got bumped from French class for throwing spitballs."

Mlle Weil blinks. "I do not know what spitballs are," she says.

"Spitballs, let me see. Well, you take a little piece of paper and you roll it up into a ball, and then to weigh it down, so that the paper holds together, you add a little spit, or maybe I should say saliva, and then you throw it across the room and try to hit someone in the back of the head."

Do you know who you are speaking to, Joe? Genevieve wants to say. This is Simone Weil, a very great intellectual, a very great thinker. And you are explaining spitballs to her. You are talking about spitting into paper just as we are about to eat.

"That's very interesting. Amusing," Mlle Weil says. Genevieve knows that she is neither interested nor amused, but at least she isn't offended, and that's better than it might be. It is possible that the encounter will not be a disaster.

Joe reaches into the sack and takes out four small wooden baskets of raspberries. Genevieve relaxes about her black market worries: fruits and vegetables aren't rationed.

She takes the raspberries into the kitchen and puts them in a pure white bowl, her favorite of all the pottery Howard's mother has provided because it is plain. The others with their fussy pattern of rosebuds—of course she is grateful for them, she can see that they are well made, perhaps even called fine, but she would not have chosen them. But this, this pure white bowl, unornamented, well proportioned: she can think of it as hers. She puts her face to the beautiful dark red of the fruit, disappointed that there is no fragrance. She doesn't have much opportunity for sensual pleasure these days. Except with her son. She breathes him in . . . the yeasty smell of his hair, when he is sweaty after sleep.

"I think we can save our sugar ration; these are sweet as sugar. And speaking of sweet as sugar," Joe says, squeezing Lily's shoulders.

To Genevieve's enormous relief, Mlle Weil doesn't seem to notice.

"Aren't these just beautiful?" Joe says, passing around the bowls of fruit. "Aren't they just perfect? There's got to be a God somewhere out there; this is the proof. But then there's Hitler, so I guess it's up for grabs."

"Are you interested in the proofs for the existence of God?" asks Mlle Weil.

A sour taste comes to Genevieve's mouth. She wants to beg her old teacher: Please, Mlle Weil, don't begin with the ontological argument. Not with Joe.

But Joe doesn't miss a beat. "Nope, I guess I'm not. I just shut my eyes, hold my nose, and hope for the best." He offers Mlle Weil a bowl of berries.

"No thank you, I am not fond of fruit," she says.

Joe seems genuinely puzzled. "I never heard of that," he says.

"You see, Joe," says Mlle Weil, "one of my shames is that many kinds of food disgust me. I have been very held back from being the kind of person I want to be because I seem to be susceptible to both fatigue and disgust."

Genevieve wants to rush across the room and put her hand over Mlle Weil's mouth. Don't talk like this, she wants to say. Nobody talks like this. Not to someone they've just met. You are impossible.

But Lily, who usually says very little, responds immediately. "I can't stand fat on meat," she says. "And I am often so tired that I just want to die."

Mlle Weil nods. "It is very difficult to work through fatigue. What is your work?"

Lily says she's a beautician, and this is another English word that has to be explained to Mlle Weil. She nods and asks Joe about his work. He tells her he's Lily's boss but that he used to be a farmer, that that was what he really loved. That the raspberries came from his family's farm in New Jersey, but his father lost the farm in the Depression and it was taken over by his cousins. That he is really happiest there, but he had to learn a trade so he got a job in a beauty salon that another one of his cousins owned. But that he really misses the farm. Genevieve has never heard him speak this way before.

"I'm sorry you won't be enjoying the fruit. But what you say makes a lot of sense," he says. "Only I never heard anyone say it before. Fatigue and disgust. You're completely right, Simone. It's okay if call you that?"

"Of course. And I will call you Joe."

"Sure thing. You know, you really know how to go to the heart of things."

And then she does something else unheard of, something that ought to be unacceptable. She asks Joe to read a poem. She reaches into the large pocket of her overlarge trousers and takes out a folded piece of paper, which Genevieve can see is covered by her tiny writing.

"This is an English poem which I love very much. And I like your voice. Its inflections. It is a voice of kindness, a good man's voice. I have wanted to have this poem read by a native English speaker, but I was embarrassed to ask. But with you, Joe, I couldn't be embarrassed."

"Okay, Simone, but I don't know if I really speak English. My first language was Sicilian, and I came to English by way of New Jersey and the Bronx. But here goes nothing."

"It will not be nothing," says Mlle Weil. "Whatever it will be, it will not be nothing. It is a very beautiful poem by a great English poet, George Herbert, who lived in the seventeenth century."

"So he's even older than me," Joe says, putting on his glasses to read the poem.

> Love bade me welcome, yet my soul drew back
> Guiltie of dust and sinne.
> But quick-ey'd Love, observing me grow slack
> From my first entrance in,
> Drew near to me, sweetly questioning
> If I lack'd anything.
>
> "A guest," I answer'd, "worthy to be here."
> Love said, "You shall be he."
> "I, the unkinde, ungrateful? Ah, my deare,
> I cannot look on Thee."
> Love took my hand and smiling did reply,
> "Who made the eyes but I?"

"Truth, Lord, but I have marr'd them; let my shame
Go where it doth deserve."
"And know you not," sayes Love, "who bore the blame?"
"My deare, then I will serve."
"You must sit down," sayes Love, "and taste My meat."
So I did sit and eat.

The easy feeling in the room has gone. Genevieve sees that Joe is uncomfortable. He hasn't understood the poem. Mlle Weil wants to talk about it, wants to explain it to him, wants to become his teacher, but he doesn't want it. He wants to be upstairs with Lily.

"I'm not much of a one for poetry, but it sure was swell meeting you," he says, and Lily, embarrassed to be in the same room with poetry, says nothing, but lowers her beautiful eyes.

"Tiens, I am once more late. My mother will be furious," Mlle Weil says, and rushes out the door without saying goodbye.

Genevieve picks up the cups and saucers, then sets them down and sits down herself on the sofa.

"She's impossible. Impossible. I could kill her for making Joe and Lily feel uncomfortable."

"Well, yes, GeGe, he was perhaps uncomfortable for a moment. But he will remember this time, remember meeting her, remember what she allowed him to think, what she allowed him to say. Lily, I think, will especially remember it. Remember how the workers she taught loved Mlle Weil, how Mama told us she would carry fifty pounds of books on her back so they would be able to read Greek poetry and geometry. Perhaps if she has more time with Joe she will convert him to Metaphysical poetry. You heard what he said—she goes to the heart of things."

"Only some people have hearts of stone, perhaps no hearts at all. And so yes, Laurent, her students loved her, the workers loved her, but many people hated her. Hated her with an almost insane violence, and sometimes for no reason."

"Joe and Lily are among the kindest people in the world."

"But she might have been with people who were not kind, not kind at all. How can she always be opening herself up as she does? She creates no shelters for herself. She's as vulnerable as a newly hatched chick. It's disgustingly easy to hurt her."

"Another vulnerable creature it is your responsibility to protect. Like your son. Like me."

"No, not like you. You, Laurent, I never think of as a child."

"And yet, of course, always in need of extravagant attention. Like a child."

The real child in the house cries out, and she is happy to go to him, knowing how easy it is to provide him with the necessary comfort.

OCTOBER 11, 1942

Genevieve is struggling with the perambulator, awkwardly carrying it down the four front steps, when her eye falls on Mlle Weil, making her way down the street towards her. She had not said she would be coming, and Genevieve is taking advantage of the last hours of light in this October, when light is increasingly precious, increasingly another commodity which seems to need rationing. She wonders what Mlle Weil would have done if she had rung the bell and found no one home. Walked away to another destination? Or planted herself on the stairs, perhaps taking a book from one of her wide, deep pockets, lighting a cigarette, just sitting, waiting, not knowing how ridiculous she looked.

Genevieve hadn't been outside all day, so she decided to be safe, to put a sweater on the baby and a hat. She often puts sweaters and hats on him when he doesn't really need them, because all of Howard's female relatives seem to have worn themselves out knitting hats and sweaters. She is not ungrateful. They have taken her in. A French woman, a non-Jew. Howard had told her the name for a non-Jewish woman. *Shikse.* An ugly word, she had thought, like spitting on the sidewalk. She had never heard any of the family use it, but she doesn't know if they do when she's not around. She chooses to believe that they are kind people, and do not.

Of course, Mlle Weil doesn't help with the baby carriage. She is looking up at the sky, lighting a cigarette.

"I'm afraid Laurent won't be home until late tonight," she says.

"Oh, no, it's you I wanted to see. And now we can go for a walk. Excellent."

Not asking if Genevieve wanted her company. Genevieve is annoyed and yet secretly pleased: "It's you I wanted to see." The old allure still in place, still in force. Genevieve condemns herself for an immature impulse. She is a grown woman, a wife, a mother. And yet the words "It's you I wanted to see" still make the skin on her forearms ripple like the skin of a horse in a light breeze.

The late sun sparkles on the river. She has not given up the habit of trying to find the right words for the color of the sky. Pearl grey, she thinks, and then changes from pearl to oyster, the inside of an oyster shell. And all at once, there is something like a rip in the matte greyness, and light pours through, as if someone had slit a grey cloth bag of sugar, and the sugar had spilt out. Only one tree is singled out by the light, and that one called a sugar maple. It amuses her to say to herself, "The sugar light falls on the sugar maple," and then she wonders if she thought of sugar because of rationing. She believes that she spends an inordinate amount of time thinking about the food she can't have. She has been told the sacrifice is honorable, and she believes it is, and is glad to do it. Only sometimes she yearns, ashamed, for the taste of sugar.

Mlle Weil says: "The tree looks like a torch thrown down by an angel."

Once more, in relation to Mlle Weil, Genevieve finds herself abashed and feels she must accuse herself. *She is thinking of angels and I of sugar.*

"I very much like New York. If France's situation didn't obsess my memory, my stay in New York would be pleasant and interesting. The skyscrapers are like cliffs and crags; I like the chaotic quality of the beauty: it is a new way of thinking about beauty. Whether the streets are beautiful or ugly, I always find them attractive. Especially Harlem. I attend a Baptist church in Harlem."

Genevieve cannot imagine what the Negroes in the Baptist church would make of Mlle Weil. She has almost no contact with Negroes, but some Sundays when she is walking with the baby she has seen whole families making their way to church, beautifully dressed, the women resplendent in dramatic hats. What do they think of this scarecrow of a white woman with flapping trousers and, instead of a beautiful hat, a not entirely clean beret? Or perhaps, she thinks, because their lives are difficult and they must have seen many things, they welcome her as respectable white churchgoers would not. Genevieve hopes that they do; once more, she feels she needs to worry for her.

Mlle Weil is standing now under the blazing tree. She lifts her hand, and spreads her arms out, as if she were ready to take flight. She closes, then opens her eyes. She seems almost young. The worn look, the look of tired discouragement, the bent skeleton—they've disappeared. And then she says, "The presence of beauty in the world is the surest sign of the presence of God."

The words are shocking to Genevieve. When she knew Mlle Weil as her teacher, God had not seemed important to her unless it was the abstract God of Plato. When the question of God was raised in class, she refused to discuss it "on the grounds of insufficient data."

In that world, the world of left-leaning intellectual Frenchmen, the use of the word "God" as she used it would have been rejected with derision. Genevieve wonders what Laurent would make of it, both she and her brother priding themselves on being "pagans" among the "unbaptized."

Genevieve longs to ask her, why she had begun speaking in this way. But she feels she has no right. She can only think of Mlle Weil as her teacher.

They sit on a bench looking at the river. All Genevieve can think of is that in a few weeks, at this hour, it will be completely dark. She dreads the coming of winter, the four o'clock fall of night, a knife blade dropping straight down to the cold stone. She can't get used to New York winters. She worries for the baby.

Mlle Weil is staring into the pewter-colored river. "The suffering of the world, particularly now in these terrible times, obsesses me and overwhelms me to the point of annihilating my faculties. I suppose you wonder why I can invoke the concept of God in this case."

Genevieve says nothing. She isn't sure if Mlle Weil is talking to her, or to herself, or to the air or the river.

"I believe there are two paths to God, seemingly divergent but in fact closely related. The soul is pierced equally by beauty and by affliction. Only when the soul is pierced in these ways can God enter."

Genevieve can no longer keep silent; her curiosity is stronger than her humility.

"Do you believe in God, Mlle Weil?"

"I don't know what it is to believe. I know only that I was pierced in my soul by the presence of God. I have felt him take possession of my body."

Genevieve is embarrassed, as if she had been given details of an amorous encounter, details she would prefer not to know.

"That's why I had Joe read that English poem, which is not, to me, a poem, but a prayer. I was at the abbey of Solesmes with my parents; we had traveled there to hear the Gregorian chant, for which it was famous. It was Easter. I was suffering particularly from headaches. Each note of the chant hurt me like a blow. I was able to rise above my body, to leave it to suffer by itself heaped up in a corner and to find perfect joy in the chanting. The Passion of Christ entered my being once and for all."

How can this be happening? How can she be speaking in this way? Genevieve remembers the pictures on the wall of their maid Louise, the one time she visited her house after Louise's funeral. High-colored prints with bleeding wounds, contorted faces, Jesus half naked, clutching a pillar, leering brutes whipping him till his flesh was shreds. And a single candle in a red glass dish in front of a tearful Jesus pointing to his red heart, the shape of a pimiento or a tongue.

"It was at that time that I met my English angel. I saw him coming back from Communion and he was truly angelic in his radiance. He gave me the poem, he wrote it out in his own hand."

It is getting worse and worse. Now she is using words that could come from the trashy novels Genevieve sees in the drugstore. "My English angel . . . in his own hand."

Suddenly, awkwardly, Mlle Weil takes her hand, probably the first time she has ever touched Genevieve. "I don't speak to people about these things. I'm always afraid people will misunderstand, purposely misunderstand, out of a mysterious desire I arouse in people to do me harm. But I believe you have no desire to do me harm. It's not that I think other people wish to harm me from malice, only from the well-known phenomenon that makes hens rush upon one of their number if it is wounded, attacking and pecking it."

Genevieve is repelled, but at the same time fascinated. She both does and doesn't want to hear more. She sees, more vividly than she would like, the wounded hen that is Mlle Weil. She remembers going to Chinatown with Joe and Lily once and watching something called the dancing chicken. You put a quarter into the slot and the chicken danced. She found it grotesque, humiliating, beneath the dignity of any animal. And yet she could not take her eyes away. Only later she learned that the chicken wasn't dancing but hopping to avoid electric shocks. When she thinks of it, she is ashamed that she looked for even a second, that she was complicit in a kind of torture. And for what? To look at something she should not have been looking at. She should probably tell Mlle Weil not to speak to her about these things. But she does not. There is something she feels she has to ask.

"Have you, then, become a Christian?"

"I will not be baptized, but I believe that I have always been a Christian; my conception of life has always been Christian. I have always had the Christian idea of love for neighbor, of the spirit, of poverty, the ideal of purity."

Genevieve doesn't say what she wants to say: But you are a Jew, as my son is, as my husband is. This is why you and your parents are here, in America, because Jews in Europe are unsafe. And she is glad she didn't say it, because Mlle Weil says, "You have always been kind to me, Genevieve; there are very few people whom I can always rely on for kindness."

Once again she is the schoolgirl, given high marks by her teacher. That quick rush. That delight.

"I remember the time I put my sweater on backwards. You were my protector then. It was only your kindness that kept those schoolgirls, who are well known for being cruel, from being terrible."

"No one wanted to be cruel to you. We adored you. To the point of idolatry perhaps."

She is no longer in New York City, at the Hudson River, a mother pushing her sleeping child in a pram; she is a girl again, in Mlle Weil's classroom in Le Puy. Mademoiselle is speaking to her students about Plato. The *Timaeus*. The class is united: a single flame of desire for understanding, for wisdom, to please Mlle Weil, who is wise and full of understanding and demands more than anyone has ever thought of demanding of them, more than any of them believed, before her, they had it in them to give.

No one sleeps much that year; dark circles under the eyes are a badge of honor, prized as once long legs and round breasts had been prized. Everyone's mother is issuing warnings: you're wearing yourself out. But the girls know what the mothers really mean: they don't want their daughters to turn into Mlle Weil, who is the very embodiment of the idea "unmarriageable." They want their daughters to be pretty, to be pleasing, to walk up and down the stone streets making clicking noises with their heels, tossing their hair back and forth to capture some boy's attention (but do not act like a flirt!), not carrying a fifty-pound sack of books to teach the workers Greek and geometry.

Genevieve recalls with pride that her mother was not like other mothers. She misses her mother, she misses her with a sharp longing. If only she had lived to see Aaron. No, she thinks, my mother did not fear that I would become Mlle Weil. Perhaps because she knew I didn't have it in me. That giftedness. That greatness of mind. Was it a kindness to me, her insistence that because I was pretty, "*jolie,*" that I need not worry: men would always love me.

It had given Genevieve an almost sickening joy to know that she was Mlle Weil's favorite, when she praised her for her attentiveness to Laurent. "Attention," she had said again and again, "is the true end of all school study."

But here she is, nine years later, blinking, smoking, saying that people wanted to hurt her, that she always had to be afraid.

"I am sure that you have had strong friendships."

"I always fear that any friendship is a mistake or an act of kindness that has nothing to do with me, that has taken place in spite of me."

Genevieve bends over to tuck the blanket around the baby because tears are forming behind her eyelids. That this great woman feels she is unworthy of love. She puts her face closer to him, doing the unthinkable, trying to wake him up. What kind of mother does that? But she needs him, she needs his help: she can't face Mlle Weil's eyes, the eyes of someone who feels herself unworthy of love. "I'll make it up to you," she whispers in his ear.

"You shouldn't think that I haven't been loved by my family. I love my parents dearly, they love me with all their hearts, and this is why I agreed to leave France with them, because they wouldn't have left without me. I have a horror of causing them pain, but I know I will, it is inevitable, because I can't stay here in safety while so many in Europe are in danger."

She lights yet another cigarette. She is never not smoking.

"I have only this one life. If I had another, I would stay here, giving my life to my parents, but I have only this one life. The only way I can relieve myself of the obsession of the suffering of the world is by getting a large dose of suffering and hardship for myself."

Her son does not let Genevieve down: he howls. She is freed of the responsibility. The responsibility of response. She walks up and down, trying to comfort him.

And then she sees her.

The woman whom she hates.

The woman who has taught her what it is to hate.

Genevieve sees that she is pregnant. She nods to the woman, who nods back, having, like Genevieve, no wish to speak.

She wants to turn away from Suzy, towards Mlle Weil, run the few feet towards her, tell her about Suzy, the woman she hates. But she is afraid to. What could she say? "That woman broke my brother's heart." Once more the cheap words from cheap novels or cheap songs. "My English angel" . . . "She broke my brother's heart." How can it be that sometimes these words seem the only ones that serve?

Suzy, the beautiful deaf girl Laurent worked with in his study of the use of language among the deaf. He takes her to dinner, to museums. He brings her home to dinner. Genevieve sees that he is in love, and that she, too, is smitten. But her parents interfere. They come to the apartment when they know Laurent will not be there, "to speak frankly," they say.

"Surely, Mrs. Levy, you agree, you must agree," they say. Agree that Suzy can do better than a man with a twisted, deformed body?

For a little while she is silent, taken over entirely by rage. And then she says simply, "Now you must leave my house."

And they turn silently and simply leave.

She did that thing, she banished them from the house. That was not enough, and always afterwards she regrets her own cowardice. But, of course, she could not have done what she really wanted to do: strike them violently, beat them and beat them until they lay on the ground in their own blood, take a whip to their smug faces, to raise it high over her head and bring it down across their self-satisfied features, cutting deep into their flesh so as to leave a lasting mark. As the younger sister of a crippled brother, she has never hit another person. But at that moment she understood bloodlust. She wanted to hurt them; she wanted to see their blood. She wanted to see it on the floor of her home. It was a powerful feeling, almost sexual. A lust for violence. Her body shook. She had to sit down and grip her hands together. She was afraid to go near the baby.

She never told Laurent. Later she thought that perhaps she should have, because he was devastated when Suzy told him they could no longer see each other. She married someone else: Genevieve did not know who. Was he afflicted in some way, or was his intact body deemed acceptable? Did he even have a mind?

Now Suzy is going to have a baby.

She hates Suzy, but she didn't want to hurt her, as she did her parents. Because she was one of the wounded, one of the afflicted. She had been hurt; she could not be, in the way that they were, self-satisfied. She would always know herself somehow lacking. Nevertheless, Genevieve could only hate her. Perhaps for all time, perhaps for eternity.

But she will not wish her ill. She could never wish ill to someone who is carrying a baby. She wonders: Does that mean I wish her well? No, she cannot really wish her well. *She broke my brother's heart.* The cheap words that somehow serve: for she could see it; something in him broke. He took to his bed, as he never did, except for a serious illness. For two days she brought him his meals in bed. And then he said: "It's over. We will not speak of it again."

When she thinks of telling Mlle Weil about it, she is afraid that her old teacher would say it was a good thing, that Laurent was too fine for ordinary love, that ordinary love was a compromise, a danger, and that he was a pure soul. But Genevieve is already too disturbed by what Mlle Weil had said about her body being pierced. And she could only have spoken about it if she also spoke about her hate, about her desire to shed blood, to leave a lasting mark. And she doesn't want Mlle Weil to know about that.

Perhaps Mlle Weil senses that she no longer has Genevieve's attention, because, without a word, she raises her hand in farewell and heads uptown.

Genevieve has no intention of saying anything to Laurent about seeing Suzy, but she is eager to tell him what Mlle Weil said in the park. She wonders if she will always feel that no experience is ever fully hers unless she shares it with Laurent. But of course, that isn't true; she doesn't share her life with Howard. Nevertheless, to have shared a childhood, a happy childhood, though marked with grief . . . this makes a connection like no other. One night, as they were having supper, he said to her, "No one but us knows what our places were at the dinner table. No one but us knows what our mother's hands looked like when she shuffled the cards before we played a game."

Laurent comes home in one of his irritable moods, impatient for his tea. The thought comes to her: If only I could give him the baby to hold while I prepare it, but I can't; he can't control his spasms, the baby would be in danger, and I, in turn, in spasms of anxiety. So she must hold the baby, pour the water into the kettle, prepare the tea, the crackers. He will be a wonderful uncle when Aaron is older. He will make up magical stories for him. She knows that they will be devoted.

And she knows, too, that her news of Mlle Weil will put him into a good humor.

"Mlle Weil has become a Christian mystic."

"The Red Virgin? Has she forgotten that she is here courtesy of Herr Hitler? And that if they were in France she and her parents would be in danger for their lives?"

"I didn't want to press her on it, she was talking about feeling that it was impossible for her to believe that anyone could feel friendship for her, that there was anyone who didn't have the impulse to hurt her. So I didn't want to say anything that might hurt."

"Genevieve, protector of the wounded bird."

She's not sure he means it kindly, because the next thing he says is "She doesn't know your son will be raised a Jew?"

She thinks of Mlle Weil's image of the hen pecked by the other birds, and of the Chinatown dancing chicken. "I didn't think I needed to tell her at that moment."

"But you will."

She raises her shoulders in a way that no one in America does, in a way that she knows is entirely French. "It is always Mlle Weil who determines the subject of the conversation."

OCTOBER 14, 1942

When Genevieve answers the telephone, she is surprised to hear Mlle Weil's voice. Surprised that she has been able to master the telephone, surprised to connect to Mlle Weil through a contrivance so modern, so American, so uneternal as the telephone. She asks if she can come to tea the next day, and once again Genevieve is pleased when Mlle Weil says, "That's fine," when she says Laurent will be at work.

OCTOBER 15, 1942

When she opens the door, it isn't Mlle Weil but her mother, who seems not to have changed in the decade since they last met.

She looks nothing like her daughter. She is short, squat, soft-looking; her large nose dominates her wide face . . . whereas it is her daughter's eyes that so dominate her face that they make the rest of the face irrelevant.

Genevieve is uneasy. There must be something wrong with Mlle Weil. But there is another cause for her unease. It is the first time a Frenchwoman has visited the apartment. She worries that she has forgotten, or overlooked, or neglected the French way of doing things. But the furnishings were not chosen by her, they were a gift from her in-laws—and it is wartime. She imagines that Mme Weil finds the furniture too large, the pattern in the carpet too pronouncedly floral.

"And what age is the baby? I myself am a new grandmother. A baby girl, two weeks old. Perhaps we should betroth the two babies immediately to save them future trouble."

Genevieve laughs, with French politesse, and asks, "Is Mlle Weil all right?"

"I am here because Simone is not well, not well at all. You know she has terrible headaches, everything has been tried; you know of course that my husband is a doctor, and every specialist has been consulted, surgery even has been considered, but there seems to be no recourse."

"It must be very difficult."

Mme Weil replies with a surprising vehemence—is it anger?—"It is only one of my daughter's difficulties, most of which she creates for herself. My daughter is romantic about danger. She runs after it, as some young girls run after actors.

"Do you know about her time fighting in Spain, with the Anarchists? It did not turn out well. She stepped in a vat of hot cooking oil and badly burned her leg. My husband and I had to sneak over the Spanish border; and it was very dangerous, in a time of war. And then for days we wandered from place to place—rooming houses, hospitals—all over Barcelona, looking for Simone. You are a mother; now I am sure you can imagine my terror for my daughter. The whole time, terrified. A daughter, in a war zone. And not any daughter. A clumsy daughter, a nearsighted daughter. But of all the dangers I had imagined, among them was not my daughter's stepping into a pot of oil. And if her father hadn't arrived in time to rescue her, she might have lost her leg. I'm sure you remember that my daughter is exceptionally clumsy."

"I never noticed it," Genevieve says; a lie, but she knows where her loyalties are.

"This apartment is comfortable and homelike. What is your husband's profession?"

When Genevieve tells her that he is a doctor, she wipes her mouth with a handkerchief. In her eyes, Genevieve sees a look of discontent.

"There was a time when I thought Simone might have an ordinary life. A husband. She was a very pretty child. People used to stop me on the street to say what a pretty child she was. I had to give up the idea that she would have an ordinary life. I realized long ago that she is not like other people. In the family, we call her the troll. The trollesse, actually."

"But Mme Weil, your daughter is a genius," Genevieve says, feeling once more that she must protect Mlle Weil. This time from her mother.

"I hope, Genevieve, that yours is not the fate of being the mother of a genius. I would much rather be the mother of a happy child."

Genevieve is offended on Mlle Weil's behalf, but there is no way of expressing her offense.

"Simone's latest scheme terrifies me. Parachuting nurses into battlefields, insisting she be one of the first. My only hope is that the authorities will find the plan unfeasible. But I know that Simone will leave America, precisely because she's safer here."

She leans forward and grabs Genevieve's wrist, not gently. "My daughter is fond of you; if you talked to her, she might listen."

"I don't think she listens to anyone, Mme Weil."

And Mme Weil closes her eyes, leans her head against the back of the chair, rubs the palm of her hand across her closed eyes. She crosses and uncrosses her surprisingly delicate ankles, of which, Genevieve imagines, as she is a product of the nineteenth century, she must still be quite proud.

"And it will be the death of her, I fear," she says, rising and walking over to the playpen. "A lovely child," she says, but Genevieve can see that her mind is somewhere else.

OCTOBER 18, 1942

The last time she saw him, Joe asked if Genevieve would be his "guinea pig." She asked him what he meant, and he laughed and explained that he needed to try out a new hairdo.

She often forgets that Joe is a successful hairdresser with a salon on the East Side. Sixty-Third and Lex, he says. She doesn't know exactly what he means by Lex, but she knows it's something she should know, so she doesn't ask. Sometimes he leaves copies of *Vogue* and *Harper's Bazaar* for her. It seems slightly wrong for her to be looking at them, but she enjoys it, admiring the beautiful women, their skin so clear, their lips so perfectly rouged, their hair so impossibly clean. She finds it strange that American women are so concerned to be always washing their hair, but, never having even heard of bidets, they are not so careful of their private parts, and often she detects a faint but unmistakable female odor.

Sometimes when she is most worried about Howard, about the War, about their future in America, it is a solace to look at Joe's magazines, and those impossibly perfect women.

When she knows Mlle Weil is coming, she hides the magazines.

Joe announces himself by playing a little tune on the doorbell, dump de dump dump dump dump. He is always excited, always enthusiastic, and Genevieve doesn't understand where this comes from, this hopefulness when his life is difficult, living with a wife he loathes, sneaking to be with his beloved. And the War, the War, which could drain anybody's hope. He arrives carrying a bunch of chrysanthemums and a bunch of purple grapes.

"Here's the deal," he says. He opens a magazine. There is a picture of an actress she vaguely knows: Claudette Colbert.

"I have to say I've always thought of you as 'a Claudette Colbert type.' You see, honey, now the fashion is for women to wear their hair long, pompadours and upsweeps. I've been on the lookout for some shorter hairdos. It makes sense, doesn't it, that women who are working have less time for their hair, they might be happy with shorter hair, but they want to be 'in the swim.' And long hair's not for everyone, particularly some of my older ladies. Now for example I think Claudette Colbert looks better in a shorter cut."

He points to an older picture of Claudette Colbert, with short hair and bangs.

"Now Lily won't let me try out my idea on her," he says. "She won't let me cut an inch off her hair. But would you do me a favor? I promise I'll make you look like a pink peony."

Genevieve touches her hair, which she has worn, since she was no longer a schoolgirl, in a chignon.

"I would quite like to look like a pink peony. I think people think of me as something much less exciting: a marigold, perhaps."

He runs over to a leather bag, rushes her to the kitchen sink, washes her hair. What a great pleasure it is to have her hair washed! The scent of the shampoo is delicious, some kind of lemon, some other kind of flower. Probably all chemical: a new invention in the time of war. She doesn't care; the War has made the worship of the natural obsolete.

Then there are clumps of hair on the linoleum.

"My hair!" she cries out, against her will. But Joe is paying no attention to her as he cuts and combs. There is something almost brutal about his attention to her hair, as if it had no connection to anyone he'd ever known. Then he goes to the bag and takes out a machine that looks something like a gun.

"It's a new gismo, called a hair dryer."

It makes an enormous noise, like an airplane. She's afraid it will wake the baby, but somehow it does not.

There is a hot wind, almost burning the back of her neck. Then he snips a bit, and combs, and clucks. He takes a hand mirror from his bag and gives it to her to hold. "You see?" he says. "A pink peony."

She has only a second to consider her reflection before the baby cries. So she doesn't know what to think, how to consider her new self. Does she look younger? Prettier? More American? She worries that Howard won't like it. It is also possible she will never see him again.

She comes out, holding the baby. "Am I a genius or am I a genius? Congratulations, Aaron, you have the prettiest mama on the Upper West Side."

She has barely got the baby down for his nap when Mlle Weil arrives at the door. She seems more flustered than Genevieve remembers seeing her.

"I must apologize for my mother. My mother can't get it through her head that I am not a child, that there are more important things in the world than her daughter's safety."

"As a mother, I must say I think it is impossible for any mother to believe anything else."

"That is a great error," Mlle Weil says. "People make idols of their children, and idolatry is always a sin. In some societies it was a crime."

Do I make an idol of Aaron? Genevieve asks herself. She considers the possibility. She is often tempted to kneel before him, to worship his beauty, the miracle that he is alive. It is the only time she has an impulse to pray, an impulse she resists, because whom would she pray to? She does not believe in a face that could protect him and receive her thanks. The only thing that really tempts her about Catholicism is Christmas. The worship of baby. A baby at the center of kneeling adults. And the animals' warm breath, comforting the infant.

"Your mother is concerned about your headaches."

Mlle Weil looks annoyed. "My mother had no business speaking of them. She doesn't understand their place in my life. I am very grateful for my headaches; they have helped me to understand suffering. But they have marked me with a cruel brand; sometimes they have made me unknowable to myself. There was a time when the pain and exhaustion were so great that I was uncertain whether or not death was my imperative duty."

"I don't understand how death could be a duty."

"It comes from a feeling of barrenness, like the fig tree Jesus cursed, and like that tree I consider it my duty not to live. In those states, I can only hate myself; I am repulsed by the idea of my barren, pain-ridden self. I become a repulsive thing to myself, and so I understand the repulsion people who have been turned into things arouse for the very reason of their affliction. They have lost themselves. They can only return the world's hatred and repulsion onto themselves. This is why

I can't imagine anyone having the impulse of friendship towards me. It would be like having the impulse of friendship towards a crushed worm."

"Did you have these headaches while you were teaching us?"

"I have had them all my life."

"Then you are very brave."

She looks displeased by the compliment. "Sometimes," she says, "when I was suffering the worst headaches, all I wanted to do was strike someone else on the forehead, to cause pain in the very same place where I was experiencing it. To make someone suffer as I had suffered. How could I understand, how could I know myself after that?"

Genevieve thinks of her impulse towards Suzy's parents: not just to strike them in the forehead, but to draw blood, to leave scars. She wants to tell Mlle Weil: You don't even begin to know. She is grateful that Laurent isn't home, and hopes that Mlle Weil won't talk like this in front of him about the afflicted person's sense of her own repulsiveness. Because Laurent is, without question, one of the afflicted. But it would be dreadful to remind him of the revulsion he causes in so many of the world's eyes, to suggest that this revulsion is inevitably turned on the self, to suggest that the afflicted might consider it their duty to take their own lives.

Genevieve suddenly understands, in a way that she knows will be permanent, that it is possible for Mlle Weil to be wrong. Grievously, dangerously wrong. Including but not limited to a category that could be called mistaken. She knows it because she knows her brother. He loves life. He doesn't want to die. He would never imagine that it is his duty to die. He has struggled with everything in his power to keep alive. This is his greatness.

Is it possible that her brother is greater than Mlle Weil? And she wonders: Which is greater, to be willing to die, or to fight death in the name of life?

The broom is leaning against the wall that separates the kitchen from the living room; Genevieve left it there to answer the door. She carries it into the kitchen, where she will make the tea. Mlle Weil follows her.

Genevieve apologizes for the clumps of hair on the kitchen floor, which she is sweeping as the kettle boils.

"Joe just cut my hair," she says. "He's only just left."

"I see," Mlle Weil says, as if this were something that required a lot of consideration. "You've got your hair cut. It will be more convenient." She says nothing about how she thinks Genevieve's hair looks. "I would like to ask you a favor. Will you cut my hair?"

What can she possibly say? The request is so strange that she can't come up with a response, and Mlle Weil goes on talking.

"I have long understood that people respond more favorably to a woman if they consider her attractive. I have never imagined for a minute that anyone could consider me attractive, but if I conformed more to the conventional idea of a proper lady it might help me at the consulate, where I must go to arrange my papers to get back to Europe. My mother usually washes and cuts my hair, but I'm trying to train myself not to be so dependent on my parents. Soon I will be living without them, far away."

A bubble of nausea forms behind Genevieve's lips. She doesn't want to wash Mlle Weil's hair. She doesn't want to be touching Mlle Weil's body, particularly knowing how much she dislikes being touched. And the truth is, she does not smell good. The truth is: Mlle Weil stinks. But Mlle Weil is a hero. So how can Genevieve not do this thing, this exceedingly simple thing?

"I will be happy to do it after I feed the baby and put him down for his nap." What is there about this woman, so devoted to the truth, that requires the telling of so many lies?

She puts her mouth and nose to the baby's scalp: the smell of his hair is a pleasure. Silk and bread and milk, safety, nourishment, desire without danger, no prospect of harm. But Mlle Weil's hair is not silky; it is almost a solid wire triangle from crown to chin. Possibly she never combs it. Genevieve opens her blouse, offers her breast to the baby, hoping he will take a long time today so that she can, in good faith, postpone the thing she dreads. Always for a mother, the unassailable moment: I have a baby at my breast. There is nothing else I can do.

While he nurses, Mlle Weil reads a newspaper. She is making notes.

Genevieve puts the baby in his crib and goes to the bathroom to get the one clean, dry towel. Olive green. A color she has never liked. A gift from Howard's parents. Kindness. Blindness. In English, the words rhyme.

She tries to duplicate everything that Joe did, hoping that she can provide the kind of pleasure Joe provided. Something in her lifts: she is pleased at the prospect of pleasing.

She bends Mlle Weil's head back to wash it. The thinness of the bones of her shoulders alarms her. How easily those bones could break. As if all the energy in her body went into the task of creating this uselessly lively, thick wire triangle of hair. No strength to spare for the necessary skeleton.

Her hair is so thick, and perhaps so dirty, that the water won't penetrate it. It is impossible to make a lather. Mlle Weil's eyes are closed. It is the first time Genevieve has ever seen her without glasses, and it seems almost indecent, as if those eyes without glasses are too naked, too vulnerable. Genevieve hopes Mlle Weil will not open her eyes. If she does, Genevieve will turn her own eyes away.

She begins humming to cover her unease. *Il était une bergère, et ron, ron, ron, petit patapon.*

To her astonishment, Mlle Weil joins in. *Il était une bergère, qui gardait ses moutons.*

And Genevieve thinks: As long as we are singing, it will be all right. It will be possible. Her hair is a disaster of tangles. Panic. Breathe in, breathe out. She thinks of the difficult things people are doing at home in France, the difficult things Howard might be doing. Soldiers facing horrifying explosions, corpses, bloodied in ditches. Surely she can untangle Mlle Weil's hair.

"My hair drives my mother wild. I am very grateful to you."

Genevieve pretends she's Joe and snips the tangled hair: if she cuts through the tangles, the process might be easier.

"It is my pleasure." Another lie, a kind of lie Mlle Weil would never think to tell.

———

Genevieve offers her a mirror. She barely looks at herself. "It's fine," she says and covers her still wet hair with her black beret. "But now I have another favor to ask you. I don't own a lipstick. May I borrow yours for just a day, just the day I must go to the consulate?"

What Genevieve wants to say is no, no, no, you may not have my lipstick. I haven't much left and when it's gone it may be difficult to get more. It is never predictable, in wartime, what will be difficult to get. You'll probably lose it or use it in some way so that it will have lost its goodness. No, you may not have my lipstick.

But how can she say that to someone who is on her way to make plans for the formation of a group of nurses, parachuting into battlefields, most likely to death? Including her own.

"Of course."

"Genevieve, you are a very good friend."

She wants to say, No I am not. I am good not out of friendship but because I fear your disapproval as I did when I was just a girl. Now I am a wife and mother. But you bring me back to being the girl I was. She thinks that Mlle Weil was never a girl. Or never girlish. A daughter, yes. But a girl? Never, perhaps.

She goes into the bedroom to get the lipstick. She uncaps it, screws up the fingertip of solid red; Cherries in the Snow, the lipstick is called. She puts some on her own lips, then twists it down, carefully, recaps it, feels the cool gold in her palm, then caresses it, as if she were petting a beloved animal she was consigning to extermination. A lamb to the slaughter.

She hears Laurent's key in the door and hears from his greeting, "*GeGe,* lock up your jewels, it's a dangerous burglar." He is in a good mood. He greets Mlle Weil enthusiastically, and asks her if she'd like to test out a new set of blocks he's experimenting with.

"Only if you'll let me smoke," she says.

"Ah," he says, "we have come to the limits of your asceticism."

"Laurent, do not be cruel to me," Mlle Weil says. Her tone is almost playful. "Come on, then, let's get started."

And Genevieve thinks: Perhaps she does not always want to die.

OCTOBER 25, 1942

It's the first time she's left the baby with anyone else, and she's doing it for what she knows may be a frivolous reason: she's going to the movies. Joe had planned everything. He has a friend, a piano player, who told him about something he calls a gig. Tonight, he is doing the piano accompaniment for a showing of Chaplin's *Modern Times* that a church in the Bronx is putting on as a fund-raiser to get money for Christmas packages to send to their relatives overseas.

Lily will babysit (she doesn't want to go to the Bronx, she hates being anywhere near it, he says, and of course Genevieve knows why: the Bronx is where Joe lives with his wife), and he's brought rye bread and salami, which he knows Laurent loves. And besides, Joe says, Laurent (he pronounces it "Lorront") isn't the kind of guy who cares that much about what he eats.

How wrong you are, Joe, she wants to say, but of course does not, because she will not betray her brother. And because she knows he will like the bread and the salami, and he likes Lily, and, although she feels a bit guilty, she will be happy to have an evening out.

The doorbell rings. It can only be something to interfere with her pleasure; she doesn't know who or what, but the doorbell can only indicate an obstacle. The university. The War. She will have to stay home.

She is only half relieved to see that it is Mlle Weil.

"I don't want supper," she says. "I was just passing your door and I thought I would say a quick hello."

"Simone," Joe says, and Genevieve stands between them so he won't be able to clap her on the back or embrace her. "We're on our way to the movies. All the way up to the Bronx. Your friend here is having her first night out. We're going to see Chaplin. *Modern Times.*"

"But that is my favorite film in all the world. I will phone my mother."

Mlle Weil automatically assumes that she is included in the invitation. Which, of course, she is, but Genevieve doesn't understand that in the light of what she said about believing that no one wants to be her friend.

She argues with her mother but only for a moment.

She pushes her beret down firmly onto her head; she's ready to leave. "I believe that Chaplin is the only really great Jew since Spinoza."

"Jeez, I didn't know Chaplin was Jewish. But I'm not surprised. Ninety percent of the really smart people I've ever known are Jewish. Which is why Hitler is scared to death of them. He knows they could run rings around those dumb Krauts."

"We must remember," says Mlle Weil, "that Germany has made enormous contributions in literature, in philosophy, most particularly in music."

Joe replies in song. "Grab your coat and get your hat."

Genevieve allows herself to wear her mother's pearl earrings, and to use some powder. Mlle Weil never returned the lipstick, and she misses it. She's sure if she told Joe he'd provide some, but she doesn't know how and from where, so she doesn't ask. It pleases her when Joe calls her pretty. But she knows she will never again be as pretty as Lily, whom she does not envy. A difficult life.

She shows Lily how to prepare Aaron's bottle, which she hopes he won't need. She will wean him soon. Perhaps in the spring, when it is warmer.

Mlle Weil is very talkative on the subway, and she is talking much too loud.

"I love the subway, all the different faces, particularly the black ones."

Genevieve is embarrassed for the Negroes in the car; she hopes that Mlle Weil's accent is so strong that they can't understand. She goes on and on about her parachute scheme, and doesn't notice that Joe's eyes have closed; he has fallen asleep, for which Genevieve envies him.

The trip takes more than an hour, and the streets are, of course, dark. Blacked out. Joe has a flashlight. He says this is his home territory and he is like an Indian in the forest, which encourages Mlle Weil to talk about some Indian myths. Something about a corn god.

They stop in front of a large church, meant to be in the style of the Baroque. These failed imitations always sadden Genevieve. She wishes

Americans would do what they do best. The Empire State Building lifts her heart.

Sitting at a table in the church vestibule is a woman collecting "donations." Genevieve is hypnotized by her hat: a wearable shrine to the basic food groups. Fruits are represented by a cluster of blood red woolen grapes; there is a dark purple bonbon, perhaps a petit four—can it be crocheted?—and then the meat group, solid chestnut coils. Are they wooden? Whalebone? She can only imagine they are representing sausages.

Joe grabs her hand, and they run down the stairs to safety. They are desperate to laugh. But it isn't really laughing, it's giggling. And she's back to being a girl again, but not the girl she was when she was Mlle Weil's student, the girl giggling with her friends, that wonderful drunkenness that can be induced by almost anything in young girls: a single shoe on the side of the road, a dog that looks like its master.

Mlle Weil has been left behind, as she was left behind when her students giggled. But no, Genevieve remembers, she wasn't left behind; we were suddenly silenced when she approached. We couldn't giggle in front of Mlle Weil. But she tells herself that Mlle Weil is no longer her teacher, and she can go on giggling with Joe if she likes.

Except that she can't. She finds Mlle Weil at the top of the stairs, standing at the table of the woman with the amazing hat. Like a child who has just found his mother, having lost her in a crowded store, Mlle Weil smiles an expression of pure relief, pure gratitude. Is it that she is always ready to find herself abandoned?

Joe greets his friend the pianist and finds seats in the middle of the room. The room is overheated, smoky; the smell of fried dinners clings to people's clothes, mixing with the smell of mothballs and some woman's scent—lily of the valley, *muguet,* a scent she'd worn as a young girl but had grown tired of.

When the lights go down, the beam from the projector traps smoke; it hangs like a heavy cloud, and then disperses, climbing to the high ceilings. This room is also a gymnasium; the smoke makes its way through the orange rims, the grayish netting of the baskets through which boys (Aaron one day?) throw those big ugly brown balls.

Mlle Weil lights a cigarette. Joe's friend begins playing the piano. "Smile though your heart is aching. Smile even though it's breaking."

She has lost her father, her mother, her country, but her heart has not been broken. If she loses Howard, it will break. And Laurent. And Aaron . . . she will not even think of it. But so many have had their hearts broken in this war.

The images appear on the screen. First sheep, being blindly herded. Then workers getting out of the subway. Then they are in a factory. She finds the equipment is rather lovely, in the way that the Empire State Building is lovely: modern, clean, free from the irregularities of natural life. But there he is, the tramp, and soon everyone can see that it is all too much for him, much too much, the boss, who can see everywhere (the eye of God?), keeps insisting that the assembly line go faster and faster. Who can keep up? Now he is in the mechanism of the gears. Now they have the machine that will make lunchtime unnecessary. The machine shoves food in his mouth, spills soup on him, covers his face with whipped cream. There is one mechanism that is meant to serve as a napkin. Every few seconds it wipes his mouth, and every time that happens, she laughs, thinking no, it won't happen again, but it does, again and again, and Genevieve covers her mouth with her hand, afraid that her laugh is too loud and someone (her dead mother?) will be embarrassed. But Mlle Weil is not laughing. She is smoking; she is eating up the screen with her weak eyes.

Mlle Weil's presence is distracting. Genevieve doesn't want to be thinking about her; she just wants to watch the movie. She just wants to enjoy it, to enjoy herself. She wants to be happy for the tramp and the lovely young girl, with whom, she wants to believe, he can be happy. Why is she always barefoot, this beautiful young girl? Perhaps Paulette Goddard has very beautiful feet. When he falls, Genevieve wants to believe he won't be hurt. When he's in jail, she wants to believe that his cell is comfortable. When he sings in his made-up language, she wants to believe she understands him. For a little while, she doesn't want to be thinking about the War, and the lives of everyone in France, she doesn't want to be wondering what has become of her friends who may have been taken God knows where. Does God know? Just for a little while, she wants to laugh with these other people who are laughing, in the dark; she wants to be taken up in this cloud of cigarette smoke and the heat of the machine, a cloud which allows her to leave her worries on the doorstep as Joe's song suggested. She doesn't want the lights to go on, because then Mlle Weil will begin talking. She hasn't laughed once.

She feels a tightness in her breasts and a spurting, and she worries: Will I leak through my clothes, will I become an embarrassment? She touches the front of her blouse. Dry. Thank God she put two handkerchiefs into each cup of her bra. Does this mean Aaron is crying for her, crying for his mother, who is sitting in the dark, laughing? Now she can't wait for the movie to be over so she can rush home. And she is distracted worrying what she can serve everyone when they get home. Crackers and some pickles. Better than nothing.

Mlle Weil of course does not take a cracker or a pickle. She starts talking as soon as she has sat down.

"You know that I have worked in several factories," she says, refusing, for the second time, the plate that Lily is passing. "I felt I had no business speaking about the rights of workers if I hadn't worked as they had worked."

"What did you do?" Lily asks, and Genevieve is surprised because Lily rarely enters conversations.

"You must help me translate," she says to Genevieve and Laurent. "I don't know the words for 'metal press' and 'bobbins.'"

"Bobbins," Genevieve says, and Lily says, "What kind of bobbins? Like for sewing?" Genevieve doesn't know what Mlle Weil means by "bobbins" but she probably wouldn't have asked.

"When I was working on the bobbins there was a time I didn't know how to avoid the flames, and for several months, I was marked by burn scars. I often exasperated the people I worked with because I made many mistakes, partly because I am not well coordinated, and then my hands, I've been told, are unusually small."

"I noticed that," Lily says. "It's the kind of thing I notice, the number of manicures I've done." She takes Mlle Weil's hand and Mlle Weil recoils, pulling her hand back as if Lily were the furnace whose flames had scarred her. Genevieve sees tears coming to Lily's eyes.

"The curse of the modern factory is that the worker has no idea what the end result of his task might be. He doesn't know what he produces, so he has the sense not of having produced but of being drained dry. Everything is simply a following of orders. From the moment you're clocked in to the moment you clock out, you have to be ready at any instant to take an order. Like an inert object that anyone may move about at will. And all these orders come from the mouth of a creature called the Boss; they are a product of his unpredictable will, a combination of caprice and brutality."

Caprice and brutality caprice and brutality caprice and brutality. The words drum themselves into Genevieve's brain, more terrible for being yoked than they would be if they were separate. And only Mlle Weil would yoke them. Only Mlle Weil speaks the unbearable truth, the glimpse of which no one else even knows to look for. But Genevieve wishes she would stop. Now she will have to wonder with every object she takes into her hand: How much brutality and caprice have gone into the making of this?

"When you are a worker you become reliant on orders; you even long for them because to eliminate them is to imagine an unbroken succession of identical moments. It is like visualizing a monotonous desert. A desert peopled with a thousand petty incidents is, to the mind, preferable to the prospect of an unalleviated present of monotony. What is most terrible about factory work is the combination of boredom and anxiety, because you could hurt yourself, or you could damage the machine. And this is killing.

"This is why I love Chaplin, like a brother, because only he has communicated the full reality of the factory's oppression with speed. Not only excessive speed, but speed without any human rhythm. Any beautiful movement implies moments of pause, that it gives the impression of leisureliness, even when very rapid. Consider the runner, who seems to glide home slowly while his rivals, lagging behind him, seem to move faster. Think of the peasant, swinging his scythe while the onlookers have the impression that he is 'taking his time.' Compare that," she says, "to the wretched spectacle of a man with a machine."

"Consider the runner . . ." "Think of the peasant . . ." Is she speaking to friends, in an ordinary room, or is she lecturing? Genevieve begins to resent being lectured at. And yet she knows she is in the presence of great thought.

Mlle Weil takes her glasses off, and wipes them on the hem of her shirt.

"When you are a worker you know that you are both an object and a slave. It takes everything that you think of as yourself, all your bases for personal dignity, and shatters them. Everything upon which I based myself, respect was radically destroyed within two or three weeks. And after a year in the factory I was in pieces, body and soul. It killed my youth. I knew quite well that there was a great deal of affliction in the world. I was obsessed with the idea, but I hadn't had prolonged and firsthand experience of it. As I worked in the factory, the affliction of others entered into my flesh and my soul. I had really forgotten my past, and I looked forward to no future. I found it difficult to even imagine the possibility of surviving the fatigue. What I went through there marked me so that still today, whenever anyone, whoever is in it and in whatever circumstances, speaks to me without brutality, I can't help having the impression that there must be a mistake.

"I woke each morning with anguish; I went to the factory with dread. I worked like a slave; the noonday interruption was like a laceration, then went home at quarter to six, worried about getting enough sleep, which I never did, and getting up early enough. The fear, the dread of what was to come pressed down on me constantly . . . until Saturday afternoon and Sunday morning. But Sunday evenings! Sunday evenings were the worst. When the prospect that presented itself was not one day but a whole week of such days. I had to try to make myself refuse to think. Because futurity itself became something so terribly bleak, so tremendously overwhelming that thought could only sink back trembling in its lair."

"Sunday evenings were the worst." Genevieve hears these words and, to her shame, recollects her childhood dread of Sunday nights: the prospect of a new week of school. But what was the source of her dread? She was not a slave, she was not brutalized, she was a privileged recipient of the learning of, on the whole, well-disposed teachers, who, however harsh, could not be called brutal and, however capricious, did not make demands that killed her soul. But Mlle Weil has invoked it—

Sunday-night dread—and Genevieve is a child again, on those Sunday nights when the sun sets too early, a doom sentence, and although she is embarrassed to link herself to Mlle Weil and the brutalized workers, she has become them, both Mlle Weil and the workers, because Sunday night is Sunday night and dread is dread. She knows that Mlle Weil would not agree with her, and she would, no doubt, be right.

"Did you make any friends in the factory?" Laurent asks.

"This was a great disappointment. I had thought there would at least be moments of fraternity. But the pressure to produce more and more at greater and greater speed, that very pressure that makes the person an object, also makes it impossible that you take notice of the person next to you. I thought that after the day was over the workers would commiserate, on the way home. But they would not meet each other's eyes, especially the women. It is their pervasive sense of shame and humiliation that makes them withdraw into themselves, far from any possibility of comradeship. I cannot explain how strong this sense of exile is. We all felt ourselves exiles, because of our hatred and loathing for the factory, the place where we were forced to spend our days.

"Once I saw some women standing in the pouring rain rather than taking shelter in the factory before the whistle blew. I'm sure that these same women would enter any home to keep out of the rain. But they felt they had no right to enter the factory before the whistle blew. Before they punched their time cards."

She looks at her watch, and jumps up in alarm. "Speaking of time cards," she says, "I must get home. My mother will be frantic." She runs out the door, not even saying goodbye.

Lily begins crying.

"Lily," Genevieve says. "Please don't be offended by Mlle Weil's acting as she did when you took her hand. It's just that she doesn't like to be touched by anyone."

"That's not why I'm crying. It's that she's so frail; when I felt the bones in her hand, even for a few seconds, I could see how frail she was. She won't live long," Lily says, "even without the War, she wouldn't live long. I could see it in her hand."

Joe is unhappy. He never wants Lily to be distressed. "So now you're a palm reader. Okay, my little gypsy, let me take you upstairs and you can show me your golden earrings."

Genevieve is glad to be alone with Laurent, because she needs him to help her understand what Mlle Weil has just been talking about.

"We have to understand what Mlle Weil doesn't understand, that her experience in the factory wasn't typical," Laurent says. "That she was always under a kind of strain that they weren't, the strain of having not to think. I'm sure that the men in the factory met for a drink from time to time, celebrated the birth of a child, the wedding of a sister, maybe shared cigarettes. I wonder if she thought to share her cigarettes. We have to understand that her story is not a worker's story, but the story of an intellectual in a factory. What would the workers have thought if they knew she was applying aesthetic theories to the way they operated their machines?"

"Don't talk like this, Laurent. She's taken all her learning, all her philosophy, her love of poetry, and applied it to factory work. She's taken the most abstract contemplation of time and brought it to the world of metal presses, of bobbins, of men who have never even heard of Plato, for whom the concept of metaphysics is as alien as life on the moon. She's brought the desert to the factory, and made both real. She is the great poet of workers' lives. I am humbled to have her in my home. Whatever else she did, she put her body on the line, as we have not."

And Genevieve wishes she hadn't said it, because of course it isn't a thing he could ever have done.

NOVEMBER 4, 1942

Mlle Weil rings the bell. The weather is unpleasant. Genevieve has always disliked the month of November; she dislikes it particularly in New York. The blackout shades make everything worse; cutting out all the light, when so little light has been offered. Or more quickly snatched away. Daylight saving time—a wonderful idea, she thought—has been randomly revoked: so daylight is no longer saved but squandered. The brilliance of an American autumn is completely gone now, the angel's torch, the spilt sugar, all long gone. The brown leaves pile up, dry, life-less; the bare branches speak too clearly about death, which is what is always in the backs of everyone's minds in these terrible days of war. She has begun to wake in fear now, not knowing whether she will see Howard again, imagining him coming home an invalid, imagining herself having the care of not one but two crippled men. She does not pray, but she allows herself to make bets with fate: I am willing to tend two crippled bodies, just send my husband home alive.

Laurent is home, nursing a cold: and as always, this brings an anxiety, not the new anxiety of the War but the old anxiety of his vulnerability to microbes. At night his cough worries her. And then, sometimes, wakened from sleep by it, she is annoyed and, in her annoyance, troubled, guilty, thinking in her half sleep: I am not a good person. Sometimes I wonder if I am even capable of love.

"Stay away from me, Simone. I wouldn't want you to catch my cold."

She jumps back, as if he'd touched her with a hot iron. She sits on the other side of the room, far from them, threatened, vigilant, as if she sat across from someone holding a loaded gun.

"And what have you been up to, Simone?" Laurent says. This is the kindly brother, Genevieve thinks, gratefully, wanting to put someone at ease.

And, distracted by the chance to report the staggering amount that she has done, Mlle Weil relaxes.

"I have been taking a course in first aid in Harlem. And of course writing endless letters, to bureaucrats and politicians, here, in England, in France. I have written two articles in English; I will leave them for you."

Stepping gingerly, not knowing what parts of the room might be contaminated by Laurent's cold, she drops two pamphlets on the coffee table. Genevieve picks them up and reads the titles. "The Problems of the French Empire." "The Treatment of Negro War Prisoners in France."

Of course she is interested. But it feels like a homework assignment, and, like a balky schoolgirl, she resents the prospect of having to read what her teacher has ordered her to read.

"If I had not been able to get to England, I would have gone to the

South of the United States to work among the Negroes. I have a very great affinity for them. But at last, I will be leaving. I've made a connection in London through an old classmate. The Commissioner of the Interior and Labor in the National Committee of de Gaulle's Free French movement has taken me on to work in the division of propaganda. In three days I will be gone."

Genevieve prepares the tea, knowing it will be their last. They settle down to it, in the dim, fading light of the November afternoon. In a way, it seems so ordinary: three old friends drinking tea in the approaching darkness. They are silent, and the silence is comfortable, as if they were resting in a light hammock, being rocked by a light wind. But then the silence is broken by the baby's cries. Genevieve brings him into the living room, and Mlle Weil reaches out to hold him.

"I have made arrangements for a very intelligent priest to come and speak to you in order to arrange for the baby's baptism, as I know you are unconnected to a church here."

Genevieve doesn't even attempt to hide her shock. "We hadn't thought of baptism."

Mlle Weil takes on her most imperious tone; imperious, but mixed with condescension, as if she were speaking to a recalcitrant student, not one of the best, who has questioned the importance of studying Plato.

"There cannot be any possible objections. He won't in any way regret having this done for him when he reaches manhood. It could possibly do him good, above all socially, and in any event cannot do him harm."

With a heat whose source she can't recognize or name, so rarely has it been hers, Genevieve says, "It could do harm to his father and his grandparents, who are Jews."

Mlle Weil takes no notice of her tone, perhaps even what she's said, and goes on, slowly, patiently explaining the obvious to the dull student.

"It will be no problem unless he turns in adulthood to a fanatical Judaism, which isn't probable, but if he turns to Christianity, having been already baptized, it will be a great convenience. If he marries a Jew, his baptism won't be an inconvenience; he won't be responsible."

It cannot be possible that Mlle Weil is using these words, "do him good . . . socially," "convenience," "won't be responsible." This cannot be Mlle Weil speaking. Perhaps because she believes a different person, different from her old teacher, is saying these words, Genevieve has the courage to speak out.

"It is not a matter of inconvenience. It would be a betrayal of his father's people, particularly now, when they are under threat of extermination."

"Yes, exactly. With the anti-Semitic legislations that are sure to become more prevalent, it would be of great advantage to be a baptized half Jew." And then she says, "It would be nice to take advantage of these things without his having to feel he'd done anything cowardly."

Can she possibly be using the word "nice"? Everything that Mlle Weil is saying is so wrong that Genevieve feels emboldened to lie: given the wrongness of all her words, the wrongness of a lie seems insignificant.

"Howard and I intend that Aaron will be raised a Jew."

In fact, she and Howard have never discussed Aaron's religious upbringing, both of them being entirely irreligious.

"No, no, you must not do that, above all you must not. Raising Aaron as a Jew would be a very grave error. You must see," Mlle Weil says, "that the tradition of the Hebrews has only been disastrous for the mind of Europe. It is a tradition of bloodshed and exclusion. Yahweh, like the Roman gods, is a god of punishment and force. The worship of force comes to us in the West from the Jews and the Romans. In choosing them, over the Greeks, we have defiled the best of the past. This is why I cannot define myself as a Jew; I have allowed nothing in Judaism to mark me, and so I have not been so marked."

Genevieve is too appalled to speak, but Laurent has not been struck dumb. Quietly, he says, "But, Simone, you and your parents had to flee France because you are Jews."

She doesn't seem to be distressed by what could be interpreted as an accusation. She leans forward in her chair, as if she wanted to be closer to him, sitting so far from her across the room. "I do not consider myself a Jew," she says. "I have inherited nothing from the Jewish religion. I have never even stepped in a synagogue. I learned to read from Racine, Pascal, and the writers of the seventeenth century. My spirit was formed at an age when I had never even heard talk of Jews. I am a Frenchwoman, not a Jew."

Genevieve moves closer to Laurent, afraid of what has entered the room. A darkness greater than the dark created by the blackout shades. She holds the baby closer. She takes Laurent's hand. He squeezes her hand three times, their old signal for "keep quiet now."

Mlle Weil looks at her watch and says she must leave. "I only came to say goodbye," she says.

She waves at Laurent from across the room, and as Genevieve moves to show her out she kisses her on both cheeks. Genevieve is not sure she wants this kiss. Which of us, she wonders, is Judas, and which Christ? Genevieve feels Mlle Weil's bones, so painfully sharp through the black wool of her cape. "Frail" is the word that comes to her mind.

"I'll be seeing you," Laurent says, almost jauntily.

"No," Mlle Weil says. "You will not see me again. This is goodbye."

When she closes the door Genevieve throws herself into Laurent's arms. What this means, really, is sitting next to him, laying her head on his chest, knowing that at any moment he might have a spasm and she'll be thrown off her spot of comfort. Strange to feel comforted being held by a body that twitches and flails, arms that can only embrace her for seconds at a time, and then become a victim of their own uncontrolled movements. But she can only be the little sister now.

"I'm glad she's gone. I'm glad she's gone."

He pats her back. "GeGe," he says, *"petit lapin."*

"What she said was terrible, it was terrible, and I was terrible not to tell her so."

"There is no point. She is very close to death, and in relation to the dying, some things are unnecessary."

"I don't know how to speak about it, how to understand it. What is the right way to describe what she said: mad or evil?"

"It would dishonor her to call her mad. And the way she lives shows she cannot be evil. No, she is a person terribly wounded, yet possessed of extraordinary gifts."

"How is she able to say these things; how did she become the way she is? She comes of a loving family."

"In the same way that it would dishonor her to call her mad, it dishonors her to look for causes in what we would call ordinary life. It's as if she's made of some excessively porous material so she absorbs more than most people. Including the greater part of French culture, including its poisons. A maimed genius. Think of a great dancer with a crippled arm. You can enjoy the breathtaking leaps as long as you don't allow your eye to rest on the deformed arm. Then your eye follows the unlovely limb, the broken line . . . but that's the only line that deformed limb can make. But then you can't resist looking at the beautiful legs, the breathtaking leaps."

"Deformed," she says, separating the syllables. "De-formed. What would Plato make of that?"

"There are horrors in Plato, too."

"I have betrayed my husband and my son."

He kisses her forehead. "No," he says, "you attended to the reality of the weakest person. Your son didn't suffer from what was said about the Jews, nor did your husband or your in-laws. But to have castigated her in her present state would have been to have fallen on a wounded bird."

"That was what she said about herself. That people hurt her from the instinct of falling on the wounded bird."

"And so," he says, "you did not cause hurt."

"But she trained us all to speak the truth. And this I didn't do."

"I never wanted the role of Pilate, but I see it is thrust on me. What is truth? The truth is, she is dying."

And his body begins to tremble: the first sign of one of his bad spasms. She knows he wants to be left alone when this happens.

SEPTEMBER 10, 1943

Nearly a year has passed. And now Mlle Weil is dead: Genevieve learns it in a letter from a priest, a priest Mlle Weil spoke of, whom she has never met and has no wish to meet. She supposes that it is the priest

Mlle Weil wanted her to speak to about baptizing Aaron. It is to his credit that he does not mention this, nor does he suggest that they meet.

It is September now, but it feels like a humid summer day. A small fan makes a noise that annoys her; she will turn it off, the annoyance of the noise is greater than the relief of the breeze it generates. Her hands are sweating. She has been gripping the letter so tightly that the ink of the words has begun to smear.

Eleven months. Since she first saw her, since the words came to her mind. "She looks ridiculous."

But that is wrong. She is not ridiculous. She is many things. Great? A saint? A madwoman?

Genevieve supposes that she must contact Mme Weil, who is still living quite near. What will she say, what words would serve, as neither palliative nor obfuscation? Neither of which would honor Mlle Weil.

Words will not serve. But she must do something.

She must bring something to Mme Weil. An offering.

Perhaps the best thing is what custom would suggest. Well, then, she will invoke custom. Traditionally, food is brought to the grieving family.

So she will bake a cake, a cake that needs no rationed sugar, only honey, honey from the hives that come from Joe's cousin's farm. Or she hopes that's where it comes from. To make the cake she will have to use this week's ration of butter. Butter will be required. Whatever else she is, Mme Weil is a Frenchwoman. Margarine will not do.

How do I understand her? How do I understand everything she was? Genevieve asks herself, looking through a collection of wartime recipes. She turns the pages. The words repeat and repeat themselves inside her brain: *I will never understand. I will never understand.*

She will explain to Laurent that she is using their butter ration for a cake to bring to Mme Weil to mark her daughter's death. He will, of course, understand.

It is, she knows, in some ways ridiculous to think of offering Mme Weil a cake to mark her daughter's death. But what is the right way to honor the dead? Is it right to deprive Laurent of the butter he so loves to make an offering that is, perhaps, ridiculous? Is it right to deprive the living for what might very well be the wrong offering in honor of the dead? Or is the deprivation itself the honor?

How odd, she thinks, to invoke the word "honor" in relation to the making of the cake.

But then, she thinks, it is the *War,* and of course the times are odd. The times demand of those who live through them certain acts, gestures, understandings that they would not have come to in ordinary times. Among the most important of these: the honoring of the dead.

She will make a cake.

To do it properly, butter will be required.

Thomas Mann in Gary, Indiana

I'VE COME TO BELIEVE it's something people say much too easily, much too quickly: "It was the greatest day of my life." At the time, though (I was seventeen), there's no doubt that I meant it. But what does a seventeen-year-old know of greatness—the kind of seventeen-year-old I was in 1939, in Gary, Indiana, the son of a happy family in safe America, which, though battered by the Depression, was still, if not one of the fortunate isles, at least a sheltered cove? Or perhaps it's right to say a backwater—undevastated, well, not even touched, by Hitler or his bombs.

"You have been chosen." Those were the first words I heard. I'd been called to the principal's office and at first I assumed I was in some kind of trouble, though I'd never been in the slightest trouble in any of my school years. "You have been chosen as the student host for the great German writer Thomas Mann, whom we at Horace Mann High School have the honor of presenting, thanks to the Hauptmanns here . . . a great honor, a great honor all around."

Thomas Mann. Horace Mann. Horace Mann was the name of our high school. Thomas Mann was a name I had never heard. But I knew I had been chosen.

My place in the school had been earned because I was considered the best actor, the star of all the plays, and I used my acting skills to pretend I knew all (or even something) about the great writer Thomas Mann. I had to pretend that I wasn't completely out of my depth trying to understand why he had fled Germany, a man of his age, his mid-sixties, which felt ancient to me. I suppose I must have heard of Hitler, heard something of the Nazis, but I had to assume an expression of sage familiarity when Mr. Hauptmann told me how extraordinary it was that he had left everything. "And when I say everything, Bill, you can hardly even imagine what he had. Absolute prestige, a life of extraordinary comfort and ease; he is German literature and German literature is his. And he gave it all up to bear witness to the barbarity of those criminals. Uprooted himself and his family to stand up against the pure evil of it all."

Mrs. Hauptmann, our French teacher, spoke more calmly; she provided more facts. He had left Germany four years ago and was living in Princeton, New Jersey. "Right there with Einstein, imagine," she said. I could not imagine; but I had to pretend I could, and I shook my head back and forth, and I think I said, "Amazing," or "My my." He was going to be in Chicago because his daughter was married to a professor at the University of Chicago.

"And my husband," she said, using the word with a sense of luxury, perhaps because it was new to her: they had been married only six months, "my husband was a student of Signore Borghese, who is Mann's son-in-law. When he visited his old teacher, he happened to mention that Mann was eager to travel around America waking ordinary people up to what was going on in Germany. And when my husband suggested he come here, to Gary—pointing out that it was a city of steel mills, a city of immigrants, that he would have access to the real America—Signore Borghese said it sounded like just what his father-in-law wanted. So, Bill, can you believe it? He will be coming here. To Horace Mann. And my husband and I have suggested— and the principal was happy to agree—that a student should introduce him. And you were everybody's choice."

I didn't know what to say. I was a bit in awe of the Hauptmanns. They were so unlike the other teachers, so unlike anyone I'd ever met. We knew he was born somewhere in Europe, but we didn't know exactly where, and we were all much too polite, not to say abashed, to ask. He taught Latin and English and one class of German that was always rumored to be on the verge of cancellation. He was fluent as well in French and Italian. People couldn't quite place his accent. It was not the accent of people who worked in the steel mills, people's fathers whose speech embarrassed their sons. Nor could we place it from the accents of the foreigners we saw in movies.

Mrs. Hauptmann was from Chicago, but had lived in France. I'd never seen a woman who looked anything like her, who dressed the way she dressed. Every day she came to class in a straight skirt, black or gray, and a thin cardigan, black or gray, a thin strand of pearls around her neck, pearl earrings in her ears. She wore her hair pulled back in a severe bun at the base of her long white neck. Mr. Hauptmann dressed differently from other men as well. His shoes were heavier than those of the other nonworking men, polished, in all weathers, to a high dark chestnut gloss. Both of them seemed thinner and smaller than other teachers, as if they were conserving flesh for some future scarcity only they could name.

Somehow their looks, their way of dressing, their way of walking and holding their heads, were a sign to me of something, a larger, finer life I hoped one day to be a part of but had no idea how to approach. It's quite incredible, how naïve I was. How innocent—although no one believes in innocence nowadays, they think it's a joke, a trap, a way of covering up, covering over. But my God, I was naïve. I try to explain it to my children and my grandchildren—but they don't quite believe me. I tell them the story of the first time I was invited to the Hauptmanns' for wine and cheese. "What is your favorite cheese?" Mrs. Hauptmann said, cutting me a thin slice of something (Gorgonzola, Camembert?) whose smell alarmed me. "Velveeta," I said, without a moment's hesitation, anxious to tell the truth.

Mrs. Hauptmann walked up to me as if she wanted to slap me or at least take me by the lapels. "No, no, no, Billy, no, no, no. Your education will commence right here."

And she gave me some of the smelly cheese (Gorgonzola, Camembert), whose taste excited me, as if it were a magic coach that would transport me to the finer world I knew the Hauptmanns lived in, owned.

How much I owe them! How they opened up the world for me. It pains me now to remember that there were times when I wasn't sure whether they were providing me with gifts or stealing my treasure.

It probably wasn't the wisest thing that Mrs. Hauptmann let me know how frustrated she was with Mrs. Ledbetter's choice of plays. Mrs. Ledbetter was the head of the English Department, and even though Mrs. Hauptmann was in charge of plays, she didn't get to choose which would be produced. Each year there had to be a Gilbert and Sullivan. My senior year we did *The Mikado*. The Mikado played by yours truly. "I am the emperor of Japan." The second play was usually a light comedy. In my memory, we were always doing *Charley's Aunt*.

Mrs. Hauptmann was the first person I ever heard use the word "middlebrow." I was helping her pack up the scripts that we'd been using for rehearsal. "Why oh why must they foist this middlebrow garbage on me? And worse, on the students."

Once I knew the term "middlebrow," I started applying it to everyone and everything around me. I felt I had to look at everything through that lens, which meant I had to question everything. I had to question my mother.

Someone recently asked me, "Was your mother intelligent?" And before I could really think about it properly, the words jumped out of my mouth: "It doesn't matter." How could I have said that, living as I have lived, among people to whom intelligence is quite simply the most important thing? I am a pediatric neurologist, or I was for many years the head of a large academic department at a large, unquestionably great university. At my dinner table have sat Nobel Prize winners (I don't tell them that I broke bread with my first Nobel Prize winner at the age of seventeen; it is at least likely that for them a Nobel Prize in Literature would count as nothing). And yet, I know that I was right, what I said about my mother. Was she intelligent? Was she middlebrow? Was her taste, well, quite frankly, bad? Did she love the sentimental? The corny? When she died I found a bundle of poems she had written, tied up with a piece of plain blue string. I've always been good at memorizing, and I memorized this one. She had written it to the switchboard operator—all the telephone calls in the Ogden

Dunes, or the Dunes, as we called it, had to go through a switchboard operator—who'd been suffering a bout of ill health.

> *There's something wrong with our telephone*
> *It doesn't sound at all like home*
> *Whenever I ask for a number*
> *I get a central, yes, by thunder*
> *I used to get a voice of cheer,*
> *"Say, how are you today, my dear?*
> > *I'm feeling fine, hope you're the same."*
> > *Oh dear, this central is so tame!*
> > *And so I say hope you are fine*
> > *And soon will be back on the line*
> > *To make us Dune bugs feel at home*
> > *When we take the hook off the telephone.*

Of course it is a terrible poem, a perfectly terrible poem. But, you see, it's also a wonderful poem, because it's about my mother's genius for connection, for making friends, for becoming a part of people's lives. My mother had the gift of consolation. People came to her in time of grief, in great trouble. They felt free to weep in front of her, and they did weep. And they left, somehow refreshed, lightened, better able to get on with their lives. She lived to be old; she lived to see her old certainties fall apart. She lived to see a beloved granddaughter get pregnant, unmarried at eighteen, another marry a drug addict, another die a hopeless alcoholic. They came to her with their troubles, and she said, "Oh, honey, I know you're good, you're a wonderful person. And it will be all right." And for a while they would believe her, even though, perhaps it wasn't true, in some cases things never were all right. And while my brother was horrified when one of his daughters became a lesbian, my mother said that she knew girls in college who ruined their lives marrying men they didn't love instead of getting to live with their "best friends." And when my daughter married a black man, in the years when this was unusual, and certainly something that had never happened to any of her friends, she embraced her new grandson-in-law saying she'd been waiting for years for someone in the family that could really listen to her stories. And when they put her new great-grandchild in her arms she said, "Isn't it wonderful. The first Morton baby with brown eyes."

When people complain of the decline of academic standards in colleges, I remember that my mother went to college, majored in German, and probably didn't know a word of German. Certainly I never heard the word "Goethe" pass her lips. And when I thought that perhaps she'd want to read Thomas Mann in the original, she said, "Oh shoot, Billy, that was a long time ago and they never made us read anything that long." It's hard to remember that my mother went to college before the First World War and that, for Americans before the First World War, Germany was a place to admire, to idealize: the home of music and culture and high, idealized philosophy. That German was something an ordinary student might study because it might come in handy sometime.

And in that time, when I was obsessed with greatness, with the anguish that my life touched nothing of greatness, I never saw my mother's greatness. The greatness of consolation. What is consolation, but the ability to be *with,* to accompany, to say, You are not alone. But that wasn't all she had: she loved life, she wasn't afraid of it. She was a person born of quite limited experience, perhaps even limited curiosity, but a limitless understanding of how hard it was for people to live a life, that the right thing was always to sympathize, and to enjoy life, because she believed there was much more to enjoy than not. Even now, I feel I have to struggle against the Hauptmanns' long-since skeletons or ghosts and say, "My mother had greatness, and yes, my mother was middlebrow."

Just after I heard Mrs. Hauptmann use the word "middlebrow"— "Why oh why must they foist this middlebrow garbage on me? And worse, on the students?"—Mr. Hauptmann walked in the classroom and sat down in one of the students' desks. He crossed his legs, and I could see how much thinner his ankles were than my father's, than those of any man I knew.

"Maybe they know their audience," he said.

"Yes, of course they do. But isn't it our job to show them something higher, something greater than what they're used to. I asked them to let me do a Shakespeare. At least some scenes from Shakespeare."

"Dream on, Macduff," he said, and she walked over and gave him a fake slap, and he gave her a fake slap right back, and then she giggled— although it seems impossible to use the word "giggle" in connection with Mrs. Hauptmann. "You can call me Lena," she said after graduation, though I never could.

I was thrilled when Mrs. Hauptmann chose a passage from O'Neill as my competition piece for the State Finals in Dramatic Interpretation. I had no idea what would be revealed to me, only by accident, when she and I were preparing my speech from *The Hairy Ape*.

"I wonder if you'd look at this O'Neill play. It's a bit unusual, a bit daring for the competition, but I have a notion you can make something rather fine of it."

I was terribly proud when she said that. When she used the word "fine." The opposite of fine was coarse, and I'd been troubled by what I had newly given a name to: coarseness, the coarseness of my surroundings. I never applied the word to my family. Certainly not my mother and my brother, Sam. I didn't like to put a name or a face to the word. I was a very nice boy, a kind boy. I understand that now. It took me quite a while to be able to be proud of it. And when I was that nice boy, I didn't feel nice; I felt monstrous. Because I seemed to be thinking of sex all the time. Like the time that I saw the Hauptmanns share a slap and giggle, and I knew it had something to do with their life in bed, and I didn't want to think about it. But I did think about it. And I believed I was a monster.

Almost anything could give me a hard-on. I remember my horror when I got hard while my mother was brushing my suit before I left the house to meet Thomas Mann.

It was because the thought of Laurel Jansen had come into my mind, and any thought of Laurel Jansen made me hard.

But how could it happen when my mother was brushing my clothes?

I was enjoying what she was doing, but I felt it was wrong for me to be enjoying it. That it was not quite manly. The manly was a crucial category to me then . . . probably because I was afraid I didn't qualify.

It was the day I was to introduce and then accompany Thomas Mann. The great day. The greatest day of my life. My mother was brushing my shoulders, brushing the new suit (an electric blue, I now remember, and I'm sure Mr. Hauptmann probably thought it was "loud" . . . because now that I think of it, that particular shade of blue must have made a rather jarring noise in the muted manly room of charcoal gray and navy).

She was using the clothes brush that had belonged to her father. It was small and fit easily in her hand, those hands which were, even for a woman as small as she was, unusually small. "Delicate," she would say when she would hold her hands up so the light fell behind them, fell through them, illumining them, turning them a reddish color like the sun going down. "My hands were the envy of all the girls I knew," she would say. "Who would have believed I'd end up with the hands of an old washerwoman."

What she didn't say: it was because my father had lost all his money in the Depression, and she resented it, resented him, because her own father had been prosperous. A banker. A pillar of the small Illinois town where both my parents were born and reared.

I loved my mother's hands, I thought they were lovely, not the hands of an old washerwoman at all. They were always wonderfully cool, the flesh was creamy, and her wedding ring sank into the softness of her fourth finger in a way that when I was a child seemed magical. Then we would sit on the couch sometimes holding hands, listening to the radio. It had made us both very happy.

But I had put a stop to it. I had to. It wasn't "manly." I knew that, after a while, with a clarity as clear as All Men Are Created Equal or A Penny Saved Is a Penny Earned. And that day I told her to stop fussing over me, although I really enjoyed her running the bristles of the silver brush over the shoulders of the jacket of my new suit. I'd always been very fond of that brush, I liked the design on its silver back, a border of raised Xs that when I was very little I'd mistaken for birds' wings. I'd liked the plain cool feeling of the matte silver against my dry palm, and the rougher, raised texture of the Xs or wings that I would run my fingertips along. When I was little, I'd ask my mother if I could hold it sometimes, after she had used it to brush her own coat and hat, and I would hold it sometimes to keep myself from feeling sad that she was going out into the world without me and to distract myself so that I could forget that I was lonely.

"Billy, you are a caution," she'd say when I asked to hold the brush. She would never tell my father because it wasn't something my father would have liked. He would have thought it wasn't quite manly, though he probably wouldn't have said anything. My father spoke very little. My father was quite manly. He built houses. The letterhead which he used to send out his bills had the heading, "Build as if you knew that it would last forever."

My father was a silent man, and I was both soothed and frightened by his silence. His silences. My brother, Sam, was much more silent than I; he was always on at me for talking too much. But my mother encouraged me to talk, to use words not just for information, but for pleasure. "Remember, you're named for William Shakespeare," she would tell me although my father insisted I'd been named for a great-uncle who'd died working in the mines.

When I was six, she signed me up for something called Expression Lessons, taught by Mrs. Alma Ferguson. I've given up trying to explain what Expression Lessons were. They were a product, a sign of a vanished America. What I can never decide is whether it's a good thing that it vanished, or bad.

Certainly there were good things about the lessons Mrs. Ferguson gave. They taught me to speak clearly and, as the name suggests, expressively. We began with breathing exercises and exercises to strengthen what she called "my midriff." Then she would have me read aloud . . . passages from Shakespeare or Byron, for example, and then she'd correct my readings by reading them herself.

Who was she? She was distinctly, deliberately unmodern looking; her skirts were long and full, and her hair was piled on the top of her head. She was rather operatic in her presentation of herself. She was a large woman, not fat, but tall and broad. When I see Margaret Dumont in the Marx Brothers movies, I think of Mrs. Ferguson. Mrs. Ferguson was not ridiculous, though. She had great dignity. She stood for something that was not foolish, that ought not be laughed away.

What was her training? What gave her the right to give lessons to other people? To children. I don't think she'd ever been on a stage, except perhaps the Little Theatre, where I remember her being very good playing Mrs. Alving in Ibsen's *Ghosts*. I think my mother sent me to her for reasons that had everything to do with who my mother was. Certainly Mrs. Ferguson was one of my mother's lame ducks. She'd been a widow for quite some time when I began studying with her. I can hardly believe that now, that my mother sent me for Expression Lessons when I was six. But she always wanted me to be an actor. She said that before I could talk, when she read me nursery rhymes, I would stand in my crib and act them out. It makes people laugh when I tell them that my mother is the only woman in America who was disappointed when her son gave up acting to become a doctor. But her disappointment was no laughing matter; it was deep, very deep. I hated causing her pain. I loved my mother.

My father harbored a lot of anger towards the late Mr. Ferguson. "He died without a penny of insurance," my father would say, pounding his fist on the table every time, in a tone of disgust that suggested that dying without insurance was equal to dying in a whorehouse or on the Bowery or running away with the underage maid. So Mrs. Ferguson was poor. Poor but middle class. Poor but genteel, and somehow she was able to support herself and her mother and her daughter by teaching Expression Lessons.

Her daughter's name was Celestine Lavonne. Mrs. Ferguson insisted that the accent be placed on the second syllable, Ce-LES-tine. I thought the name very romantic. I imagined it was French. But Celestine was anything but romantic. She was a stocky, good-natured redhead, and it was to Mrs. Ferguson's credit that she accepted her daughter's lack of dramatic talent, entire lack of romance, with a generous grace. Celestine went to business school. She became a bookkeeper. I don't know what happened to her. I assume she married someone. I assume she had a happy life. There's no reason to assume otherwise. Or maybe there is; maybe it's true that most people don't have happy lives. But it's not the way I like to think about people like Celestine.

The apartment they lived in was very small and very dark. I took my lessons in the living room, two thirds of which was taken up by the piano, so there was no room for a couch, only two berry-colored overstuffed chairs. There was a statue of the Venus de Milo on the top of the piano; its whiteness shone out like a small moon in the room that was always dark. The curtains were heavy, plum-colored; velvet. They were lined with a satiny material the color of rich cream.

When I say that my Expression Lessons with Mrs. Ferguson were a product of a vanished America, I mean it in more ways than one. That kind of emphasis on being "a good speaker," the very word "elocution," is something that was disappearing even as I came of age. But there was another way in which what happened in the Ferguson apartment was a vanishing America. Mrs. Ferguson's mother, whom we called Grandmother Geer, was in her nineties when I was taking my lessons. She spent most of her time in bed, lying on a cot in the back room. But she liked seeing people, and I was a nice boy, old ladies tended to love me, and Mrs. Ferguson would bring me in to say hello when our lesson was done. She loved telling stories, and her favorite one was to say that her father had shaken George Washington's hand and had put her up on his shoulders to hear the Lincoln-Douglas debates. She made the point that her father was very old when she was born—in his sixties, she said, with a shy pride in his late virility, I now understand. I've calculated the dates, and they work: if she was born in the 1840s and her father was in his sixties when she was born, then he was born in the 1780s, and Washington didn't die till 1799. So there I was, with the history of America embodied in an ancient old lady, with a face that looked like a walnut shell, but a pleasant one, lying on a cot in the back room of an apartment that was paid for by Expression Lessons, taken by people like me, because of mothers with some half-baked idea of a higher culture.

But when I think of what Mrs. Ferguson gave me as the poem that was meant to be my pièce de résistance, that I performed for the women's clubs and the Rotary Club and the Lions, I am appalled and ashamed for all of us. Was there any excuse for the kind of ignorance we all lived in? Could you call it innocence? If you did it then, you can't now. This is nothing I've talked to my children about.

The poem was called "The Glory Road." I wish the words weren't in my brain, but that's the curse of early memorization: it's cut in the grooves of the mind forever. "The Glory Road" is about a black man being visited on his bed by God himself.

> *O I lay upon mah pallet*
> *Till about one o'clock*
> *And de lawd came a-callin*
> *All his faithful flock*
> *And he called Hooee*
> *And he called Hooee*
> *And I cry Massa Jesus is you callin me*
> *And I riz upon my pallet and I cry*
> *Ere's me*

Mrs. Ferguson made a point of my emphasizing the difference in tone and emphasis as the "hooees" are repeated. This was a way of using my vocal exercises, showing my vocal range. Up to this point, except for the insult implied by the imposition of uneducated dialect by a person of a different culture and a different diction—there's not so much to object to. But the objectionable enters quite soon.

> *Nigger, you must travel back*
> *To help poor sinners*
> *Up de glory track*
> *To help poor mourners*
> *And de scoffing coons*
> *By shoutin loud*
> *Halleluiah tunes*

I now understand that it fell under the category of white people's appropriation of black folk material. I suppose they thought it was a kind of homage, a kind of sympathetic attention. But now it's impossible to see it as anything but grotesquely insulting.

Can we be excused for this, pardoned on the grounds that we meant no harm? I sometimes think that we cannot be pardoned. It's why I'm not patient with people my age who bathe in the warm stream of nostalgia. That stream had horrible breeding creatures on the bottom, and if we happened not to be attacked and destroyed by them—well, that was luck, or privilege. But there is no sense pretending that the killing creatures weren't there.

So do I have to say that the people whom I loved and lived among were poisoners and if not killers then implicated in the killing that went on? Do I have to say that about my mother, whom I adored?

My poor mother. It must have been confusing for her, trying to understand me in those years. Trying to figure out the right way to deal with me. God knows I was confused. I loved my mother; I loved her till her death at ninety-six, and all through my childhood I loved her unequivocally. I knew I was the favorite of her sons, and that it was a secret we both felt bound to keep, so that we were only entirely free when we were alone and could express our delight in the other's company. But then I became a teenager and feared that my love for my mother was not quite manly. That I had to create a distance between us, a distance I wanted only half or perhaps less than half the time, to escape a closeness that I loved and feared . . . so I was often saying things to her I didn't mean and acting in ways I didn't want to.

Like the day I was going to introduce Thomas Mann when she was brushing off my shoulders. I was enjoying it very much but felt I had to say, "Cut it out, Mom, it's no big deal."

Did I say that so she would have to say, "No big deal? No big deal. Why, Billy Morton for land sakes, what's a big deal if not interviewing onstage the most famous writer alive in the world today? A winner of the Nobel Prize. Shoot, Billy, you were the one chosen to interview Thomas Mann. It's a very great honor. It shows how highly everyone thinks of you. Your teachers. The principal even told me he couldn't think of anyone who would be more of a credit to the school."

And as she said that, as she was running the bristles of the brush over my shoulders, I was thinking, If they only knew what I was really like. If they only knew I am really a monster.

And then came the thought of Laurel Jansen, who had not chosen me, the girl of my dreams, the thought that maybe I was the choice of Mr. and Mrs. Hauptmann and all the teachers and even the principal, maybe even the whole student body would have chosen me, but Laurel did not. And I thought of Laurel and the smell of her hair, and, even as my mother was running the bristles of the silver brush over my shoulders, I got a hard-on. And I knew myself to be a monster. But then the thought of Dolph Johnson, whom Laurel had chosen over me, Dolph who was playing halfback for Purdue and wouldn't have known Thomas Mann from Tom Mix, and my hard-on went down. I hated Dolph Johnson with a ferocity that made me suspect I was another kind of monster, and I hated myself because I thought that maybe Laurel, who was the smartest girl in our class, had chosen that chuckle-head over me because she thought I was not quite manly. And then I thought, If that's what being manly is, I want no part of it. I will have to think of another way of being a man. But what I really believed was that I would have been willing to be any kind of man at all if Laurel would have chosen me. Would have loved me. And sometimes I hated her because she could make me feel these things, and I had fantasies about doing terrible things to her, tying her up, hitting her, and sometimes that would arouse me and then I knew I was truly a monster and it was only a matter of time before everyone would know.

It was enormously helpful to me when Mr. Hauptmann said, "The most important thing to remember about *Death in Venice* is that it's about the impossible paradox of having both a mind and a body." But that was much later, and it didn't seem to help for long.

A mind and a body. Because of my mind, my body was more and more a source of anguish to me now. There would be times when my body was the pleasure to me it had always been. But more and more it was unruly, shameful. I almost thought I should talk to the doctor about it, but I would never have made a special appointment to do that. I was glad to have to have a tetanus shot when I stepped on a rusty nail, glad that it was he who brought it up. "Old Man Sex getting you down?" he asked, after I'd put my shirt back on. I didn't know what to answer. He was a good man, Dr. Larkin, and he said, "Just remember a lot of things that seem troubling are entirely normal. Entirely normal."

Do you mean that I am not a monster? I wanted to ask. But I said nothing and finished buttoning up my shirt.

Then when I got home I worried that there was something about me, some telltale sign that had given me away: that sex was giving me trouble. I'd heard it called self-abuse. I knew some of the things I'd heard couldn't be true: that it could make you blind. But I also knew that when I'd spent whole days in my room doing nothing but masturbating I could see a kind of pasty look when I looked in the mirror, and I was pretty sure there were dark circles under my eyes even though I'd got plenty of sleep. I wanted to ask Dr. Larkin if it was a sign of mental illness that I masturbated so much. That I woke up every morning in a pool of my own semen no matter how many times I'd jerked off the day, or even the night before. Was I afflicted with some sort of excess fluid that could lead to a future of invalidism, perhaps an early death?

This is another story I told my children, that I've even told my grandchildren (they're old enough for it now) that makes them understand the kind of foolish boy I was. I'd been very worried that my mother would know about what I considered my obsessional masturbation because she'd discover the caked handkerchiefs in the laundry. That she couldn't possibly ignore the stained sheets. But of course nothing was ever said.

There was a laundry chute that led from the second floor, where the bedrooms were, to the basement, where the washing machine sat. You simply threw your dirty laundry down the chute and it landed in the basement, right into a basket that my mother could carry to the washing machine. Sometimes, for some reason, some of the laundry would miss its mark and would land on the concrete floor and my mother would have to bend to pick it up and I could hear her—if I happened to be in the kitchen—saying "Oh shoot" and something about old bones.

One night at supper, she said to my father, "Dan, the strangest thing. You know how sometimes the laundry misses the basket and falls onto the floor? Well today I bent to pick it up from the floor and every single thing I picked up was full of little holes, little holes with brown rings around them as if something had eaten into the clothing some way. Luckily it was just a pile of handkerchiefs and so it's no big loss."

My children, my grandchildren now get almost sick with laughter as I reenact the panic that I felt when I heard my mother say those words. I was terrified; what I'd feared was true. There was something inside me, some toxic substance that was dangerous and poisonous and destructive to anything it touched. Here was the proof.

My mother was surprised when I excused myself before dessert and said I had to study for a math test. But of course I couldn't concentrate on math or anything, I was so appalled at myself, at what had been discovered or revealed. Then I heard my parents laughing downstairs, laughing in that way that reminded me that they had a life outside me, that had nothing to do with me or my brother, that had begun before we were born, that would go on after we'd all left the house. Too often now they argued. It was always about money. The Depression. My mother was tired and disappointed. My father was tired and ashamed. But now they were joyous, light. They were laughing. My mother was laughing louder than my father. My mother was famous for her laugh. People who liked her loved her laugh, they said it was infectious, but they employed the metaphor of infection in a positive sense, as if she were without their will infusing joy into their bloodstreams. But people who didn't like her—some of the women in the church—said she was loud. She'd been terribly hurt when she'd overheard the minister's wife saying: "Why is it that wherever Mae Morton is, there is always a noise?"

I went downstairs to see what they were laughing about; I needed the relief from my own misery and self-loathing and terror at being exposed.

"Your father's solved the mystery. The mystery of the small holes in the laundry."

I was terrified again. Why were they laughing at what so clearly was not a laughing matter?

My father explained that he'd left an old car battery in the basement, absentmindedly putting it in a place where it shouldn't have been (that wasn't like him. A place for everything and everything in its place was one of his favorite sentences). The clothes had fallen on top of the battery and the battery had been leaking acid. The little holes in the handkerchiefs came from the leaky acid. "End of mystery," he said.

I heard a sound come out of my mouth, the same mouth that had, only minutes before, tasted of ashes, the ashes of shame, and now was sluiced with a wonderful, cool relief. I think the sound I made could only be called a hoot.

"It is pretty darn funny," my father said.

It had been a long time since I had loved my parents so much.

But I was still worried about what I felt was excessive masturbation, and since Dr. Larkin had raised the topic, I asked him if he thought there was such a thing.

"Not a tall, not a tall," he said. "You're perfectly normal. You're perfectly healthy. In time, it will sort itself out. The important thing is not to worry. You have a fine healthy body. The least you can do is to enjoy it."

And when Dr. Larkin said that, I remembered that there were things I loved, things I loved about being Bill Morton, about being alive and seventeen years old. Things I loved on the surface of my skin and in the depths of my muscles and in the speed and strength and lightness of my limbs. That I loved all kinds of weather, the cold, blue-white snow, the slow light summer breezes, carrying the wonderful smells, my mother crushing some herbs in her fingers and saying, This is thyme, this is the mountain thyme, Billy, and even thunder and lightning, and the feel of the cool sand under my bare feet. And swimming, how I loved swimming—jumping into the cold lake, knowing my body would forget the shock soon and the cold would be exhilaration only. Making my way so easily, simply through the water, effortless, and putting my head under the water and seeing the colors changing as the light fell differently, and made shadows and patterns on the sand below, and the sun's rays striking straight down through the bottom like gold spokes and the reflection of the trees when the lake was still, like a sheet of lime-colored spun sugar, so you were surprised when you tasted it that it wasn't sweet at all, only the complicated lake taste that reminded you that somewhere you couldn't see some rich life was going on and now you were part of it and it of you. And the light on the water, wonderful, at any time, in any weather.

That was what I talked to Mrs. Hauptmann about—the light on the water—when she gave me that passage from *The Hairy Ape* to read.

I had no idea that this would be the beginning of a conversation that would blast a hole right through my easy life, my easy happiness.

In her copy of *The Hairy Ape,* Mrs. Hauptmann had underlined one of Paddy's speeches for me to deliver. Paddy the old Irish sailor, a foil for Yank with his dreams of force.

"The Irish are the true poets of the English tongue."

I'd never thought of the Irish in that way. Jimmy Riley and Mike Costelloe were Irish. I thought they were great guys, imaginative, interesting, with good senses of humor. But poets . . . No, I would never have connected the word with them. Their fathers worked in the steel mills and they didn't seem to have a whiff of romance about them. They were always kidding me for being too much of a dreamer. "Billy has his head in the clouds so he falls on his ass. I have my nose to the sidewalk, and someday I might find a diamond." That was what Jimmy Riley said to me one day. I didn't think of that as poetry.

I've never seen a production of *The Hairy Ape* and I can only imagine that some people would find the language overwrought, but I thought it was wonderful; it was thrilling to me that what I felt about the water—although it was only Lake Michigan and I had never been on a boat that could hold more than four people—had been written about by someone acknowledged to be a great writer. I can call the words up in a second, three quarters of a century later.

"Oh, to be scudding south again wid the power of the Trade Wind driving her on steady through the nights and the days! Full sail on her! Nights and days! Nights when the foam of the wake would be flaming wid fire, when the sky'd be blazing and winking wid stars. Or the full of the moon maybe. Then you'd see her driving through the gray night, her sails stretching aloft all silver and white, not a sound on the deck, the lot of us dreaming dreams. . . . And there was the days, too. . . . Sun warming the blood of you and wind over the miles of shiny green ocean like strong drink to your lungs."

I guess I must have made a good job of it—maybe Mrs. Ferguson's lessons counted for something to someone like Mrs. Hauptmann—for I could see she was pleased with me, and the pleasure she took, the extravagance of her praise, freed me to talk about my happiness on the water. And she allowed as how she was happiest by the water, how the light on the water, the smell of the salt air, the clarity of the sunlight, the sound of the waves—always made her feel renewed. She told me about a summer she'd spent on Cape Cod, in Massachusetts, in Provincetown, where Eugene O'Neill had lived.

"One day I'd love to have a house by the water," she said.

And that was where my enthusiasm got the best of me.

"You could, Mrs. Hauptmann, you really could. You could have a house in Ogden Dunes, where we live. My father builds houses for people, and he does them very reasonably. I'd be happy to introduce you to him. I'm sure he'd be able to help you out."

And then she said the thing that made it impossible for me ever to love my parents in the same way again.

"But you see, Bill, that would be impossible. We're Jews and Jews aren't allowed to live in Ogden Dunes. It's the first thing you see when you drive into the town: a sign saying 'Restricted Home Sites on Lake Michigan.' Didn't you ever think of what that means?"

I don't think I'd ever felt so ashamed. The fact was, I'd never thought of what the sign meant. And I'd seen it every day. I was ashamed for myself, but I was ashamed for everyone I'd ever known, a shame that spread like the blood I felt spreading from my neck and heating my face straight to the roots of my hair. I knew I should say something, but there was nothing that seemed right to say. And so I said something I knew to be ridiculous.

"I'm sorry, Mrs. Hauptmann. I just didn't know."

"No, Bill," she said. "Of course you didn't. That's part of the problem, isn't it? That's why Thomas Mann is so insistent upon traveling around America. That's why it's so important that ordinary people hear what he has to say."

I couldn't imagine that she'd want anything to do with me again. But she ruffled my hair, as if I were a child, and said, "You're a nice boy, Billy. You'd never do anything to hurt anyone. I know that."

A nice boy. That was what everyone thought of me. That was what everyone said about me when they signed my yearbook: "Dear Bill: To think that the sweetest, most considerate guy in the senior class is also the handsomest." "Dear Bill, Thanks for your kindness . . . Horace Mann is losing its Gary Cooper." And at that moment, I was disgusted with myself for being the boy people thought nice when I wasn't nice, because of sex, and now because I had allowed myself to be blind to prejudice.

How can I explain to people that in 1939 I didn't know about anti-Semitism? That what was going on in Germany—that fellow Hitler—didn't seem to have anything to do with me, that I knew that the First World War had been over only four years before I was born, that it was a terrible thing, and it seemed right that everyone I heard speaking said that above all we shouldn't allow ourselves to be involved in another war. That the term "isolationist" didn't seem like a bad thing to me. That everything I learned from Thomas Mann was a shock and a surprise.

But how can it be, that I had never heard of Kristallnacht, or the defeat of Poland, to say nothing of the deportation of Jews? I can only say it's the truth: before I met the Hauptmanns, before they prepared me to meet Thomas Mann, none of it had penetrated my mind.

What had penetrated my mind? That was what I had to ask myself, diving up from the swamp of self-loathing that Mrs. Hauptmann's words had plunged me into. What had I been thinking about all day? Decorating the gym for dances? Preparing for the state finals in this or that? Being in love with Laurel Jansen, earning money for college with after-school jobs, keeping my masturbation secret so my mother might believe she had a decent son.

I had to ask my mother if she knew that Ogden Dunes was a restricted town. I could tell she didn't want to talk about it. Didn't want to listen to the words that I was using. She was peeling vegetables for dinner: carrots, potatoes, onions, celery; she would boil them with pieces of chicken for a stew. She would dip a mix of flour and water into the broth for the dumplings she knew I loved.

"I never really thought about it, Bill," she said.

"But now, Mom, now that we know, we have to do something."

"I don't know about that," she said, wiping her hands on her flower-printed apron.

"But you know it's wrong. You know it's wrong to keep people out because of their religion. Because of who they were born."

"Of course it's wrong. Of course I know it's wrong. But maybe it's for the best. Maybe they just wouldn't feel comfortable. Maybe in time they will. I tend to think that things work themselves out in time and it's better not to go stirring up a hornet's nest."

And for the first time, I wondered if I loved my mother.

But I couldn't even hold on to that thought for a minute. I knew my mother was the kindest, the most loving person in the world. She'd taken a job for almost no pay teaching English to foreigners, and, at the end of every class, she invited her students to our house for a party. Many of them went on to be her friends. She was the most loving person I knew. But was it possible that she lacked courage?

The courage I was just then learning about as I learned about Thomas Mann.

What I came to understand was: Thomas Mann was great. Thomas Mann had greatness. And my mother did not.

I was tormented by the idea of greatness, and that so much of everything that made up my life could not ever be thought of as great.

Certainly, the daily life of my high school was not great. But at least I knew it, and I was proud that Mrs. Hauptmann knew that.

I realized that Mrs. Hauptmann had singled me out, saw me as different from the others, an outstanding teen. I had come upon her impatiently shuffling papers and saying, "This is not what I did my thesis on the dream plays of Strindberg for." Had she not noticed I was in the room? When she finally did, she laughed and said, "Oh, Bill, it's this damned dance. Mr. Hauptmann and I are meant to be the chaperones; we're supposed to stand on the balcony like some minor Greek gods looking down at the kids and making sure they're not having a good time. Of course I loathe these dances and everything that they imply. I'm awfully glad that you're not one of the crowd that devotes themselves to all this ballyhoo."

How proud I was to be able to tell her that I had stopped going to the dances because I thought they were "for snobs." That I didn't like the way some of the students who thought themselves so important, the leaders of the Latin Club and the newspaper, made others feel left out . . . and that was why I didn't go with them to Walgreens after school, to the soda fountain. What I didn't tell her was that I went with my friends Jimmy Riley and Ted Pezinkowski to a tavern. To drink beer. To talk about real things. Like about Roosevelt, whom they taught me to admire to the point of idolatry, whereas even the mention of his name in our house caused my father to slam his fist on the table in outrage.

"It isn't just the ordinary kind of high school exclusion. Think about the class implications," she said.

I wondered if Mrs. Hauptmann was what my father would call a pink.

"In order to go to the dances you have to have the right kind of clothes. Am I right, Bill? You have to have black pants and a white dinner jacket, the girls have to have the right kind of dress, you have to know the right kind of dances, you have to have at least access to a car. That lets all the working-class kids out—they can't even think of going to the dances. They're only for the Four Hundred. God, what a hateful concept."

"The Four Hundred?" I asked.

She showed me an article in the local paper, complaining about the discrimination at Horace Mann in favor of the wealthier students, calling this select group "the Four Hundred." The article said there was a favoritism nurtured by the parents, and in which the teachers were complicit. I wondered who had written the article. I wondered if it was my friend Mike Costelloe, who wanted to be a newspaperman. He did become one. I often wonder how many of us actually became what we wanted to become.

"I'm against all of that, Mrs. Hauptmann. I really am," I said. I was full of myself, of my own importance.

"I'm so glad, Bill," she said and put her hand on my shoulder. I felt that hand on my shoulder as a young knight would have felt the touch of the king's sword. I was anointed, chosen.

But quite soon, I would learn that my anointing was only partial, and that Mr. Hauptmann had not quite shared in it. I was standing outside Mrs. Hauptmann's classroom after school, unwilling to interrupt what I knew to be a private conversation. They were, after all, husband and wife.

"Bill Morton. He's no genius, but he's our best bet. And he has the looks of a young blond god, and let's face it, that will probably engage Herr Mann more than a great mind. Oh, yes, I'd be willing to bet on that."

"He is a beauty, and, yes, you're right. No, he's no genius, but he's a pure soul, a sensitive soul. And he has it in him to be greatly responsive."

"And you, my dear, should know." I saw Mr. Hauptmann stroke his wife's cheek with his knuckles.

I felt a fool. I had imagined that the Hauptmanns thought about me in a new way, a way that would open all sorts of doors for me, in that it would allow me to think I had the right to walk through those doors. I thought I had kept my mediocrity hidden from them, the middle-brow side of myself I was trying so hard to be rid of, my taste for the sentimental, the merely pleasing. But I believed then that they had seen through me.

Mr. Hauptmann had stroked his wife's cheek with his knuckles. And she had given him a play slap again. And I found the gestures not only arousing but the sign of something I wanted one day for myself. That kind of talk. That kind of marriage. Stroking a woman's cheek with the rough knuckles, knuckles that were meant for fighting, knuckles that could draw blood rather than the gentle fingertips that were of no possible danger. Not in the least. And then a slap; not a kiss but a slap.

And then it happened again. A hard-on. At the sight of Mr. Hauptmann stroking his wife's cheek with his knuckles rather than his fingertips, and her pretending to slap his face. A double shame: a shame at the foolish tyranny of my body, shame that the Hauptmanns believed I was not great, but only the best of the mediocrities available to them.

In order for Mr. Hauptmann to get me ready for Thomas Mann, he had not only to give me a cram course in Mann's fiction but also to shove the whole of the Great Books down my throat. That's why I'm thinking about it all now, why I'm reliving it all after all these years.

My brother, Sam, just died, older than I: the Morton boys seemed to be blessed or cursed with extraordinary health and access to the best medical care in the world. So I am, at ninety, free of all major afflictions and I still have all my marbles. But my brother's death . . . a quick death from an embolism . . . made me understand in a new way that I myself will die. Apparently, he was in a department store and he turned to a perfect stranger in an elevator and said, "Something quite unusual is about to happen," and he fell to the floor, almost immediately dead. My wife, my second wife, is much younger than I, and today it occurred to me that the least I can do for her and my children and grandchildren is not to leave them with the burden of a lot of useless junk. So I'm going through things, getting ready to get rid of almost everything. It's terrible to take old photographs of people I have loved and put them in large black plastic bags, kind of like the body bags they use for corpses. But I will do this. However, I'm going to keep the books that Thomas Mann signed for me, and the copy of the speech he gave the day I introduced him.

I make a pile of them, putting them on the table in the order that I read them. The novellas and short novels: *Death in Venice, Buddenbrooks. The Magic Mountain. Joseph and His Brothers, Tonio Kröger.*

I think I realized even then that Mr. Hauptmann wasn't helping me read Thomas Mann for me, that what I was required to learn had nothing to do with me, it was like cramming for any other exam: no one really cared if I forgot everything the day after Thomas Mann's appearance. But maybe I'm not being fair to Mr. Hauptmann, certainly not to Mrs. Hauptmann. They cared deeply about literature; for all their snooty remarks about the students and their families, it was important to them that what they loved not be lost, that the torch be passed on, the flame kept alive. I suppose Mr. Hauptmann would jump all over me if he heard me using that kind of cliché. So would Mrs. Hauptmann. But of course they're long dead. I never saw them after I'd left for Europe; he'd enlisted in the army—I didn't know the details. I don't even know if he survived the War. Somehow I got the idea that after he was in the army she moved away to be with her family. New York, maybe. Or it might have been Los Angeles.

The first thing of Thomas Mann that Mr. Hauptmann gave me

to read was *Death in Venice*. I don't think it was the very best choice, but maybe he did it because it was short and he thought the subject would grab my attention. But you see, at that time, the only way I knew how to read was to identify with one of the characters in whatever I was reading. The minute I got to Chicago, I was taught to be ashamed of that, that it was something I had to give up, a mortifying sign of an almost pathological immaturity, like sucking your thumb or wetting the bed. Mr. Hauptmann didn't have time to instruct me on the breaking of that childish habit; he had to make sure I'd read things, so that if Thomas Mann asked me something, or some reporter from the local paper, I wouldn't look like a fool. By which they meant that they wouldn't.

No, there was no way I could identify with Aschenbach. I was much closer to Tadzio's age, but I couldn't identify with the spoiled rich boy who did nothing all day but be looked at—except for one fight almost at the end of the story. Mr. Hauptmann had told me that it was about the impossibility of having a body and a mind and a spirit, and that, as I've said before, was a help . . . but I couldn't help thinking of Aschenbach as a queer.

I'd known that there were men who were interested in men. There was the librarian who was the head of the little theatre who took an interest in me, and my friend Jack Scully said, "Just make sure you're never alone in a room with him. He's been known to make passes at guys like you." And I was shocked, but I was careful to keep my distance from him. Of course when we were younger, just starting Boy Scouts, we played at jerking each other off. But we told ourselves that had nothing to do with being queer. It was just "horsing around." And it all stopped when we started being interested in girls. We would never have imagined that we had anything to do with Aschenbach, with the kinds of feelings he had for Tadzio.

So I listened to Mr. Hauptmann when he said *Death in Venice* was not really about sex, not in the ordinary way, that it was about eros, rather than sex, that I had to understand everything in Platonic terms. Which meant I had to read Plato. Which meant he had to take me through the *Phaedrus,* and I had to consider the problem: Is beauty a distraction? If we can only get to the spirit through the flesh, are we prisoners? Hopeless? Trapped? It didn't seem to have much to do with me, but I was proud to walk around with *The Dialogues of Plato* under my arm. I even thought it might impress Laurel, but it *was* hopeless. If she wasn't impressed by my being chosen to introduce Thomas Mann, she wouldn't be impressed by my reading Plato. It only occurred to me just now, after all these years, that maybe she was jealous or resentful that I was chosen instead of her. She was a much better student than I: she'd read much more, and with much more sophistication. But she was going to Purdue to study home economics and I was going to the University of Chicago. To study whatever I liked. And she was a girl. Or perhaps it's better to say: she wasn't a boy.

I had a much easier time with *Buddenbrooks,* even though it was much longer. I remember telling Mr. Hauptmann that it was a very sad story of a family that didn't seem to be able to make each other happy.

How contemptuous Mr. Hauptmann was when I said that, how he spat the word "happiness" out, as if it were a piece of spoiled meat. "Happiness! An American invention like Coca-Cola. Life, Liberty, the pursuit of Happiness . . . Happiness"—he spat the word again—"what a comedown from the other two, life and liberty. The paltriness of it: it cries out to heaven."

I nodded, and acted chastened. But I didn't give up my sadness for the Buddenbrookses, and I thought of my own family, particularly my mother, how we were a family that people wanted to be around, maybe because we liked being around each other. We were a family that many people wished was theirs.

Like Old Ladislaw.

Old Ladislaw—did we ever know his last name? If we did we never used it. He worked for my father as a painter. My mother saved rags for him . . . he seemed to always be in need of rags for his painting. Of course my mother was always kind to Ladislaw, and sometimes they would chat a bit as he came to collect the rags. He never took his hat off in the house, and I knew that was wrong, something a gentleman didn't do, but I was proud of my mother because it didn't bother her. It probably bothered my father. Although he never said anything either. Maybe he knew it would make Ladislaw feel bad, and then he might not have come back. But maybe he wouldn't have felt bad, would have been grateful that my father was teaching him something about America. How would you ever know?

One night the doorbell rang as we were all at dinner. My father answered the door. It was Old Ladislaw. He was there to collect rags. My father started to say we were eating dinner, but my mother rushed up—she knew that the way my father was talking would make Old Ladislaw feel bad—and said, "Please join us, Ladislaw, you're very welcome to join us."

"No," Old Ladislaw said. "But is it all right if I just sit and watch?"

There was no way that they could say no to him, and after a few tries at insisting that he join us, met with resolute refusals, they agreed to let him sit and watch us eat.

And from time to time, with no regularity, so that it was nothing we could plan for or expect, Old Ladislaw came and asked if he could sit and watch us. I could see that it filled some large emptiness in him, just to watch us, and after a while we stopped offering him food. It was just something that happened: Old Ladislaw rang the bell, he was shown into the dining room, he took his chair at the side of the room. And watched us. Watched us eating an ordinary dinner, an ordinary happy family.

And then one day he said that he was going home. Going home to Lithuania, to his family. He was going to leave us a car, to thank us for having been kind to him. "A jalopy," he said, pleased at his use of the American. My brother and I were thrilled.

We never heard of him again. From time to time during the War, and afterwards, in the Cold War, I wondered if his family were safe, if they were alive . . . if they were Jewish. It's another thing that I will never know.

Having got me through *Buddenbrooks*, Mr. Hauptmann thought it was time to accompany me up *The Magic Mountain*. I was overwhelmed at the prospect, and Mr. Hauptmann told me just to skim it: he'd tell me the most important things to know about it. But I didn't want to skim it; I was fascinated by it . . . maybe it was a sign that all along I was meant to be a doctor, although I must admit I skimmed the parts when Settembrini offers his theories, and I skipped his arguments with Naptha. I didn't care that much that Naptha died.

I felt very sad for Hans Castorp. I could very well understand his kind of passivity . . . I knew I had it in myself to do what I was told, to listen to people in authority. And I was sad for his cousin Joachim. I remember being shocked that, as he's leaving the sanatorium, he calls Hans by his first name for the first time. And I thought of my cousin Bob, whom I'd had so much fun with for our whole lives, and how odd it would have been if we'd called each other by our last names. Bob, who was a polio victim, walked with a limp but insisted on playing baseball. I kept thinking of him when I read *The Magic Mountain,* how he would never have allowed himself to sink into that seductive invalidism. Bob, who was my only real contact with serious illness. To think, except for Bob, I had a whole childhood free of contact with anything more threatening than mumps or tonsillitis. A privileged childhood in clean, well-fed America, even in the Depression a fortunate country, even in the horrorstruck 1930s, a privileged life.

And of course I identified with his hopeless love for Clavdia. Although I thought it was very weird that she gave him her X-ray. Just this year, I reread it, and I thought the detail of the X-ray was wonderful. I remembered a patient of mine when I was just an intern, doing an orthopedic rotation. She'd been in a car accident and had broken several ribs. The attending doctor was showing her her X-ray. And she said, "It's really rather disappointing. It could be anybody's rib cage. There's nothing special about it. I would never know that it was mine. And all my life I've considered myself quite special. Now I have to think of myself as a skeleton like any other skeleton." I liked her very much for that, but I never saw her again; she hadn't been badly hurt and she left the hospital. If she'd stayed longer, I might have asked her on a date. I might have told her about Clavdia.

And reading the book now, after a lifetime tending to sick bodies, I found it even a little arousing that Clavdia had given Hans her X-ray. Was she telling him what my patient was telling him: that she was nothing special, that he could love her or any other woman, it didn't matter? Or was she telling him that beauty is skin deep, that we are the envelope that covers us and without that we're anyone or no one?

Reading it again I remembered copying a passage in the notebook I kept specifically devoted to Thomas Mann. It's a conversation that a fellow patient has with Hans, someone even more hopelessly in love with Clavdia than he is. Would there be any sense, he asked Hans, in making a declaration of love to a woman whom he adored but who made absolutely no response, a declaration, in other words, of hopeless love? He thought there would be boundless happiness in the experience. Even if the act of confession aroused nothing but disgust and involved great humiliation, still it ensured a moment of intimate contact with the beloved object. The confidence drew her into the circle of his passion, and after that, all was indeed over, yet the loss was paid for by the despairing bliss of the moment, for the avowal was an act of force, the more satisfying the greater the resistance it encountered.

I remember reading that with a great sense of relief: I was better than that, I wasn't tempted to make a hopeless confession to Laurel, I wouldn't have opened myself up to that kind of humiliation; I had more pride than that. If I'm honest about my thoughts at that time, the time that I met Thomas Mann, and if there had been some sort of calibrating apparatus to measure the amount of time my thoughts ran to particular subjects, I have to admit that I spent much more time thinking about Laurel than about the rise of Fascism or the admirable President Roosevelt or the prospect of World War. Soon that would change. It had already begun to change when the Hauptmanns began their tutelage. The temperature jumped after I had met Thomas Mann. But when I was reading him, before I had met him, what I was most able to attach to were the passages about unrequited love.

There was nothing about unrequited love in the Joseph novels, and when I finally got to them there wasn't really enough time for me to do more than skim. And I have no impulse to reread them now: I have had no impulse to reread them in all the years between. What I remember being excited about were the ideas about the past, the past of humans as unfathomable, like a deep well, the bottom of which can never be seen. And that there is no such thing as the present because it is always only the remembrance of the past or the anticipation of the future. Alongside my boundless self-involvement, I was capable of being excited by large ideas. Particularly by the idea of large ideas.

———

And so the day arrived. My mother saw me off, standing at the door I knew till she couldn't see me anymore, till I'd turned the corner and was out of her sight, in the world. I experienced for the first time a sensation, or more a way of being that would last me a long time. As I approached the school I wondered, *What will Thomas Mann make of this?* I've heard that some religious Christians wear bracelets that say, "What would Jesus do?" I might as well have worn a bracelet that said, "What would Thomas Mann think?" Only at times it felt more like a shackle than a bracelet.

I'd been so proud of the school, the grand staircase leading from the parklike grounds—the pond, complete with swans, the high Gothic windows, the whole building based, we'd been told, on the English architecture of the sixteenth century: it was meant to recall an English castle. But I'd heard Mr. Hauptmann call it pseudo-Tudor, and of course Thomas Mann had seen real castles. And the swans were not peaceful and graceful; if you got too close to them they made an ugly squawk, worse than a quack, and there had been stories of a little boy who tried to feed them and had got his arm broken for his pains.

I tried to banish the feeling that the Hauptmanns had stolen things from me. Of course it was better to know what the real thing was, what the truly beautiful was, what the good really consisted of. As it was better to have been told (why had I never found it out on my own?) that across the town was a black high school, which had been built to replicate Horace Mann but was vastly inferior, with none of the facilities or equipment that Horace Mann had and where speakers were never invited, where Thomas Mann would not have been brought to speak. "Haven't you noticed, Bill, that there's not a single Negro student here?" I hadn't noticed, and I was shocked that I hadn't, and I was grateful that they'd pointed it out. I knew it was better to know, but I hated knowing it. I knew things, but I believed there was nothing I could do about them. Remember it was 1939. It would be twenty years, at least, before I began to see that there might be something I could do.

But walking into the auditorium that day, I couldn't forget that it was a place I had been happy: the site of my greatest successes, what I knew now was a ridiculously small venue. But I knew I was a star, the star of the high school plays, *The Mikado, Charley's Aunt.* And walking down the stairs, seeing the rich red velvet curtain, which I'd both stood behind and pulled the ropes to open, I remembered that happiness, that sense of being outstanding, of being gifted, of being admired. Loved by strangers. Praised.

By the standards of high school auditoriums, or I guess they should be called auditoria (what would Thomas Mann say?), our auditorium was quite grand. You entered from the outside through one of those open tunnels like you see in football fields. It was a kind of amphitheatre; on either side of the aisle there were sloping rows of seats: around five hundred, as I remember. Below was the stage, which stretched across the entire space. It had a rich velvet curtain, far enough back to allow for a sizeable apron. That day, there was a podium set up on the left side, with a pitcher of water and a glass. At the back of the stage was a set of stairs that led to two smallish classrooms; the lower one was used as a greenroom. We made up there, changed costumes. Thomas Mann would be showed to one of those rooms.

There would be coffee and something to eat: the Hauptmanns were in charge. I didn't know if he was there yet. I was very early.

But they were already there: Mr. and Mrs. Hauptmann. And the great man himself. Thomas Mann. Looking exactly like his pictures. The stiff hair, the stiff moustache, the stiff spine, the stiff shoulders. Holding a cigarette (smoking was not allowed but who would stop him?) so that I felt I couldn't offer my hand for a handshake, certainly because he hadn't offered his. The Hauptmanns introduced me. Mr. Mann inclined his head. He seemed to be looking at nothing, focusing on nothing, staring at the sickly green walls as if there were a message there he needed to decipher before he knew what the next thing would be for him to do. He looked uneasy. It didn't seem possible to me that he was nervous. But I knew his English wasn't good, and all I wanted to do was to reassure him: that he was a great man, one of the greatest men in the world, that he could do anything, anything at all, and everyone in the audience would revere him, would feel honored simply to be breathing the same air.

I had memorized my speech. I had delivered it for the Hauptmanns at least twenty times; they said that they were satisfied. I understand now that it didn't really matter what I said: what mattered was how I looked and the way my body moved across the space of the stage. And that I wouldn't embarrass them if Thomas Mann asked me something about one of his books.

"Bill here has actually shaken hands with someone whose father shook hands with George Washington," Mr. Hauptmann said.

Thomas Mann shook his head several times, as if he had water in his ear.

"But how can that be possible?"

I told him the story of Grandmother Geer. I reminded the Hauptmanns that not only had her father shaken hands with George Washington but also she had seen Abraham Lincoln, both in his debates and the train that carried his body.

"You see, Herr Mann, we have here a real American. As the Americans would say, the real McCoy."

"And what is the etymology of that, I wonder," Thomas Mann asked. "The real McCoy."

"I haven't the faintest idea," Mrs. Hauptmann said. "But then I'm not a real American. Do you know, Billy?"

I felt paralyzed by my own ignorance. "I think they were what we call hillbillies that kept feuding with other families. They seemed to keep killing each other. But I don't know why this entitled them to be called real."

And everyone laughed, as if I'd been purposely witty, whereas I was just saying anything at all, to cover my mortification.

"Bill's going to start the University of Chicago in the fall."

"And what will you study, young man?" Thomas Mann asked.

I had no idea what I would study. I said the first thing that came to my mind. "Philosophy," I said.

"Ah, the queen of the sciences."

"I fear he's not a Platonist. Much too much devotion to the real world. An Aristotelian in the bud," Mr. Hauptmann said.

"I object," said Mrs. Hauptmann. "Bill is a devotee of the ideal."

Just then the principal and his wife came in. I could have fallen at his feet in gratitude. I was afraid that they were going to ask me whether I was a Platonist or an Aristotelian. I had never read Aristotle, and my only Plato was what Mr. Hauptmann had made me read, the *Phaedrus,* so that I could talk to Thomas Mann about *Death in Venice.*

"A very great honor, a very great honor," said Mr. Prendergast, the principal, whom everyone knew to be a timeserver and an idiot. Thomas Mann looked again at the green wall. He accepted a drink of water. "I am grateful that it is not iced," he said. "Americans seem to have a mania for ice."

And then it was time for us to go onstage. The principal led us out, and I was next, Thomas Mann last. I have no memory of what the principal said. When I stood up, all my friends clapped very loud; some of them, to my mortification, whistled. I have almost no memory of what I said. What was there that someone like me could have said? It was something about the honor of having a great writer, about the eternal value of literature. What else could it have been? I sat down, wrapped in a kind of blankness; I hadn't disgraced myself, but I hadn't done anything wonderful either. I had done what was expected of me. I had done what I was told.

And then he made his way to the podium, walking slowly, as if he hoped he'd never actually get there. He coughed. He took a sip of water. He took off his glasses and put them back on. We'd been told he was going to read his lecture; he didn't trust his English. In fact, his accent was so thick that we all had to work very hard to make out what he said.

It's a word people use much too easily, much too carelessly, but you must believe me when I say that Thomas Mann's speech was electrifying. Because I felt in all the nerves of my body a heat, a luminosity, as if they were the first time real to me, palpable, almost visible. I felt a thrumming up and down my back, and then a sense of a match having been lit under my ribs. It was almost as if I were being given shock treatments, the old consciousness emptied out, but instead of torment being replaced by nullity, the nullity of my own life would from then on be replaced by a torment. A torment that was the knowledge of the world, of the implication of what it meant to be human in a world that was full of evil and greatness, of terms and conditions larger than I had ever imagined.

Now I'm opening my Thomas Mann notebook, a black-and-white cardboard composition book, the most common kind, the pattern aspiring perhaps to an impression of marble. The journal I kept of my thoughts about meeting him, and after meeting him. Pasted on the cover, the paper so brittle I'm afraid to hold it in my hand, yellow and fragile and somewhat pathetic, is the speech itself, which was reprinted in the Gary newspaper the next day. I look at the title and I can hear his voice.

"The title of my speech," he began, "is 'The Problem of Freedom or the Crisis of Democracy.'"

He began talking about the conflict between socialism and individualism, between the common good and the good of the individual. I'd forgotten that he spoke about Western civilization, or Occidental civilization as he called it, as Christian and that he saw Nazism as an attack on Christianity. I find that odd now; I know he wasn't a religious man. But perhaps he knew his audience. Perhaps he knew that he had to convince Americans that they were fighting not just people who wanted to kill Jews but people who wanted to do away with Christianity. I can see what he was trying to do, he was trying to refute the argument that Fascism, particularly Nazism, was a bulwark against Communism. He was trying to convince them that Nazism wouldn't protect their property, or anything that they held dear. Oh, how Germanic so much of it is, turgid, dense; he invokes Goethe and Heine and tries to distinguish between the claims of the individual and the larger society.

But finally he gets to his point and he's as passionate as any Neapolitan. He says that, unlike any other revolutionaries, Nazis are devoid of any humanity, any ideal, that they are devoted only to extermination and to force. He calls for a forceful response to their love for force; he insists that, like the church of old, the church militant, there must be a democracy militant. He says that no moral person can be outside the fight.

It was thrilling to be in the presence of someone not afraid to use words like "evil" and "force" and "revolution" and "humanity." It was shocking to hear someone insist that, at the very moment that we were drawing our safe breaths in safe, middle America, blood was being shed in the defense of democracy and liberty and the individual. That there were clear choices to be made: between freedom and tyranny, between liberty and annihilation. And that we must not hide our faces from it.

But most electrifying were his final words, when he spoke as himself, a man, an artist. Seventy-three years have passed and I still feel the same heat, the same illumination of my nerves, the same match-lit blow to my ribs when I read those last paragraphs.

"Before you stands an individual who never expected in former years that he should be called upon to make statements and efforts such as these.

"I have spoken to you of truth, justice, civilization, democracy. In my purely aesthetically determined youth, it would never have occurred to me to deal in such terms. Today I pronounce them with a wholly unexpected note of joyousness. For the position of the spirit has changed upon Earth in a peculiar way. Civilization is in retreat. A period of lawlessness and anarchy reigns over the outward life of the people. Yes, we know once more what is good and what is evil. Evil has been revealed to us in such crassness and meanness that our eyes have been opened to the dignity and the simple beauty of the good. That is, if you like, a rejuvenation of the spirit, and I often have thought that this period of spiritual rejuvenation and simplification, this moral epoch, into which we have entered, might well be the great hour for America. May America stand forth in an abandoned and ethically leaderless world as the strong and unswerving protector of the good and the godly in mankind. I salute you as a country that is conscious of its own human inadequacy but knows what is good and what is evil; that despises force and untruth, a country that perseveres in a faith which is sound and utterly necessary to life—faith in goodness, in freedom and truth, in justice and in peace."

Are you surprised that I stand here, holding the old notebook, the old pages in my hand, and weeping? I suppose I am above all weeping for myself, weeping for the young man who was shocked, electrified by these words, who felt the force of clarity: we knew what was good, what was evil, and we would die for it. I would have followed him anywhere, felt humbled that I could follow him off the stage, into the room with its ugly green walls, to offer my hand and say, Thank you, thank you, you have changed my life.

"And do you think, Mr. Bill, Mr. American, that America will do as I have said? Will save us, will save Europe? Or will you hide from it, protected by the miles of ocean; will you leave us to our perhaps just deserts? Our just destruction. Will American boys be willing to give their lives for us? For what we call civilization?"

"I'm sure we will," I said. "I'm sure the best of us will want to."

He shook my hand and sat down heavily on the inadequate chair. "I'm afraid that the best might not be enough."

He'd insisted that he be showed directly to the car: he said it took too much out of him, this speech, and he didn't want to talk to the press or anyone in the audience. Mr. Hauptmann gave me the signal to bring the car around. I was hoping Thomas Mann would sit beside me in the front seat, but he walked towards the back door, and Mr. Hauptmann opened it for him and got in beside him.

I didn't know what I could possibly say to him after those words that shone and burnt and pierced me like hot arrows. Now I had to drive him to Chicago. Because that was another reason Mr. Hauptmann had chosen me. He didn't like to drive. He was afraid of driving in Chicago. And I was known to be an excellent, supremely responsible driver.

I think he fell asleep in the backseat. I drove him to the Palmer House, and Mr. Hauptmann got out with him; he was going to spend the night in Chicago. "Thanks for everything, Bill. You did us proud."

I got out of the car to shake the great man's hand. "Thank you, sir, I'll never forget this day."

"You very well may, my son," he said. "You have your whole life ahead of you. I hope it is a beautiful life." And he made his way into the formal doorway, Mr. Hauptmann walking a few paces behind him, as if he walked behind a king.

And then I just drove home. I wondered what my mother thought of it, or my father, who thought that Communism was the greatest evil under the sun, who was even against labor unions as something getting in the way of his ability to do his job. But they weren't there to see Thomas Mann. They were there to see me, their son, sitting transfixed, electrified, ready to change his life. Perhaps they were relieved that my shoes were shined, that my tie was straight, that I'd got a haircut. That I hadn't stumbled over any of my lines or mispronounced any words. In fact, we never talked about it. We never said a thing about what Thomas Mann said. They told me they were very proud of me. But that was all they said.

I don't want the relief of too easy tears, because I am, in a way, crying for a young boy, a whole way of life that took its tone from a kind of deafness. Deafness and blindness. Thomas Mann told us that good and evil were clear, but I hadn't even noticed the evil of living in a restricted town, going to a segregated school . . . and my parents died without grasping it. Does that mean they were good Germans? That we all were? That we can love ourselves only because of the accident of not being put to the test?

And I wonder what he would think of his idealistic words about America now? He left America in disgust during the McCarthy years. What would he have thought of Vietnam, when the world and we ourselves no longer thought us worthy of the faith and hope that we'd believed in? What, I wonder, would my children, my grandchildren make of Thomas Mann's speech? Or of an old man, in an attic, wiping the dust off on his trousers, weeping.

I'd like to say that my life was changed from that day forward, that I thought about Fascism and Nazism and evil and good and that force must be used against force all day, every day. But I was just seventeen years old, and although Thomas Mann's voice was never far, it wasn't always at the center of what I heard. I was still the self-absorbed moon-struck boy in love with Laurel Jansen. And I was still the midwestern boy who hoped that war could be avoided, hoped for that above all.

Nevertheless, I had the image of Thomas Mann, the sound of his words as a lodestar. When I remembered to—it wasn't always, but it wasn't rarely—I measured things against him. I wrote letters to him, which I of course never sent. I have no idea what happened to them, and I'm not sure whether or not I'm sorry that they don't exist anymore. Let me be honest: I am sorry. Any trace of the boy I was, whom I loved for some of the very reasons that he hated himself, is precious to me, and any loss of the trail, a sadness.

I know for certain that I wrote to him about the real tragedy that struck all of us in the Dunes, the terrible death of Betsy Laird. The death of a young girl, right in Ogden Dunes, on a night in June: a full moon, and a sky full of bright stars.

I suppose the night began with my lying on my bed, sulking. I knew I was sulking, knew that what I was doing wasn't admirable, not manly, but the obvious deep wrongness of it granted it a kind of grimy voluptuous allure, as if I were putting my nose to something filthy, but the filth was my own. The way I sometimes liked the smell of my own dirty shirts. Is it something that everyone does, sniffing their own clothes to see if they're good for another day's wearing? Or telling yourself that's what you're doing. But is it really that, secretly, everyone is a little in love with his own stink?

So there I was, lying on my bed while everyone I knew was outside on this glorious June evening. A perfect night, everyone said, for the hayride we'd all been planning for weeks.

I'd had some part in planning it, but it was my brother, Sam, who ran the show. He'd arranged with one of the local farmers to rent his tractor, arranged that the farmer would both drive the tractor and provide the hay. He would load it onto a flat-bottom cart that the tractor would be attached to, that the tractor would pull. We were expecting ten people, five couples: Sam and his fiancée, Mabel, two other couples that were friends of Sam's from Purdue, Betsy Laird and her boyfriend from Northwestern, and the youngest among them, Laurel and myself.

I'd dreamed of it for weeks. I'd lie on my bed as the nights grew steadily warmer, the days steadily longer, breathing the heavy air, the breeze just lively enough to move the white muslin curtains, occasionally. I thought about lying on the hay in the wagon next to Laurel, how the smell of the hay would mix with the smell of her hair, the light lovely smell of her skin that in my mind had its source on the insides of her arms, particularly the bends of the elbows. I had smelt that wonderful smell when my face came close to her arm when I turned her as we danced a jitterbug. I knew just how the stars would be, flat as saucers, and the moon, which we knew would be three quarters full. I knew there would be singing and I'd practiced the song I'd sing to her, though I'd pretend I was singing it for the whole group. I'd spent a lot of time choosing the song, studying the songs on the hit parade as carefully as I later studied for organic chemistry finals. I narrowed it down to three. I was tempted by "Change Partners," because it was such a clear expression of my fervent wish that she free herself of the beastly Dolph Johnson. But I rejected that: too obvious. I was drawn to the high drama of "All or Nothing at All," but I was afraid it might scare her off. So I settled on "Moonlight Serenade." It was romantic, but gentle; it spoke of the touch of a hand and roses and the stars and the moon, but it hinted of something larger, "break of day . . . love's valley of dreams . . . you and I . . . summer sky . . . heavenly breeze, kissing the trees."

I stood in front of the mirror, practicing, closing my eyes at particular moments, opening them, moving my head closer to and farther away from the phantom Laurel. I'd been told I had a good voice: after all, I'd had the lead in *The Mikado*. But I had to use my voice now to suggest to Laurel that she'd be happier with me, a gentle but no less passionate lover, the kind of man who didn't rely on muscle power, but would listen to her dreams, than with Dolph.

And then the morning of the hayride, she had telephoned and said she couldn't make it: a cousin was visiting from out of town. But I knew it wasn't a cousin, it was Dolph, home from Purdue for the weekend.

All I wanted to do was sleep, sleep so I could forget the humiliation, but maybe it was because the moon was too bright, I couldn't get to sleep. I decided to read. I decided I would read *Tonio Kröger,* and the thought allowed me to salvage some vestige of pride in myself. Laurel Jansen had stood me up, but I was reading *Tonio Kröger,* and I had been praised by Thomas Mann. I was sure Dolph didn't even know who Thomas Mann was.

I read the beginning quickly, the encounter between Tonio and the boy Hans, stupid ordinary Hans, who doesn't want to read a great book; he only likes books with pictures of horses. And then like a detective finding the right clue—the footprint, the piece of string, the crushed grass, the discarded envelope—I came to the place I had been looking for, and it filled me with a rush of excitement. This is me, I thought, reading by the light of the three quarter moon, so bright was it that I didn't need to switch on my bedside lamp. These words, I thought, will tell me who I am.

I still have my old copy of *Tonio Kröger,* and I see the passages I underlined. To say that I was self-dramatizing would not be the half of it, but then Tonio is a master of self-dramatization.

"To feel stirring within you the wonderful and melancholy play of strange forces and to be aware that those others you yearn for are blithely inaccessible to all that moves you—what a pain is this! . . . But yet he was happy. For he lived. His heart was full; hotly and sadly it beat."

So I turned my sense of shame into "the wonderful and melancholy play of strange forces," and I took a deep, unkind pleasure in Tonio's description of the people who were more successful in the world than he, though he knew himself to be superior. Of the despised dancing master, Tonio says, "To be able to walk like that, one must be stupid; then one was loved, then one was lovable."

So I lay in the bright moonlight in my thin pajamas (it was only ten o'clock but I'd taken off my clothes in despair) and thought: Laurel doesn't love me because I am not stupid enough, and to be loved one needs to be stupid, like Dolph.

But soon *Tonio Kröger* failed in its work of consolation. I was not Tonio Kröger. Laurel was not Ingeborg. For one thing, Ingeborg was stupid, as stupid as Hans; her phrases were "commonplace," her thoughts "indifferent." And I knew Laurel wasn't; she was the smartest person in our class. It upset me terribly that she planned on studying home economics in college because that was the only thing her father would pay for, the only thing he said it made sense for a girl to study. I had dreams of marrying her the day after graduation, running away and putting both of us through college, waiting tables, working in a factory, anything so she could study whatever she wanted: literature, philosophy. I dreamed of us sitting at our kitchen table, reading the tragedies of Aeschylus, Shakespeare's sonnets. No, Laurel wasn't Ingeborg. If Laurel didn't want me, there must be some good reason.

It must be because she knew I wasn't Tonio. Tonio despised the dancing master because he loathed dancing, loathed everything about it. And I loved dancing, everything about it. Holding the lovely girls in my arms, the light silkiness of their dresses, the fresh smell of their hair and their skin, moving to the music, singing the words in some girl's ear, or silently, in my own heart. The most wonderful night of my life had been the freshman dance, walking with Laurel through the trellis of artificial roses, dancing under the synthetic moon.

It was true that I had given up going to the dances, but it was also true that what I considered the most wonderful night of my life had happened at a dance, the freshman dance that Laurel and I had been in charge of, the first time we'd danced together, the beginning of what was for me (but not for her) what I believed to be the great love story of my life.

There were four of us on the dance committee, Laurel and I, and Rose Blaine and Tom Nelson. We'd decided what the theme of the dance would be: spring. God, weren't we original! Spring. We planned on setting up trellises in the girls' gym and covering them with paper flowers. We decided to take a look in the school attic to see if anything like trellises might be up there. But what we found was much more wonderful than trellises that could be covered by paper flowers: a sky painted on scrim, clouds and stars on a background of what could only be sky blue. We brought it down to the gym. It stretched from one end of the balcony to the other. Rose Blaine's father was the electrician who was in charge of the lights of the Christmas tree and also the lighting of the little theatre; she talked him into getting involved. He set up two lights behind the scrim. One would revolve and change the shade of the scrim as it revolved so that the sky seemed to be turning from dark to light, and he would get his pal to train a spotlight on a particular couple and follow their progress across the dance floor. And on the night of the dance, Laurel Jansen and I walked through the trellis together.

I knew what the Hauptmanns would say about it, that it was the kind of thing that one had to have risen above, that only the unimaginative members of the Four Hundred would have fallen for it. But I had fallen for it, would always fall for it; even now I remember it as one of the magic nights of my life. The sky turning, as if we'd captured our own moon, from light gray to pure blue to midnight, and the two beams, one revolving behind the thin cloth, one focusing on the dancers, rendering all the girls magic, beautiful, suggesting that what was between the beautiful girls and the gallant boys was wonderful, and magic, and could only be true love.

And even though I'd given up the dances because I didn't approve of them on ethical grounds, it was a sacrifice. But if I'm really honest, I'd have to say that there was a pleasure in the sacrifice: I knew that Laurel would not go to the dances with me, and going with anyone else was a falling-off from the ideal. My sense of myself as ethically heroic was something of a compensation. But it had been a sacrifice; it had been a loss. The truth was, I loved the dances. I loved to dance.

Tonio Kröger couldn't help me. Tonio was great, Tonio was an artist. At first, he suggested that he didn't know what he wanted to become. Asked what in the world he meant to become, he gave various answers. He was used to saying—and had even already written the words— that he bore within himself the possibility of a thousand ways of life, together with the private conviction that they were all sheer impossibilities. But really he had always known that he meant to be a writer, an artist. He was perfectly ready to give up everything for art. He loathed the spring because it disentranced him from writing.

I knew I had no idea what I really meant to become. When you were a child, people were always asking, "What do you want to be when you grow up?" But they didn't really want to know, whatever you said was fine with them. A fireman. A policeman. President of the United States. Mostly adults found whatever answer you gave funny. But Tonio Kröger knew he was meant to be a writer: he said he felt it as a curse, but even then I knew that wasn't real. And I knew I had never felt anything like a calling. And I was face-to-face with my own meagerness. I knew that there was nothing in me that was great, and there would never be. I was better at some things than most of the people around me. A better actor, with a good comic timing and a good voice. But I knew I wasn't a great actor: I knew what a great actor was. Laurence Olivier. I'd seen *Wuthering Heights* six times, because I had a job as an usher in the movie theatre. I'd seen him as romantic Orlando in *As You Like It* and as a cold-blooded spy in *Clouds over Europe*. That was greatness. Thomas Mann had greatness. But all I could say about myself was I was better than some people at some things.

I wondered if I could never be great because I wanted to be happy.

I was sure Thomas Mann didn't want to be happy. Certainly, Tonio didn't. He didn't require to be loved; he was happy to love hopelessly. Happiness is not in being loved—which is a satisfaction of the vanity and mingled with disgust. Happiness is in loving, and perhaps in snatching fugitive little approaches to the beloved object. I wasn't satisfied with fugitive little approaches to the beloved object. I wanted to make love to Laurel Jansen, then to marry her, to have children with her, to live with her forever, to grow old beside her, to die at an advanced age in her arms.

Tonio Kröger didn't even seem to want friends. He called his friends "impious monsters." I thought of my best friends, Larry Held and Ernie Townsend. We could talk about anything. I could trust them with everything. I could trust them with my life.

And I knew that there were times in my life I had been happy. And that I wanted that as much as possible. I lay in my bed holding *Tonio Kröger* wishing I could think of something better to wish for than happiness. But I could not. And I wondered whether I could never be great because I wanted to be happy or whether I wanted to be happy because I knew I could never be great.

And so a new layer of self-loathing covered the original one, the one whose source was Laurel's rejection. For a moment I could imagine she had rejected me because she knew I was better than Dolph and she preferred stupidity to tenderness. But then I came to believe that she was right to reject me, because I was nothing, not one thing, not the other, not Hans, which was to say not Dolph. Not Tonio. Certainly not Thomas Mann.

Looking at my copy of *Tonio Kröger*, seventy-three years later, I remember the boy lying in his bed in the moonlight, thinking these young man's thoughts. But more strongly, I remember waking up at midnight and hearing my father and my brother, Sam, in the kitchen. I heard chairs scraping across the wood floor. Then I heard my brother's voice and my father's. It's a strange thing, but you know right away when something terrible has happened. The air changes: it becomes electric, like just before a storm, and both heavier and lighter. But charged with something. Overfull.

I went downstairs to the kitchen. Sam and my father were sitting at the kitchen table. Sam was sitting with his head in his hands. It was hardly credible. My brother was crying. I'd never seen my brother cry. Even as a child, he had refused it.

"You mustn't blame yourself, Son," my father said. "It was an accident. Nobody could have seen it coming . . . Nobody would have imagined."

"But the light, Dad," I heard my brother say. "The light."

My father saw me standing in the doorway. I hung back: I thought it was not my business. It was not my world. It was the world of men like Sam and my father, who always knew what to do. I knew something terrible had happened and I knew that they would know what to do. And I would not.

"You've done everything you could," my father said. Then he pulled up a chair for me. "Have a seat, Bill," he said. "There's been an accident."

I had never heard my father's voice like that. Tender, like a woman's. Like my mother's. As if, to tell the terrible story he knew he had to tell, he had taken on my mother's voice. Where was my mother? Away at her sister's for a week of playing bridge. We all knew we needed her; we needed our mother, he needed his wife. But she wasn't here. She couldn't help us.

He told me the story in my mother's voice.

They had planned to do all the driving along the soft berm at the side of the road; it was more than wide enough for the wagon. But there was just one place where the berm wouldn't take them because there was an old store on the side of the road, so the farmer, Mr. Thompson, drove the tractor pulling the wagon into the road itself. Just to avoid the store. It all happened in a minute, Sam kept saying . . . less than a minute. A truck came up behind them. It mistook the white lights of the wagon for the lights of the store and so it didn't stop until too late. The driver jammed on his brakes. The truck rammed into the back of the wagon and the people in the front of the wagon couldn't see it coming. The ones on the back of the wagon saw the truck and jumped off in time—"I was one of them," Sam kept saying. "Dad, it easily could have been me." But the people in the front couldn't see anything; they didn't have time to jump. Mr. Thompson was killed.

"Betsy Laird died, too," my father said, and he put his head in his hands so that he and Sam looked like matching statues, facing each other, as if they were at the entrance to something, as if they guarded the space between them, which was nothing but night air and the white deal table.

Nothing of what was happening seemed possible. My brother weeping. My brother and my father sitting with their heads in their hands like each other's reflections. Everyone awake, long after midnight now, the air cool, silky, but heavy with this new wrongness that hung over the white deal table. Betsy Laird dead. The smartest girl I'd known, even smarter than Laurel. A student at Northwestern, not home ec, but literature. Modern poetry. She wanted to be a professor.

One night after a beach picnic, we were all lying around the dunes and she said, "I don't think I'll get married, Billy. Who would have me once they knew what I was really like? And besides I don't see myself doing dishes and changing diapers."

She'd always talked like that to me, seriously, although most of Sam's friends thought of me as Sam's kid brother. We lay looking at the stars and talked about poetry. About life. She had long tan legs and her hair was a cap of crisp dark curls.

She'd been thrown from the wagon and broken her neck. A broken neck didn't seem like the kind of thing you needed to die from, I thought. "I broke my neck." It was a statement people used when they were exaggerating something: some difficulty that had nothing to do with death. When you heard the words you didn't think of blood or a stopped heart. I thought it sounded like something you could get over, if you lay very still, perhaps for a long time. But eventually you'd get over it. Eventually you'd get up again.

But Betsy Laird would not. Betsy Laird was dead. She would not be getting up; she would not be all right. I saw her body, flat, sprawled on the white road in the clear moonlight. I saw that Betsy Laird was dead. She was twenty years old.

I tried to think what was the right thing to be doing now. Should I sit with my father and my brother or should I let them alone? When I was trying to decide, a terrible thought came to me, a thought that I believed was the worst thing I could possibly be thinking. What I was thinking was this: Betsy Laird is dead and I am alive. I am glad to be alive. If I had to choose which of us was to be alive and which was to be dead, I would choose what happened: that Betsy Laird had died and I had lived.

I excused myself and stepped outside into the darkness. I was glad to feel myself shivering. My impulse was to strip off my pajamas and run into the lake, which would be freezing at this hour, at this moment in June. But I knew my father and my brother would think that was ridiculous, embarrassing: it would reinforce everything they thought about me. That I was not the man they were. That I was not quite a man.

I stood for a while looking at the water and then I was seized by the urgency to write something, to write something down. I went back to my room and wrote a poem. God, how I cringe looking at it now among the papers my mother saved, that I now save. How false it was, and I see the falseness in every syllable. If I were going to write truly, I would have had to write a poem about being glad that I was alive and Betsy was dead. But of course that wasn't what I did. This is what I wrote:

> *She filled the lives of those she knew*
> *With richness born of earnest love*
> *And like a candle, snuffed anew*
> *By Him who watches from above*
> *Leaves still a glow, so then will she*
> *Which through our lives will ever be*
> *Reflections of eternity.*

When my mother got home the next day, all the tears were over. My brother was dry-eyed, and my father returned to silence. She took up the work of weeping; they were glad to pass it on to her. And I was glad to be able to hide my real self from her once again, to show her the poem I had written, as if I were a nice boy, a loving boy, a poetic boy and not the horrible person I knew myself to be. Oh, God, how it pleased her, to have a son who wrote poetry. She held my hand and kissed it and said what a blessing it was to have a son like me, and how we were all alive in this world just by chance, and how we could lose what we most loved any minute. She copied the poem in her own handwriting. I don't know when she took it down to the local newspaper, but that fall, after I'd been at the University of Chicago for two months, she sent it to me. By that time I knew enough to be mortified by it; I hid it in the back of my bureau, the way some other boys hid French postcards. And I knew it was another thing that I had lost: pride in my mother's pride, replaced now by a necessary skepticism, a necessary coldness.

I started college at Chicago that fall, and it was almost as much of a shock as the news of the world I got from the Hauptmanns. Except that, after the first shock, no shock has the same power. I can hardly believe that I was only there for a few months before I left; I can hardly believe the speed and force with which my old ideas were blasted and new ones put in place. I had already learned from the Hauptmanns what a naïve reader I had been, but now my naïveté was not tolerated kindly: anything personal, anything having to do with the life of Bill Morton had to be excised from what I read, under pain of literal failure: a paper scored through with red lines and marked at the top with a red F. It was no wonder I lived in dread of anyone finding the poem I had written about Betsy Laird's death.

I was living away from home for the first time, in a dorm, and the excitement of the day's classes went on all night: we sat on the floor, we smoked endlessly, we talked about God and death and sex. Platonic forms. The existence of the unconscious. Relativity. It was the age of Robert Maynard Hutchins: The Great Books curriculum, the Socratic method, the insistence on a rigorous scientific education. The electrification that had taken me over most violently was fully in force then: I woke up every morning, my mind running like a torrent, like a water-fall powering an electric plant. I lit a cigarette, headed to the john, and talked about sex or death with one of my roommates as we shaved and discussed Spinoza looking at each other in the mirror.

But it was 1939 and what we talked about more than anything was war: the War that was going on in Europe and what our part in it should be. I never told any of them about my encounter with Thomas Mann; it would have seemed too much like bragging, and maybe I was ashamed of how small a part I would have had to play in my own nar-ration of the arguably quite small event. We debated Aquinas's theory of the just war; we spoke about pacifism and the horrors of the Great War: was force justified, was force necessary . . . what did it have to do with us as Americans?

And in the library I wrote to Thomas Mann, trying to sort out all the ideas that had been thrown around by my friends as we shaved and smoked and drank coffee and ate our hurried, unattended-to meals. I wrote him a long letter, I remember, about Mr. Lyons, because as important as my teachers and fellow students were to me in trying to understand what I felt about war, no one was more important to me than Mr. Lyons.

When I wrote to Thomas Mann about Mr. Lyons it was, as I said, a way of trying to understand my troubled feelings about pacifism, but it was a way of presenting myself—although it was a presentation that existed only in my mind—to the great man as someone who would interest him. An exotic. Which is the way I was presented to him by the Hauptmanns: Herr Mann, you have before you a specimen of the real American. As if I was a creature in a zoo, or an exhibit at the world's fair. Chinese jugglers, Indian snake charmers, Peruvians play-ing wooden flutes. As I had charmed him talking about Grandmother Geer, I knew he would have been charmed by, or at least interested in, Mr. Lyons, such an anachronism, such an anomaly, a sign of something in America that one need not be ashamed of, that I could, even under the gimlet stare of the Hauptmanns, love.

Mr. Lyons was the minister of our church, the Congregational, on Taft Street. He was universally beloved because of his great kindness.

When there was illness or death, he was there: you could count on him to show up. He had been trained in the Chicago seminary, with an emphasis on a kind of Gospel Christianity that was almost entirely based on moral responsibility. He was the lowest of low Protestants. There was no ritual element to his services; once a year Communion was provided, and instead of wine, grape juice was passed in special small silver cups, only large enough for a sip. No chance of excess of appetite being tempted . . . even with grape juice. He dressed in a way none of us had ever seen before. He wore a long swallow-tailed coat, a grey wool vest in all weathers; around his neck, a white silk cravat. Oddly, he gave me my first copy of *Life* magazine.

Only now I realize how courageous he was, to preach to a congregation that only wanted platitudes and anodynes, that Jesus wanted us to treat everyone as brothers. He spoke about racial tolerance when it was a concept as foreign as space travel. And he was a pacifist, as he said Jesus required us to be. He reminded us of the horrors of the First War. He reminded us to think of shattered flesh, and not abstract ideas, to remember that what was called patriotism so often ended in shattered flesh. And so, by the time I was two months into the University of Chicago, I realized that I had encountered a genuinely good man, a genuine moral hero. And yet Thomas Mann had said that we must do our part to keep back the monster Hitler and his monstrous plans for the world. And that included taking our place beside the British, joining the war effort. This was before Pearl Harbor. By 1942, Mr. Lyons was fired from the congregation for his pacifism. But by that time, I was in the thick of it. I had written to Thomas Mann about Mr. Lyons long before that. Or perhaps it was only a few months earlier, but the time before my entering the ambulance corps and everything that followed seemed like centuries, impossible to calculate with a paltry metric like months.

How do you tell what is a genuine moral concern, real pacifism, and what is simply a desire for self-protection, or isolationism? I read Gandhi, and quoted him in my letter to Thomas Mann. I assured Thomas Mann I understood the depth of Hitler's menace. (Of course I did not. Of course I believed, at eighteen, that I did.) I asked him if he thought it was possible to be a pacifist and a realist. A warrior and a peaceful man.

So many elements were involved in my decision to volunteer as an ambulance driver for the American Field Service that it's impossible now for me to say which was the most important. I can say, though, that meeting Thomas Mann made me feel it imperative that I do something about the situation in Europe. But we were not involved, at that point, in the War. And the influence of Mr. Lyons made me gravitate towards something nonviolent, and so when a guy on my floor, who was a Quaker, volunteered for the American Field Service Ambulance Corps, I went along.

But I'm not here to talk about my war; there's nothing more boring than an old codger reminiscing about the glory days, about the Great Generation. I drove an ambulance from January through May 1940, first in France, and then, when France surrendered, we made our way to Egypt. And then of course we entered the War, and I seemed to have lost all taste for pacifism; in any case, I didn't feel I could fail to put my life on the line when other people were doing it. And I didn't feel certain enough of my beliefs to register as a conscientious objector . . . and I certainly wasn't certain enough of them to risk going to jail. I enlisted before I was drafted, and, because I'd had experience in the ambulance corps, I was sent to work in the army hospital in Paris. I never had to fight; I never even had to hold a gun. Certainly, I never even came close to killing anyone.

After that, it was only natural that I thought of becoming a doctor. By that point, I understood that I wasn't going to be a great actor, that, although I loved literature, I wasn't going to be a great literary scholar. And there seemed no point doing those things if you weren't going to be great at them. I believed I could be a good doctor, and that it was a good thing to do. I'd seen enough pain, enough broken bodies, to believe that what I wanted was to do something to make those kinds of things better. Sometimes I thought of the broken body of Betsy Laird and I wished I'd been there. Maybe I'd have been able to do something.

I think I was a good doctor. I loved my work. Was I a great doctor? It doesn't seem a worthwhile question. I was good at what I did. I can honestly say I've had a good life, and I know that even that is quite a rare thing to be able to say.

For a few months, though, I was an ordinary college student, as though anything in that year could have been ordinary. I went to classes, I did my work, I stayed up all night talking with the guys on my floor, I had a few dates, but nothing spectacular: I was still a virgin. I was working my way through school, having to supplement my scholarship: my parents couldn't afford to give me any money. So I got a job, first as an usher at the Apollo Theater on Randolph Street, and then, when the doorman had a heart attack and died, I was hired to take his place.

It was a great job, everybody wanted it. I was hired right away because I'd been an usher at the movie theatre in the Dunes. I guess I was considered experienced. Once again, I got to see movies for free; my boss was a terrific guy, I realize now he must have been pretty old, maybe in his seventies, I don't know why he was still working. He'd had something to do with the making of movies, not just running a movie theatre. He talked to us about movie stars he'd known. Norma Shearer. Jean Harlow. William Powell. Edward G. Robinson. He told us that Jimmy Cagney was a good friend of his. We thought he was exaggerating, maybe making everything up, and then one day Jimmy Cagney came by to see him. Looking just like Jimmy Cagney, a small fellow, walking on the balls of his feet, reminding me of nothing so much as a bantam cock, though he was very nice to us, signed autographs. I have no idea what I did with my autograph of Jimmy Cagney. Of course I've moved around a lot. But I have managed to hold on to the books signed by Thomas Mann. And my silly Thomas Mann notebook.

It was a great location, the Apollo, everyone passed by, everyone going to the fancy stores on Michigan Avenue, everyone coming out of the train station. I saw some amazing things, some things I'd never seen before. Drug addicts stumbling along, falling into the gutter. At first I thought they were drunks, but then Mr. Rosenberg, my boss, said, "No, kid, they're junkies. They're that way because of dope." I guess I'd heard of people taking drugs but I'd never seen it. And once I actually saw a bank robbery, and just like Jimmy Cagney looked exactly like Jimmy Cagney in the movies, the bank robbery looked exactly like a bank robbery in the movies. First a guy came running out of the bank and jumped into a car that sped down the street, but it was caught in traffic, then there was a police car with a siren, followed by a taxi with a cop on the running board brandishing a gun. He shot at the tires of the getaway car and of course it had to stop, and the robbers got out of the car with their hands up over their heads. And then a man in a suit and a fedora—he must have been the police detective—got out of a taxi and put the robbers in handcuffs. When I told one of my grandchildren that, he said, "You know, Grandpa, for a lot of people that would have been the most exciting thing that ever happened to them. But you just tell the story like it was just another thing that happened in your life."

I don't know whether he was telling me that I wasn't very good at telling stories or that my life had been unusually eventful. I sometimes find it difficult to distinguish praise from blame.

Mr. Rosenberg liked putting us all in snazzy outfits. The ushers had white pants and short red jackets and red caps with white bills. But when I was promoted to doorman, I was all in white pants with a red stripe up the side of the leg, a red jacket, a white Sam Browne belt, gold epaulets, a red cap with a lot of gold braiding. I thought I looked quite fine; it was a good way to get girls to notice me.

And this is how it happened, that I met Thomas Mann again. I guess he was coming out of the train station; he was walking with a young woman and a man who was near his age. He seemed unhappy, agitated, on the verge of being angry. But of course, being as young as I was, having thought about him so much, having had him in my mind's eye so intensely for so long, it didn't occur to me that he didn't seem in the mood to be greeted. And I couldn't get over my good fortune in seeing him just then: I'd be able to tell him that I'd volunteered to drive an ambulance in France. I was sure that he'd be pleased; I'd tell him I was inspired by him to do it.

I left my post and ran up to him. I grabbed him by the arm. He looked alarmed, then furious.

"Mr. Mann," I said. "I'm Bill Morton. I introduced you at Horace Mann School in Gary, Indiana." He still looked furious, and I could tell that he didn't recognize me or remember me. But some demon in me pushed me to go on. "Then, remember, I drove you to Chicago."

He looked me up and down with a gaze that frightened me with what I knew could be nothing but contempt.

"Ah, the all-American boy. And now you're dressed up like a toy soldier in an operetta. Perhaps one day you'll be in a real uniform, not playacting, but doing your duty, fighting and dying along with all the other young men."

The young woman took him by the arm. "Come, Papa," she said. I think she was embarrassed by her father's outburst. She didn't look at me, nor did the man who walked beside her.

And I never saw Thomas Mann again. I never got to tell him that I was going to Europe because of his words. The only consolation I had was that no one had heard what he said to me, no one had even seen me approach him, no one had seen us speaking on the street.

Of course this is a part of the story I never tell anyone. But I almost never tell anyone about my meeting with Thomas Mann. I don't think most people would be interested. It doesn't make a very good story, not the kind of story most people like to hear. So because I don't talk about it much, I haven't thought about it as much as I once believed I would. No, I can't say I've thought about it very much at all.

But even now I can still feel the hot lashings of shame that I felt when Thomas Mann's daughter pulled him down the street and I saw his angry back and his stiff shoulders, the three of them making their way down Michigan Avenue, to someplace I was sure was more important than I could imagine.

From time to time, I've taken the books down from the attic to read them, the ones with his name in his strict, formal handwriting, but I always bring them back up here. I keep them hidden. I don't think of them as I think of other books. Because I don't think of him as I have thought of any other person I have ever met.

He was a great man. I knew it then, and nothing has changed my mind. He believed it was his duty to wake us up from our stupid sleep, pulling off our blindfolds, unstopping our ears. The waking was a shock, a laceration, but it was one we needed. His words lanced the infection of our refusal to understand who we were, who we were in the world. That America was not the world and that we, as Americans, had no right to the lulling music which was not of the spheres, not even of the sirens, but the low hum of cave dwellers who didn't even have the wit to see the shadows.

When I met him, I knew I was in the presence of greatness. And in some way I can't explain, I know that I was marked by it. Marked indelibly. Permanently.

I would like to say eternally, but then I am American, an American man born in the Midwest in the first quarter of the twentieth century, and "eternally" is not a word people like me believe we have a right to use.

Fine Arts

O N THE TRAIN from Pisa to Lucca, Theresa looked up the word "weak" in her Italian-English dictionary. *Debole.* She said the word to herself. Then she made a noun of it. *Debolezza.* Weakness.

He was a weak man, he was very weak, she said silently, to no one in particular. Or it wasn't to no one; it was to many people, to whom she felt an obligation to explain. At twenty-five, she still felt herself a girl, and therefore someone who owed things to people. Especially the ones who believed in her.

She was a girl in whom many people had believed. The nuns had been the first; her mother had needed the example or the prodding of the nuns in order to believe. Even Yale, it seems, had believed in her. They had accepted her into the doctoral program in art history; she was traveling on a grant they had provided, allowing her a month in Lucca to explore her dissertation topic: Matteo Civitali, a fifteenth-century sculptor, most of whose work was in Lucca.

"She's an unusual girl, Mrs. Riordan; uncommonly intelligent. But it's more than that. She has tremendous powers of concentration."

She'd heard Sister Patricia say that to her mother when she was only nine years old. Was it a gift or a burden? Normally, it wouldn't have occurred to anyone to pose that as a question. Normally, belief, confidence was thought of as a gift.

But now, she'd been through something. It was natural that she'd look at things in a new way. She'd gone through something with a man. A kind of thing neither her mother nor the nuns would understand. When people thought of nuns, they thought of censorious, judgmental, even sadistic joke figures, holding a ruler and a rosary, laying down the law. But the nuns in her life had not been like that. They hadn't worn habits. They didn't seem angry, not nearly so angry as her mother, as most of the mothers she knew. They had seen that her family was troubled, and that Theresa had promise. They had stepped in.

But they wouldn't understand what she'd been through.

Their special girl. Their prize.

From the train she saw the fields and towers she'd seen in five-hundred-year-old paintings. She was surprised that her heart lifted as she'd always thought it would at her first sight of Italy. That even after what she'd been through, her heart could lift. Despite everything, she could still write the postcard she'd always imagined writing to Joan Gallagher, the professor who had trained her, who had singled her out and arranged her passage from Divine Word College to Yale. A postcard of the countryside. And on the back, she would carefully print one word: "Beautiful." And she would write one to her friend Maura, with whom she'd fantasized about traveling to Europe. Maura had got there before her; a week in Paris with a boyfriend whom she ditched when she arrived home. "I made it," she would write. "I'm here."

She looked out at the olive trees and cypresses and the calm hills, some bare, some cultivated. At first she was delighted. There they were: the trees of her imagination, trees she'd only seen, not in actual paintings, but in reproductions before which she sat in the libraries that she believed were her real homes, the places where she felt safe and strong and certain of herself and her own right to speak. But there they were now, these trees. Real, solid. If she jumped off the train she could touch them, lean against them, smell them. But then she began to be disappointed. There they are, she said to herself, using the present tense. There they are. They were there for everyone. They weren't hers anymore. Anyone looking at them could make anything of them they wanted. And being only themselves, they were vulnerable. They could be burnt, cut down, their bark made ugly by lovers' initials, their leaves the victims of disease, something to be turned away from. And as soon as she saw them, they were gone, as the train sped forward, lost to her forever. Looked at through the window, one was indistinguishable from another. Not placed in a work of art, they were only themselves. Interchangeable. Then gone.

She could hardly believe that cypresses were trees like other trees she'd known: oaks, maples, pines. Slim and self-enclosed, they seemed not really natural; they had more in common with the campaniles, and the towers, which, you had to remind yourself, were about onslaught and attack.

She did feel she was riding through a dream. But she was not a dreamy girl. "Dreams are a luxury the likes of us can't afford." That was the kind of thing her mother always said. "Dreamy" took its place in her mother's mind with other words like "vain," and "frivolous."

Theresa knew very well that she wasn't dreamy, although sometimes the way she looked at things gave them the intensity of things seen in a dream, the intensity that stemmed from the force of having been seen so closely, looked at for so long that the trees in the pictures she loved seemed to melt, to surround themselves with haze. She was a city child, born and raised in Milwaukee, and, except for the occasional view of the lakes, nature hadn't meant much to her. The first things she remembered looking at with the kind of intensity that made their borders melt were the holy cards Sister Imelda had given her.

Sister Imelda must have been in her eighties then, still wearing her habit, cared for but condescended to, Theresa would learn later, by the younger nuns. She helped with the cooking, answered the phone. She gave Theresa a holy card every time she got a good report card. Slipping it to her as if it were a kind of pornography, knowing the younger nuns she lived with didn't approve of that kind of pious bad taste. Later Theresa would come to think of the holy cards as in bad taste. Guido

Reni. Carlo Dolci. Sugar-sweet Madonnas. Jesus pointing to his sacred heart that looked like a pimiento, the Good Shepherd leading sheep that looked like marshmallows or stuffed toys.

But as a nine-year-old, she'd loved them. Perhaps because there were, in her house, no pictures at all. A crucifix on the wall. Her First Communion photo, her parents' wedding photo. A wooden board for hanging keys, with little girls in polka-dot bonnets painted around the hooks, and in polka-dot script the words "Don't forget."

And perhaps Sister Imelda's shame and secrecy about the holy cards had made them doubly precious to her, made her look at them only in secret, in the privacy of her room. She loved sorting them, arranging them into categories. Crucifixions. Agonies in the Garden. Resurrections. Annunciations. Visitations. Nativities. Virgin Marys. So when her colleagues at Yale marveled at her facility in spotting iconic patterns, they thought it had been achieved through a kind of scholarly grunt work. They didn't know that she'd learned it sitting on the shag carpet of her bedroom in Milwaukee, hoping her mother wouldn't shout that she had to set the table. Or do something for her father. That was how she'd found herself, what she believed would be her life's work: looking carefully at images, being carried to a past which at first was lodged in her imagination but now, because of her training, was propped up by a firm knowledge of the time, the technique that the images represented.

But Sister Patricia had found her out and said, "Theresa, it's very nice that Sister Imelda gives you these things, but let me show you some other images that are really much more interesting." She gave her a book of images of Joan of Arc, and holy cards with slanted script by another nun, Sister Corita, that said things like "Hope," and "Our Hearts Are on Fire."

"That's the kind of thing you want to keep in your mind, Theresa," Sister Patricia had said. Being hopeful, being on fire, like Joan of Arc, who stood for what she believed in, stood up to powerful men, afraid of nothing. A girl, only a girl, just like you, poor and uneducated, much poorer, much less well educated than you, but powerful because of her own belief in herself and what she knew to be right. That's the kind of thing you should be thinking of, Theresa, not these martyrs.

She'd taken Joan as her confirmation name, and so, when she met Joan Gallagher, it seemed another confirmation: of the rightness of her choice.

She was here because of them, she could trace everything to them. The nuns, who had sent her when she was still in high school to Joan Gallagher.

For the medieval section of her world history class in junior year, Sister Jackie had allowed her to write on Giotto. They had spent a very long time studying St. Francis, the Franciscan movement, much longer than they spent on the Crusades. Sister Jackie loved St. Francis; the Crusades upset and shamed her. She told her students that the Crusades were a blot on the history of the Church, but St. Francis was a pure flower. Pure. It was a word they were not afraid to use, the nuns, and afterwards Joan Gallagher. Sister Jackie and Sister Maureen often spoke of purity of intention; Joan Gallagher spoke of purity of line and form. But when she lectured about Giotto and his work on the Assisi basilica, she pointed out that if Francis's followers had followed his lead, his insistence on austerity and simplicity, there would be no basilica. If Francis had been obeyed, she said, there would have been no Giotto.

They had sent her paper on Giotto to Joan Gallagher, who taught art history at the college run by the order: Divine Word College. Joan Gallagher had invited her to come to the college for a day. She had been offered a full scholarship, including room and board. Joan Gallagher had assured Theresa that she would give her very full attention. And she had, insisting she learn Latin, reading her papers with a demanding exigent eye that Theresa would learn only later was extraordinary for an undergraduate teacher. Working with her hour after hour on her application to Yale, where Joan Gallagher had determined she should go. To work with her old friend, Professor Tom Ferguson.

A heart on fire. Purity of intention. Purity of form. What a joke it was now, their faith in her. They'd be ashamed of her if they knew. They'd be terribly disappointed. Their prize a fraud: Theresa Joan Riordan. Well, she was hardly Joan of Arc. What name should she have taken for confirmation? Magdalen? No, that would have been too grand for what had happened, which had been, after all, quite a small thing, undistinguished.

It wasn't long after Confirmation that she developed breasts. Breasts that she believed were an embarrassment to everyone. When she was twelve, her mother took her shopping for her first bra and she felt her mother was mortified. "I didn't mean for this to happen," she wanted to say to everyone, as she now wanted to say to everyone, "He was a weak man."

None of the women she admired had large breasts. Joan Gallagher was straight and slim and boyish. She wore trouser suits and flat shoes and her hair was cut very short. You wouldn't say that she was mannish, only that her femaleness didn't get in the way. You didn't have to think about it. But Theresa knew that how she looked was something she had to attend to. Making sure people weren't thinking about her body. She deliberately bought clothes that were too big for her. Once Sister Ann Claire, who Theresa would never have believed thought about clothes—all she ever wore were navy blue skirts and white shirts or sweaters—said to her, "Theresa, you should wear clothes more appropriate to your age. You're a lovely girl, it's a gift from God, don't try to hide it."

But if all that started up, "all that" was the way she thought of it— boys coming around, boys wanting her attention—it would be one more thing for her mother to contend with. And with Theresa's father, they had their hands full. There wasn't room in their lives for one more difficult thing.

She had some memories of a healthy father. Being held in strong arms, being pushed on a swing. Her father had been a construction worker, and a beam had fallen on his spine. He'd walked out of the house in the morning a healthy man, a strong man, husband of his wife, father of his four-year-old daughter. He had come back ruined, a cripple, a child.

He was away from them a long time, two years in rehabilitation, where they were teaching him to walk or walk a bit with the aid of a walker, so at least he could take himself back and forth to the bathroom.

Or they would never have sent him home. If he hadn't been able to take himself to the bathroom, they would have kept him there forever.

He had the mind of a child, a pleasant cheerful child. They had no idea what he understood. He was almost wholly silent.

They'd longed to have him home, the both of them. She was nearly seven the day they went to pick him up. For two years, her weeks had been shaped by Sunday visits. Wake up now, you don't want to be late for Daddy, don't wiggle while I braid your hair, Daddy wants to see a pretty girl. She'd dreamed of a life not shaped by those Sunday visits and their accompanying dread. Wards of grey-skinned men, their legs disgustingly bare in short hospital gowns, tubes coming from their arms or noses, bags full of liquids whose source and provenance she didn't want to know.

For a while, just having him home made everyone happy. For a while. But only for a while. For a while, he was her mother's prize, her big child, whom she would help dress and help to settle himself in front of the television. For a while they believed he would get better. Theresa was happy just to be in his presence. But after three months, or six months was it, she and her mother realized that the happy time of their life was over. Without saying it, they both knew that they missed their leisurely breakfasts, just the two of them, without the father to be tended to, their evenings of watching TV in a living room that was a living room, not something dominated by a hospital bed. Days when they could go shopping or to a movie without the fear that he had fallen, hurt himself, died.

Her mother, never a patient woman, now grew chronically short-tempered. The part-time nurses were undependable; some days they wouldn't show up and Theresa's mother would have to stay home. The insurance company she worked for was understanding, but Theresa's mother knew her husband's needs jeopardized her position. "I've given up all hope of job advancement. I'll just stay where I am till I die. If I'm lucky enough that they keep me."

Theresa knew her mother wished there was some way to send her husband back to rehab, some way that wouldn't lead the parish, especially Father Anstey, who was strict about family obligations, to think of her as an unloving woman, a monster of selfishness. A failure as a

Christian and a wife. But Theresa didn't want her father to go away again. His presence nourished her; she always felt his goodwill towards her was unequivocal, as her mother's was not. They would often sit quietly, watching television. She would talk to him about what she'd learned at school. She had no idea what he understood. But he smiled and nodded, and she told herself that he was pleased. Sometimes if she came home early, she'd see him with his head in his hands. He might have been crying; she didn't want to know.

"Your mother's a saint to keep everything up," Sister Peg had said to her, when she was ten years old. She was the first to tell her, but by no means the last, "You must never let her down."

She had understood that. She had never given offense, never failed, taken every honor. She treasured the half smile on her mother's face with the news of every prize, every time her name was called for special recognition. Her abashed pleasure when Joan Gallagher had said to her mother, "She's the real thing, your daughter. The real thing."

It was Joan Gallagher who had put her in the path of Tom Ferguson. They'd been graduate students together at Penn. Sometimes she wanted to shout at Joan Gallagher, "You ought to have kept me from him. You ought to have known."

But it was no one's fault but her own. Tom Ferguson was a weak man; she'd been the one to make things happen. It was all over now and no one was the wiser. She was grateful, at least for that. And if she'd gone through what she'd gone through because Joan Gallagher had put her in Tom Ferguson's path, well, she was here for the same reason, on the train from Pisa to Lucca.

When, leaving for New Haven, Theresa had thanked Joan Gallagher for everything she'd done, she'd said, "It's in my interest. You'll come back here, teach in the department next to me, we'll keep something going. We'll make sure it's not all lost. But you'll go farther than I, I can tell. You're not so distracted by ordinary life as I am."

Theresa had been hurt by that. She had wanted to say, "Ordinary life was a luxury my mother and I couldn't afford." She had read Tom Ferguson's *Italian Sculpture 1300–1500,* in awe of the daring, the bravado, so different from Joan Gallagher's careful exigent prose. She couldn't believe she would be studying with him.

"First of all, Theresa, you're a wonderful student, fantastically well qualified. And second, Tom Ferguson will do anything I tell him. I've known him since he was twenty-two, straight out of the University of Illinois. Before he met the lovely Amaryllis. He was the son of someone who owned a stationery store in Normal, Illinois. Parents who loved him but thought it would be better if he went in for something practical. Oh, how he rails against his parents, even now, twenty years later, compares them with Amaryllis's fabulous forebears. It makes me quite sick, and I tell him that. I think he likes it that I keep him in line. When he doesn't resent it, that is. He's made all the right moves, married a rich woman, tenure at Yale. The fact that he's lost his soul in the process seems to be, to him, neither here nor there. Nevertheless, he has a first-rate mind. Nothing's affected that."

"I've come a long way, a very long way. You and I, we know about something that a lot of these others don't," he'd said to her in bed one night. Perhaps he was tired, or had had too much wine. Usually, he made no allusion to his past.

For a while, she believed the choices he'd made had rendered Joan Gallagher's pathetic. He'd pushed his way to the front. Were his initial gifts superior to Joan's? She knew they weren't, but they weren't inferior, she couldn't diminish his accomplishments, his learning. His Latin was the envy of all the classicists. His memory for images was so great he could use it as a party trick. And he could understand all the theoreticians, although, on the whole, he dismissed them. Learning that there were treasures to be explored in Budapest, he was teaching himself Hungarian, a language everyone agreed was impossible.

And yet everyone sort of knew that the kind of career he had was partly due to his marriage.

The face of Amaryllis Ferguson is suddenly on the Italian train. *Leave now. Don't you see what I've done to be away from you. I am in Italy. You can't follow me.* But the words didn't sound right in her ear. Theresa wasn't the kind of person for this overwrought diction. For crying out, even in the privacy of her own mind. Particularly crying out to a woman sitting comfortably in her living room in Stonington,

Connecticut, listening to bluegrass while she sat at her loom. "We can't afford that kind of dramatics," her mother would say if Theresa ever seemed upset about something.

She made herself focus on the silver leaves of the olive trees. She made herself listen to the women gossiping in the seat behind her, trying to make out their Italian. I will not, will not, she told herself, think of Amaryllis Ferguson. Or her husband. Because that is who he is.

"You can't imagine how impressed I was by her family," he'd said, when they had hardly been lovers for two weeks. "I owe them so much. I was a lump when I met her, a lively lump, but a lump nevertheless. The original overachiever. The original overachieving boy. My God, then I thought everything was exciting."

And now, she wanted to say, you think nothing is.

He explained to her, making sure that she understood the significance, that when he met Amaryllis her father was the Sterling Professor at Princeton. "Author of the landmark, and I mean the landmark, Theresa, you can't understand how important his work was then, the landmark book on the Rococo. A period that still isn't given its due: He was a real pioneer. A most remarkable man, my father-in-law. After a while, I think, he grew to like me, though I know for a long time he thought I was a pretentious upstart. Just before he died, he said to me, 'You know, Tom, I've spent a life studying the decorations of a frivolous and wasteful people. Was it a frivolous and wasteful pursuit, would you say? A frivolous and wasteful life?' I think it meant a lot to him when I said, 'Oh now, John, what you've done will live after you. Will live forever.'"

But would it? Theresa wasn't sure what would live forever; she wasn't sure if anyone would even be reading books in twenty years, by the time she had children, to say nothing of grandchildren. And was it something that was worth a life, analyzing the social implications of things almost no one cared about? But she wouldn't say that. Not to Tom Ferguson, whom she so admired. With whom she was in love.

"And of course the marriage was a great romance," Tom said. "You know who Amaryllis's mother was?"

"I don't," Theresa said apologetically. Although she didn't know why he was telling her all about his wife's parents when he was in bed with her. When he had just become her lover. Her first lover, though she believed he didn't know that. What had happened to her hymen? She'd been afraid of the pain of her first encounter, but it hadn't arrived. Had she fallen off a bicycle? Had she been born a freak? Or was it just a lifelong habit of stoicism that made her not notice what other people would call pain?

"You've heard of Millicent MacCarthy?"

"I'm afraid I haven't," she said. Shame at her ignorance caused her to cover her breasts with the sheet.

"I'm sure you'd recognize her face. She was a great star in the thirties. British of course. Playing opposite Alec Guinness and that lot in the early Ealing films."

"The Alec Guinness that was in *Star Wars*?"

"God bless your limited little brain. Is it that you haven't seen anything produced before nineteen seventy? No, that's not true, you've seen quite a lot produced before sixteen hundred. But my God, my darling, there are serious gaps. Which I'm thrilled to be filling in." He made a comic lascivious face.

"Of course," he said, "you're streets away from some of your cohort, who believe that because they've seen every film noir ever made, it doesn't matter that they haven't read Dante."

"I've read Dante in the original," she said, and then was mortified at how she sounded, how ridiculous it was to be saying this when she was naked in her lover's bed.

"Of course you have, my darling," he said, nuzzling her. "I used to think they'd done you a terrible disservice, keeping you in that backwater little college. But I had to understand that, intellectually, you're better prepared than almost any student I've had. But it's as if you were some sort of princess of a minor country, educated in the palace, but forbidden to walk the streets. Joan, of course, crammed you with an incredible amount of good stuff. But you've never taken part in the rough-and-tumble, the scrimmage with your peers that's so good for sharpening and toughening the mind. So in some ways you're a sort of innocent savant, aren't you. Luckily, you have the skin and breasts of a Titian so I'm entirely at your feet."

"Rapture" was the word that went through her mind as he put his mouth on her breasts. I am feeling rapture. And she could hear her mother's voice saying, "Rapture is not something the likes of us can afford." But her mother's voice was quite soon very easy to drown out.

She had never been happier. Part of her joy came from the element of surprise. She had never thought of this happening to her. When she thought of her future in relation to men, she felt hopeless. She had no model into which she could fit herself in relation to a man. Sometimes she thought it would be nice to be married to someone like Harrison Ford. But what would it mean to be married to Harrison Ford? She hardly knew any men. Her father hardly qualified as a man. And she'd gone to school apart from men and boys until Yale.

She knew she didn't want a marriage like Joan Gallagher's; she was married to someone she couldn't talk to about her work. Her husband was a podiatrist. Tom had said she'd married him just because she had an instinct for the perverse. "I think it's because her father was an undertaker. Actually made a fortune in funeral parlors." Theresa didn't know what the connection was. But she would never have wanted to be part of a marriage that anyone could so easily mock.

Without even knowing how to dream of a man, she realized that Tom Ferguson was the man of her dreams. A partner in looking. A man who looked at her with the same joyful attention with which he looked at great works of art. As she looked at him.

She was the one who'd made the first move. She waited until she was no longer taking courses with him, waited until the summer after her first year. At first he resisted, but she knew that it was just a gesture; he rather easily gave in. She knew all about his wife. She knew he could never be hers, not really. But it didn't matter. For now, they shared everything important. And she knew she was important to him, was giving him something his wife couldn't give. Hadn't he said to her, "It's like a miracle, working with you, guiding you, bringing you along. It's brought me back to life"? Hadn't he said, "It's as if we saw with the same pair of eyes"? He sent her a postcard from the Art Institute of Chicago; he was in the city for a conference. It was of a Titian Danaë: a nude stretched out, yearning, her eyes fixed on the gold about to be showered down upon her from the invisible god in the sky. On the back of the postcard he wrote, "Ever think about acquiring a little dog? But don't worry, I'm not asking for a golden shower." It was only then that she noticed, beside the Danaë's bed, a small brown dog curled up like a mushroom. She didn't know what he meant by a golden shower, so she Googled it, and was shocked that such a thing existed, and very glad that he didn't know that she'd had no idea what the phrase meant.

She understood that by sending her the card he meant to say he thought her beautiful. Oh, he'd said she was beautiful, but by comparing her to a Titian he was saying her beauty had the importance of a great work of art. So she began to look at herself in a new way. She'd always liked her hair, but now she began to admire it. Her breasts, which had been nothing but a vexation, now seemed a prize. She wondered what she could do to highlight her eyes' greenness.

For the first time, she was really living away from home, and not in a dorm down the street from the nuns. She felt lucky in her roommate, Leila, who knew about clothes and makeup. Lucky that their coloring was similar. She asked her about eye shadow. Leila was glad to advise and then began to invite Theresa out for evenings with her friends at a student bar. So now Theresa was part of a crowd of people her own age. After a while, she grew bold enough to ask Leila's advice about where to get sexier underwear. She was embarrassed at her sensible underwear, which, as she told Leila (hoping to make a joke of her inadequacy), could have belonged to her high school principal, who was a nun in her seventies.

"Who's the lucky man?" Leila asked.

"No one you know," Theresa said. She could tell Leila was disappointed not to be taken into her confidence. Leila was studying physics; she'd never have heard of Tom Ferguson, wouldn't have recognized him if she saw him on the street.

He wasn't a popular teacher. Medieval sculpture, 1300–1500, wasn't, as he said, a sexy topic. As a lecturer, he was both dry and sarcastic. Students felt he was reading the same lecture over and over; she'd heard them say that. His graduate students were more complimentary, but he was only working with one other besides Theresa. Graduate students didn't want to work with him because he wasn't a departmental star; he'd written only the one book, which, though highly praised, was thought to be a bit arrière-garde by the more theoretically minded. She liked to think that most people didn't appreciate Tom as she did, that she was the one who saw his greatness, treasured his brilliance, understood the full implications of his thought. He wasn't afraid to show his enthusiasm for the things he loved, to use words like "greatness" and "beauty." Even "purity of form." He had introduced her to Civitali, shown her the polychrome sculpture *An Allegory of Modesty,* which was part of Yale's permanent collection, but not on view. She had seen it, and her heart had been on fire. The seated figure, her knees apart, her face confident, even mocking, her delicate hands indicating a calm certainty, a balance, a sure sense of who she was. She had felt the hair on the back of her neck stand up when she saw it, and the words came to her, "This is mine."

And later, when they were lovers, it was a joke between them, that Modesty had brought them together, that Modesty had brought them to abandon, to extravagant pleasure, rapturous bodily joy.

With Leila's help, she bought a peach-colored underwire bra, half lace, half satin, and matching bikini underpants.

"Jesus, you're lucky to have those tits," Leila said. Theresa was shocked to hear someone use the word "tits" in relation to her body.

"They can be a real pain," Theresa said. "I could never really run without real discomfort."

"Oh, spare me," Leila said. "Any woman with half a brain would give her eyeteeth for what you have."

"It's not true, Leila. I have a terrible time buying clothes that fit."

But they both knew Theresa didn't really mean it. Once she would have. But not now.

She wasn't very good at going out with people her own age. Some of Leila's friends flirted with her, but she had no idea how to flirt back and Leila agreed that she was, "for some reason, sort of hopeless at it. You just have to relax."

But it didn't matter. None of those boys mattered. They were boys. She had Tom Ferguson. He was her lover, the man who called her a Titian. Who said the two of them saw with one pair of eyes. She slept with his book next to her bed. When she was lonely for him, she ran her fingers over his name, embossed in gold on the book's spine.

How could weedy graduate students with earrings and ponytails compare, with their pitiful come-on lines? ("Shall I tell you a dream I had about you last night? I'm afraid it was X-rated.")

He never said he loved her, and she respected him for that. He made a point of it. "I can't stand saying those words. 'I love you.' They always sound false, as if I were doing something expected of me. The expected thing. And I've had a bellyful of that."

He said that was the thing about his parents that was unbearable to him. Why he only went back to Normal, Illinois, once a year. Even the name, he said . . .

"What drove me around the bend about my parents, what makes them so incredibly different from Amaryllis's parents, is that they assume there's only one way of doing things, one right way, and either they know it or they're terrified that they can't figure it out. It always made me feel suffocated. Whereas, the first time I had dinner with Amaryllis's parents, it was like heaven. People talking about ideas, people from all over the world, in and out of their home, taking their places at the table, living such immensely various lives. The range of possibilities they represented! The range of responses."

"But of course your parents wouldn't have had the opportunities of your in-laws," she said.

"There speaks the little democrat, as always in the voice of truth. But my dear, you see, however right you are, and I don't deny for a moment that you are right, nothing you say can stop my sense of suffocation when I'm with my parents, or my sense of pleasure when I'm around intelligent, sophisticated people. However inferior they may be in the eyes of God, who has the good fortune never to be bored."

She took his words about suffocation to heart. She knew she must be on her guard: never to bore him, never to make him feel suffocated. If she saw that happening, she would make the move to leave, as she had made the move to become his lover.

He often talked about his wife. "She hasn't had an easy time of it. She often feels she was a disappointment to her parents. They were such stars, you see, in every way, in so many worlds. And I'm afraid that Amaryllis felt she couldn't keep up. It's only recently that she's really found herself. With her weaving."

"Weaving?"

"Yes, she's wonderful at it, absolutely wonderful." And he talked about her summers away in Maine, working with "a master weaver." And Theresa thought: If she's away in the summers, he'll have more time for me.

"It does her a world of good, I think, getting away from here, going to a place where she's her own person, where no one's even heard of her parents. Or me, for that matter. I don't want you to think of Amaryllis as pathetic. She's not pathetic, you know. She's quite a going concern."

A going concern? she wanted to say. What kind of way is that to talk about your wife? As if she were an investment you'd been afraid you were going to lose money on that seemed to be, just recently, in the black.

She wanted to tell him that it was a terrible way to refer to his wife. And she wanted to ask him not to talk about his wife to her. She wondered if he told Amaryllis he loved her. She was sure he never told his wife she was beautiful. That would have been impossible. She was not beautiful. Not by any standards. Not by any standards in the world.

Theresa had seen her only once, dropping something off at Tom's office. She was much too thin. It had been said it wasn't possible to be too thin, but there were kinds of thinness that were undesirable. Amaryllis's hair was thin and taffy-colored, and she pinned it to the top of her head in a way that looked uncomfortable. The hairpins were too visible; you could too clearly imagine them painful against her scalp. There were thin red veins all over her face. Was she a drinker? And she dressed in vivid colors—ruby-red tunic, sapphire wide-legged pants— that exaggerated her starved look.

Theresa disliked herself for having these critical thoughts about another woman, a woman close to her own mother's age. She wished somehow that he'd arranged it so that she'd never seen Amaryllis. But that, of course, wasn't his fault. She had seen the wife before she was his lover.

Then he insisted on her coming to dinner at his house, the dinner they gave every year for graduate students and particularly serious undergrads.

"I just wouldn't feel right, Tom. I just couldn't."

"It's important to me to normalize the situation as much as possible. So that if the two of you met on the street, it wouldn't be awkward. I've mentioned you. She knows I think you're an excellent student."

So I must go through hours of Purgatory to save you a minute of awkwardness on the street, she thought, wondering where the word "Purgatory" came from. Was it from Dante or was it from Sister Imelda, telling her to pray to the souls in Purgatory so she would never oversleep? She hoped it was Dante. She didn't want to be thinking of Sister Imelda now.

The house he lived in wasn't the one she expected. She supposed it should be thought of as *her* house. Amaryllis's house. The house of his wife. She'd found herself, Tom had said, in weaving, and when he said that, Theresa had imagined the woman looking into a tangle of threads and finding an image of herself—her thin, unlovely countenance part of a larger fabric. None of the people who had been important to Theresa had had any respect for the domestic arts. The people she knew—they were all women—feared the entrapment of such things, the distraction from what was really important or, in her mother's case, one more demand threatening her survival. She couldn't imagine that Tom really respected his wife's weaving. She thought it was kind that he pretended to.

Theresa had imagined them living in a converted farmhouse, with exposed beams, old pottery (French or Italian), brought back from his travels: the head of a saint given to him by a grateful collector, perhaps a small polychrome wooden statue, since that was his area of expertise. But the house was modern Scandinavian: light wood and glass, the furniture all white but draped with what Theresa assumed were Amaryllis's weavings, all in what Theresa imagined were called earth tones but which seemed to her only various shades of brown.

Four of Tom's students had been invited, three undergraduates and his other doctoral student, who had just arrived from a research trip to Siena.

"Leif Erikson," a young man said, thrusting a reddish hand in her direction. At first, Theresa thought it was some sort of geography quiz. Then she remembered that Tom's other doctoral student was named Leif Erikson. He was slight and well made; his feet, though, seemed like doll's feet, too small for an adult; his eyelashes were white; she wondered if he were albino. But no, he was merely very light blond, and his thick glasses, fashionably red-framed, made his eyelashes look even whiter. She couldn't stop thinking of rabbits, and the combination of rabbits and Vikings made her want to laugh, so instead of introducing herself, she simply nodded. But she was glad that she could even think of laughing at him. She'd feared him, jealously. Suppose Tom thought he was better than her.

"I've heard you're disgustingly learned, that's what Herr Doktor Professor says."

"Oh, no, I've just . . . I don't know . . . there are just some things I seem to have under my belt."

The words "under my belt" made her think of what was under her belt, and she thought of her own body and she wanted to say to Leif Erikson, "Tom is my lover," and fearing that the words would somehow slip out, she once again went silent.

Where was he? Where was Tom? Shouldn't he be greeting his guests, making introductions, easing the way? Theresa hadn't had much experience at adult parties, or parties of any kind, and her eye wandered desperately around the living room, looking for him. Finally, he appeared from the kitchen, carrying a tray with a pitcher of clear liquids and six glasses, beautifully shaped, and inviting.

"Martinis," he said, "guaranteed to loosen everyone up. Theresa, you've arrived. Let me serve you."

Oh yes, serve me, comfort me with apples for I am sick of love, she wanted to say to him.

Amaryllis came out of the kitchen then, carrying a tray of hors d'oeuvres. She passed them around: pigs in blankets, pastry triangles, squares of brown bread with smoked salmon and thin fronds of dill.

"Now I know everyone really wants the pigs in blankets, but fears that will reveal them as déclassé, forcing them to select what they in fact do not desire, but resist the impulse, follow your bliss."

Tom laughed much too loud at this. Theresa thought it wasn't that funny. Would she have to introduce herself to Amaryllis? Shouldn't Tom have done that? He wasn't a good host, she thought, even her limited experience of host behavior told her this.

"Mrs. Ferguson, I'm Theresa Riordan," she said, not holding out her hand because Amaryllis was holding a tray and she didn't want to make things awkward for her.

"Oh yes, the Titian," she said, looking Theresa up and down. "But you're not working on Titian, you're doing those boyish Madonnas, aren't you. Working against type."

Why had she called Theresa the Titian? What had Tom told her?

"The great movie stars of the thirties were all androgynous," one of the undergraduates said. She herself was pencil-thin with a shock of straight black hair. She was dressed entirely in black except for a pair of orange suede boots, high-heeled with toes so pointy they made Theresa's own toes ache. Theresa thought what she said about the movies was in response to Amaryllis's comment about boyish Madonnas.

The mention of movie stars—or was it the martinis—suddenly engendered a kind of conversation that reminded Theresa of puppies falling out of a basket.

"Garbo, Hepburn, Katharine I mean, Dietrich. All a bit iffy in the femininity department," said another undergraduate, whose name, Theresa remembered, was Tristan, and whose father was a diplomat.

"Of course we really don't know what we mean when we say 'feminine,'" said the woman with the impressive boots.

"Oh, get off it for one minute, Camilla," said Tristan. "Stop playing more feminist than thou."

"Well, anyone's more feminist than thou, Tristan," Camilla said.

"It's an interesting distinction, though, isn't it, the difference between the words 'womanly,' 'feminine,' 'female,'" Tom said.

He was the professor, so everyone nodded and waited for the next thing he would say. But Theresa knew he was talking about her, talking to her, sending encoded messages that meant *you are desirable.*

"I mean to say," he went on, "you wouldn't say Marilyn Monroe was feminine. But she certainly was female. But would you say she was womanly? With all that implies of the maternal, the protective. She always seemed so in need of protection, impossible to imagine her mothering anyone. But female: absolutely, absolutely that."

"With his usual brilliant incisiveness, my husband has jumped to the heart of the matter. Asserting that Marilyn Monroe is female. Absolutely top drawer, darling," Amaryllis said.

"Thank you, darling, for the spousal vote of confidence."

And Theresa was thinking: You are all talking about the bodies of women, but none of your talk is real. What is real is his desire for my body, which, whether or not he loves me, is absolutely real.

"Your mother was an actress, wasn't she, Mrs. Ferguson?" Tristan said.

"Yes, but she'd never have wanted to be called a star. She loathed the whole Hollywood star system. She simply thought of herself as a professional. Acting was what she did. It was her business, her livelihood. She never took herself too seriously. Or anything else, for that matter. My God, she could make mincemeat of my father's colleagues who thought their little ivory tower was the world, and that the center of the world was Princeton."

"She was someone who was able to portray both intelligence and desirability," Tristan said.

"Oh, God, yes, my mother had no trouble broadcasting sex, in her hypercivilized way. Believe me, I know more about my mother's sex life than I ever wanted to."

Theresa was mortified, but the others seemed to be enjoying the revelation and they all laughed. She was disturbed by both Tom's and his wife's habits of saying critical things about their parents. In public. To strangers. She would never have dreamed of saying anything critical about her mother, never have dreamed of saying that now she looked like a third-rate country-western singer and her new husband was a bore and a slob. Or that she didn't know what a fellowship was. She would never have exposed her mother in that way; her life had been too hard. And it would have been unthinkable to say anything critical about her father, whose life had been a ruin. But perhaps criticizing their parents in public was something Tom and Amaryllis had in common. Maybe criticizing their parents brought them closer. They had, Theresa reminded herself, been married over twenty years. But although she was his wife, and got to have a life beside him and to call him hers, Theresa didn't envy her. Amaryllis Ferguson was not a desirable woman. Tom would never say to her as he said, over and over to Theresa, "I adore your body. Yours is the body I adore."

And of course Amaryllis couldn't understand his work. "She takes a kind of pride in not being intellectual," Tom had said. "Growing up as she did, she's fed up to the teeth with it. Of course, she's highly intelligent. But she puts more stock in the intuitive, and what she calls the intelligence of the hand."

"What movies do you like?" Camilla asked Theresa. Theresa knew she was trying to be kind, trying to include her in the conversation. But it was always the case when anyone asked her a direct question—her mind went blank.

"I don't go to the movies much," she said.

"Yes, well, there is something premodern about Theresa, isn't there?" Tom said.

"Maybe she's been alive for hundreds of years," said Camilla, giggling. "Maybe she's a vampire."

Was she drunk? Theresa wondered. Was she trying to be friendly, to include Theresa in a joke? Or was she being aggressive because she thought Tom favored Theresa? The last, she believed.

"Maybe we should stay away from her during the full moon," Tristan said.

"Vampires are the new locus of the sexual imaginary," said Leif Erikson, who hadn't spoken.

"As long as it's just imaginary," Amaryllis said. "The curry needs me. I hear it crying out, Help me, help me, I'm ready."

Where had they learned it, all of them, this way of talking, this exaggeration, this leaping from branch to branch like frantic monkeys, not knowing if any branch would hold or, if it broke, what the damage might be? Tom was following his wife into the kitchen, carrying two trays.

Theresa couldn't taste anything. Lamb curry, she'd been told, but it might have been anything. She had said nothing through the whole dinner. She wondered when it would be possible for her to leave.

Amaryllis tapped her wineglass with the edge of her knife.

"Those of you who've been here before know that we always end every dinner party with a ritual. I'm afraid we're boringly famous for it. Everyone must sing for his or her supper. One song, a song from your childhood, or whatever you consider your home."

Apparently, they'd all been here before. None of them seemed surprised. They all seemed ready. Camilla sang a song from the Auvergne, where her parents had honeymooned and where, she said, she may very well have been conceived. Leif sang a sea shanty; his father loved to sail. Tristan, of course, sang a melody from *Tristan und Isolde*. Tom and Amaryllis made a duet of "Foggy, Foggy Dew." Theresa was in a panic. She couldn't think of a single song. There had been no singing in her family; there had been no family dinners. Only the problem of getting her father fed and ready for bed, and then Theresa and her mother settling down in front of the TV, eating their dinner off trays. Because of her father, they didn't join her mother's sisters and their families for holidays. It was too difficult to get help on Thanksgiving and Christmas, and, quite soon, they never even thought of it.

"I really don't sing," she said. "I have a terrible voice."

"Nonsense, we're all friends here," Amaryllis said. "Nobody's judging you. It's all just good fun."

The table went silent. Everyone's eyes were on her. Fun, she wanted to say. You think this is fun? I think it is simply hell.

He wasn't looking at her. He was looking at his plate. She didn't want to embarrass him; she didn't want him to find her wanting, pathetic. She thought of Joan of Arc. A song came to her. She would sing it now.

"Puff, the magic dragon, lived by the sea," she began.

But the minute the words were out of her mouth, she saw that she had made a mistake, that in trying to save him and herself from embarrassment, she had embarrassed him even more. It was a ridiculous song. They had invoked Auvergne, Wagner, the Appalachian, the great Atlantic. She had invoked her own impoverishment, her own lack of right to be where she was.

"Wasn't that supposed to be a song about marijuana?" Tristan asked.

"Well, they didn't tell us that in Catholic school," Theresa said, and everybody laughed, as though she had at least been witty. But she had simply told the truth. She understood that the necessary ingredient in all their talk was mockery; self-mockery was fine if it included a mockery of one's own past, one's own family, one's own education.

"I suppose by the time you came along, they'd completely given up the Latin and all the wonderful traditional trappings," Amaryllis said. "I don't suppose you learned Gregorian chant? Such a perfect form, so simple."

"Theresa's a fabulous Latinist though," said Tom.

"Sweet to think of you among those little nuns," Amaryllis said.

She wanted to say: They're not little nuns. They visit people on death row. They hire ex-cons to do their yard work, and face up to their neighbors' complaints. They stand up to the bishops, who could ruin them financially. One of the "little nuns" you think you know something about is traveling around the country with other "little nuns" gathering support to resist an imposition of male authority, restating the Vatican's order that they have a male cleric supervising all their meetings. What have you ever done that takes one tenth their guts? she wished she could say. But after all, she was implicated in the woman's betrayal; she was her husband's lover. She could only be silent as Amaryllis Ferguson made a crude parody of the lives of women she loved.

"Well, she's a protégée of Joan Gallagher's, Ammie," Tom said.

"Oh, my Lord, the terrifying Joan. It always took me a week to recover from an evening with her. Such an exhausting display of intellectual energy. Positively Amazonian. I had no choice but to take to my bed afterwards. That is, when I worked up the courage to encounter her. Usually I just hid. You can imagine my ecstasy when I learned she'd married a podiatrist. I adore imagining what kinky things they get up to with corn plasters and arch supports."

Theresa wondered how Joan Gallagher would have behaved at this table. But Joan Gallagher would not have had Theresa's secret. That hers was the body the host adored.

And she wouldn't have had the other secret that washed over her when her mind wasn't entirely engaged. That her period was six days late.

"Your wife knows about us," she said, the next time they were together in the Days Inn near Bridgeport.

"Don't be an idiot," he said. "That's just your Catholic guilt."

"She knows about us, Tom. I can tell."

"Even if she did, we have an understanding, and we have for years."

The words sickened her. She always knew she wasn't the first. But now he'd made it clear.

"You're lucky I'm addicted to you, or I'd say you were too much of a silly goose to waste my time on. And I have a bit of good news. Amaryllis is going to a crafts fair in Vermont all next week. So we have a bit more time. And we can stop throwing away the family fortune on this hideous room with the blankets made of some petroleum product."

I love this room, she wanted to say. This room and all the other rooms exactly like it. Because it is where I am with you.

When she was with him, she felt she was inhabiting a world as full and beautiful as any of the paintings she loved. A world that had the intensity of Bellini's skies, the vividness of Mantegna's apples, the richness of Bronzino's draperies. It had nothing to do with the rest of their lives. With his wife or her mother or Joan Gallagher or Sister Maureen or Sister Imelda. It had nothing to do with the past or the future. They were together. They were happy. The time they had was the only time.

"I wouldn't feel right being in your wife's bed."

"Neither would I," he said, "there's a foldout couch in my study."

"Can we spend the night?"

"Can't risk it," he said, kissing her shoulders. "Nosy neighbors. One day I'll take you somewhere fabulous. For more than just one night."

"Promise," she said, knowing she sounded like a child. She put her arms around his neck.

She felt odd sitting on the toilet that she knew his wife had sat on. On the rack across from it, a bra and underpants were drying. She knew it was wrong, but she couldn't stop herself touching them. They were white cotton, stiff from the wash. She picked up the brassiere. The cups were small; she checked the size: 34A, it said. She stopped herself from holding her own bra against it so that she could compare.

"What's happened to you in there? Are you all right?"

Did he know she might not be all right? Did he know how many times she went into the bathroom to check if her period had come? It was nine days late. She told herself she would wait till day ten, then buy a pregnancy test at the drugstore.

He was sitting at his desk in the study. He'd put what had been their bed together; now it was an innocent monkish couch. For the first time, she looked at what was on the walls; they were covered with pen and ink drawings. A woman with the body of a bird carried the tiny body of a terrified-looking man in her beak. In another, she pecked at his intestines. In another, the bird carried wool in her beak, the remainder of what she'd used to tie up the helpless male.

"What do you think?" he asked.

"Very well done," she said, her voice tight with anxiety. She thought they were ugly, almost wicked in their ugliness.

"Are you saying that just because you know they're mine?"

"I didn't know they were yours."

"Are you too formalist a critic to comment on the subject matter?"

"I'd rather not."

"Don't be a coward."

"I don't have any thoughts."

"You always have thoughts."

"I don't, Tom, honestly."

"I call them 'Portrait of a Marriage.'"

"Don't, Tom please," she said.

"Why not? Amaryllis is crazy about them. She's always after me to do more."

"She's not hurt by them?"

"She thinks they're hilarious. She's a terrific sport, you know."

No one should have to be that good a sport, she thought, feeling, for the first time, a withdrawal from him.

He told her to sit on the couch and read something while he made coffee. The couch was covered by one of Amaryllis's weavings, reddish brown, like everything else she made. Theresa was trying not to look at the drawings. She saw on the shelf a book about Simone Martini, which she'd wanted to take from the library. She thought she'd ask him if she could borrow it for a while.

Focusing on the Assisi Freschi, she felt, quite suddenly, a loosening in her lower body. A wetness. Then a gushing. And she knew she had to move quickly. Her period had come. She stood up. Her underpants were drenched in blood. She was horrified at what she knew was a disgusting sight. Then a new horror overtook her. She looked down at the weaving that covered the couch. It, too, was drenched.

She felt covered in panic, wanting to run to the bathroom but afraid she'd leave a trail of blood. He appeared at the door, holding two mugs of coffee.

"Tom," she said. "I need your help."

She extended her hand, then beckoned for him to come closer. But he stayed in the doorway, as if he were poised for a quick escape.

"I didn't want to tell you because I didn't want to worry you. But my period was late. I was afraid I was pregnant."

"Oh, God, darling, oh, my poor sweet dear. We must do something about it. You weren't thinking of keeping it. I know how Catholics are, of course it would be a wonderful dream, we would make a beautiful child and it would be a whole new lease on life for me. But you understand it would be impossible."

"Tom," she said calmly, as if she had to quiet a child on the verge of hysterics. "I'm not pregnant. That's what I'm trying to tell you. I just got my period. But, I'm afraid it came kind of dramatically and I need help cleaning up. Or, no, I don't. But I need you to get me some towels, just so I can make my way to the bathroom."

"Of course, darling, of course. Are you all right? Are you feeling weak or faint or anything?"

"No, I'm fine, just the towels please."

She sat on the couch feeling the blood seeping out of her, pressing her legs together in a useless attempt to keep more blood from seeping into the fabrics on which she sat. He came into the room, finally, with not only towels but a basin filled with soapy water. She had forgotten that he had been a father, or still was, the two children at boarding school. Putney was the name of it, someplace in Vermont. Or New Hampshire. He had told her how wonderful it was the boys were learning about nature and animals. And that they had learned to knit.

"Thanks," she said. "I'll see you in a minute."

She knew he was glad to be out of the room, and she was glad to have him gone. She made a kind of diaper for herself out of one of the towels, and waddled to the bathroom, holding the towel closed with one hand, the bowl of soapy water in another. She took off her underpants. They were saturated in blood as if she'd been stabbed. She put them in a sink full of cold water, and got into the shower, watching the blood stream down her legs, mesmerized by watching it spiral down the drain. She washed her hair, uneasy at using Amaryllis's shampoo but feeling the need to cleanse herself fully.

She would have to go home without underwear. And she would have to fold a washcloth into eighths to make a temporary sanitary pad. Thank God she had been wearing her jeans. She would make it home, carrying her filthy underpants, rinsed but still telltale, in a plastic bag.

As she dried her hair in a yellow towel she was moved by tenderness at his having brought her a bowl of soapy water. And almost giddy with relief: she wasn't pregnant. Not for a minute had she considered having a child, but the practical implications of an abortion had distressed her when she allowed herself to think of them, and she realized now that she'd expended a lot of energy pushing these thoughts away. She was light with gratitude and relief, and although she knew they couldn't make love, she walked quickly into the study, eager to embrace him.

He was on his knees in front of the couch, and when he looked up, she saw that he would not be pleased at the offer of an embrace.

"This is a disaster, an absolute disaster. Look at what you've done to Amaryllis's beautiful blanket. It's one of her favorites. I think it's ruined, completely ruined. I'll have to make up a story, say I spilt coffee on it. She'll be furious. And I don't blame her. All her wonderful work . . . the design, the execution. All those hours. She'll be absolutely livid. I just don't know what to do."

She was standing above him. He was on his knees, and her greater height accentuated her feelings of contempt for this frightened, grovel-

ing child, terrified of his punitive mother. She knew that he meant her
to feel shame, to share his shame, but there was no room in her for
shame, so taken over was she by contempt. And the clanging ring tone
of the end of love.

"Oh, for heaven's sake, Tom, I'll deal with it. It's only blood. It will
come out with cold water."

"It isn't a cover for a motorboat, Theresa, for God's sake. The wool
is very special, very delicate."

"Just go away. I'll take care of everything."

She took the blanket into the bathroom. She filled the bathtub
with cold water and dropped the blanket into the full tub. The water
quickly grew red. She gently rubbed, squeezed, wrung, emptying the
tub and filling it with fresh water, then rubbing, squeezing, wringing
again and again, until the water was clear. She was grateful that Amaryllis favored earth tones; even if some residue remained, her blood was
so much the color of the wool that she knew it wouldn't be visible.

She looked under the sink for a blow dryer. She sat on the floor and
held the dryer, at its lowest setting, blowing warm air onto the sodden
wool. She didn't know how long she sat there; she allowed the whirr of
the dryer to hypnotize her. Was it an hour, or two, later that she walked
out of the bathroom carrying a perfectly clean, perfectly dry blanket?

"Oh, darling, you're wonderful, wonderful," he said. "And most
wonderful wonderful! And yet again wonderful, in Shakespeare's
words. Let me drive you home."

She would have liked to walk, but the bunched-up washcloth
between her legs would have made it too uncomfortable.

That ought to have been the end of everything, she thought, looking out at the Tuscan countryside. But it wasn't. Because although she
no longer loved him, although her dominant feeling for him was contempt, she still desired him.

And whatever else he was, he was her advisor. And a good one. It was
he who'd recommend Civitali, he who coaxed and prodded and lightened her stiff prose, he who pointed her in the direction of a nineteenth-
century biography, the proceedings of a conference on Civitali in the

year 1912. And he who arranged the travel grant so she could go to Lucca for a month. And when he suggested that he come with her because he could introduce her to a great friend who actually owned two Civitalis, there was no reason for her to allow her contempt to loom large enough to stand in the way.

He said he would meet her in a week, after she was settled. "Good-bye, my beauty," he said, his hair damp from the Days Inn shower, smelling of the inferior motel soap. He handed her an envelope. "Euros," he said. "To tide you over."

And yet she wasn't surprised when, checking her email in the air-port, she read the words "Darling, it was all so wonderful, so perfect, let's not take the chance of diminishment. A clean break, shall we? I know you'll be so absorbed in your new work, the new world you'll be discovering, that there'll be no room for thoughts of your always ardent but rather exhausted lover, who will always be grateful for your luminous presence in his life and at your side, observing with pride and pleasure what I know will be your brilliant career."

The conductor came by and she handed him her ticket. He had an untidy-looking red goatee and smelt of cigarettes; in his right ear was a diamond stud.

"Non ha convalidata," he said.

She had no idea what he was saying. She looked at him dumbly, like a dog whose food dish has just been snatched away.

"Parla italiano?" he asked.

"Un po," she answered, knowing that she'd forgotten every word she'd learned, that not one word would come to her mind now no mat-ter how hard she tried. "I am American," she said.

"You have to validate," the conductor said, flapping the ticket and then putting it down on the tray in front of her. "You not validate."

"I don't understand," she said. *"Non capisco."* Those two words at least had floated up.

A very short man with round glasses walked down the aisle and stood next to the conductor.

"You're supposed to validate your ticket, stamp it in a little machine in the railroad station. Otherwise they can fine you. But they usually don't."

The conductor shrugged his shoulders as a sign of his helplessness.

"Fifty euros," he said, "is rule."

She felt sick. Fifty euros. Almost seventy dollars. Why in all the instructions Tom had given her—don't order cappuccino after noon, don't dip your bread in olive oil or ask for butter, don't say "Ciao" to someone you don't know, especially if they're older than you—why didn't he tell her about validating her ticket?

"It's things like this that make you understand the success of Mussolini," said the young man, having tried, and failed, to reason with the conductor. "It's not all sun and wine and olive oil and dolce far niente. They also have a fantastic love of bureaucracy."

She reached into her bag for her envelope of euros. She was determined not to cry. She couldn't say anything to the young man, except to thank him, because words would have released her tears. She waved to him from the platform.

"Enjoy Lucca," he said, through the window. "It's very beautiful. It's as civilized as you can get."

"That's a nice place you're going to," said the taxi driver in English. "You'll be happy."

"I hope so," she said, thinking she needed at least to try to use her Italian. *"Spero che si."*

Tom had explained that the place she'd be staying—although when he first told her about it she thought they'd be staying together—wasn't really a hotel, it was a residence, an apartment with very basic necessities: coffeemaker, microwave, and that her room would be cleaned and her bed made every day.

She didn't know what she expected, but the lobby was disappointing. The desk was modern, functional, undistinguished; there were mauve-colored silk flowers in a cream-colored vase; on a glass-topped table were brochures advertising language courses and olive oil, and a pile of cards that said "Google si." On the landing going up the stairs was a Roman head, white marble, on a black marble table with gilded legs.

A young woman walked through turquoise silk curtains to the reception desk. Her hair was dark brown, long and curly. Her scarf, grey with a black stripe, was cunningly arranged in a soft series of waves that Theresa knew to be entirely beyond her. Her skirt was grey; her T-shirt long-sleeved and white; she wore black stockings and black ankle boots, which Theresa thought odd for July, and then felt foolish in her flowered sundress and sandals.

"I know you will be happy here," she said, when Theresa had filled out the registration form and handed over her passport.

Theresa wondered if everyone in Italy believed that everyone would be happy, that happiness was the expected thing, ordinary, unexceptional as food or air.

"I will be glad to carry your bag up the stairs," she said. "There is no elevator."

"Oh, no, you mustn't," Theresa said.

"But it's my job."

"Well, let's do it together then."

"You are clearly not a spoiled American. What is the new word, 'entitled'?"

Theresa laughed. "I never think I'm entitled to anything. I'm always afraid I've been given too much by mistake and a terrible price will be exacted that I'll never be able to pay."

She didn't know why she was babbling like this. It wasn't like her. Was it that she was very tired, or was it that being in this new, strange, but long-desired place had brought a kind of wild freedom?

"I know exactly what you mean," the woman said, looking at her with eyes that were certainly brown but had within them tiny flecks of orange.

Each of them took one of the straps of Theresa's bag. It was a hard climb, forty-one steps, and they stopped in the middle. "I guess this means we are not fit," said the young woman. "Many more hours in the gym required. Oh, my God, what a thought. Too horrible. I am, by the way, Chiara."

She opened the door and put a card attached to the key ring into a slot in the wall near the door. "Now this may make you crazy," she said. "You must never forget this card. It turns the lights on and you need it to get into the front door, which is a lot. We're only here from nine to twelve and four to seven. But I'll give you my mobile number in case you need it."

"You're very kind," Theresa said. "*Molto gentile.* Can we speak Italian, so I can practice? I really need to learn."

"*Certo,*" Chiara said. She patted Theresa's bed and turned down the cover. Theresa remembered Tom's advice about not saying "ciao." But it was all right if someone was your age. Or considered you a friend. "*Ciao,*" she said to Chiara, as a sign that she was hoping they might become friends.

The room was a combination of ancient elegance and contemporary motel: there were exposed oak beams in the ceiling; the walls were thick plaster, and the floors red tile. But the table and chairs were very like the ones in the Days Inns she went to with Tom. She took a shower in the stall that was like a little phone booth. The water was hot and plentiful, but she wished the towels were thicker. She would unpack later. Now she would begin what she was here for. She would visit her first Civitali. She would start her work. Here in Lucca. In Italy. In Europe. In the world.

It was an easy walk up a street called simply Fillungo to the church of San Frediano. She would have to learn who San Frediano was eventually, but it wasn't important now. What was important was that she was going to see the Rose Annunciation, which she had studied so carefully in reproductions, knowing they could only give her a hint of the real thing.

The church was at the end of a square surrounded by quite ordinary establishments: a shop that repaired computers, one that sold sweaters and lingerie, a toy store, a café. And rising above it, the great warm pinkish brick basilica, at the architrave a golden mosaic glistening in the sun. But she would look at all that later; her heart beat fast and hard, as if she were about to meet a lover she had known only through letters and the occasional blurred photograph.

The light in the church was dim. She had never experienced herself in space in quite this way, never been in a place so large and dark and empty. And yet the darkness and the emptiness didn't make her feel alone and insignificant. There she was, herself, Theresa, twenty-five years old, her body young and healthy, ardent, warm, and there was the cool darkness, and she took her place in it, content, and yet full of an excited apprehension. Any minute she would see it: the Rose Annunciation. Which she had traveled all these miles to see.

It was almost hidden in a side altar, halfway up the nave to the main altar, only partially visible in the light from the opaque, white glass window with its series of octagonal panes. She walked up to it with her eyes shut, afraid to look, afraid to be disappointed.

But it was more wonderful than she had been afraid to hope. The slender girl, her blond hair elegantly coiffed, surprising for a Madonna: you expected either a veil or long flowing hair. Because she was made of wood rather than stone, she seemed more approachable, and the deep rose of her dress provided a warmth that marble would have denied. She was so slender as to be almost boyish; her simple dress was high-waisted, the rose color deepened and then faded as it traveled to her shoes. Up close, the shoes were surprising. The elegance of the hair, the delicacy of the hands were contrasted by the sensible earth-bound shoes, peasant shoes. She stood flat-footed on unadorned earth. It was meant to be an Annunciation, but there was no angel. Only the position of her arms and hands suggested an exchange. The arms were bent at the elbow and the hand gestures were self-contradictory, ambiguous. The palm of the left hand faced the imaginary angel, a clear message of refusal: I'm not ready, I will not, go away. The other hand beckoned. The palm was open, facing inwards, towards her body, the middle finger was bent, seductive; the thumb and middle finger touched, suggesting resignation, supplication, assent. The ambivalence of Mary's position was absolutely clear. I would and I would not. I am willing but I am afraid. And the firmly planted feet. I am where I am. Here.

She would have to explain the significance of the thumb and third finger. That would require a lot of research, perhaps culminating in an article. But what she couldn't write about, because there was nothing to be said about it because it was fleeting, an accident, a trick of light, was the shadow cast by the Madonna on the plain, stone wall. She kept looking at the shadow, feeling herself drawn to it, and wished there was some way to mark that, as Fra Angelico had marked the shadow behind the Virgin in his less famous Annunciation fresco. But that kind of marking was not her work. No one, though, could stop her from focusing on the shadow for as long as it was here.

She felt the slow, deep pleasure of knowing she was exactly where she wanted to be, doing exactly what she wanted to do. Her breath came easily; the damp coolness seemed to refresh the fragile skin around her eyes, abraded from fatigue and the dryness of plane travel. She felt lapped in a nourishing, consoling air. I am here, she kept saying to herself. I am here, and the word "here" seemed to her the most beautiful, the most desirable word imaginable.

She took the binoculars out of her bag and looked at the mosaics on the wall across from where she sat. She became aware of the sound of weeping. She lowered the glasses guiltily, tracking the sound. A young woman, probably about her age, was sitting in the darkness, her head in her hands. The church's emptiness freed her to sob without restraint, like a child, holding nothing back, with no sense of shame or exposure. Theresa felt that looking at her was a violation. She put her glasses back into her bag.

The door of the church banged, and she heard the parade of loud feet and the sound of German. It was over. She would leave.

Tom had written to the curator of the art museum, the Villa Guinigi, and the curator had written Theresa urging her to be in touch as soon as she arrived: she would be glad to be of help. But Theresa didn't want to meet her yet, to present herself, as if she were a diplomat presenting credentials to the court. She wanted more time alone with the work; she wanted to know what she thought before she had to say anything to anyone, before anyone asked her anything. She wanted to be looking innocently, as she had looked innocently at the Rose Annunciation. She would go to the museum as an ordinary tourist.

But not just any tourist; she had a destination in mind. She would bypass the Romans, the trecento crucifixions, and make her way to the Civitalis. She knew that there were four of them in one room alone. Probably more than in any other room in the world.

She made her way into the room, past a guard who seemed nearly asleep, opening his eyes to look at her neutrally, then going back to his cell phone to text. She knew that she would be seeing the suffering Christs, so different from the Rose Annunciation she had seen the day before.

The largest of them was a standing figure, nearly six feet high. Life-sized, she thought, but it was not a representation of life. The place where the spear entered Jesus' torso was a thin line, the width of a pencil mark. The loincloth was simple, nearly colorless, making almost no contrast with the flesh.

Her first glimpse of the Rose Annunciation had filled her with delight, and she was able to move from that place to a position of close scrutiny, her training taking its place easily beside her visual pleasure. But what she felt looking at the figure of Jesus was not pleasure, but shock. Because this Jesus was, himself, shocked, unable fully to understand what had befallen him. His face expressed a stricken incomprehension. His arms, open at his sides, his palms facing upwards, said most clearly, "How can this be happening? To me? In this world? Here? Now?"

She thought of the uncomprehending look that sometimes took over her father's face. His bafflement at what his life had become.

And for the first time in all the years since her father's accident, certainly the first time since his death, Theresa wept. She looked around, hoping the guard hadn't seen her. He seemed to be absorbed in his texting. She knew she could not weep here. She wished that she were in the dark church where she had heard the girl freely weeping. You could weep freely in a dark church; this was one of its last public functions, one of its last civic services. But in a museum, you might be thought mad if you wept, seen as a danger, perhaps asked to leave. She was glad that Chiara wasn't on duty. She would go back to her room without speaking to anyone. She would weep.

She woke after a three-hour nap. She hadn't realized how tired she was. Was it too late for lunch? The day stretched ahead of her, its open-ness luxurious and threatening. She had a month. Thirty days, and she had to determine the best way to use them. What Tom had written in the recommendation for the grant was that she would use the month in Lucca to solidify a dissertation topic. But what did that really mean, "solidifying a topic"? It could mean anything or nothing.

Not much had been written on Civitali. There were articles; one book, a hundred years old, was in French, and the most recent one was in German, which she couldn't read. Would she have to learn a new language to read one book? Not having an army of scholars ahead of her was both a gift and a burden. She didn't have to sift through moun-tains of dullness or misinformation. On the other hand, she felt she had no hand to hold.

Tom had told her she must find a special pizzeria that made a spe-cial pizza; instead of tomato sauce, the thin crust was covered with a paste made of chickpeas, oil, and garlic. It was near the Cathedral of San Michele. She wouldn't open her map on the street, so she wouldn't leave her room till she felt confident of her route. She had a glass of wine with her pizza, and then made her way across the square to the statue of Civitali.

It wasn't a good statue: bronze, imposing, seventeenth century, with nothing of the tenderness and delicacy that marked his work. It didn't make him look anything like what she'd imagined; she was sure this wasn't how he looked; for one thing he was a fifteenth-, not a seventeenth-century man. It pleased her that there was a statue in a large town square dedicated to an artist that most of the world hadn't heard of. But she also resented it. People passing him every day, lean-ing against him as they smoked or kissed—this made him less hers. They don't know him as I do, she thought, and she laughed out loud at herself. I sound like a possessive wife in the face of a parade of casual lovers unworthy of the beloved husband. Who would always be, most importantly, hers.

She walked up the Via Roma. I am pleased, she heard herself saying. I am so pleased. The word sounded wrong, but she knew it was the right one. "I'm so pleased" sounded false, affected, a hostess's words or something from an English movie, and you knew the person saying the words—it was always a woman—wasn't really pleased at all. But she didn't care, she kept repeating in her mind, "I am pleased." She felt that everything had been arranged, not to make her happy, "happy" seemed too risky a term, implying some expectation of continuance. This, this being pleased, was happening right now and it might never happen again. But the things that unfolded before her eyes, that pleased her, seemed like the work of good manners, the product, not of a particular affection, but of a sense of what was right.

The windows of the shops of the Fillungo were a sign of something, of a way of living she had never experienced, but had somehow intuited. How, she wondered, how did I always know? They had, she thought, been waiting for her. The candied violets, the marzipan fruits, the cakes as beautiful as fashionable ladies' hats, the artful pyramids of oranges and lemons in the markets, green-gold grapes resting on a bed of dark leaves, carefully arranged trays of cheeses, even the meat in the butchers' windows (chops decorated with white collars or parsley necklaces), the children's clothes, lace, crocheted, embroidered, all spoke of a care for the look of things that was somehow free of the element of punishing exclusion or self-aggrandizement that she associated with American commercial display.

I am in Europe, she kept saying to herself. I made it. I'm here. And all at once, the word "pleased" wasn't enough. She knew that what she was experiencing was delight.

She was very glad that she was by herself, because she could allow the words that she knew were clichés without banishing them for fear of someone accusing her of a cliché. Thank God Tom wasn't here. If the thought of ordering cappuccino after noon was an abomination to him, what would he have thought if she'd allowed the words that were now going through her mind to slip out? "Things are so old here, so much older than in America." "I have never seen stones this color. I love the way the light falls on the sides of the buildings, and I remember the names of colors I knew in my first Crayola box. Ochre. Burnt sienna. The stones are kinder here."

There was a life lived in the open, on the streets, but, unlike on the streets of Milwaukee, where almost no one walked except as a sign of some kind of ruin, or the streets of Chicago, where everyone walked in response to weather that was nearly always insupportable, the street life here was elegant and leisurely. People spoke to each other, kissed each other—men and women—on both cheeks. They carried flowers or you could see the tops of vegetables—the complicated asparagus, the mathematically precise carrot leaves—peeping like well-behaved schoolchildren out of cloth market bags. She thought that everything she saw must be some sort of sign, some hint of a larger connection, and she believed she would, eventually, put the pieces together. But she knew she couldn't will it; it would have to happen on its own.

It was up to her to get in touch with Gregory Allard, the American collector whose name Tom had given her, and she had let a week go by without doing it. She told herself that it was all right, that this was her first time in Europe, her first time anywhere by herself; she could allow herself a little latitude. But she knew the truth: she dreaded making contact with Gregory Allard for reasons that had everything to do with who she was, and where she felt she had no right to be.

The problem with any sentence she could imagine saying to him overwhelmed and paralyzed her. "I would like to look at your Civitalis. I am a student of Tom Ferguson." And what if he asked what would be normal questions: "Why do you want to look at my Civitalis? Why isn't Tom here now?"

She spent most of her days in silence, and she was happy in that silence, happy even in her growing ease speaking her simple Italian. But this made the prospect of phoning Gregory Allard all the more daunting. Words were so rare in her life now that they seemed newly precious and significant. The ordinary polite lies—I'm planning to do my dissertation on Civitali, I don't know why Professor Ferguson cancelled his trip—well, they weren't lies, but the truth they yielded was so partial she felt she was misusing the words in saying them. Misusing or wasting.

But eventually she began to feel ashamed that she was squandering the university's money. She knew that wasn't really right; she was looking at Civitalis every day and she had made an appointment with the curator of the archives. The curator seemed to be away for two weeks, a gift. Theresa told herself it was another sign, but of what? And her being here was really a gift of Tom's. "A wonderful opportunity, you must always be very grateful." That was the kind of thing her mother would have said. She hadn't talked to her mother. She knew she could buy a phone card and speak to her mother in Arizona very cheaply, but it was another thing she couldn't bring herself to do. She spent a whole morning trying to find the right postcard to send her mother. Her mother, who wouldn't have the slightest interest in anything depicted on any postcard she could find. For her mother, Europe was pretension and discomfort. Italians were Mafiosi or pizza makers. At least she had said that she was sure Theresa would be eating some delicious food. And so Theresa was relieved when she found a postcard showing many different kinds of pasta. "You were right, Mom, the food is great. It's beautiful here." She knew the words were empty, but they had no falseness to them.

She was paralyzed whenever she thought of contacting Gregory Allard. And then she thought of a way out of her paralysis. She needed to be in touch with Maura.

They had been friends since they were thirteen. A friendship that was encouraged, nurtured, possibly engineered by the nuns who taught them. Maura and Theresa were invited by the nuns to help them after school in the office; they felt it as a signal honor, being trusted to file receipts and run various errands. It was only much later that they realized the sisters could have done it themselves. But they asked this favor of Theresa and Maura because they knew how depressing and painful their home lives were, and they understood that the girls could be a solace to each other. Theresa's misfortune was public knowledge, but only the sisters knew about Maura's troubles: two alcoholic parents, and a brother three years younger for whom she had the primary responsibility. Maura told Theresa that she guessed the nuns figured it out because they noticed that Maura was coming to school without lunches, and with unmatched socks and unmended clothes. And that the Shaughnessy parents came to teachers' conferences—when they came—smelling of alcohol, with bloodshot eyes and broken veins.

And so the nuns made a place for the two children of affliction, afflicted themselves but refusing to admit it. It took five years for Maura to confess her problems to Theresa, and after that she spoke about her parents only with contempt and rage. Her tenderness was saved for her brother, Rory, who wasn't half the student Maura was, although Maura insisted, to Theresa's sadness, that he was "really, really bright. He just has a different learning style."

And so both girls knew they couldn't go away to school; they were needed at home, Theresa because she wouldn't leave her father to her mother's care, for both their sakes, but particularly for her father— she understood her mother's position, but didn't trust what outcomes her harshness might engender. And Maura because she wouldn't leave Rory to those two "assholes who can't even take care of themselves."

Their freedom came at just the same time, their sophomore year of college, when Theresa's father died and Rory joined the navy. The next year, Theresa's mother married George Hoffman, a man she'd worked with for years, whom Theresa thought of as a Coors drinker who combed his one existing strand of hair over his bald spot. His crudity hurt Theresa, and she felt it an affront to her father, who, whatever he had been, had never been crude. And she had to wonder if her mother had been sleeping with George for years, coming home from assignations with him to check her husband's oxygen. She and Maura moved into a room in the dorm, provided, of course, by the sisters. By that time, Maura, who had thought of herself as a poet, had decided she would major in nursing because it would give her the freedom to travel, which was her romance, as the study of art history was Theresa's.

But it was Maura's only romance, because she was determined to be hardheaded, practical. Having lived with alcoholics whose ordinary register was exaggeration, she refused extremes of language, even of thought. Having endured the hourly swerves—"I love you/I hate you/ you are the devil's child, you can't be mine/why did I ever have you?/

you are my angel girl and I don't deserve you/you're goddamn lucky to have us as parents, you ungrateful little shit/how can you ever forgive us for what we've done to you? . . ."—she was determined to inhabit a solid unmoving ground, a temperate, coldish climate. Unlike Theresa, she was determined not to take things too seriously. And to trust to luck.

Maura had an instinct for pleasure, as Theresa did not. Sitting on her bed in the warm air of Lucca in July, Theresa thought of her only happy Christmas, one she'd shared with Maura. It had happened her first year at Yale, when Maura won a raffle—she had bought an environmentally friendly fire extinguisher from a friend who was selling them on a pyramid scheme. The prize was a round trip to Disney World, and Maura figured out how to make a good thing of it. She and Theresa would take the airline tickets and the three days at the motel in Orlando. They would not go near Disney World. They would sit by the pool and drink, and eat pizza in their bedroom, watch movies on the TV, play cards, maybe go outside a bit if it was warm. It was the first Christmas either of them had enjoyed; Christmas with alcoholics was always a nightmare, and there was never room for a Christmas tree in a room that was completely taken over by a hospital bed. And now that her mother had married George and moved to Arizona, Christmas would be another kind of nightmare, which Theresa was grateful to be spared.

The second night they were there, two men came to them at the side of the pool carrying extra beers, clearly on the prowl. When one of them asked if the girls would like to come to their room for more drinks, Maura said, "We'd love to, but we really can't. We know what you have in mind, and it would be great, but we both have these terrible vaginal discharges. It might be a yeast infection . . . it might be chlamydia," and the men were waving goodbye before she could finish her sentence.

And the two of them ran to their room so they could lie on their beds giggling in the way that had always been the sign to themselves and to each other of their liberation, their victory over what might have been considered impossible odds. And because of this, because they had been children together, trying to discover a way out to a larger life, but with no one to help them, stitching together the hints they had picked up accidentally from the accident of being alive, having got out ... Theresa to Yale, Maura to the island of Tortola (where she was work-ing as an emergency room nurse), Theresa knew she could make any atavistic, embarrassing request with complete freedom. There was no shame in traveling with Maura to the place they had once been, repeat-ing patterns that were fine for a fourteen-year-old ("make an appoint-ment with the doctor for me, I'm embarrassed to call him and tell him I have to pay cash because we have no health insurance ... Open this envelope for me, it's from Yale, I can't stand it if I haven't got in"). The only gap in the utter safety of their friendship had occurred because Theresa never told her about Tom Ferguson. Maura wouldn't approve, not only because he was married but because she knew that Maura would include Tom in her overlarge category of "asshole" or, more lately, "pretentious asshole." But her fear of calling Gregory Allard was something Maura would be more than ready to help with; Theresa didn't doubt that for a second.

The cell phone reception in Tortola was erratic, and Maura's hours in the emergency room were unpredictable. The five-hour time differ-ence was one more problem. Theresa only got Maura on the fifth try. "Where the hell have you been?" she asked.

"Working, you know. I'm a wage earner, unlike some."

"I can't call this guy. I just can't. If you were here, we could do what we always did when we were afraid to call someone. You could call him and say you were me. But it wouldn't work from your island."

"Just email him then."

Theresa felt like a fool. Why hadn't she thought of that? She wouldn't have to talk to him at all. Not just yet.

"And when you email him, think of him—he's kind of an old guy, right? Think of him sitting at this big old, totally out-of-date computer in a white T-shirt, maybe like a V-neck, and white boxers and black socks."

Theresa lay on her bed and laughed. She realized she hadn't laughed out loud since she'd left America. Anyone but Maura would have said,

Think of him naked, think of him on the toilet. Only Maura would have thought of the black socks.

"Do it right now. I'm not hanging up till you tell me you've pressed Send."

She'd chosen a good time to email Gregory Allard because she'd been invited to Chiara's family for lunch, so she couldn't sit in front of her computer all day waiting for a response. They'd agreed to meet in the square by the cathedral, because Chiara didn't want the owners to see her "fraternizing with a guest." She was straddling her Vespa, and she held out a peacock-colored helmet for Theresa to wear. Theresa hadn't imagined she'd be riding on the back of a Vespa. When Chiara said her family lived on the road to Bagni di Lucca, Theresa had imagined they'd be driving there in a car.

For the first five minutes, she was terrified. The seat seemed narrow; the distance from the pavement was extremely slight, and slight, too, was Chiara's torso, to which she had to cling. She thought Chiara drove very fast, but she had no idea what was considered fast on a Vespa, and, after a while, Chiara's confidence, the complete relaxation of her body, induced a kind of relaxation in Theresa as well. No sooner had she got used to the feeling of relaxation than it was replaced by something else, something she'd never felt, a kind of elation at moving very fast through space, through air, covering ground at a great rate, eating up the road, climbing up hills, barreling down hills, and then, with a judder and a quick stop, an arrival at a low, white house with lemon trees in pots on either side of a dark wooden door.

Chiara took Theresa's hand, pulled the helmet off her head, and pushed her into the hallway, which was white-walled, the floor tiled with plain brown tiles, full of rubber boots in various sizes. How did it happen: suddenly everyone was in the hallway, everyone was embracing Chiara and then Theresa, and she was being introduced to Chiara's mother, who was younger than Theresa could imagine anyone her age's mother could be, wearing lime green capri pants and golden sandals. Chiara's father's bald head gleamed with pleasure at seeing his daughter, who towered over him by three inches. And suddenly she was in the midst of it, people laughing, people pressing drinks on her, introducing her to Chiara's grandmother, Chiara's younger brother, who Theresa guessed was around fifteen. There was food and more food: first thin crackers with pâté and capers the size of grapes, thin delicious slices of ham and small pieces of cheese: some sharp, some mild. The grandmother demanded: Tell the truth, did she ever in her life encounter olive oil to equal what could be found in Lucca? Theresa was guided to the table, where everyone knew exactly where to sit, and Chiara's mother brought out a huge white bowl of pasta with tomato sauce, and then cold pork and a salad of cold green beans, and four different cakes. People wanted to know everything about America: Does she love President Obama as they love him in Italy? He is so much better than any of our politicians, and had she been to the Grand Canyon or Hollywood? She said she was from the Midwest and someone said the word "prairie" and someone else said Chicago and they all laughed at the impossibility of pronouncing the word "Milwaukee," and then there was more food and she found herself laughing at jokes she didn't quite understand, and some man's name was mentioned and Chiara pretended to slap her brother's face, and then, suddenly, they were on the Vespa again. "My family is very loud and probably talks too much. They didn't ask you anything about your work, because they wouldn't have anything to say about it. Or they would, but would feel too embarrassed because they'd think of you as an intellectual, a *professoressa,* and then that would be the end of fun."

In the dark quiet of her room, Theresa felt quite lonely. This was what a family could be, this was what it was to have ease and pleasure with the people you were related to. She felt a slashing bitter envy of Chiara and knew that, as much as she liked her, they could never understand each other enough to be real friends.

She checked her computer. Gregory Allard had asked if it would be convenient for her to meet the following afternoon at a café on the Fillungo called Di Simo. She answered that it would be perfect, and that she was grateful for his time.

He wrote back one word: "Fine."

She stood against the wall of a pharmacy on the street that intersected the Fillungo so she could watch him from a distance, knowing, somehow, that he'd be early. He was wearing a seersucker jacket. Theresa had heard of seersucker jackets, or read about them, but she'd never seen a living man wearing one. She knew Gregory Allard was in his eighties, but he looked younger. His hair was the color of silvery hay; it hung over his forehead like a boy's, like that of someone whose mother had cut his hair at the kitchen table. He was pacing up and down. She saw that, somehow, he had never quite got the knack of his long thin legs, and the stiffness that characterized his walk wasn't the stiffness of old age, it was the stiffness of someone who had at a young age adopted certain habits bred either of unease or of a lofty unconcern for how he looked. He would walk a few paces and then swing one leg over the other and turn around. She thought of one of those compasses she had used in grade school, then in high school geometry, when one was required to draw mathematically precise circles. She thought of a grasshopper: the colorless tuft of hair, the stiff overly long legs, the sense that at any minute, he might leap, alarmingly, and then land somewhere out of sight.

He offered his hand to be shaken. Theresa had very rarely shaken hands with anyone, although she had heard often enough that it was important to have a firm handshake. But she had no idea what that really meant.

She had looked in the window of Di Simo but had been afraid to enter it. It was so elegant that she felt she had no right. The gold art nouveau lettering of the sign, the bow windows, the beautifully wrapped confections . . . and she had heard that it had been the meeting place for great poets. She preferred her pizzeria with the corny poems pretending that Dante and Beatrice had met there and fallen in love over *ceci* pizza. She was worried about what to order. What was the right thing at four? She thought probably an espresso couldn't be too far off the mark, but she was never sure whether to order espresso or just *caffè,* as she was never sure, when she wanted a glass of tap water, to ask for natural or normale, because she didn't want to pay for bottled water, and was too embarrassed to refuse it when it was offered.

Gregory Allard ordered something called Punt e Mes. She was surprised when it turned out to be a dark-colored drink, accompanied by a separate glass of ice cubes.

She noticed the dark spots on his hands, and that his watch was like something from a movie about heroic pilots.

"So, Miss Riordan. You are at work on our friend Matteo. May I ask how you came to him?"

"Professor Ferguson suggested it. He's my advisor. I'm very grateful."

Saying that made her realize that she was grateful to him, grateful and disgusted at the same time.

"I have the privilege of owning two Civitalis. A marble head of a woman and a polychrome Madonna and child. I'm hoping you will come to my home and see them. Of course I wanted to meet you first. If you'd turned out to be some version of ghastly, I wouldn't have invited you."

How could you possibly know whether or not I'm ghastly? she wanted to say. We've only just met. She understood that it had to be something about the way she looked.

"I of course came to Civitali because he's a Lucchese and I have lived here for over forty years. His reputation has been hindered because he didn't work from Rome or Florence or Venice or Naples. A local boy. Of course, the fact that he's not better known is something of a joy to me. I almost resent it when anyone else knows about him. I'm not sure I don't resent you a bit. Obviously, I want him to be better known. But not too much better. I like very much the idea of a fit audience but few."

"Yes, I know what you mean. If I'm looking at him, and someone else comes by, I want to tell them they have no right to be there, and they simply have to leave. But you really don't have to worry, Mr. Allard. I don't think my dissertation's going to be sold at airports."

Gregory Allard raised his glass to her. "A good thing, that," he said. "I think you should have something more than a coffee." He gestured to the waiter and ordered her a Punt e Mes.

Reaching into his pocket, he took a folded piece of paper from his wallet and passed it to her. "A local antiques dealer, someone I rather trust, suggested that this piece is a Civitali. He's offering it to me for twenty thousand euros. What do you think?"

What could he be thinking? He was asking for her opinion, as if she were an expert. Which she knew herself not to be.

"I couldn't possibly say. Not from a photograph. Probably not at all."

"Tom was supposed to give me his opinion when he came. I don't know why he bailed out."

I am the reason, she wanted to say. Do you know that he is a very weak man? *Debole.* That he has *debolezza.*

"Would you like to look at it? The Civitali, or the putative Civitali. Possibly only *scuola di?*"

Was it the alcohol that had given her courage? Dutch courage, she remembered it was called. Well, she had liked the Netherlandish painters. Their attention to detail. The Italians and the Spanish had learned from them. "I would be happy to look at it, as long as you don't ask me whether I think it's authentic or not."

"Not-at-all, not at all, just think of it as a kind of window shopping. Isn't that the kind of thing young women like to do? Or do you just live a life of the mind?"

"Mr. Allard, I've never shopped for anything with a twenty-thousand-euro price tag."

"Tom Ferguson said you had spunk. I'm glad to see it. So many serious young women are bundles of nerves. Afraid to eat. I hope you're not afraid to eat. My friend Paola owns the best restaurant in town. If I say I am bringing a young friend, she'll outdo herself."

I am in Europe, Theresa said in her mind. He is a rich man. A rich American. He thinks of me as his young friend. "That would be very nice," she said.

"Shall we walk around the walls until Paola will receive us?"

"That would be very nice," she said, wishing she hadn't repeated herself.

It was still full light, and the heat of the day had not lifted; the cicadas were making their noise in the large plane trees. The sun shone strong through the rich leaves of the plane trees, new to her, and the oaks, familiar. He was telling her things about Napoleon's sister, who'd lived here, and Chet Baker, the jazz musician who'd been jailed here for heroin. But she couldn't really listen; she was hypnotized by the honey-colored light. The buildings seemed to shift angles, the corners to open into views down narrow streets and then close, the campaniles of churches to slide in different directions. Runners in immaculate tracksuits with immaculate matching headbands; mothers in jeans and high wedge sandals pushing strollers; old couples, the men in jackets and ties, the women in low heels and neutral-colored skirts and long-sleeved blouses—everyone was doing some version of their *passeggiata,* everyone very aware that what they were doing was not simply taking exercise, it had something importantly to do with being looked at. She probably shouldn't have had a drink, she told herself. She still wasn't sleeping well and she often forgot to eat lunch. It was a relief when they walked down from the walls onto the main street and he opened the door of the restaurant which was called, not surprisingly, Paola's.

She assumed it was Paola herself who greeted them, embracing Gregory Allard and thanking him for something, something to do with medication for her daughter. She was impressed at the woman's sophistication. She wasn't young, perhaps in her late fifties. How did she convey sophistication although she was wearing only jeans and a light blue T-shirt? Was it her hair? So well cut, so subtly colored, as opposed to the aggressive metallic impression that her mother's hair, and the hair of all Theresa's mother's friends, conveyed.

Gregory explained that Theresa was a student and was studying Civitali. Theresa couldn't tell from Paola's response whether that meant anything to her at all. What was clear, though, was her affection for Gregory Allard.

"You're very lucky to have a friend in Lucca like Gregory. The most generous man in the whole of the city."

Was it possible that Gregory Allard blushed? He bared his strong yellowish teeth, the teeth of a strong, healthy, but no longer young horse. Theresa couldn't read whether the baring was a grimace or a shy smile.

"Shall I leave it to you to order for us?"

"What else?" Paola said.

The prosecco arrived, then a golden local wine, a small plate of squid and mussels, then another of eggplant, and then another of polenta and mushrooms. Pasta tossed with only tender green peas in their shoots, and then a grilled fish: Bronzino. Theresa giggled, thinking of the painter, and shared the joke with Gregory Allard, who didn't laugh.

She realized that she had never been in a restaurant alone with a man before. She'd had a bowl of soup and a sandwich with Tom in small casual places from time to time, but mostly they couldn't appear in public together. This was a real restaurant, serious, impressive, its offerings complex. She felt with a sense of pride and pleasure that a man was spending money on her, and this had never happened before. Oh, she supposed that Tom had paid for the motels, but the transaction was by necessity secretive and rather sordid. Possibly before the accident, her father had bought her an ice cream or the three of them had eaten in a Chinese restaurant. But she couldn't remember a specific instance, and her sense of her father as someone who needed to be cared for, provided for rather than providing, overcame all other ways of thinking about him.

This was like something that happened to people in movies. She wished she had seen more movies, not what her fellow graduate students would calls films, serious, ironic, but movies that would have given her information, the kind of information she never thought she needed until now, about how to be a woman with a man, even an old man who reminded her of a grasshopper and a compass and a horse.

But somehow, coming from somewhere—her blood, the air— knowledge arrived. She knew how to sit, how to arrange her arms and legs, how to hold her head, so that she indicated a relaxed readiness, tilting her head like an expectant, eager bird, her hands palm upwards on her lap so that he, Gregory Allard, a man, would understand that she, Theresa Riordan, a woman, wanted more than anything in the world to hear what he had to say.

"How did you come to settle in Lucca?" she asked, not feeling impertinent or intrusive, understanding that this was what people did. They wanted to know things, they asked questions.

"My late wife was Lucchese. It was rather a late marriage. After Harvard—sorry, I know you're at Yale, but I'm afraid I'm a Harvard man—I went into the army, because I was drafted, and then for years I just traveled and collected and lived a very aestheticized life. I went where I liked, bought what I liked, made very few deep human attachments; my attachments were much more to places and things than to people. And then, when I was in my forties, I met Elisabetta. She was working in an antiques store. I suppose I couldn't have loved her if she weren't so lovely. She was very lovely. Not only physically, but with a tremendous vitality, a rather scalding wit from time to time, but a great open heart. And she died a terrible, tragic death. A death that took far too many years of her short life to arrive. Lupus, it was called, her disease. The wolf. And she was so beautiful, she had something of the Civitali Madonna in her, a rather cool beauty, perhaps a bit austere, with a great, innate elegance. So that when she was afflicted and not only her health, but her beauty, was taken from her, it was a terrible thing. A terrible thing for her, but for the world, too. This beautiful woman, with clear, beautifully pale skin, a victim of this lupus rash, the wolf rash, so that her face was covered by horrible, red eruptions, and then she had strokes so that one side of her face was distorted, lopsided. And then the terrible pain, the difficulty breathing. Years and years of it. One learned that death was not the worst thing that could happen, that death could be something of a relief."

For the first time in her life, Theresa thought it was all right to speak about her father. She hadn't even spoken about her father to Maura.

He nodded, when she had told him about her father's accident and what followed upon it, as if she'd just been explaining something complex and mentally taxing to him.

"Your mother kept him at home," he said.

"Yes, for a long time. Until we couldn't do it anymore."

"And you grew up with that. You grew up with affliction in the center of your home, in the center of your life."

"Yes, literally. His bed and all the equipment he needed were in the middle of the living room."

"I suppose your mother had no choice. I suppose, like so much else, so much more than the likes of us will credit, it was about money."

"We had to worry about money," she said, realizing it was the first time she had spoken of it. "We had to worry about money all the time."

"I have never worried about money," he said. "Not for one moment in my whole overlong life. It has made many things possible. Not everything of course. There was, in the end, not much I could do for my poor lovely Elisabetta. Oh, I could make her more comfortable than she would have been if I hadn't had money; I could surround her with beautiful things and people who cared for her gently. But I couldn't spare her pain. And I couldn't spare the damage it did to our son. Although I tried. We both tried. We didn't want him to live with what you had to live with. We didn't want to have his mother's illness be the thing that most importantly shaped his life. Partly, it was Elisabetta's vanity. She didn't want him to see her ugly. She wanted him to remember only a beautiful mother. So we sent him away. A Swiss boarding school: how's that for a cliché. He didn't see his mother for five years; she died without saying goodbye to him, except over the phone. He and I would go to marvelous places on holidays. The Galápagos. Cambodia and Vietnam. Kenya, Montana, Machu Picchu. But he will never forgive me. A very important part of his life is not forgiving me, finding ways to punish me. And of course, I don't blame him. How could I? He is, by the way, a first-rate photographer. He's having a show in a gallery here in a week."

"I hope to be able to see it."

"I'm not sure it will be exactly your cup of tea. His work is very often not mine, though I admire his skill. But let's talk a bit about you. Why Civitali? I'm assuming it's not just a clever career move. I would be surprised if you were a person who made clever career moves. If it is, don't tell me. It's important to me that someone like you is as moved by him as I am. By like you I mean, someone young."

She leaned back in her chair, which was upholstered in a soft burgundy velvet, and looked into his eyes, which were the color of the green grapes she'd seen in the market.

"I love him for his mixture of containment and tenderness."

He jumped to his feet and came over to her, took her chin in his hands, and kissed her on both cheeks.

Then he sat down, and bared his horsey teeth again, and once again she didn't know whether or not he was pleased.

"Have I embarrassed you unbearably?"

"No," she said. "I think I'm having fun."

"I hope you do more than think so. I hope you really are having fun, although I'm not sure that talking about illness and death with an old man would be most people's idea of fun. But I'm having fun, too. May I come for you tomorrow at four or so, and I will give you dinner at my house and show you my Civitalis?"

"Yes," she said, once again. "That would be very nice."

He drove a light blue Mercedes, which she imagined was at least twenty years old. He got out of the car to open the door for her, and waited to start the engine till she'd fastened her seat belt. She liked this very much, but she forbade herself to go on liking it. It was too predictable, pathetic in its predictableness. The fatherless girl, the scholarship girl taken under the wing of a rich man old enough to be her grandfather.

He asked about her day and she was happy to describe it: her morning *cornetto* and cappuccino, at the café on the corner where they recognized her now and served her without her asking, a morning reading and taking notes, a walk around the walls, a lunch of bread, cheese, and tomatoes, which she bought in the market and ate in her room while she read. A half-hour nap, and then more reading.

They drove out of the city into the countryside. Quite suddenly, a fog developed; the cypresses grew indistinct and she lost sight of the mountain. Gregory Allard beeped his horn at each curve. They drove down a hill, and out of the mist there appeared something that Theresa thought could not possibly be real. A white horse galloped through the fog, his whiteness the only thing distinguishable, a brightness against the duller whiteness of the fog. If you concentrated, you could see the horizontal bars of the fence behind which you could hear the sound of his galloping, but he, too, had grown invisible, the white bars separating him from them and the road. Rolling down the window, she imagined she could hear the horse's breath.

"I feel like I'm in a dream," she said. This was something she would have been embarrassed to say in front of everyone she knew. Except Gregory Allard. Tom, certainly, but even Joan Gallagher. Maura would tease her for being overly romantic. Perhaps she could have said it to Sister Imelda, but Sister Imelda thought everything Theresa said was wonderful.

"The Tuscan dream of the white horse. It sounds like a painting by de Chirico or Magritte or one of those surrealists I loathe. But thinking of a Tuscan dream of a white horse when I connect it to your pleasure in it, that is quite wonderful. You'll remember that, Theresa, you'll remember the white horse in the mist when you've forgotten most of what you've experienced in these days."

"I don't forget things," she said.

"We all forget things. We must."

The house was barely visible in the mist, but as she approached, she saw it was pink, with mottled pink walls and green-shuttered windows. Gregory Allard took a key out of his pocket and then put it back. "I forgot, my son is here. You'll meet Ivo. And his companion, whose name is Sage. I'm not sure whether it's about wisdom or cookery, that name. I don't like to ask."

They walked into a high room with white walls and blood-colored floor tiles. The walls were covered with photographs, many of which Theresa assumed were of Gregory's late wife. She would have liked to look more closely, but was embarrassed to. He showed her into the sitting room. The fog was beginning to lift, and she could see outside the window two large palm trees growing on either side of the double staircase and terra-cotta pots with lemon trees, leading to a loggia that overlooked a lotus pool. She thought the surrounding garden was stuffed with flowers, so profuse were they . . . perhaps, she thought, a bit too profuse. The land outside the gate sloped down to terraces planted with vines and olive trees. She could see, pricked out of the greyness, poppies and some lavender flowers whose names she didn't know. The dark red roses stained the fog; there was a glimmer of fireflies in the bushes.

A woman wearing a white apron over a black wool dress appeared and nodded unsmilingly. *"Ecco la studentessa Americana,"* Gregory Allard said. *"Theresa, ecco Rosalba."*

Theresa didn't know whether to extend her hand to be shaken, so she stood with her hands at her sides and the woman didn't approach her. She disappeared and then reappeared in a second carrying a silver tray covered by a white cloth, two glasses, and a green bottle. She had not yet smiled nor even met Theresa's eyes.

"Prosecco," Gregory Allard said. Rosalba returned with a blue and white plate of olives and another of almonds on a smaller silver tray. Theresa felt wild with impatience. Why were they eating and drinking when what she was here for was to see his Civitalis?

From another part of the house she could hear what sounded like a buzz and a rumble; she knew it was a kind of music called techno, something that didn't seem like music to her, but people she knew, and even liked, admired it. She assumed his son was listening to it. Gregory Allard seemed to be taking a ridiculous amount of time finishing his drink. He would take one olive at a time, in his long spatulate fingers, and fastidiously place the pits in the small white dish which was there for the purpose. He took three almonds, chewed each one separately, then wiped his fingers on a linen napkin.

He began slowly, a rumbling laugh that reminded her a bit of the music coming from the other part of the house. "Oh, Theresa Riordan, you're not good at hiding your feelings. Or your thoughts. You are nearly bursting out of your skin with desire to see my Matteos. I will not torment you any longer. Come," he said, stretching out his long grasshopper arm.

He led her to the adjoining room and switched on the complicated lighting. He took her hand and led her over to a glassed-in cabinet.

These works of art belonged to him; he owned them, and so they would be available to her, would be hers, in a way that no works of art had ever been. He would allow her to touch them; he might even allow her to be alone with them. She felt a kind of dread and at the same time a kind of supersaturated elation.

He opened the glass doors with a small key. He took the marble statue out first, rubbing it with a chamois cloth. He placed it down on a small marble-topped table. She had no idea what she would do in relation to it, what she was allowed to do.

"Don't be frightened of her, hold her if you like, she's been around for a while and I know you'll treat her well."

She felt her throat close with anxiety. The marble was cool and smooth. It felt as she thought it would: like marble. People were always saying things were like marble, and this was, this was marble that was just like marble. She ran her fingers around the graceful contour of nose and chin, around the coiffed rolled hair, and the raised design of the ribbons that kept the hair in place. She put it down. She walked away from it, and then walked closer. She closed her eyes. She was afraid that when she opened her eyes it would no longer be as beautiful as what she had first seen. But then she opened her eyes, and nothing had changed. She knew what she meant to say—I could look at this forever—because time was about change and forever was about no change and she couldn't imagine there would be a time when she would want to be doing anything else than looking at the *gentildonna,* would want any change, any sense of moving on. And she knew that, like most of the things that came to her mind when she saw something beautiful, she couldn't say what she meant to anyone. There was only one word she wanted to say, and if she couldn't say that she would say nothing. So she would say it now.

"Beautiful," she said.

"She is beautiful," Gregory Allard said. "And she is mine. And now, I feel, in some way, yours."

And almost without her willing it, a reflex, like sweat, or the leap from an electric shock, a smile came over her face, she felt her whole face was only a smile, and she couldn't stop it, couldn't reduce or modulate it, she could only nod and smile. She was aware of possibly looking foolish. But she didn't care. I have never been happier in my life, she said to herself, and then she remembered saying that about being with Tom. But that had been a mistake. The happiness she felt now had no tincture of wrongness in it, no voice that had to be silenced telling her she shouldn't be where she was.

He took down the small wooden Madonna and child. How eagerly the mother leant towards her baby, as if she could barely restrain herself from picking him up and holding him to her. The intense stillness of the marble head was not a part of this—was it the difference between marble and wood? The head gave a sense of endless serenity; the mother and child were full of a kind of vitality, as if at any moment they might spring into motion.

"How would you date them, if you had to?" Gregory Allard asked. She tried to read his expression. He was testing her, but what was the motivation behind the test? Was he going to reward her for a right answer or punish her for a wrong one, refuse her another look or grant her the access she needed?

She knew she was good at this sort of thing, noticing the small details in the course of a career that marked early from late work. She had studied images of Civitali for many hours, but she had only seen four or five actual works. He had a perfect right to ask her. She knew she was here because of her training, her position, which she knew to be false, as an expert.

She thought of Maura, and imagined Gregory Allard in his underwear and black socks. She thought of Sister Imelda, who would have had a saint in her hip pocket for just this sort of thing. Or she would have told her to pray to the Holy Spirit. Even Sister Maureen or Sister Patricia might have done that. But she had lost her faith, and it was many years, years of looking at her father's ravaged face, since she had believed there was a face with an ear that would respond to her prayers. She ran through everything she knew of Civitali's work; the *gentildonna* was marble, she was small, she was probably commissioned by a private client, and her hair was coiffed in the same way as the Rose Annunciation's. And the posture of the Madonna suggested the influence of Mino da Fiesole. She closed her eyes, as if she were diving from a high board. What would happen now? A perfect swan dive or a broken neck?

"Midcentury," she said, "I would say perhaps the sixties, fourteen seventy at the latest."

Gregory Allard laughed that rumbling laugh, that sounded like a reluctant winter engine.

"Well, well, well, Miss Riordan, Professor Riordan, that is to be, you've got it spot-on. Just what your elders and betters have said. Almost to the year. I will leave you alone here for half an hour and then we will have some very good and very cold champagne."

He backed out of the room, as if he were departing the presence of royalty. She was aware that she had broken out in a sweat, and she was afraid that she stank. She wanted to lift her arms and sniff herself, but she felt she couldn't. Certainly this was something the *gentildonna* would never have done, would never have thought of doing, and the Madonna was too busy with her child to care how she smelt. And if she did stink, Theresa told herself, there was nothing she could do about it. But then she realized it wasn't true; she could go into one of the bathrooms and surreptitiously wash. She lifted her arms and sniffed.

She seemed to herself all right. Now she could approach them, these beautiful ones, without the distraction of anxiety about her stinking flesh, flesh that unlike theirs, would rot and putrefy as these would not. "I'll do my best for you," she whispered to them; "I'll try not to say anything that won't be worthy of you." Thinking about her responsibility to say something about them, her elation disappeared. It was another burden, this sense of having to say something, of having to use them in some way to make something else: an argument, an article, a book. She wished she could just be with them, in silence, making nothing of them, making nothing.

There was a gentle knock at the door. Had half an hour really passed? She could hardly believe it possible. Gregory Allard showed her into the sitting room. The furniture was old and almost, she thought, deliberately rickety and uncomfortable. On one of the sagging chintz sofas sat two people whose good looks made Theresa want, simultaneously, to gasp and to hide. She guessed that they would both be called blond—but they didn't really have hair: instead, standing up from their skulls were silvery yellow spikes, and they had almost no flesh on their bodies. The woman wore a very short skirt and a top that seemed to be made of dragonfly wings, and her legs were so well muscled that Theresa wondered if she was a professional athlete. Neither of them changed their posture when Theresa walked into the room. Their legs were both very long, but the man's were the longer of the two, and Theresa could see in their thinness, their disproportionate length, the grasshopper features of Gregory Allard. She wondered why she kept thinking of insects.

"This is my son, Ivo, and his friend Sage," Gregory said. "They are joining us for champagne."

"Hey," said the woman.

"*Salve,*" said the man.

They both lit cigarettes. "I'm very grateful to the old man for letting us smoke."

"My parents won't let anybody smoke within a hundred yards of their house. But then, it's Marin County. My mother's always throwing me out of whatever room I'm in and basically sending me to another zip code if I want to smoke."

"But this is your home, of course," said Gregory Allard. "And it's Italy, not California."

"Yeah, home sweet home, Dad. What have I spent, like maybe sixty-five days total here in my life?"

"That's your choice, Ivo, of course. But let's not spoil Theresa's time with unpleasantness."

"No, Theresa, Gregory here never allows unpleasantness," he said, taking a heavy glass ashtray from the table and cradling it between his knees.

Everything about these two made Theresa feel clumsy, foolish, unfashionable, almost middle-aged, although she knew that Ivo was at least fifteen years older than she. "You're a photographer," she said, hoping to get him off the subject of his father and their past.

"Ivo has a show coming up. We hope you'll be there for the opening next week."

"I'm sure it's not your thing, any more than it is Gregory's here."

"I'd very much like to go. I really admire good photography."

"Who do you really admire?"

Her mind went blank, as though she had never seen a photograph in her life. The only names who came to her were all of dead people, and she knew that, unlike the test that Gregory had set for her, this question, also a test, was one that she would fail.

She felt herself blushing and she hated this man for making her do it.

"She's probably a real Ansel Adams girl," said Sage. "Don't you think? Good old American values."

"Actually," she said, "I've never been very interested in America."

"Well, Gregory, you've snagged one right out of Henry James," Ivo said. "Watch out, Theresa, they never come to a good end, these Henry James girls. And it's always about money. Gregory knows all about money. Or no, he doesn't know anything. He doesn't have to."

Theresa saw that Gregory would not say a word in her defense, or in his own. He opened the champagne. "To Theresa and her brilliant career," he said and poured them each a glass. Sage took one sip and held it in her mouth for at least half a minute before swallowing. Ivo downed his and said, "We're out of here. Nice meeting you." He pulled Sage to her feet.

"I'm sorry, Theresa," Gregory Allard said. "I think I've told you that Ivo can't forgive me. And he seems to enjoy not forgiving me. I don't think he'd know what his place was in the world if he weren't the person who couldn't forgive his father."

Theresa knew that she did not forgive her mother. Still, she would never have dreamed of speaking to her like that. But, she wondered, did that mean that she had more in common with Ivo Allard than she did with his father? Or ordinary nice people like Chiara, who loved their parents and enjoyed their company?

The grim-faced servant brought them their dinner: *tortellini in brodo* as a first course, then a roasted chicken and a plate of spinach surrounded by sliced lemons, leaving on the sideboard a salad in a crystal bowl rimmed with silver.

"It pleases me to be able to tell you—I suppose it is a sort of bragging, but, well, what of it?—that the chicken was reared here and the olive oil is from my trees and the wine is ours. It pleases me very much indeed."

"It's wonderful here," she said. "Everything is so beautiful."

"It requires a tremendous amount of attention, the upkeep is staggeringly expensive and difficult; well, everything is difficult in Italy, except when it isn't, which is when you know somebody who turns out to be the cousin of a cousin who can open any door."

"Speaking of which," she said, "I may need your help. One of the pieces I most want to see seems to be in a church that is never opened. Santa Maria dei Servi. And there's another in a church in the countryside, Mugano, that can't be got to by public transportation."

"Nothing easier," he said. "I'm sure I can find someone who's the cousin of a cousin. And we'll make a jaunt to Mugano; have lunch out-doors in a little trattoria I know there. Nothing simpler."

For dessert there was a sweet wine and *cantucci,* and Gregory Allard offered coffee, which he said he would not drink himself. She refused it, too; she knew she would already have trouble sleeping tonight because of what she'd seen.

He showed her his Roman medals and a bronze that he'd brought back from Cambodia, and some watercolors of Naples from the late eighteenth century. After a while he sat down and stretched his legs and raised his arms over his head. "And now," he said, "I'm afraid I must take you home. I fade rather early. People say that the old don't require much sleep, but actually I require quite a lot. And I do adore sleeping. Everything about it: my bed, my covers, my lovely pillows. Yes, sleeping is one of my greatest pleasures now. Perhaps that says something about a nearness to death."

"Oh no," she said. "You seem so young and so alive."

"We're all alive until we're not," he said.

The fog had thickened and Gregory Allard beeped his horn every few seconds as they made their way down the winding narrow road.

"You mustn't worry, I'm an excellent driver," he said. "It's one of my two real physical skills. Driving, and carving meats. You know my father went to a special course just to learn how to carve. And I must say he was a dab hand at it, and I'm offended by the hacking that passes for carving at most tables, I must say."

She tried to relax her grip on the handrest, but she did find the drive on the nearly invisible road rather alarming. She was glad when she saw the lights of the city, and even the narrowness of the streets, where it seemed you might always be scraping your car against some ancient wall, seemed a relief after the near-blind drive.

"I wonder if I might ask for the pleasure of your company tomor-row," he said. "I want your opinion on that piece the antiques dealer is saying is a Civitali."

"Oh, Mr. Allard, I don't think I'm qualified to make that kind of judgment."

"My dear, I'm not bringing you as an expert, just a friend with a very good eye. And by that time I may have found the cousin of the cousin who might be able to get us into Santa Maria dei Servi."

They agreed to speak in the morning. Theresa thought she would be awake all night, from the excitement of having seen the two Civitalis, but she fell immediately into a deep dreamless sleep, from which Gregory Allard's phone call awakened her, asking if they could meet at the antiques shop in an hour. He was already standing there when she arrived, pacing up and down, looking more than ever like a grasshopper in his green Lacoste shirt and khaki pants.

She could see it in the window a hundred feet before she got to the storefront; a statue, four feet high, that was once polychrome but the color had faded to a pocked beige. The arms were missing and one of the shoulders was degraded. But the posture was unmistakably Civitali's. But she told herself, it would be very possible to make a mistake. Perhaps it was Civitali's, perhaps it was only by someone in his school, perhaps it was only someone who had seen his work and been influenced by it.

Something in her was aroused by the statue, by the kind of puzzled supplication that she had seen in both the suffering Christ and the young virgin of the Annunciation. But she would not say anything yet.

The owner of the antiques store was younger than she expected, and more nervous than she believed it was in his interest to be. He kept rubbing his hands together and putting his first three fingers to his lips, then moving them away and rubbing his hands together again.

It was clear that he and Gregory Allard had had many conversations about the piece, and even Theresa's Italian was enough to let her know that they used their words only as placeholders, not using them as vessels of information.

Gregory Allard introduced her to Signore Calvi as a graduate student of art history at Yale, a specialist in Civitali. He mentioned Tom Ferguson's name. This seemed to make Signore Calvi even more nervous, and Theresa wanted to say to him: "You needn't be afraid of me. I'm nobody. I have no authority at all. Nothing I say will be of any consequence."

But seeing the intensity of Gregory Allard's gaze as it fell on her, she knew that was only partly true.

It seemed entirely remarkable that she was in the company of someone who might be able to make this beautiful object his, take it into his home, purchase it as you might purchase a refrigerator or a telephone. Or a perfectly ordinary, perfectly serviceable chair or desk.

"I think it's earlier than your pieces," she said to Gregory, speaking English. "You can see the gestural energy, but he hasn't quite achieved his full refinement, and he's still heavily under the influence of Rossellino and Mino da Fiesole."

Gregory Allard nodded and said, "Not in front of the children."

So he would be bargaining, she thought, as she had seen women in the market bargaining about tomatoes.

She tried to understand what it was about this statue that made it stand out, almost jump out from the other things in the shop, some of which were very lovely, some as old, or older. What made it more desirable, as you might desire one person standing among a clutch of perfectly attractive, perfectly presentable others? Some charge emanated from it, some envelope surrounded it, so she could feel the hair stand up on the back of her neck and the skin on her forearms prickle. She told herself she must be cool and analytical. She looked at it from all angles. She ran her fingers over the wood. And again all she really wanted to say was "It's beautiful, it's wonderful." But actually, that wasn't all. Now she wanted to say, as well, "You should buy it."

They excused themselves and made their way to Paola's for lunch. She could tell that Gregory Allard didn't want to talk until they were seated, until, perhaps, they'd had something to drink.

"So, what do you think?" he asked.

She said aloud the words, words she knew to be daring, that had been in her mind. "I think it's beautiful. I think it's wonderful. I think you should buy it."

"But do you think it's a Civitali? I'm a bit suspicious. Even with the missing arms, the price seems a little low. Calvi says he's giving me a break because he'd like it to stay in Lucca, but I'm unwilling to trust that kind of sentimentality in a dealer."

This was a side of Gregory Allard she hadn't seen: a rich man who bought beautiful things but wanted his money's worth. But what did worth mean? She wasn't sure she liked this in him. No, she was sure, she didn't like it, and the dislike made her bold.

"Does it really matter if it's a Civitali?"

"One doesn't like to be cheated."

It occurred to her that she had probably never worried about being cheated because she had never owned anything that anyone would want to cheat her of, had never had enough money so that anyone would want to do her out of it. And in the same way that Chiara's happy family made Theresa feel alone and a freak, Gregory Allard's wealth made her feel the strangeness of the way she had, until now, lived. The question arose: What was he paying for? The look of the thing, or the name attached to it? Was he buying something that would give him pleasure every time his eye fell on it, or was he looking ahead to the moment of resale, and the hope of making a profit? Or was it something else; would he be paying for a connection, a physical proximity to someone long dead, the primitive need to touch what the beloved dead had touched, a lover's desire for anything that proved that the beloved had inhabited the world, a consolation for the loss or the impossibility of presence? An ancient magic, but one that money could buy. So was it love, or commerce, at work in the decision Gregory Allard would now make? Or was it possible to separate them?

"You should buy it if you think it's beautiful and wonderful. Do you love it?"

"I like it very much. It often takes me a while living with something to experience what I would call love. I suppose that's very New England."

"If you don't love it, you shouldn't buy it. If you love it, or if you think it's beautiful and wonderful, you should buy it whether it's Civitali or not."

Gregory Allard blinked his grape green eyes, as if he were surprised at being spoken to in this way. "But you see it isn't just money I'd be cheated of. I'd be cheated of the real. So little in this world is real, is authentic; anything can be a copy of anything. I suppose one reason one desires objects like these, by an artist one feels attached to because the attachment seems like a living thing. And so if that turned out to be a lie ... Well, one would feel a terrible fool for being cheated of it."

She instantly regretted what she'd said, remembering how disrespectfully his son had spoken. So he wasn't unused to being spoken to in this way, and the thought of being in some way like Ivo appalled her.

"Please forgive me, Mr. Allard. I had no right to speak as I did. It's all very new to me."

"On the contrary, dear Theresa, and you must call me Gregory. You raise questions that I certainly ought to have thought about, but somehow never have. The question of what I'm paying for. What an extraordinary person you are, and now, stung a bit by your candor, I'm trying to discern whether you are extremely naïve or disproportionately wise for your years."

"Perhaps I'm simply rude."

"Believe me, my dear, I know rudeness when I encounter it. You were taken up by an idea, aroused by it, and what a rare thing that is. As a collector, I think a lot about rarity. And you are a rare person."

Paola came over and shook her finger at Gregory. "Are you going to eat or just discuss, discuss, discuss?"

"We will, I hope, Paola, do both. What do you recommend?"

"It's very warm today, so a cold tomato soup, some chilled prawns with garlic and parsley, and then a wonderful goat cheese which I found in the market in Orvieto. For dessert, a lemon ice."

"A summer meal from a dream of summer," Gregory said.

Theresa remembered that he had used a similar phrase about the horse. "The Tuscan dream of the white horse." Was it that he believed that everything good was only a dream, only unsusceptible to loss or snatching if you called it a dream, out loud?

"Gregory, you are a failed poet," Paola said.

"A failure in many things," he said.

"But in greatness of the heart, a very great success." She turned to Theresa. "My daughter has many troubles of the mind, and Gregory helped her to find the right doctor, the right medication. She has very nearly a normal life now, and it is all because of him. And what can I do in return? Recommend chilled prawns and a lemon ice. Not, dear Gregory, what we would call a just recompense."

"That's quite enough out of you, Paola, when my tongue is hanging out waiting for the tomato soup."

Money, Theresa thought. He was able to do good because of money. It made so many things easier. She wondered what it made more difficult, as it was reputed to do.

"I have good news," he said. "The cousin of a cousin . . . he happens to be a cousin of a cousin of the man who cleans my drains . . . has arranged for us to be let into Santa Maria dei Servi later in the week."

Theresa clapped her hands and actually said, "Oh goody," and was embarrassed, until Gregory laughed with her.

"How wonderful that you can be as pleased as a child by what will, after all, be your life's work. I think it is the most fortunate thing in the world to be able to make a living doing what you love."

"I've always thought that was such a strange phrase," Theresa said. "Making a living. As if living was something that could be made. Or not made. And all because of money."

"Money," said Gregory. "Let's not think of money until at least the sun has set." He raised his glass of Pinot Grigio. "To not thinking about money," he said.

"Agreed. And thank you, Gregory, for everything."

He lowered his head and said, "My dear."

The next five days were peaceful and harmonious. She breakfasted at her café, took a picnic on the walls, or treated herself to a *ceci* pizza— unless Gregory had phoned to invite her to Paola's. She worked four hours in the morning, sometimes in archives, where she would leave with dusty fingers and a cache of information which she believed would be of no use to her but which she equally believed she had to have examined. She lunched, napped, and then worked until dark, when she had a late dinner and took herself to bed, exhausted, pleased with herself and the sense of days well spent. Some days she talked to almost no one; some days Chiara was free for a coffee or a drink, but some days Theresa didn't come home until she was off duty.

She wanted to take another look at the Rose Annunciation, just to refresh her spirits, hoping that sitting in front of it in the dim quiet would inspire her to focus her thoughts and coalesce some of her ideas. The day before, at lunch, Gregory had asked her what she thought she might write about for her dissertation. He had said it very lightly and calmly, and this allowed her to speak calmly, in a way she never could have to anyone else, particularly anyone at Yale. Something about him suggested a large leisure, space and time for things to unwind themselves; the exact opposite of the professional anxiety that was part of her academic life.

"I have very conflicting ideas. I want to look closely at the work, and what I most like is doing formal analyses, so after I see the other Annunciations I could certainly do some sort of comparison, but I find it so difficult to write about what I see in a way that's not stultifyingly boring. I could do a monograph, but that's very out of fashion: it certainly wouldn't help my job prospects. It's very difficult, Gregory, to find the right words for what is beautiful. And yet that's what I have to do, or, as my old professor says, things get lost if you don't nail them down in writing. I could go in a completely different direction," she said, eager to speak, using him only as a wall on which to project her ideas, not noticing the marks that might already be there. "I'm very interested that a lot of the restoration work done on the Civitalis was done in the thirties. I'd like to explore what the aesthetics of restoration were under Fascism. Restoration is always about a view of history, and I wonder how that played out then. Civitali seems the antithesis of that overlarge Roman aesthetic, that Mussolini brand of looming, but anyway it might be interesting."

"You know, I first came to Italy in 1954. The War had only been over for nine years. But no one talked about it. They still don't, not really. The Italians like to believe that everything bad that happened under Fascism was forced upon them by the Germans. Just recently, I was at a dinner party with very close friends, all around my age, and they tried to come up with a definition of Fascism and said it was impossible. I thought: it's not impossible, it's about the abrogation of free speech, and civil rights, and the punishment of dissent by brute force. But I didn't say anything because they had all lived through it and I had not. It's a very interesting idea, your idea about restoration under Fascism."

"But I feel I'd be abandoning Civitali for a more general topic, and that makes me feel a bit guilty."

"Well, of course you'll come back here when you decide. And please know that I would be honored to have you as a guest in my home if you need to stay in Lucca for an extended period. As you see, I have an almost shameful number of rooms."

"That would be wonderful," she said. His offer, made as they sat in his garden waiting for lunch, gave her a sense of relaxation that was supported by the sweet smell of the new hay. This was the atmosphere she lived in, a mood of calm lightness that surrounded her as she approached San Frediano. But as if it were a protective glass covering, like the glass cabinets Gregory had built for his Civitalis, it shattered as she approached the steps of the basilica and saw Ivo Allard, Sage, and two men, with identically shaved heads. One was wearing white jeans and a black T-shirt, the other black jeans and a white T-shirt. The jeans and the T-shirts were tight, emphasizing the well-muscled bodies of both men.

She didn't know if they would have greeted her if she hadn't greeted them first. Certainly, they didn't seem glad to see her.

"Taking in the great churches?" Ivo said, with something like a sneer.

"There's a wonderful Civitali Annunciation here," she said.

"Oh, yes, but that's not the jewel of the crown here. We're here to see the mummy. Santa Zita. I believe the term is the 'incorruptible body.' But I think of her as Mrs. Bates. Norman's mother. Right out of Hitchcock."

Theresa didn't know what he was talking about, and he was quick to pounce on her puzzled look.

"Don't tell me you've never visited Mrs. Bates? Oh, my dear, you must. It's the biggest hoot in Lucca. Maybe in the whole of Tuscany."

The woman who worked in the little shop where Theresa had bought a postcard of the Annunciation opened the door slowly, with a pronounced reluctance. Theresa understood why the woman would be reluctant to welcome Ivo and his friends, but she wanted to say to her, I'm not with them, I'm not like them. I belong here.

Sage put her thin arm through Theresa's. "You've got to see this, honey, it's absolutely awesome."

She steered her past the baptismal font to a side chapel, and brought her over to a glass casket. Sage, Ivo, and the two men, to whom Theresa had not been introduced, began to laugh, too loudly for a church, and Theresa was afraid the woman who had let them in would now feel it her right to throw them out. She didn't want to look in the glass casket, but she couldn't help herself. She also couldn't help looking away. She had rarely seen anything that made the horror of deadness so real. Lying inside the glass casket were the remains of the dead saint, the skeletal hands folded, a rosary threaded through the bone fingers, and on the grinning skull a veil and a wreath of flowers.

"You must definitely do something with this, Ivo," said one of the men in what she assumed was a German accent. "Some kind of installation would be more than fabulous."

"I'm way ahead of you, Hermann," said Ivo. "I've already got sketches.

"She was a housemaid," he said, "famous for her devotion to her employers. One day she left her stove to go and help the poor, and one of the other houseworkers, who was jealous of her employer's regard, ratted her out. But when the employer came back, angels were at the stove, baking the bread that Zita was supposed to be baking. Now she's the patron saint of lost keys. You pray to her if you've lost your keys. Particularly your house keys. I don't know whether she's good at car keys, it may not be her field."

He was looking at Theresa with his sharp dark eyes, waiting for some kind of response. Was she supposed to laugh, was that a requirement? But it was his father, not Ivo, who was her benefactor. She owed him nothing. She was free not to laugh. She was free to walk away.

"I've got to take a look at the Annunciation," she said.

"What a good girl you are," said Ivo. "No wonder the old man's crazy about you. See you at the opening, I understand you're Pa's date."

"I look forward to it," she said. She felt that it wasn't wrong to lie politely in that way. But it was a complete lie; she dreaded going to the opening, and she was made uneasy by Ivo's calling her Gregory's date. But that, of course, was what he wanted. To make her uneasy. Congratulations, Ivo, she wanted to say. You've wrecked my peace.

She wanted to run away from them, but she knew that they were watching her and so she walked very slowly towards the chapel where the Annunciation was. It was 4:30 but the sun was still high, and it fell through the white octagonal panes of the window and struck the rose-colored dress of the Madonna with a soft clarity. She took her binoculars from her bag; she wanted to study the modeling around the lips.

She needed to take in the Madonna's calm. She felt the contact with Ivo and his friends a defilement; and she felt foolish that she'd never known about the horrible mummy just near the entrance of the church where she had come day after day. They were right, of course, to mock the whole thing: the "incorruptible body," the wreath of flowers and the bridal veil on the grinning skull, the legends and the devotions and the foolish credulous belief. She wanted to say: it has nothing to do with me, I have nothing to do with it, and, more important, it has nothing to do with Civitali.

She heard a low rumble in the main part of the church. Ten or twelve women, most of them at least in their seventies, two of them younger, plainer, wearing head scarves and cheap shoes, were saying the rosary. If they came into the chapel where she was sitting, if they knelt before the Madonna, they would be inhabiting a different universe than the one she inhabited, a universe where style and provenance and restoration and attribution were the coin of the realm, and the subject matter, the Virgin visited by an Angel, was entirely beside the point. But to these women it was the point, they based their lives on it, as Civitali had. So was she in fact closer to Ivo and his friends than to these women? And to Civitali, who had created these figures as objects of devotion, as objects of believing prayer? She felt a sudden shame, as if she had no right to be there, no more right than Ivo and his friends. What would Civitali say to her if he appeared now, in the basilica, looking through her binoculars while, a few feet away, old women prayed the rosary? Would he have said, "You understand nothing of what it was I did. Nothing at all. I made what I made for them, not you." Was Civitali, in his beliefs, closer to the people who prayed to the mummy than to her, who believed in nothing?

The Annunciation happened to be in a church, but it would have served her purposes as well if it were in a museum or a private house. Better, perhaps. She wouldn't have dreamed of praying to the Virgin. She was not someone who prayed. If she believed in transcendence, it was the transcendent power of beauty. There was no one she could speak to among the dead who she believed could make anything happen in the world or in her life. She did not even speak to her poor dead father, whom she could not imagine, even in eternity, having any effect at all.

She thought she would buy something new to wear to Ivo's opening; all her clothes seemed too floral and girlish and unurbane. But the prices in the shops on the Fillungo terrified her. She decided on a long scarf, which she thought would at least add an element of seriousness to her dress. Only after she'd paid for it did she realize that it was a deep rose color, almost the color of the Rose Annuciation's dress. She bought a bottle of nail polish that pleased her by matching the scarf almost exactly. She polished her toenails. She remembered the first time she'd ever done that, when she and Maura went to Florida. Was that almost two years ago? Where would she be in two years?

Gregory was waiting for her in the lobby. He was pacing up and down, eating up the small space with his long legs, his jerky strides. She knew that he was nervous. He was nearly silent on the ten-minute walk to the gallery. She wanted to say, "It will be fine, everything will be fine." But she had no confidence that those words were, in fact, true.

The gallery was actually a private museum, founded by a local industrialist Gregory didn't know much about. It had been a palazzo built by a Renaissance banker, and the outside kept its ancient look, but once they were in the door, the present and the future declared themselves with a breezy insistence. The walls were white, and there were video displays flashing from every wall, and flashing signs recommending small plates for early to late luncheon. She saw immediately that she and Gregory were overdressed; everyone else was in jeans, except for some of the women, who wore short skirts that fitted their buttocks like bandages.

Just at the top of the staircase leading down to the exhibition itself, a screen flashed the words "Lucca Then and Now, the Sacred and the Profane." She and Gregory stopped to watch the screen. Alternating with the lettering was the image of a man whose body was almost entirely covered by tattoos. Theresa felt a wave of nausea rise up inside her. The tattooed man was standing in the posture of Civitali's Dolorous Christ she'd seen in the Villa Guinigi, his arms opened in baffled supplication, his face despairing.

She wanted to take Gregory's hand and say, let's go quickly, before we see something terrible. But she knew that wasn't possible. They made their way downstairs, entering a room that a sign on the wall informed them was a cellar that housed the remains of a Roman well. But she couldn't pay attention to that. Now she had to read the words on the wall, Ivo's words, explaining his work.

LUCCA THEN AND NOW

One of the major sources of Lucchese pride is the fifteenth-century sculptor Matteo Civitali. He didn't travel much outside Lucca, so his fame is not as great as many believe it should be. Perhaps he is most famous for his (contested) contribution to the history of art: some say he was the first to depict the male nude. Without fig leaf, without even a loincloth. I like to think it's true, because even then Lucca was a stuffy town. I'm trying to rescue Civitali, as a kind of trope for the mummification of the past (see the "incorruptible body of S. Zita in the basilica of S. Frediano"), to dislodge Lucca from the frozen place of a museum city—let's hope it doesn't go the way of Florence—and, in my work, to mix up categories, the gift of the postmodernist imagination. So, dressed in the clothes of Civitali's Madonnas, we see one of Lucca's proudest residents, Campari, born Giorgio Alcante, now star of one of the coolest drag clubs in Tuscany, CLUB SEXI LADY. In the posture of the suffering Christ, our own Lauro Z., owner of TAT TATTOOS, wearing a creation by one of the most innovative designers here, an Australian expat, Bonnie Lederer, whose reinvention of the tuxedo has

been a big seller in her store, THINK OUTSIDE THE BOX. I'd like
to thank my beloved Sage Brooke for her work with costume, hair, and
makeup—without which nothing of my work would be possible. Art
lives, Lucca lives . . . and not just for tourists.

Theresa had to acknowledge that he'd described his work quite well. The show consisted of paired photographs. There were photographs of two Annunciations and, beside them, dressed in identical costumes, his hair done exactly like the Madonna's, was Giorgio Alcante, Campari, the drag queen. In the posture of the Dolorous Christ was the tattooed man. In the place of the mark of the spear, there was a tattoo of a dragon and, instead of the loincloth, a miniature tuxedo, with a bow tied exactly at the center of the clearly erect penis.

She was afraid to meet Gregory's eye. But looking around the room, she couldn't see him. She went upstairs, thinking perhaps he'd gone to get himself another drink. But he was nowhere to be found.

She had never been so angry in her life. She knew that was something people said all the time, and it wasn't literally true for them, but it was for her. The circumstances of her life had made her feel that anger was one of those luxuries that, in her mother's words, she simply couldn't afford. She was the only child of old-fashioned parents who didn't countenance anger in a daughter, and then she was the child of tragedy, the child of a destroyed father and an overworked, exhausted mother whom everyone called a hero. When she felt anger, it was a fire that was kept banked, well protected by walls of impermeable stone. But now she felt anger as an explosion; she saw herself a cartoon character; she imagined smoke coming out of her ears, so on fire did her brain seem.

What Ivo had done was disgusting. It was perverse. It was wicked. What, she wondered, was the difference between wickedness and evil? Evil, she supposed, suggested a greater scope, and Ivo's adolescent display would affect no one but his father and herself. He had mounted a small show in a provincial gallery; the notice that might be taken would be small and provincial. But he had defiled something that she believed to be of the very highest value. Purity of intention; it was a phrase that Sisters Jackie and Maureen used in describing some of the saints they admired, to encourage Theresa and Maura to work hard even at subjects, like math, that they didn't like. She'd applied the words to the artists she loved as Sister Imelda did to her saints. Defilement. But no physical thing had been harmed. Could you defile an idea? Could you defile love and fineness and effort and skill and patience and an original vision? Certainly, he had tried.

Never had the desire to punish someone seized her so entirely. People had hurt her before; her mother's going off with George had seemed a kind of betrayal, not that she had chosen another man but that she had chosen such a coarse and vulgar braggart. But Theresa could forgive her mother, because her mother had had such a hard time. And she could forgive Tom because she had got a great deal out of what they'd had. Also because she felt he was too insignificant to want to punish; thinking of him as the husband of his wife, she despised him too much to want to direct the energy of punishment his way.

But Ivo and what he'd done left her no room for compassion, gratitude, or the indifference made possible by a sense of one's own greater power. Ivo was powerful; he acted from a position of strength, his gestures were strong, his aim exact. His desire to punish fed her own. She felt it in her mouth; it had a bitter taste, and its texture was sharp and cutting as if she were biting down with a ragged tooth on a capsule that released pure bitterness. The sharpness and bitterness were not without pleasure; she felt enormously alive; small seed pearls of sweat broke out along her hairline, and her blood seemed quick and thin, like an athlete's primed for speed.

She knew exactly what she would do. But it would have to wait till morning.

She showered and tried to sleep, but sleep was impossible. She packed her bag. She counted the money left in the envelope Tom had given her: she still had two hundred euros in cash. She checked the credit balance on her MasterCard. She looked up the Trenitalia timetable, and the Alitalia website, and then Delta's, and United Airlines, and USAir.

She made herself stay in the room until 9:00, and she phoned and booked a taxi to take her to the station at 11:30. She wrote a note to Chiara: so sorry, had to leave at the last minute; will be in touch. She made her way to the café, where the owners seemed pleased to serve her cappuccino and *cornetto* without being asked. She told them she would be leaving that day, a work emergency, no no, nothing wrong with her family. Her family was fine. She looked up "hardware store" in her phrase book, and asked the owner of the café to recommend one in the neighborhood.

In the hardware store, she asked the salesman for cans of spray paint, and picked up three. Yellow. Color of cowardice. Color, she hoped, of shame.

The gallery opened at 11:00, but she knew that no one would be there that early. She smiled politely at the bored young woman at the desk, who was busy reading the Italian edition of *Vanity Fair,* then made her way downstairs, glancing over her shoulder to make sure she wasn't followed.

She looked at the photographs as little as she could. She didn't have to look closely to do what she'd come for. She took the top off the first can, shook it, and covered the photograph of the drag queen Madonna with yellow paint. She did the same with all the others, and then put the cans back into her navy blue cloth carrier bag. Then, smiling pleasantly, she walked out of the gallery, bidding the *Vanity Fair*–reading girl goodbye.

She brought her bags down to the hotel lobby, settling her bill with the sullen young man whom she'd spoken to only perfunctorily in her time there. Part of her planning included the knowledge that it was Chiara's day off. She asked the young man to give Chiara her note, and he shrugged his shoulders, as if it were one more incomprehensible request from one more incomprehensible guest. The taxi arrived on time. The train was not late.

She boarded the train, looking around her in case she was being followed by police. For the first time in her life, she had to think of herself as a criminal. Movies and detective novels had been no preparation for this sick feeling of anxious vigilance. The word "capture" suddenly became real, with its attendant images of confinement, darkness.

She was surprised how easy it was at the last minute to trade her first-class ticket for an economy seat. She smiled her way through customs, hoping she wasn't giving herself away by smiling too much, but the fat clerk merely wished her a good voyage.

She'd booked her ticket through to Milwaukee. She couldn't bear going back to New Haven; certainly she couldn't face Tom. She had no idea where she'd go when she got to Milwaukee. Her mother had sold the house. Sitting at the gate half an hour before takeoff, she realized she was homeless.

The thought of her own homelessness made her feel especially vulnerable to the law. She searched around in her mind to imagine a place of safety and could think of only one. She would call Maura. What time was it in Tortola? She would have to wake her, and Maura would be crabby, she was always crabby waking up. But she had no choice.

It was almost a relief that Maura's response was so predictable. "T, what the fuck. It's five o'clock in the morning here."

"Maura, I've ruined my life."

"That's pretty hard to do nowadays, even for someone with your work ethic."

What Theresa didn't expect, but probably should have, knowing Maura, was that when she told her what she'd done, Maura laughed. "That might just be the coolest thing you've ever done," she said.

"But, Maura, you don't understand. I probably can't go back to Yale now. I can probably never go back to Italy. I may be wanted by the police."

"I think they're too busy with pedophiles and arms dealers to worry about you. And maybe the Yale people will never find out. Their heads are so far up their tiny asses they might not even notice."

"Of course they will, my advisor will find out, the guy's father is a friend of his." She remembered that she hadn't told Maura anything about Tom.

"Where the hell are you, T, on what continent?"

"I haven't left Italy. I'm landing in Milwaukee, but I don't know where to go when I get there."

"Sure you do. Go to the convent."

The convent. Of course. There were plenty of empty rooms there; the house had been built for many more nuns, and the ones who lived there now had no desire to sell it. She tried to imagine who would be there in the summer, who she hoped would be there. She hoped it wasn't Sister Jackie; she would ask too many questions, offer too many solutions, not understand at all what had upset Theresa so much that she would commit what Sister Jackie (who was devoted to nonviolence, to the point that, as Sister Maureen said, it made you want to do violence to her) would call a violent act. She hoped it wasn't Sister Imelda on her own, because she would just be puzzled. She wanted Sister Maureen there because she would get the situation, might come up with some ideas, would probably be annoyed at Theresa's unwisdom, but wouldn't go on and on about it after what might be a quick initial blast. As long as Sister Maureen was there, she realized that she wanted Sister Imelda, too, because of her unquestioning acceptance, her unquestioning belief that Theresa was "a wonderful girl."

"Just email them. Maureen is on her computer around twenty hours a day."

"I'm afraid to open my email. Will you do it?"

"You still have the same password? Matteo C?"

"Yes. See if there's anything from somebody named Allard. Or Ferguson. Or from Joan Gallagher."

"She always scared the crap out of me. I always thought she expected me to be interested in paintings on velvet. But her husband's really great. He does all this work with diabetes patients, particularly on Indian reservations. He's saved a lot of people from being amputated."

Theresa remembered how Tom and Amaryllis had made fun of Joan's husband. How he had called Joan's marrying him "perverse."

"There's one from Ivo Allard. The subject line is 'Mille grazie.' I take it that means a thousand thanks."

"Oh my God, it's a trick, it's some kind of a trick. You have to open it, Maura. No, don't. No, do it now but don't tell me. No, you have to tell me. But don't tell me if it's terrible. No, you have to tell me in case I have to watch out for the police."

"Be quiet, I'm going to read it to you. It says, 'Dearest Theresa. I can't thank you enough for what you've done. You'll put me on the map. The gallery has been on the phone to the newspapers in Rome and Milan . . . they might actually send someone to cover the show.

You've turned a minor show in a minor provincial gallery into something that will get national attention. The sales will go through the roof. I will have to buy you champagne next time you are in Lucca. By the way, everyone knew who you were. The girl at the desk said no one was around but a red-haired American with big tits. Pa doesn't know yet. He'll probably be shocked, but secretly glad. Mille grazie."

"What an asshole," Maura went on. "But he doesn't sound like he's sending Interpol out after you. So I don't think your life is ruined quite yet. On the other hand, he really feels like he beat you. And maybe he did. Whatever game it was you thought you were playing."

"It wasn't a game, Maura, and what he did was horrible. What am I going to do, Maura? Where am I going to go? I can't stand to go back to Yale, I just can't stand it."

"Well, it's only July, so you can just put that on the back burner. Listen to me. Just listen. You'll go to the convent and you'll talk to Professor Gallagher and you'll let the nuns pet you and feed you lots of junk food, and then you'll come down here. It's almost hurricane season, the flights are really cheap. Call me when I wake up."

"What time is that?"

"Think Margaritaville."

She rang the convent bell. At first no one seemed to be answering the doorbell. But then she heard slow, light footsteps; she knew it was Sister Imelda. And the look on her face was one of unalloyed, unmodulated joy. She opened her arms and took Theresa to her with such a delighted intake of breath that Theresa let herself (although she was much taller) fall onto Sister Imelda's breast and cry. "I've made a mess, Sister," she said. "I've really made a mess."

"Well, I'm sure you haven't, you couldn't possibly, you're such a wonderful girl. But let's hear what Sister Maureen thinks. And come and have some tea and cookies; Sister Maureen and I were just going to have some and then watch Dr. Phil. He's got a show today about the fattest bride in the world. This girl whose goal was to be eight hundred pounds at her wedding. And her fiancé was all for it; it seemed to be what he wanted."

Sister Maureen appeared at the door. "Yeah, Theresa, I'm sure that's the thing you most wanted to see just off the plane. So you've made a mess. You're not the first in the history of the world; I'll bet you're not the last."

She followed Sister Maureen up the stairs. "Do you want a shower first? Maybe you just want to sleep. Why don't you shower, we're having BLTs for supper, then you can just crash. You can tell us everything in the morning. Or tonight if that's what you want."

"BLTs with mayonnaise?"

"Specialty of the house."

She couldn't think of a more desirable meal. It was so American, so much the food of home, so entirely unlike anything she'd eaten in Italy.

She hadn't realized how hungry she was, and to her embarrassment she had finished her sandwich before the other two were half done. Sister Imelda stood up and made her another without her asking. She felt like the indulged, perhaps even spoiled child of the house, but she craved the indulgence, like a balm on abraded skin.

They took their iced tea out to the back porch and sat on identical white wicker chairs with identical red and yellow striped cushions. She told her story. Sister Imelda just kept blinking, as if Theresa were speaking in a foreign language. Sister Maureen whistled.

"Well, you have made a mess. I don't quite understand the implications for your future, which you are so convinced are dire. I think the best thing is to call Joan Gallagher. I'm out of my depth."

Theresa nodded, as though a doctor had just told her that she needed a course of treatments that would be painful and expensive, and whose usefulness he couldn't guarantee. Sister Maureen went into the room where the telephone was, and came back in less than five minutes.

"She's coming over now. I told her the outlines."

"What did she say?" Theresa asked, her throat dry with anxiety.

"She laughed," Sister Maureen said. "She couldn't stop laughing."

When Joan Gallagher walked into the room, Theresa remembered what Maura always said about her: she looked much more like what people thought nuns looked like than Sister Maureen or Sister Jackie. Sister Maureen had simply been born a beautiful woman; she had those blue-violet eyes people associated with Elizabeth Taylor, and in the years in which Maura and Theresa had invented exotic pasts and romantic histories for the nuns who taught them, they were convinced that those eyes would have made her susceptible to a grand passion. "They're almost wrong on a nun, okay for Elizabeth Taylor, but you've always got to be thinking of sex somehow when you think of violet eyes, and, hey, you're not supposed to be thinking about sex when you're thinking about nuns," Maura had said. Sister Maureen's hair curled softly and naturally; she wore it simply, but there was no severity to the simplicity, and today she had on simple black cotton pants and a white cotton shirt. Joan Gallagher was nearly six feet tall. "You just have to think of the word 'beanpole' when you see her, you just don't have a choice," Maura had said.

Tonight, she was wearing a khaki skirt that fell two inches above her ankles, a short-sleeved madras shirt, and Birkenstocks. Her hair was a clench of tight, almost furious curls, which had once been blond but were now turning half gray, and the turn was not in Joan Galla-gher's favor.

"Sit down, honey, let me get you a glass of iced tea," said Sister Imelda. Theresa found it astonishing that anyone would think of call-ing Joan Gallagher "honey." She had very little sweetness in her; she was rigorous, demanding, honest, ironic. The word people used about her most often was "tough." Theresa could never imagine her as the mother of children. Sister Maureen and Sister Imelda were a hundred times more maternal. With Joan Gallagher, you always had to watch your step.

And she knew she had lost her step, lost her footing, fallen on her face. She would have to prostrate herself now—but she was already in the abject position. She would have to confess, and humbly, almost helplessly, ask for advice.

"No, thanks, Sister, I'm taking Theresa out for a drink." She turned to Sister Maureen. "We'd invite you, but I've given up on teaching you how to drink properly. You'd probably order Baileys Irish Cream and I'd have to move to another city from the mortification of it."

"You forget my M.Phil. year at Oxford, Ms. Gallagher, when I became quite discerning in the matter of beer."

"Oh, yes, the brew that made Milwaukee famous. How do I know you're not just reliving your riotous youth?"

"Well, you just have to trust me."

"I have, and where has that gotten me? Oh, wait I forgot. It all worked pretty well."

Theresa had never imagined that Joan Gallagher had it in her to be playful; she could see how she and Sister Maureen enjoyed this smart girl banter, and she wished she could just listen to them for the rest of the night instead of having to sit through this required tête-à-tête with Joan Gallagher. She wanted to take Sister Maureen's hand and say, "Come with me. Don't leave me alone." But Joan Gallagher was jingling her car keys. "I have two hours' leave, and then Michael puts some bloody masterpiece on the table. God, his experiments in the kitchen are exhausting. Of course it takes me seven hours to clean up."

"Oh, you're a pitiful woman. A man who cooks for you, what a curse."

"Yes, and you encourage him, although God knows you've never done anything above a grilled cheese sandwich."

"I'll have you know we had some excellent BLTs for supper."

"My son Jeremy would say, 'Oh great, dead pig.'"

"Pigs are not high on my list of worries," Sister Maureen said. "I don't like the look in their eyes. Shifty."

"Neither do I," said Joan Gallagher. "But I don't tell Jeremy that."

They were silent in the car, and then Joan Gallagher said, "Shall we go to Valentino's? It's a bit quieter than other places."

Valentino's was an upscale pizzeria that had some tables outside. Theresa knew Joan Gallagher went there often and they would probably find her a quiet spot.

She ordered a bottle of Nero d'Avola and without a pause looked into Theresa's eyes and said, "You'd better tell me everything."

She would not tell Joan Gallagher everything. She would not tell her about Tom Ferguson, who theoretically was her friend. She told her about Gregory Allard's collection, and his helping her get access to the Civitalis. She told her what she believed was available in the archives if she decided to pursue that kind of thing for her dissertation.

She described her possible dissertation topics. Only then did she talk about Ivo, about his show, and about what she'd done to it.

"Well, to be completely practical, you really didn't ruin anything irreparable. You probably didn't even hurt the photographs, just the glass in the frames that was covering them. And from what you say, this little shit probably doesn't want to take any legal action. The father sounds like a nice, sad man; he probably fantasizes that you're the daughter he never had and always wanted, so I bet in time he'll take you back to his bosom. But what you need right now is a little time off. You've never taken time off in your life. Take next year, go somewhere fun and different, let your dissertation ideas simmer, or bake, or whatever cooking metaphor you want to use, or that my husband would be happy using."

Something about Joan Gallagher's straightforwardness gave Theresa a kind of courage, the courage to be straightforward herself. "The thing is, I don't know if I want to go on with a Ph.D. There are so many things against it."

"Like?"

"Like, even though Ivo was completely disgusting, he made me have to think about the connection between the kind of art I love and the money that goes into its preservation and display. And then there's the way you have to talk about things in the academy nowadays. You can't use the word 'beautiful.' You can't use the word 'value.' I can't stand the theory, and other kind of stuff bores me to tears. How the pattern of the wormholes proves some kind of dating. Or the influence of A on B. And who's going to read what I write? Three Ph.D. students, two of whom have private incomes, and one who's married to a hedge fund owner."

"Everything you say is right. We are an endangered species, people who like to look at beautiful old things, not because we can make money off it, but out of love. 'Love'; oh, 'love,' it's another word like 'beauty' you can't use. But love and beauty, yes, that's why we do what we do."

It was a little frightening for Theresa to hear Joan Gallagher speak that way. She wasn't sure she liked the heating up it implied, the melting of the cool surface she had come to depend on for its very coolness.

"You're worn out, or burnt out, something like that. You need a bit of a rest." She looked at the man's watch on her thin wrist. "And now, I must go back home to my husband. How long will you be in Milwaukee?"

"I don't know, exactly. My friend Maura is working as a nurse on an island in the Caribbean. I might go there for a while."

"Sounds perfect. Have a drink with an umbrella for me."

They drove back in silence. As Theresa got out of the car, Joan Gallagher took her hand and kissed it. "You'll make it," she said. "You've got the stuff."

Once, she would have been thrilled by this kind of praise from Joan Gallagher. But now it just seemed like another burden.

Sister Maureen was sitting on the back porch. She was holding a very thick book. "I'm rereading *War and Peace,*" she said. "I think I was too young for it when I read it first. I may just be old enough for it now. How was Joan?"

"She was great. She was very encouraging. She thinks I should take time off."

"And will you?"

"Yes. You remember Maura Shaughnessy? She's working as an emergency room nurse on Tortola, it's an island in the Caribbean. She's invited me to come down there for a while, just get some kind of simple job."

"Sounds great. I've always had great regard for Maura. The two of you were so important to each other. Two brave girls, given not a very good hand of cards. She was an excellent poet, you know. Remember I was your English teacher before I was your principal. Is she still writing poetry?"

Theresa felt ashamed that she didn't know. In high school, they had been the editors of the literary magazine, Maura bullying their classmates into submitting poetry and stories and essays, and Theresa coaxing drawings out of them, and finding images that were striking but not controversial for the cover. But since she'd decided to do nursing, Maura didn't talk about her poetry anymore. And Theresa hadn't asked. Once Maura had settled on becoming a nurse, the attention had shifted to Theresa, and her move into the great, dangerous, larger world. She would ask Maura about her poems as soon as she saw her. Or maybe not right away. But it would happen; she would see to that. She hoped it wasn't too late.

"You know, Theresa, you never had a youth. I think it's time you get one, or use what you have before it's past its sell-by date."

She knew that Sister Maureen was trying to be helpful, to give her some kind of permission, but she felt her words as another weight on her shoulders, as she had felt Joan Gallagher's "You've got the stuff." Would she never get away from the sense that people wanted something from her, were waiting to see what she had "made of" whatever they had in mind: her intellectual gifts, her well-trained eye, and now her youth? She didn't want to make anything of anything. She didn't know what she wanted. She felt she had never known less about more in her life.

"I sometimes feel that we did you a very great disservice keeping you here at Divine Word. That we should have pushed you out to an Ivy League school, or maybe UW Madison, someplace where you'd be in a crowd of peers, introduced to new things, challenged, trying your wings. I think we wanted to keep you in our nest because we liked our nest, and we never considered that it might be too small for you. You probably didn't belong here. You were grateful to us, and, yes, in the very hard times when your father was so ill we were good for you, we gave you a place to go. But we probably kept you here out of nostalgia, out of a remembrance of things past and a hopeless hope in a nonexistent future that we didn't even believe in, maybe didn't even want, but couldn't give up because for us it represented a past that for us had been beautiful. And had a kind of luster, simply in its pastness.

"We didn't want things to end with Joan Gallagher. She was the last of something, one of the last classes of smart girls who didn't think, or whose parents didn't think, that they belonged in the big, scary secular colleges. In those days, our biggest majors were English and philosophy and art history. And the sisters teaching those things—I count myself among them—had very good training. Jackie went to Berkeley, I went to Oxford, only for graduate school, of course, but never mind; we came back with very good training. And we'd been smart girls ourselves. So we really believed, in the days after the Second Vatican Council, God, we were so young then, that we could do something that would allow us to hold on to the best of the past but open some new windows. But you see, it didn't work. When the smart girls knew they could go other places, they didn't come to us. And why should they? We got their point, even though it hurt us. We knew something had come to an end.

"My life has been about the end of a lot of things. When I entered the community, there were fifty of us in my class. Now only two of us are still around; everyone else left or died. Left to get married or just because they should never have been here in the first place. We knew we had to change, and we did. Now Divine Word is a place for people who need to be here, need us in a new way. Now our most popular majors are nursing and business and accounting. But I'm still teaching Shakespeare, and Joan is still teaching Medieval and Renaissance art, and we teach it to people who wouldn't be getting it, and, for some of them, it's very important. They're better educated than they would be if they were somewhere else where people weren't looking after them as we do. Only they're not educated as we were educated. When I entered, we spent hours learning to sing Gregorian chant. I learned reams of Latin poetry. Well, that's over now, and it's probably a good thing. We weren't paying so much attention as we do now to the people our order was founded to pay attention to. Our founders started the order to teach the children of immigrants, not the children of the comfortable middle class. And now, again, we are.

"But I think we saw you and we thought, Well, maybe something will last from the old ways. We weren't thinking of the cost to you. We never worried about Joan. For one thing, she came from a wealthy family, and, for another, she never seemed much affected by what people thought about her. I'm not sure she even notices; it might be the money, I don't know. But she's always done exactly what she wanted, and what she wants now is to teach here, to teach the kind of people she's teaching, which she knows she's good at, is happy to tell you she's better at than anyone she knows. But you're a different case. You don't have her self-confidence. You don't have her money. I think we may have served you very badly. It's not enough that I have to ask God's forgiveness. I ask you to forgive me now."

"Forgiveness? Of all the people in the world, you have nothing to be forgiven for. You always took me seriously. I'll never be able to repay that."

"Well, maybe you need to be a bit less serious for a while," Sister Maureen said, and Theresa knew her words hadn't meant much to Sister Maureen, and she felt like a parent who hasn't been listened to by a recalcitrant child.

"You always have a place here, Theresa," she said. "Please know that you always have a place."

The days that made up her life on Tortola were unlike any she had ever lived. She read almost nothing, she became a runner, training herself to run on the beach, working up to six miles a day. She took long swims in the turquoise sea. That year, the hurricanes were not a devastation, the storms dramatic and interesting rather than life-threatening disasters. She almost never thought about Yale, and, when she did, she quickly changed her clothes . . . into a bathing suit or running shorts or a sundress, as if a change of costume might banish the thoughts of graduate school, which it seemed again and again to do. She got a job in a wine bar owned by a friend of Maura's boyfriend, a young Dutchman who appreciated her knowledge of French and Italian, and insisted that she wear a black sleeveless dress and high, strappy sandals to work every night. She learned a great deal about wine; she began to consider that it might be a sensible way to spend a life, becoming an expert in wines, using her talents for discrimination in a way that would bring immediate pleasure, a way that had been honorable for centuries.

She and Maura lived together easily; Maura was happy to have Theresa to share the rent, since she had thrown out the anesthesiologist with whom she'd got the apartment. It turned out he had a gambling problem, and was stealing drugs from the hospital to pay his debts. He hadn't been sent to jail, but he'd lost his job and was now back home in Arkansas, refusing any kind of help.

After Theresa had been there nearly three months, she opened her email to find a message from a lawyer in Italy. He asked her to phone in relation to the estate of Gregory Allard, who had died in an automobile accident.

At first she thought it was some kind of trick, something Ivo had thought of to entrap her, a way of finding out where she was so he could send the police after her. But Maura said, "He said you were left something in a will."

"Poor Gregory," she said. "I hope he died a good death. He was a good man. I don't know how old he was. In his eighties."

"Call the lawyer now. Don't you want to know what he left you? Maybe one of the Civitalis. Or maybe it's just a set of teaspoons."

Notario Lambrino spoke perfect English. He told her the details of Gregory's death. It was an automobile accident; the young signore was driving; both of them were killed instantly. It was a wet night, and they crashed into a stone wall on the road outside Signore Allard's villa.

Theresa's first thought was: That was where we saw the white horse, and her second was rage at Ivo. Driving too fast, his carelessness taking the life of his father, who was ten times the man he would ever have been.

"Well, signorina, Signore Allard has provided very handsomely for you. The villa and its contents belong to you; he has arranged that the staff be kept on, that they be paid an annuity only as long as they continue to work there. And he's left you a very large sum of cash because he makes a point that you will be responsible for the upkeep of the villa as he left it. Except for this and a bequest to the Lupus Foundation, you are his sole heir. I hope you can come to Lucca as soon as possible. There will be some complicated negotiations."

"The villa and its contents?" Theresa said, sitting down heavily on her bed. She had put the phone on speaker, so Maura could hear everything. Maura was jumping on the bed, running in circles, taking Theresa's hands and twirling her around.

But Theresa didn't feel like dancing. She felt frightened. A villa and its contents. A fortune. A fortune she knew she didn't deserve, in a foreign city, a foreign country famous for the Byzantine incomprehensibility of its laws.

She told the lawyer she would be in touch with him when she had made travel plans, and assured him it would be very soon.

"You are a very fortunate young woman," the lawyer said. "Very fortunate indeed."

"I don't understand. We'd only just met."

"He changed his will two months ago. When I asked him why he was making this change—one has to, of course, with persons of a certain age—he said you were a person of courage, taste, and standards. Of course, you would only inherit in the case of his son's death. And, by the way, his son had made no will."

She wrapped her arms around her torso and sat on the bed rocking.

"Will you tell me your problem, for Christ's sake?" Maura said. "You look like someone told you you have to have your leg cut off without an anesthetic."

"It's all wrong. It's all wrong. I hardly knew him. He hardly knew me."

"I guess he thought he knew you well enough. Jesus, T, you're an heiress. That's a sentence I never thought I'd be saying. My friend is an heiress. My friend owns a villa. My friend is rich."

"I don't know what to do. You'll come with me, won't you, to straighten it all out?"

"Of course."

They rented a car at the Pisa airport, and Maura drove while Theresa read the map and translated the road signs. Theresa kept telling her to slow down. Gregory's accident had made her nervous every time she got in a car.

"I wonder where it happened, exactly," Theresa said. "I wonder where he died."

"I wonder how much of this is yours," Maura said.

"I guess we'll find out. The lawyer said he'll meet us here at one, but Italians aren't famous for punctuality."

Maura stopped the car in the drive in front of the double stairway. They walked down the hill and sat on a green iron bench in the garden that Theresa remembered from one of the times she'd been here with Gregory. The valley spread out like a lap; stuck into the various shades of green, like the heads of pins, were the pinks and yellows of the small farmhouses, an insistence of sheer colors among the black cypresses, the silver olives.

The colors spun; the shapes grew indistinct. She knew she ought to be feeling joy, but what she felt was dread. Was this another one of those gifts that the giver failed to see was also a great burden? It was all too much. She had owned almost nothing in her whole life. She hadn't even owned a car. She tried to think what she had owned. Her clothes, her books, a computer, a cell phone. And now she was meant to be the *padrona,* a great landowner. She felt overwhelmed. Why had he given this to her? Why hadn't he just given her the Civitalis? Even that would have been too much, but it would not have been the burden that this was.

"I bought champagne at duty free and I stole these plastic cups from the plane," Maura said. "They won't make much of a satisfying clink, but we'll do what we can. And of course the champagne won't be cold. But look at this, we have to celebrate, and we have to do it right now. Look at all this. It's all yours."

"But suppose I wreck it, suppose I destroy it, suppose it falls to ruin in my hands. Suppose it catches fire or the pipes burst and everything is destroyed in a flood."

"Jesus, T, get a life. This is a fairy tale. Do you think Cinderella spent a lot of time worrying that glass slippers could lead to plantar fasciitis?"

"I don't know what it all means. I don't know what to do. I don't even know where to begin."

"I don't think you have to. Not right now. The lawyer will be here in a little while and he'll tell you where to begin. And then you'll do the next thing, and then something else." Maura raised her plastic cup. "Here's to not knowing what to do," she said.

Theresa took a sip of champagne. She knew that there was one thing she would do. She was thinking of Tom Ferguson, that she hadn't been in touch with him at all since she had read his email telling her he wouldn't be joining her. She wondered if he had ever heard from Gregory or even knew that they'd met. She imagined the words she would use when she wrote to tell him what had happened.

"Dear Tom," she would write. "I wanted you to hear my news. It seems that I am Gregory Allard's heir. He has left me his villa and its contents. You won't be seeing me for quite some time. Details to follow."

Afterword

Simone Weil

Simone Weil was born in Paris on February 3, 1909, the daughter of assimilated Jewish parents; her father was a doctor, her mother a home-maker ambitious for the intellectual achievement of her two children, Simone and her brother, André, who grew to be a world-class mathematician. She studied philosophy at the École Normale Supérieure in Paris. But from an early age, her astonishing intellectual commitment (she became fluent in ancient Greek by the age of ten) was joined by a heartfelt identification with the poor and suffering. Simone de Beauvoir, a fellow student at the École Normale, encountered Simone Weil weeping after learning of the deaths of victims of Chinese famine. Simone Weil told Simone de Beauvoir that the most important thing in the world was the coming revolution that would feed all the starving people of the earth. Simone de Beauvoir responded that the most important thing was to help people find a reason for their existence. Simone Weil snapped back: "It's easy to see that you've never gone hungry."

She saw herself allied with the politics of the left, but always on her own terms. At the age of ten, she declared herself a Bolshevik, but she earned the enmity of committed Communists when she repudiated

Stalin in the early 1930s, among the first to see in him the same tyranny of force that marked Hitler and Mussolini. Also as early as the 1930s, she was writing against the evils of French colonialism, meeting with Vietnamese and Algerians working in Paris for the liberation of their homelands.

In 1931 she got her first job as a teacher in the *lycée* of Le Puy, a small city in the Haute-Loire region in the south of France. This is where I locate the first meetings of Simone Weil and my fictional character Genevieve.

In 1933, convinced that she had no right to speak about the lives and conditions of workers unless she had shared their lot, Simone Weil worked for a year at a series of factories owned by the Renault company. In 1936 she joined the forces of the Anarchists in fighting on the Republican side in the Spanish Civil War. Unlike most of the participants on both sides of that war, she was able to see the horrors inflicted not only upon but by her comrades, whose casual brutality shocked her. She felt compelled to bear witness to the lust for violence which appalled her on both sides—but it was particularly painful to her when she observed it among the Anarchists, whom she had idealized.

In 1937 she had experiences of a mystical and visionary nature, in which she felt herself penetrated by the presence of Jesus Christ. Deeply drawn to Catholicism, she would not submit to baptism in the Catholic Church because, she said, of its history of "anathema sit," of excommunication on intellectual grounds—the Church's insistence that Catholicism had a monopoly on truth. She said she could not be part of an institution which deprived anyone of intellectual liberty.

Devoted to solidarity among the oppressed and suffering of the world, she nevertheless failed to identify with the plight of Jews under Nazi persecution. She would not wear a yellow star; threatened with the loss of her job, she wrote to the Ministry of Education explaining why she did not define herself as a Jew, since she had had no contact with the Jewish religion and considered her intellectual formation Christian and French. But her alienation from Judaism was more thoroughgoing. She was deeply critical of Jewish tradition, referring to Yahweh as a God of force and punishment, and the Jewish people as a people devoted to exclusion and persecution of the other. She traced all the evils in Western thought back to the Jews and the Romans, the following of whom, she believed, led to the rejection of the tradition of the Greeks, which stood, in her mind, for purity and freedom.

In 1942 she and her parents had the opportunity to flee occupied France for America, where André Weil had a position at Haverford College in Pennsylvania. She lived in New York City for a time. After three months she sailed to England, where she worked in the Propaganda Department of the Free French. There, she was diagnosed with tuberculosis and hospitalized. Always uncomfortable with many kinds of food, with everything having to do with eating, she worsened her condition by refusing to eat what the doctors recommended, insisting that she eat only what she imagined was the ration of those suffering in occupied France—an amount that she had arbitrarily determined. She died in Ashford, Kent, in August 1943, at the age of thirty-four. The circumstances of her death were as controversial as the rest of her life: some, particularly her doctor, believing she starved herself, others insisting that there was nothing that could have prevented her death by tuberculosis.

The work on which her reputation is based was published posthumously. Among the strongest supporters of the publication of this work was Albert Camus. Camus paid a visit to the Weil apartment on his way to receive the Nobel Prize in Stockholm, asking Simone's mother if he could have some time alone in Simone's writing room. Camus referred to Simone Weil as "the only great spirit of our age."

Thomas Mann

By the time of Hitler's rise to power, in the 1930s, Thomas Mann was indisputably the most famous, most honored, most "German" of German writers. He could have supported the regime and lived comfortably and safely in Nazi Germany but, urged and inspired by his son and daughter, outspoken anti-Fascists, he criticized the regime and paid dearly for it. His luxurious and privileged life was threatened; he fled first to Switzerland and then, in 1939, to the United States, where he made numerous broadcasts and tirelessly spoke to American audiences about the dangers of Nazism and the threat to democracy. He did not, in fact, speak at the Horace Mann School in Gary, Indiana, but he was in Chicago in the early forties, as his son-in-law was a professor at the University of Chicago. Disgusted by America's failure to live up to its promise and appalled by the rise of phobic anti-Communism, he returned to Europe in 1952 and died in Switzerland in 1955.

A NOTE ON THE TYPE

This book was set in Granjon, a type named in compliment to Robert Granjon, a type cutter and printer active in Antwerp, Lyons, Rome, and Paris from 1523 to 1590. Granjon, the boldest and most original designer of his time, was one of the first to practice the trade of typefounder apart from that of printer.

Linotype Granjon was designed by George W. Jones, who based his drawings on a face used by Claude Garamond (ca. 1480–1561) in his beautiful French books. Granjon more closely resembles Garamond's own type than do any of the various modern faces that bear his name.

Typeset by Scribe, Inc.,
Philadelphia, Pennsylvania

Printed and bound by Berryville Graphics,
Berryville, Virginia

Designed by Cassandra J. Pappas